EVA SLEEPS

Francesca Melandri

EVA SLEEPS

*Translated from the Italian
by Katherine Gregor*

Europa
editions

Europa Editions
214 West 29th Street
New York, N.Y. 10001
www.europaeditions.com
info@europaeditions.com

Published by arrangement with Marco Vigevani & Associati Agenzia Letteraria
First Publication 2016 by Europa Editions

Translation by Katherine Gregor
Original title: *Eva dorme*
Translation copyright © 2016 by Europa Editions

Library of Congress Cataloging in Publication Data is available
ISBN 978-1-60945-312-1

Melandri, Francesca
Eva Sleeps

Book design by Emanuele Ragnisco
www.mekkanografici.com
Cover photo © Sally Mundy/Trevillion Images

Prepress by Grafica Punto Print – Rome

Printed in the USA

To my children, happy multilinguists,
and two dads full of love: theirs and mine.

"One evening in the *Stube*, old Sonner put an end to the usual mumblings about betrayal, saying, 'It's all nonsense! Even children know we won the war. But I would never have dreamed that they'd give us the whole of Italy!'"
—CLAUS GATTERER, *Bel paese, brutta gente*

"But, I mean, they're all Germans there!"
—MARIANO RUMOR, after a holiday in Val Pusteria in 1968 revealed to him the existence of a language minority in the country of which he was Prime Minister.

"So you're Italians ruled by Germans? Lucky you!"
—INDRO MONTANELLI

"Call the world, if you please the 'vale of Soul-making.' Then you will find out the use of the world."
—JOHN KEATS, Letter to George and Georgiana Keats

"Let Eve (for I have drench'd her eyes) Here sleep below, while thou to foresight wak'st."
—JOHN MILTON, Paradise Lost, book XI

CONTENTS

EVA SLEEPS

PROLOGUE

It was a small parcel wrapped in brown paper and tied with thin string. The names of the addressee and the sender were in neat handwriting. Gerda recognized it immediately. "*I nimms net,*" she told Udo, the postman. I'm not taking it.

"But it's for Eva—"

"I'm her mother. I know she doesn't want it."

Udo nearly asked if she was sure. But she looked up at him with her transparent, almond-shaped eyes and stood there, motionless, staring at him. He said nothing. He took a pen out of his breast pocket and a form from the leather bag. He handed them to her, without looking her in the face. "Sign here."

Gerda signed. Then, suddenly gentle, she asked, "So what's going to happen to this parcel now?"

"I'll take it back to the sorting office and tell them you don't want it"

"That Eva doesn't want it."

"—and they'll send it back."

Udo put the parcel back into his leather bag, folded the form, and slipped it in with the other papers. He replaced the pen in his breast pocket after checking that it was closed securely. He was about to leave. The upper part of his body was already turning toward the road and his feet were about to follow when he had one last scruple. "Where's Eva, anyway?"

"Eva is sleeping."

The brown parcel traveled backwards along the road it had taken to arrive at that spot: two thousand, seven hundred and ninety-four kilometers in total, there and back.

1919

I f anyone had asked Hermann, Gerda's father, if he had
ever known love (no one ever did, least of all his wife
Johanna), the image of his mother standing at the entrance
of the barn, handing him the bucket of lukewarm milk from
the first milking, would have flashed before him. He'd sink his
face into the sweet liquid and raise it again, a creamy mustache
on his upper lip, before setting off on the hour-long walk to
school. Only after covering a certain distance would he wipe
his lip with his wrist. When Sepp Schwingshackl joined him
from his *maso*[1] to walk with him. Or, when along came Paul
Staggl, who was the poorest boy in the whole school—his
father's *maso* was not only uphill but north-facing, so never got
any sun in the winter. Or, if he'd tried thinking about it (something he never did in all his life, except for just one time, and
then died immediately afterwards), he would have remembered his mother's hand, cool but also as rough as old wood,
cupped over his childish cheek in a gesture of total acceptance.
By the time Gerda was born, though, Hermann had long ago
lost love. Perhaps he'd lost it on the way, like the hay in his
dream.

The first time, he was a boy, but then the dream recurred
throughout the rest of his life. His mother was spreading a
large white sheet on the field, filling it with freshly scythed

[1] Rural house typical of the Italian Trentino-Alto Adige region. It generally
consists of a barn, a stable and a small room for cooking food and making
cheese.

hay. Then she closed it by bringing together and tying the four corners, and put it on his shoulders, so he would carry it to the barn. It was a huge load but he didn't care. His mother had given it to him, so the weight was all right. He would walk up from the scythed field, swaying, like a monster flower. His mother watched him with her blue, almond-shaped eyes—the same eyes as Hermann, then his daughter Gerda, and also her daughter, Eva. Stern, gentle eyes like in some portraits of Gothic saints. However, another Hermann—ageless and invisible—realized with alarm that the corners of the large cloth weren't tied properly and that he was shedding hay behind him on the ground. A few stalks would fly out at first, then entire handfuls. The Hermann who saw and knew everything couldn't alert the Hermann who was the character in the dream, so when the latter reached the barn, his bundle would be empty.

The first night he dreamed this, the peace treaty was being signed in Saint-Germain, with which the victorious powers of the Great War—France, especially—wishing to punish the dying Austrian empire, assigned South Tyrol to Italy. Italy was very surprised. There had always been talk of liberating Trento and Trieste, but never Bolzano—let alone Bozen. It was perfectly logical. South Tyroleans were German people, perfectly at ease in the Austro-Hungarian empire, and didn't need anyone to liberate them. Even so, after a war that had certainly not been won on the battlefield, Italy ended up with that stretch of the Alps as their unexpected booty.

That same night, his parents died three hours apart, swept away by the Spanish flu. The following morning, Hermann found himself orphaned, just like his land, South Tyrol, deprived of its *Vaterland*, Austria.

After their parents' death, Hans, the eldest brother, inherited the old *maso*. The property consisted of a house with a

Stube[2] blackened by smoke, a barn full of wood beetles, a field so steep that in order to cut the hay you had to put your weight on one leg at a time, land so poor and vertical that it kept having to be carried back up on your shoulders in a wicker basket after every rainy season had sent a large part of it sliding down to the lowest point of the field. And Hans was the lucky one.

The three elder sisters got married in a rush, just so they could sleep under a roof they could call their own. Hermann, the youngest, had to go and be a *Knecht*, a servant, in the wealthier *masos*, the ones with level slopes you could scythe with your weight on both legs. The ones where the land stayed in its place even after a heavy downpour, and didn't slide down into the valley. He was eleven years old.

Every night, until he was twenty, never having been away from his mother for more than half a day, he wet the bed from fear and loneliness. In winter, in the drafty loft where the masters made *Knechte* like him sleep, Hermann would wake up enveloped in his own frozen urine, as in a shroud. When he got up from the straw mattress, the thin tegument would shatter with a light crackle.

It was the sound of loneliness, of shame, of loss, of homesickness.

---

[2] Stove. The term also refers to the timber-paneled room at the heart of traditional Tyrolean houses, with a wood stove in the centre.

KILOMETER 0

J et lag is worse when you travel East. That's what everybody
says. When you go against the sun, they say it then retali-
ates by depriving you of sleep. As if I had sleep to waste.

Carlo is coming to pick me up at Munich Airport, but I
can't tell my mother, because I know she doesn't like him.
She's never liked him. Maybe it's because when I first introduced him, he didn't try to butter her up, not even a little. He
was just polite. Still, we must remember that he's an engineer,
so his job is to take things literally. Otherwise, the bridges and
viaducts he builds wouldn't stay up. He probably thinks I'd
take his chivalry toward my mother as a slight. How little he
knows about me. About me and, especially, about her.

I introduced him ten years ago. We'd gone to visit her for
All Souls weekend and she'd had us at Ruthi's—my patin's[3]—
farm. She'd installed herself in the fir-lined *Stube,* looking like
something in a tourist office brochure. She was wearing a lace
blouse under the boiled wool jacket with the buttons made of
bone. Only thing more Tyrolean than that would have to be a
Dirndl. Maybe she was keen on being seen by Carlo in that setting that was ever so rustic and picturesque, like a staging of
her own identity—even though, to tell the truth, she's never
been a peasant.

Carlo talked to her, enquired after her health, and held the
door open for her when we went out. However, he never

[3] Godmother.

stared into her eyes and laughed, never told her that now he could see who I got my beauty from, and, what's worse, did not agree to play a hand of *Watten*. And that was something my mother has really not forgiven him. Carlo justified himself by saying he didn't know the rules of that particular card game. The rules! He really hadn't understood a thing.

That's why I don't take him to visit her anymore. She doesn't like Carlo, but not because he's married or because he has three children I've never met. And not even because, in the eleven years we've been together, he's never mentioned the possibility of divorcing his wife.

These aren't the things that matter to my mother.

I come out through the glass door of International Arrivals. A fifty-something man is pushing my luggage cart: Jack Radcliffe, from Bridgeport, Connecticut, a farming machinery manufacturer on temporary transfer to Munich for a trade fair. Tall, salt and pepper hair, impeccable navy-blue suit. As for me, even after a nine-hour flight, I'm dressed and made up as if for the New York art previews, which is indeed where I'm coming from. Pistachio green Donna Karan jersey ensemble, pendant earrings, pumps. We make quite a handsome couple. Shame about the American's slightly beady eyes and that purplish nose (he enjoyed the in-flight bar service). When Carlo sees him next to me, he rolls his beautiful dark eyes, as though asking the sky to witness the stamina needed to keep up with a woman like me.

The American, on the other hand, takes a while to work out that someone has come to pick me up, or maybe I forgot to inform him. In any case, he stops smiling. It's as though he's watching the fantasies he's entertained about me melt away in the presence of another man, like ice in a glass of whisky you've been holding too long. His eyes become even more translucent—tearful almost—as he gradually realizes that this handsome, Latin-looking man is there for me. Without any surprise or embarrassment, Carlo shakes his hand, thanks him for helping me with my baggage, then sweeps me away with those broad shoulders of his I still like so much.

As I walk away, my arm around him, I turn to look back, flash him an encouraging smile, wiggle my fingers and twitter, "See you later, Jack!"

That's enough to confuse athe baggage cart and, as a matter of fact, Jack Radcliffe, of Bridgeport, Connecticut, remains in the Arrivals Hall, devastated by incomprehension even more than disappointment.

"Poor thing . . . " Carlo says, kissing my hair. Not a reproach but an observation.

"Why? He was a nice gentleman"

"'Eva's nice gentlemen,'" he sighs. "A category of the spirit."

"He let me rest on his shoulder during the entire flight."

"And what did he do for nine hours with your lovely weight upon him?"

"He picked up the blanket when it slid off me, drank spirits, and told me about his unhappy marriage."

"Actually, the exact category is 'the nice gentlemen who tell Eva about their unhappy marriages.'"

He squeezes my shoulders, all lovely and male, the doubt never even crossing his mind that he might belong to this despicable category. I must say it's true that he doesn't belong to it at all. After all, Carlo never mentions his marriage, so I have no way of judging whether it's a happy or unhappy one. Not that I care, actually.

He's pushed the cart to his car and loaded the baggage. A baby blue three-piece set I just bought in New York: trolley suitcase, holdall and beauty case—and with such handy compartments too. My mother would like it. In fact, I'm thinking it's a color that suits her rather than me and that I'll probably take them to her when I go there for Easter lunch, the day after tomorrow. I remain on the sidewalk with the computer case over my shoulder—I never let anyone take that from me. I like it when a man does muscular, physical work for me. Like lifting and arranging suitcases in the trunk. I assume a calm, patient air and enjoy the moment, looking away from Carlo so he doesn't think I'm rushing him. There's a man coming toward me on the sidewalk, heading to the taxi rank. A little younger than I, in a steel-gray, freshly pressed, woolen pinstripe suit, with an overnight bag that suggests he's flying on business. German, but not Bavarian, rather a Northerner: from Hamburg, perhaps, or Hanover. When I catch his eye, his pupils dilate and he assumes that expression men have when I look them in the eye—that unmistakable blend of rapacity and yearning. Desire makes them bold but also vulnerable and I become the keeper of a secret: chances are, their mother has never seen that look in their eyes—at least I hope not.

Carlo slams the trunk shut and sits down behind the wheel. I open the passenger door and, as I sit down, crossing my legs, I look up at the man who may be from Hamburg or Hanover, and who is now walking past me. I don't smile at him but barely squeeze my eyelids, the way thirteen-year-old fashion models do when they want to make their expression more intense. Then I slam the door, and Carlo starts the car.

I'm not beautiful. Nice-looking, but nothing special. There are so many other tall blond women.

I'm not even young anymore. There are many girls around young enough to be my daughters, with fresher bodies, smoother faces, and a more desirable innocence. And yet men still look at me. I inherited my mother's features but in an approximate version. Her Russian aristocratic cheekbones have been passed on to me with a more rustic cut. Her lips have an elegant design to them, while mine have something of the *maso*, of fresh, still warm milk, of butter. Like her, I have slim legs, a full bust, and North-European height, but when it comes to bearing, we're poles apart. Gerda Huber spent her life sweating over cookers and chopping boards while I wear Armani and organize society events. And yet between the two of us, she's the one who looks more like a queen.

It's a three-hour drive and two borders from Munich airport to my home. When I was a girl, I found this double frontier behind our land very exciting. It made me feel close to a big wide world, to other places, to the unknown. It was back in the days when Schengen was just a small town in Luxembourg no one had ever heard of; when European customs houses were indicated by real red and white grade crossings, and humorless men in uniform who looked like they could deny you access and even arrest you. And then there was the Brenner Pass, which certainly made quite an impression as a border: dark, oppressive, with its cavernous railroad station like something out of a spy movie. The thrill of those days is gone. Now, when you go through the narrow doorway that leads from Northern Europe to Italy, they don't even check your car tax disc.

Well, almost. After Sterzing/Vipiteno, just before Franzensfeste/Fortezza, Carlo stops at the *Autobahnrast-stätte/Autogrill* and we have a *belegtes Brötchen/panini*. Then we leave the Autobahn/autostrada and pay the toll at the *Mautstelle/casello*. All this while driving his Volvo which, thankfully, is Swedish so doesn't have to be translated into German or Italian. Welcome to Südtirol/Alto Adige, the land of bilingualism.

We pass various exits before getting off the highway and entering a wide valley full of light, that is welcoming even now after the first thaw has made the sunlit slopes muddy and patches of brown are already discoloring the mountain pastures still covered in snow. All around, the slopes are thick with larches, fir trees, birches, and dense forests that don't, however, threaten human activity on the valley floor. On the contrary, their impenetrable nature almost seems to frame the civilization of work—the *masi* with large lawns, bridges over the still-torrential river, and churches with their bulb-shaped bell towers. It's in this valley that I was born.

Carlo takes me home. We make love the way we usually do, with the usual gestures. It's the advantage of eleven years of secrecy: sex follows established, reassuring patterns, like in a marriage, but doesn't end up being taken for granted, or become a duty. This blend of habit and precariousness suits me. Afterwards, the two vertical lines between Carlo's eyebrows always relax a little, letting in less shade. I first noticed it eleven years ago, in this very bed, and it has been happening ever since. So this, I tell myself, is my power over him. I'm the one who smooths his forehead, I'm his personal anti-wrinkle cream. It's a comforting thought because the older he gets, the more he'll need it.

We remain in each other's arms between the linen sheets. White ones. I can't bear to have my sleep—scarce enough as it is—surrounded by colors. Carlo turns on his side and wraps me from behind. He smells my hair.

"You travel too much, you," he says.

I smile. When he talks like that, I know he means it. The phone rings. Carlo holds me tight. Don't go, his arms are saying. I don't go, and the Telecom answerphone kicks in. "This is the answering service for zero, four, seven . . . "

An excited, adolescent voice with a strong Roman accent, says, "Listen, it's coming now . . . "

The answerphone continues, unperturbed, in German now,

"Hier spricht der Anrufbeantworter der Nummer Null Vier Sieben Vier . . . "

"What's that—German?" a second voice says. A slightly clucking voice that hesitates between high and low tones. Fourteen—fifteen years old at most. Perhaps younger.

"Hey, how long does it go on for?"

" *. . . Hinterlassen Sie bitte eine Nachricht nach dem Signal.*"

At this point the two boys are guffawing and the first one has started screaming into the receiver, "Krauts! Krauts!"

"Actùn, cartoffen, capùt . . . !"

The other one has joined in but is laughing so hard he can't carry on. My back remains glued to Carlo's stomach, his arms around my chest. We stay there, listening without moving.

"Go back to Germany!" the first one screams, then hangs up.

"Again!" I say. "Don't they ever get fed up?"

There's a scene in all the TV soaps my mother watches every day after lunch. The married man knots his tie while standing at the foot of his mistress's bed, gives her a kiss on the forehead, then leaves, while she remains lying on an unmade bed, staring sadly at the door that has closed behind him. Often, she'll hug her knees and put her chin on them, always modestly covered by the sheet. In eleven years, it's never been like that with Carlo. Before he says goodbye, even if he's in a rush, he always takes the time to move from the bed to the sofa, or the kitchen, or balcony, in other words somewhere that isn't the place of pleasure, to allow me also to get dressed or at least put on a robe. Then we have a coffee, a chat, a laugh. I feel that's quite a lot.

This time, before leaving, he helps me unpack my bags. Together, we leaf through the catalogues of the exhibitions I saw in New York. Gerhard Richter at MOMA. A young Korean artist in a gallery in Chelsea—twenty-two years old and he's already selling his paintings to billionaires on the East Side. An exhibition of wood art by the people of Dogon. I've seen more than one African statue in my clients' homes, often family castles redecorated with skillful additions of glass and steel. The South Tyrol rich like ethnic art. It makes them feel like citizens of the world.

Before he leaves, Carlo says, "After Easter Monday, if you like, I'll come inside."

"That would be great," I answer.

Don't panic. We haven't suddenly decided, on the spur of the moment, to have a child together. All he's saying is that, after the holidays, he'll come back to me, inside my valley, from Bolzano, where he lives. If you're from Alto Adige—even if, like him, you have Venetian and Calabrian blood—you translate into Italian many of our German dialect idioms. You go inside—*inni*—when you go into valleys that run outside—*aussi*—towards the plains and the big wide world.

Last summer, for instance, I was in Positano. Carlo phoned me. His wife and children had gone away and he was free to fly out of Bolzano.

"I'm coming out tonight," he said, meaning he was going to join me, not that he would be using a form of contraception approved by the Church.

And now Carlo gives me a kiss (not on my forehead!), then goes home. To his home.

Of course, every so often I get questions. There's always someone—generally a woman—who feels it her duty to communicate that she feels sorry for me. "How can you bear it—so many years with a married man?" they ask. Many, almost all of them, add, "I could never do it."

Every time, it takes me a little while to remember that there are people out there to whom my situation seems untenable. Sad, if not desperate. Ulli, however, would never have asked me that. He knew there's only one person I can accept being bound to. The only one I can belong to without feeling that I'm sinking into sticky mud, into an unknown marsh. The only one I could, if need be, look after and take care of without feeling trapped. And it's not a man.

Shortly before dinner, Zhou comes by to say hello. Ten years old, two pigtails from which small pink plastic strawberries hang, and a dangling molar. Almond-shaped eyes, like a Chinese girl. Well, she is Chinese. She's very clever at school. Her favorite subject: Geometry.

"I saw the light on, so I knew you were back."

I haven't seen her for a couple of weeks and looking at her face as she talks makes me feel as disorientated as I did the first time. It's like watching a Bruce Lee movie dubbed by a choir of yodeling Alpini.

Signor Song, her father, was the owner of a shoe factory in Shandong, in Southern China. In the late eighties, he sold it to a party official. The total proceeds obtained from the sale of the establishment, including warehouses, machinery, and goods ready to be shipped: two passports with authorization to leave the country—one for himself, and one for his wife. As a memento of China and of his family, which, for a time, was very prominent in the area, he managed to take with him just an ornate wooden box containing the instruments necessary for raising fighting grasshoppers, an activity typical of Shandong, and in which his father was an expert.

After a few months, the Songs arrived in Italy, first in Trieste, then Padua, where their children were born, and, finally, in South Tyrol. That's where Signor Song was living when, during the 2001 census, they asked him to tick one of the following boxes: Italian, German, or Ladin. There was no room for any other option, since these are they only three ethnic groups recognized in South Tyrol. In order to receive the benefits of the Region with special status you had to fill in and sign a declaration of belonging to the language group. The heading on the form said, in German, *Sprachgruppenzuge-hörigkeitserklärung*.

Signor Song told me he stared at that word for a long time. Thirty-six letters. Eleven syllables.

Although he is a polyglot (Italian, English, Mandarin, and now also some German), his mother-tongue is Shandong dialect: a tonal and especially monosyllabic language. For the first and perhaps only time in his life, he skipped over the practical side of the question and experienced a gut reaction: he could never even have started to speak a language which can form a single word with thirty-six letters and eleven syllables. He considered the possibility of ticking "Ladin." He knew little about those somewhat marginal people but felt a vague kind of warmth toward them. However, he wasn't planning to relocate to Val Gardena or Val Badia, the only places where that would carry a distinct advantage.

So now, Zhou, as well as her parents and older siblings, is to all intents and purposes ethnically Italian. She keeps me company with her accent that smacks of a North East tavern, while I finish unpacking my bags. When it's time for dinner, she leaves.

On the bookcase, I keep two two photos in pale wooden frames. One is that of a boy with eyelashes that are too long, like those of roebuck, and an apologetic smile: Ulli. The other one is in slightly yellowed black and white. A ten-year-old girl stands between two slightly older children—not sure if they're cousins or more distant relatives. They're on a sunny mountain pasture, slightly against the light. They're minding the cows grazing behind them. The little girl's dress is too short, clearly handed down several times, and exposes bare legs filthy with mud. There are blades of grass and a daisy sprouting between her toes. She looks straight in the eyes of whoever is taking the picture. She's the only one doing so—the other two children are staring at her, stealing a glance, mouths open, in their eyes the terror and awe of someone witnessing a wonder of nature.

My mother, as a little girl.

It's pointless trying to sleep after crossing six time zones—and in the wrong direction at that. I spend the night awake, tidying up. Now I open the window.

Even though it's April, the air still smells of snow in the middle of the night. Yet the larches are starting to awaken, the resin is already rising from the dark depths of the trunks, and its oily essence is beginning to spread through the air. I breathe in deeply. On sleepless nights like this, I remember how lucky I am to be living somewhere that smells good. The pale blue stars are throbbing, promising a fine but still chilly day.

On the mountain across from the balcony, snowcat lights go up and down, as they do every night. All in line, like obedient little spaceships. With the advance of spring, the upkeep of the snowy slopes for end-of-season skiers becomes an increasingly thankless task, since the snow melts quicker and there's less of it falling. Watching those lights climbing up and down, there are many things I don't think about. About the warmth inside the driver's cab of Marlene, the snowcat with a woman's name, thoroughly heated during icy winter nights; about the music wars between Ulli and me—my Eurythmics against his Simply Red, shot through the stereo he had installed in the cab by himself; about the absurd, zebra-striped covers on the seats, as though Marlene was a Texan truck and the ski slope US Route 163 in Monument Valley. I don't think about these things. At least not every night.

Up on the summit, in the crisp air 2,000 meters, right beneath Orion's Belt, the permanently lit beams of the factory glisten as relentlessly as those of a prison. I look at them for a long time. Another thought that doesn't even brush past me:

the factory could have been mine one day. Instead, it will never be so.

I take in another breath, and close the window.

I sip my first coffee before dawn. It's not to wake me up, I'm not sleepy yet—not even tired—but what else can you drink at six o'clock in the morning? The night is wasted anyway, I tell myself, so no point in trying to sleep anymore. I'll go to bed early this evening and tomorrow I'll get to my mother's rested. At least I hope so. I know she's been preparing Easter lunch for three days with Ruthi and the other relatives. *Schlutza, Tirtlan, Mohnstrudl, Strauchln.* And *Topfentaschen, Rollade* and grappa made of last summer's cranberries. I wouldn't wish to fail in my duty to pay homage to the treats they're preparing but if I don't get enough sleep, I don't have an appetite.

The mountain still looks black against the opalescent sky while in the east a lonely little cloud stands out, glowing pink—almost orange. The snowcats are now asleep in the hangars dug out of the rock. The factory is still lit up but not for much longer. Two hours from now, the steel cables, taut between pylons, will start transporting the thousand, ten thousand, one hundred billion skiers on which our valley depends to perpetuate its own wealth. I'm the first to agree: without the factory, there'd be no tourists. Without tourists, no hotels. Without hotels, no wellbeing. Without wellbeing, no events to organize. For me that would mean no trips, no Prada shoes, no previews in Chelsea full of promises of Asiatic art, no trips to Indonesia or Yucatan. Not even Jack Radcliffe from Bridgeport, Connecticut, with his perplexed beady expression, or his thwarted erotic hopes.

God bless the factory for generating happy skiers for us all.

I sip my coffee, wrapped in the blanket my mother gave me: a patchwork of knitted squares made from the leftovers of my childhood pullovers. It has subdued, ill-matched colors. The sign of a time when if you were lucky enough to have any clothes at all, the way they looked was the least of your concerns. Loden blue, apple red, mousey gray, forest green. An orange square (I've no idea which pullover this one comes from) sticks out like a sore thumb. This blanket is totally out of place in my elegant home, all in lime green and aquamarine shades. It's also rough, like barbed wire, and feels like wool that hasn't been carded. I can still remember how that coarse kind of wool used to make my arms itch. How did I ever put up with it? No wonder I have only cashmere or mohair sweaters now.

The telephone rings.

In the stillness of dawn, that sharp sound makes me jump and I almost spill my coffee. I'm about to answer but freeze. Who'd be calling me at this hour? It's probably a wrong number. I let the answering machine start.

"This is number . . . /*Hier spricht der Anrufbeantworter* . . . "

I let Signorina Telecom/Fräulein Telekom finish her elaborate homage to bilingualism, and keep listening. There's a protracted silence. There's a presence on the other end of the line. Then, a little louder, comes the faint sound of breathing. I can't believe they play tricks even at this hour! Before even going to school! Maybe it's the sleepless night, or perhaps the jet lag but the adrenaline starts pumping in my veins. I grab the receiver. "Stop it! I'm fed up with this!"

"Eva . . . Is that you?"

It's a man's voice. Not a young man. Perhaps he's tired or ill, or both. Taken aback, I say, "Who's that?"

A pause.

"My *Sisiduzza* . . . May I still call you that?"

I stare at the absurd square in the blanket. The orange one. I really must ask my mother which pullover it comes from. Perhaps it wasn't mine but one of Ruthi's.

"Is this a joke?" I whisper.

"No, it's me—Vito."

I look up. The sun has risen. A golden light is bathing my kilim.

Woe betide the daughters of loveless fathers: their fate is that of the unloved. Only once in my life has my mother, Gerda, been sure of a man's love, and I of a father's. All the other times have been like summer downpours: they came, made our shoes all muddy, but left the fields dry. With Vito, though, it was the real thing. Both for her and me, his presence was like a rainfall in June, like water that makes the hay grow and refills the springs. But even then we weren't spared the drought, before and after.

In a tired voice, Vito tells me he hasn't got long left to live.

He also says, "I'd like to see you again."

A few hours later, I'm already on my way. I'm going South, I'm going to him.

1925 - 1961

Vofluicht no amol!" Hermann burst out in a loud voice. "Vofluicht, scheisszoig!"[4]

The basket his master had given him to take to the market had fallen on the ground. All the wheels of gray cheese had rolled on the ground.

He hadn't sworn in Italian, as demanded by the Fascist laws now in force, which dictated that only Italian be used in public. He hadn't even used a blasphemy, which would have been frowned upon but not considered illegal, as long as it was in Italian. He had sworn, and sworn in German. And, to be more precise, in dialect. An employee of the Fascist land registry office, who was walking past, heard him and, wishing to defend the Roman spirit of Südtirol, now Alto Adige, struck Hermann right across the face with his ink-stained open hand, then decisively tore off his *Bauernschurtz*, the blue work apron.

No German to be spoken in public, no Tyrolean clothes, no dirndl or *Tracht* or *Lederhosen*. Nothing to imply that the new Brenner border wasn't the holy limit of Italic land. It was the Fascist law. Among the peasants and *Knechte* at the market, nobody looked up or defended him.

Some time later, despite the slap and the humiliation, or perhaps for that very reason, the badge, the fasces pin of party members began to gleam on Hermann's collar. The local party officials looked on this favorably and taught him to drive a

---

[4] "Shitty contraption!"

truck. They entrusted him with the transportation of timber between the valleys, and turned a blind eye if he spoke dialect with the lumberjacks. In any case, up there among those forgotten crags, even il Duce wouldn't have been able to hear them.

The years passed and one day, Hermann saw on the main road of the main town a group of Golden Pheasants—it was what they called the SA. Their eyes were like blades ready to cut down any obstacle to the creation of the magnificent Thousand Year Reich. They walked straight, impeccable, Aryan, infinitely German. Hermann thought they were beautiful demi-gods.

He decided to become one of them.

Maybe Hermann lost love completely just as he was deluding himself that he'd found it—when he saw Johanna, an eighteen-year-old girl with black hair, thin and pale, who never spoke but walked with her head down as though wishing the world would overlook her existence. Maybe having at his side a woman whose every gesture apologized for her being alive would make him forget the shame, powerlessness, anger, and loneliness. That's what Hermann sensed, although he could not have said it. Therefore, even though he didn't love Johanna, he asked her to marry him. She immediately saw the coldness in his pale eyes. However, she also thought she saw a hint of concealed tenderness convinced herself that she had discovered, in this tall man who walked so rigidly, an all-consuming truth that was reserved for her alone. It wasn't true, or perhaps it could have been true, but that's not what happened. In any case, she married him.

The first child, Peter, was born with his father's saturnine temperament and his mother's dark eyes. He was three years old when Hermann lifted him onto his bony shoulders and joined the crowd gathered where the highway met a valley-bound road. Perched up there, the child felt important, almost as important as Crown Prince Umberto, guest of honor at the unveiling of the monument to the Italian Alpine troops, which had been so keenly desired by the *podestà*. The statue was covered with a white cloth that was being lifted and lowered by the summer wind, like giant breaths. Peter thought it looked like a huge ghost, something inhuman yet alive, throbbing. After the formal speeches and the band playing, the cloth fell with an almost animal rustling sound, in a sinuous ectoplasmic movement. But there was nothing evanescent about what it revealed: that was very solid—almost obtuse—matter.

A granite Alpino with a thick neck and not very slender—appropriately Italic—legs, directed his grumpy gaze to the northern glaciers, to the spot where the new border had been for the past twenty years. The not exactly sparkling expression of the stone soldier symbolized the blind, obedient and ruthless force that Fascist Italy would unleash against anyone daring to state that Alto Adige did not belong to her. This was not a superfluous clarification, and not only because of the reluctance of many, too many, South Tyroleans to recognize their very Roman lineage. The Fascist government had a more pressing reason for needing this clarification: on entering Vienna only three months earlier, Hitler had declared Austria, through the *Anschluss*, part of the Third Reich. And Austria, the lost homeland, was right there beyond the glaciers.

But this, as the Alpino stated with his presence, and as the authorities gathered for the occasion repeated, this was Italy.

Mussolini's project to Italianize Alto Adige had been thorough. However, he soon realized that to make the place "very Roman, Latin, imperial" it wasn't enough just to prevent the peasants from speaking German and wearing traditional clothes. Nor was it enough to forbid school children to study their mother-tongue and force them, instead, to learn Giosuè

Carducci's poem about the serene, wholesome bull "Pio Bove" by heart. Besides, those poor women sent over from Caserta, Agrigento and Rovigo could only weep at the thankless task of trying to make these blockheads produce the musical sounds of the Italian language. Brave teachers throughout the territory carried on teaching German in *Katakombenschulen*,[5] the clandestine schools. Italianizing place names hadn't sufficed either. Now, people would look up at the bell towers to work out where they were: if it was bulb-shaped, they knew they were in Völs, if pointy, then in Blumau. As for "Fiè," "Prato Isarco" and all the other names invented by Mussolini's topographer, Tolomei, nobody used them except bureaucrats.

There was only one solution for truly Romanizing that beautiful, vertical land: allowing only Italians to live there. It was not enough that the flow of immigrants from other regions was motivated and supported by Fascism in the hope that, someday, German-speaking South Tyroleans would become a minority in their own land. No, they actually had to leave.

Hitler embraced this idea enthusiastically. Ensuring the purity of nations by moving (or erasing) larges masses of people across the map was his favorite occupation. So he promised Mussolini that if the *Südtiroler* wished to carry on being German, they would be welcomed with open arms by the Greater Germany, and by their brothers who belonged to the pure Aryan race. He would give each and every one of them a new maso as large as the one they'd left behind south of the Brenner Pass, the same size fields and pastures, the same number of cows and, so assured the propaganda, of the same color coat as those left in the hayloft by their ancestors. The Sudeten, Galicia, Styria and even Burgundy then, later on, the boundless lands taken away from the worthless

---

[5] Literally "catacomb schools," illegal institutions that taught the German language (which was forbidden) and were widespread in the Alto Adige region during the Fascist era, from 1924 onwards.

Slav people: Tatras, in Poland, the immense Hungarian *puszta*, and soon also lush Crimea. Anyone who left Alto Adige would find fertile lands that only needed a virile German workforce to become paradise on earth.

Mussolini, at the same time, was threatening the *Dableiber*, those who remained, with forced Italianization: speaking German was totally forbidden, even in private, and anyone not adopting Italian—in fact, Roman (with a capital "R" on the flyers)—customs and practices would be deported en masse to Sicily, to grow prickly pears—what they were exactly, nobody really knew. The choice wasn't between staying or going, but between declaring yourself to be either a *Walsch* or a *Daitsch*: Italian or German. You could not remain a German on Italian soil.

Whether or not you left was presented as a matter of free choice. However, the decision to leave, so said the Nazi flyers, would be rewarded as a clear sign of love and devotion to the Great Germanic cause. Whoever loved their *Heimat* was certainly ready to abandon it and rebuild it elsewhere, exactly the same, in the bosom of the Thousand-Year Reich. Remaining, on the other hand, was an unequivocal sign of betrayal, insubordination against the National Socialist cause, cowardice.

These were your options; actually *die Option*.

No peasant would have chosen to leave his *maso* but they all felt *Daitsch*, and the vast majority ended up doing just that. They opted to, as they used to say. Still, there were too many peasants who would whisper to their wives under the goose eiderdowns at night, wondering: but what about their field, deforested by their great-grandfathers with saws and axes a century earlier? Would they really never see it again? And what about those lands, where cows of the same color awaited, *masi* with the same extensions, the same number of trees as what they'd leave behind—were they uninhabited? And if they weren't, then where would the inhabitants go?

Hermann enthusiastically took part in the persecution organized by the regime against the *Dableiber*. With the blessing of Fascist party officials, he maimed heavy draft horses. He killed guard dogs. He smeared his own excrement on the jambs of the doors of those who weren't planning on leaving; then he'd go and wash his hands in the streams, feeling in his chest a strength he'd never felt before. During those moments he almost forgot the shame and solitude of the little *Knecht* who pissed himself in the freezing cold.

There was an old peasant who had been widowed for many years and had no children. He was born in the *Stube* of the *maso* where he was living and had never been more than just a few kilometers away. He hadn't even gone to fight in the Great War because he was born blind in one eye. He had two cows, Lissi and Lotte, which he was reluctant to leave in the hands of strangers: one could say they were his family. In any case, he couldn't quite make up his mind to hand in his Option form signed. Hermann and two of his comrades set fire to his hayloft. The old man spent all night running up and down with a small bucket of water, trying to bring the fire under control, crying with his good eye. The mooing of Lissi and Lotte, trapped by the fire, sounded like the wailing of two enormous babies. They fell silent only when the burning roof of the hayloft collapsed on top of them and, together with the smoke and the flying fragments, a delicious smell of steak wafted out. The old man let himself fall to the ground and did not get up again.

Hermann also took part in the ambush on Sepp Schwingshackl. Unlike so many of his fellow countrymen, his old schoolmate had never shared that pagan fascination with the Führer, and the way he had quietly and firmly declared that he would not be leaving his maso made him a very dangerous *Dableiber*. The *Gauleiter* ordered Hermann and two others to teach him a lesson—they could decide just how hard it should be. And so, even though he and Sepp had walked to school together every day when they were children, even though every time his truck had broken down while carrying a load of timber Sepp had always lent him his hand cart, Hermann went.

Sepp did not die after being ambushed. He remained with his hands shaking, slightly deaf, and with a white scar on his forehead, which lifted his eyebrows in a puzzled expression. As though the astonishment of seeing a childhood friend kicking him in the face was printed on his face forever.

A joyful crowd saw off the first *Optanten*, pioneers of the new *Heimat*. Very blond children (chosen expressly for the color of their hair) placed daisy chains on the heads of all those leaving. The red, black, and white of the swastikas stood out against the deep blue sky, the whiteness of the glaciers, the dark gold of larches in the fall. Everybody said it looked magnificent. When Hermann Huber got on the train with his family, Peter was four years old, and his wife Johanna was expecting her second child, Annemarie. Hermann wanted to set an example, as appropriate to a true Nazi, and was one of the first to leave.

Also one of the last. Just a few months later, Italy entered the war and the departures of the *Optanten*, even though these were the majority of South Tyroleans, were suspended. Those who left, instead, were men called up to the front. As for creating the German paradise on earth, the *Daitschn Himml*, everybody forgot about it.

The Hubers came back to the valley after the war. Nobody, including the *Dableiber*, wondered where they had been. On which front Hermann had fought, in which division of the Wehrmacht, if he had moved over to the SS, if he had murdered many civilians or only his uniformed counterparts, enemy soldiers whom it was right and moral to strike down—nobody asked him. And especially, nobody asked him to give an account of the paradise on earth promised by the Führer. In everybody's eyes, he might as well have been finished.

The war cemetery of the valley's main town had—and still has—plain wooden crosses in the midst of very tall larches: a small forest of the dead in the midst of a larger forest of real trees. On the crosses are written the dates and places they fell. Specific information, like Woroschilowgrad, Aletschenka, Jehsowetowska, Trieste, Cassino, Pojaplie, Vermuiza; or more general, such as the Caucasus, Finland, Normandy, Montenegro. In some cases there's just the continent: *Afrika*, or the direction: *im Osten*, in the East. On many crosses there is also a photograph. Young men looking impeccable in well-pressed uniforms, striking poses. Almost no one looks straight ahead, but rather up to the side. Some have gentle expressions, others excited, others uncertain. It's impossible to tell whether the expression in their eyes that has been fixed forever is consistent with the way they acted in this planetary slaughterhouse. Perhaps that lost-looking nineteen-year-old boy machine-gunned a pregnant woman. Perhaps that SS *Unterscharführer* with eyes like ice performed an act of mercy toward a prisoner. Of course, many had the opportunity to do both. But nobody wanted to know that. They were the sons, the fathers, the brothers of those who were now rebuilding the houses that had been destroyed. Nobody wanted to know if they had died as humble heroes, as cowards, or as torturers.

Optanten and *Dableiber*, once enemies, found themselves united by the wish not to give things too specific a name. Nazi, collaborator, informer, war criminal, *Konzentrationslagerführer*: these were not words but unexploded grenades around which you tiptoed so as not to trigger the worst kind of explosion— the truth. There was still too much war rubble to be cleared, too much hunger to endure, too many dead to mourn, too much loss they had all suffered. Even the monuments to the

Italian Alpine troops had been erased by Allied bombs. No, there was no need to ask anyone anything, not even Hermann.

The agreement was made in silence, but it was respected by all.

Alberto Ruotolo, an employee of the railroads, was now occupying the house where the Hubers had lived before the war. Like thousands of other immigrants, Mussolini had called him up from Vomero in order to Italianize Alto Adige. Now, the new Republican government still needed him, along with the rest of the Fascist-era white-collar workers, to operate the country. Through the windows of the house where Hermann had conceived his first child, there now wafted the sour smell of tomato sauce; Ruotolo's fat wife would summon their children to dinner in a very high-pitched voice, letting out a burst of truncated words. "Pepè! Ueuè! Totò"—that's how her Neapolitan delivery sounded to South Tyrolean ears. The Ruotolos remained in the house and the Hubers had to go and live in Shanghai. *Rücksiedler* was what they called—and not affectionately—the cluster of houses on the side of the mountain in the shadow of the Medieval castle, assigned to those who'd returned to live there. It was now the most insulting name, given to the Hubers as well as all the ones who had opted and who'd come home. South Tyroleans seemed to have forgotten that at the time of *die Option* almost all of them had said they were ready to leave and the only reason they hadn't was because the war had broken out, and that nobody had stood up for the *Dableiber* who'd resisted. All the ones who had signed "*Ja*" on the orange Option paper were now calling the few who had actually left "traitors to the *Heimat*." The same people who had waved swastikas and flags at the departure of Hermann and his family were now calling him a bastard. That dark load that would press on his chest from when he used to piss on himself, as an eleven-year-old orphan, became even more oppressive.

Shanghai was nearly a *mile* away from the nearest shop and almost two from the center of town: its good inhabitants insisted on keeping their distance from the *Rücksiedler*. It was a cluster of low houses coated with a gray mixture of plaster and stones from the river. The sun would disappear behind the looming hill at the end of September and not reappear until May. During thunderstorms, water from the highway would come flooding in through the front doors and even in summer the washing would never dry. The Shanghai residents were considered good-for-nothing, treacherous, Communists.

Shanghai was also called *Hungerburg*—from *Hunger*, hunger—or *Revolverviertel*, the district of handguns, because of the continuous coming and going of customs officers, Alpini and Carabinieri, and not for patrolling. When, years later, Gerda was seen escorted by an Italian in uniform, some people said, "No wonder! She grew up in Shanghai."

Peter was ten years old and didn't have a single friend. He'd spent his early childhood elsewhere and spoke with a strange accent (a Bavarian accent: the Hubers hadn't actually gone that far). No mother would allow a child of his age to go and play at his house in Shanghai. His schoolmates bullied him then said, "Don't like it here? Well, nobody asked you to come back."

Annemarie was old enough to help around the house, and Gerda was a baby. Johanna's milk had dried up in Munich in the bombing, but Gerda learnt to digest *Knödel* before she was even four months old, and survived. You could already tell that she was nothing like her mother.

Johanna wasn't old: she'd married Hermann at eighteen and was now about thirty. Nor was she ugly. She just looked even more mortified about being in this world than before. Perhaps it was the war, or perhaps the fact that her husband had stopped speaking to her since he'd returned.

"*Ostfront*," is all Hermann would say to the rare people who asked where he had fought. The Eastern Front.

Gerda was growing up. Peter and Annemarie had inherited their mother's black eyes, while hers were blue and almond-shaped like her father's, and her cheekbones were high and . Johanna, on the other hand, became more and more stooped, like a woman twice her age. As though there were a limited amount of vital force available in that house and that it was no longer for the mother but only for the youngest daughter. And that's where it flowed in its entirety and with a vengeance.

Peter began spending more and more time on his own in the woods. Every step he took on the thick layer of humus, the billions of larch needles that had accumulated over thousands of years, made the live rock several feet deep resound like a drum; that light thud as he advanced gingerly, holding a sling, seemed to him the most welcoming sound in the world. That was his home, and the squirrels, foxes, martens, grouses, and magpies were his companions. He learned to kill them, of course, but first he got to know them, to watch them patiently, and wait for them for hours. He was an excellent shot and soon, with the money from the furs and feathers he sold to the milliners, he bought his first gun.

Although she was still very young, Gerda was to remember for the rest of her life the day Peter brought home his first stag. He loaded it on his shoulders, wrapping it over his neck and holding its legs almost tenderly. The stag's head was bobbing up and down on his back, its mouth open, its tongue hanging out, like a bloody version of the Good Shepherd. Gerda was struck by the contrast between the inertness of the dull eyes and the fur still soft to the touch. The sickly-sweet smell of blood remained in her nostrils for a long time while Peter was skinning the deer, and also the stench of nerves and animal fat that emanated from the largest pot Johanna owned, and over the edge of which protruded long, elegant antlers. If Gerda hadn't seen Peter cut the head clean off the animal's body, she would have always believed that the stag was playing hide and seek in a pan with magic powers.

The skull was boiled and the flesh stripped off completely. Peter was planning to make good money by selling it as a trophy.

When they had left, those who had "opted" had renounced Italian citizenship, so now the *Rücksiedler* were stateless. Without documents, without work, and without respect, times were hard for the Hubers, at first, like for all the other Shanghai residents. The mother of the town dentist, a baroness, offered to take Johanna into her service but Hermann wouldn't hear of it: as long as he was alive his wife would not be bringing money home. And so to top up the family income, at the age of twelve, Peter went to work in a sawmill. Annemarie started cleaning the stairs of the primary school when she turned ten, and was therefore still younger than the pupils in the final year. Their efforts weren't in vain: after a couple of years driving other people's trucks, Hermann managed to buy himself one.

Three years after the end of the war, with a merciful gesture, the Italian government made a clean slate of the effects of the Option: it gave back Italian citizenship to the *Rücksiedler* who requested it. The old Hermann could never have imagined the relief he felt the day he obtained once again, for himself and his family, the documents which declared them to be Italian Citizens.

Shanghai became once again part of what was now Republican Italy.

When Gerda was eight she began replacing her mother in the task of warming up the engine of Hermann's truck. She would wake up at three in the morning, put on her coat without even washing her face, and go out into the winter frost when the night was at his darkest. Interrupting her sleep was even more painful than the cold slapping her drowsy face. At night, her father's truck was parked outside the front door, and in order to start the engine in the morning you first had to scrape the ice off the crank on the front. Gerda's hands were already as rough as a washerwoman's. She would light a small fire with shavings and paper under the belly of the vehicle, taking care not to waste the matches. She stayed there in the cold, on all fours, to make sure it wouldn't go out, spreading the fuel in a circle with an iron shovel. You had to be careful: if the flame was too high the oil tank and the entire truck would explode, and she with them. Once the starting crank was warm and the ice vapor that blocked it had melted, Gerda would go back home, pick up the cup her mother had meanwhile prepared on the wooden stove, and wake up Hermann with the coffee. While her father climbed into the truck and started the engine, Gerda would get ready for school.

One morning when it was still dark, Gerda handed her father the coffee but he didn't wake up straight away. He was still dreaming. His opaque eyes opened with difficulty.

"*Mamme*," he muttered.

His mother was back! And now she was there next to his bed with a cup of steamy white coffee for him, just like when he was ill, as a child.

Gerda got frightened: she had never seen him with this helpless, trusting expression before.

"*Tata . . . i bin's. Die Gerda*," she said.[6]

Hermann blinked and opened his eyes again. The same eyes, the same mouth, the same cheekbones as his mother; except that it was only his daughter. He realized what he had just called her and never forgave her.

---

[6] Daddy, it's me. Gerda.

In the summer, when the truck engine didn't need warming up, Gerda would go to the mountain pastures with her cousin, to mind the cows of uncle Hans, Hermann's eldest brother, the one who had inherited the family *maso*.

The pasture was half a day's walk from the *maso*, too far to come back every night. Gerda and her cousins, Michl and Simon, who were more or less the same age, and little Sebastian, known as Wastl, would sleep on the hay in a hut. They would spend their days showing one another those anatomical parts that they didn't have in common, stuffing themselves with blueberries, spitting juniper berries at one another, and carving twigs. Only when absolutely necessary did they run after cows that were wandering off. When it rained or, even better, when there was a thunderstorm, they would plunge into the warm hay and tell one another scary stories, with evil spirits of the mountain as protagonists. Three times a week, Hans's wife would bring crisp rye bread, called *Schüttelbrot*, speck and cheese.

Gerda was the only one who never needed to use the stick with the cows, since they followed her around like huge lapdogs. Her cousins, too, would have followed her anywhere. Several decades later, when Simon and Michl thought back to those nights in the hay with Gerda, with little Wastl asleep right next to them, the memory of her sparse, blond pubic hair, revealed by her raised shabby dress, could still make the blood rush to their nether parts.

One of those summer mornings, an English mountain climber who'd lost his way saw her from afar. Gerda was sitting under a Swiss pine, her eyes half closed. She was emitting high-pitched whistling sounds, like glass, with a blade of grass held tight between her lips. Her bare legs and feet caked with mud protruded from a threadbare cotton dress, and her dirty hair was tied back with a string of braided bark. High cheekbones, rounded forehead, fleshy lips, elongated blue eyes. The Englishman thought she was the most beautiful girl he had ever seen. The thought of going away and never seeing her again seemed unbearable. He contemplated her for a long time before making his presence known. He forgot about his planned climb and remained all day at the hut.

The English climber shared his packed lunch with Gerda and her cousins. When he heard her laugh he decided he would do anything to hear that sound again. He began chasing after the cows, brandishing his *Alpenstock*, and barking like a sheepdog. He hung a cowbell around his neck and grazed, ruminating and actually swallowing the grass in the field. He mimed the solemn gait of young Queen Elizabeth, placing a crown of daisies on his head with which he then crowned Gerda, declaring her the one and only queen. However, when the moment came for him to leave, the Englishman respectfully asked her permission to take a photo. At the end of the summer, Hans's wife handed Gerda an envelope addressed to her. Sender: John Gallagher, Leeds, United Kingdom. In it was Gerda's photo at the age of ten, which Eva would one day put on her bookshelf. On the back, in large, spiky letters, was written: *In eternal gratitude for the best day of my life. Forever yours, John.*

During one of those summers, the monument to the Alpini had been rebuilt—a little more slender than the previous one, and a little less grumpy. At the solemn inauguration, the army bishop declared that this time it underlined the reconciliation between the Italian government and its faraway province. It symbolized defense, he stressed, not aggression.

However, the South Tyroleans didn't change their minds. That was a Fascist monument and always would be, even though there was no more Fascism. Except for the authorities, none of them attended the inauguration. Not even Peter, who was now sixteen, or his father. Hermann didn't want anything to do with these things anymore.

One night, a couple of years later, Peter came back home at dawn. His mother, who could never get to sleep until her first-born was back, knew immediately: Peter hadn't been hunting. His clothes didn't smell of forest or gunpowder, but were soiled with red and white paint. However, Johanna asked for no explanation. The following morning, the Carabinieri surrounded the monument to the Alpine troops and closed to traffic the intersection where it had been erected. During the night, its granite pedestal had been painted red and white, the forbidden colors of the Tyrolean flag. Thus derided, it inspired more an almost ironic affection than fear or resentment. From that moment on, the town residents started calling it by the common diminutive, Wastl. The Carabinieri had to spend an entire day scrubbing it with brushes and soap.

Peter couldn't find a job and got by on seasonal work. He picked potatoes, hired himself out as a laborer to peasants whose sons were conscripted when they needed an extra pair of arms to gather the hay. Only occasionally, when there was a particularly heavy load, he would help his father with the truck, but there was never enough money. One winter he found a good job as a custodian in the house of a noble family from Vienna that spent the summers in South Tyrol. His duties involved lighting the stoves three times a week so the pipes wouldn't freeze, checking the windows, and sweeping the snow from the roof. The work wasn't arduous but it wasn't well-paid. Peter wanted to start a family. He was twenty-two now and there was a girl he quite liked. But at this rate he'd never be able to do it. That was until he heard that Falck steelworks in Bolzano were hiring workers.

Johanna was the only one in the family who could read and write in Italian: she was the only one to have gone to a Fascist school. Hermann had gone to primary school in the Austro-Hungarian Empire and suspended his studies when his parents had died. His children had gone to the schools of the Republic created by anti-Fascism, which had not returned South Tyrol to Mother Austria, as its residents had deluded themselves it would, but at least it had recognized their right to study in their own language. All the bureaucracy, however, was still in Italian.

It was therefore Johanna who helped Peter prepare all the documents: certificate of good behavior, dispensation from obligatory military service, a strong and healthy constitution. It was she who accompanied him to the various offices. There was no form or sign in German, no state employee spoke German; nobody understood German. The fact that the population that frequented these offices was German-speaking was totally ignored. Applications had to be written in correct Italian or you risked having to start from scratch. For Johanna, having to speak with these impolite clerks in a language that wasn't her own was a source of anxiety and embarrassment but, in the end, Peter obtained all the certificates. She then ironed his Sunday suit, and one Monday at dawn Peter took the bus to the main city.

He remained in Bolzano for a few weeks. He stayed with a distant cousin of his mother's in a tiny house with four children aged between two and eight. At night, Peter slept on the floor next to the stove, but he could not remain there during the day. Those were the days of the three *Eis Männer*, the ice saints in the middle of spring, the last cold and nasty stretch of winter, and the air was frosty. Peter had no money to go and warm up in a tavern so he spent his afternoons in the waiting room at the station. That's where he saw them get off the trains.

They were mainly men. Although Peter didn't know it, they were identical to those who during those same years were arriving also in Turin, Liège, Düsseldorf. They had peaked caps, checkered jackets, cardboard boxes tied with string and the odd leather suitcase. Every so often there would also be a woman between twenty and thirty, seldom any older, with thick black hair. She would get off the train alone or else with three or four children, but there was always a man waiting for her, with a face identical to those who had arrived alone though perhaps a little less hollow, a little less anxious, a little more self-confident: the face of a man who has a job and can now take on the responsibility and dignity of the head of the family.

Nobody had explained to the immigrants from southern Italy what kind of place they were going to, before they left. It hadn't occurred to anyone in the recruitment offices in Enna, Matera and Crotone, where the Bolzano factories were obtaining their workforce, to let them know that they were about to go and live among people who spoke German, who did not eat spaghetti or even polenta, but things they called *Knödel, Schlutzkrapfen, Spatzlan*. They were still in Italy, weren't they? That was all an immigrant needed to know.

When Peter arrived in Bolzano, wearing his Sunday suit all clean and ironed, he went to the Falck recruitment office. There, he left his job application and all the painfully obtained documents. Over the following days he also went to Lancia, then the railroad company and even the road company: the life of a road worker wasn't great but it was still better than being unemployed.

Not one of his job applications was answered.

It took a while for Peter to understand. The economic miracle of the industrial area of Bolzano, with its social housing and almost acceptable wages, had been devised only for Italians. It's not that they didn't want a German-speaking worker. It was simply not factored in.

Yes, now you could teach in German once again in Alto Adige schools. There was no more need for *Katakomben-*

schulen for pupils and teachers to be able to speak and study in their own language. The new Italian Republic had not tackled the Germanness of South Tyroleans the way Mussolini had done. It had chosen to adopt a different attitude toward the problem: pretend it didn't exist.

Peter went back home. Johanna was horrified when she saw the state of his suit: he hadn't taken it off for three weeks. Peter did not explain why he hadn't found work and nobody asked him. The following summer he remained in Switzerland for the entire season. He found a job as a herdsman and supplemented his income selling hunting trophies, especially chamois. Once, he got lucky and killed an ibex. Only German tourists bought anything from him. The few Italians who ventured in those parts weren't particularly interested in trophies.

One November day, when Gerda was almost twelve, Peter suggested she go with him on an excursion near Bolzano. He said there would be lots of people, like at the church fair, *Kirschta*, only much bigger.

An excursion! Sometimes on a Sunday automobiles, carts or groups of bicycles would drive along the highway past Shanghai, and Gerda would hear people singing and laughing. On Sundays during the summer, her father's colleagues would also load their families and friends on trucks and take them to the shores of the river that comes down from the glaciers, or to the fields at the start of the adjacent valley. The wind would carry to Gerda the smoke, the smell of grilled Würstel, waves of music, laughter, and she would be overwhelmed with longing at the joy of these strangers. Sometimes, without needing to go too far, there would be a party even in Shanghai, in the courtyard in the middle of the houses on the upper part of the road. At the end of the summer, that's where they would pile up freshly-picked corn, then tear off its long, sharp, pointy leaves by hand: once dried, they would use them to stuff mattresses for the whole winter. The workers and the peasant women would set the pace with songs and jokes and afterwards, in the evening, when the heap of leaves in the courtyard corner was taller than the front door, they would start dancing to the sound of the zithern and the accordion. All the residents of the district would come, some with bottles of cider, others with a slice of speck, others with chairs for the elderly. Everybody came except for the Hubers. When Hermann heard singing during those light evenings that smelt of hay, his face would darken. "It's alright for some who are rich and can afford to party," he would say, "but I have to work tomorrow." Then he'd go to bed.

Gerda had never heard the sound of her father's laughter. On the other hand, she remembered exactly the last time she had seen her mother laugh. A pail with soapy water had been knocked over on the kitchen floor, Hermann had walked on it and slipped. The sight of her husband falling stiffly and hitting his behind entertained Johanna, and for a long time Gerda remembered her mother's delicate laugh, in whoops and hiccups that shook her skinny chest. Hermann did not tell her to stop, did not shout at her, and did not make fun of her in his turn. But when he got up, he gave her such a look of deep contempt that laughter dried on her lips like a flower touched by a firebrand. Gerda never heard her mother laugh again for as long as she lived.

Gerda did not know her older brother Peter very well, either. He was ten years her senior and she had spent much less time with him than with her cousins. There was no intimacy between them: separated by sex and age, they had never had much to say to each other. They had lived under the same roof, eaten the same bread, but that was all.

Peter had become a tall, well-built young man but his movements were somewhat graceless, like his mother's. More than uncertain, he looked furtive; like a hunter lying in ambush who has to conceal the power of his firearm. He had also inherited his mother's dark brown eyes that didn't reflect the light. There was something opaque in his eyes that had frightened Gerda as a child. Now that he was grown up, Peter looked nothing like Hermann, except when he spoke—which, like his father, almost never happened—and when he really had to speak he did so with his mouth half-closed, as though words were precious objects you could only part with reluctantly.

Peter had never even brought a friend home. The girl he would have liked to marry had never yet been to their *Stube*. He would visit her in the courtyard of the *maso* where she was born. He took her small gifts: the long antler of a stag, which he had carved with geometrical figures; a bunch of capercaillie feathers with a steely sheen; a handkerchief he bought at the market. Leni, the girl, would accept them with a smile that made them precious, just as a sunbeam lights up a cat's eye and makes it look like a gold nugget. However, even with her Peter wasn't very talkative.

No, the Hubers were not known for being good company.

An excursion. With Peter. Gerda wasn't sure which of these novelties was more extraordinary. *Tata* and *Mamme* wouldn't come, he explained, they weren't interested. Nor would Annemarie: she worked as a servant in a family and had only half a day off on Sundays.

They left long before dawn. That year it was a mild fall, but it was still dark and cold. Gerda was surprised to see so many people in the street even though it was long before early mass. They were all going to the town center where a few trucks and a bus were warming up their engines. Gerda was wearing her confirmation dress. Twice already Johanna had let it out, but it was still tight over her chest and soon you wouldn't be able to fix it anymore. Over it she wore a boiled wool jersey, gray with green borders; and she had a red handkerchief around her neck. Peter was wearing the same suit as when he was looking

for work in Bolzano. Johanna had restored it to life with
patient darning and cleaning.

They climbed onto one of the trucks along with a couple of
dozen other people. Some were in *Tracht*: the women were
wearing long skirts, heavy satin aprons with an iridescent glow
and lace bibs, like on a *HerzJesu* parade; many men wore waistcoats with red and green stripes, embossed leather belts over
Lederhosen, and felt hats with capercaillie feathers. Even those
not in Tyrolean costume were wearing their Sunday best.

Gerda was the youngest there. When she got on the truck
the men made room for her as if she were an important person,
the women offered her rye bread and elderberry juice from
aluminum flasks wrapped in felt. Never had so many people
smiled at her all at the same time. When the column of vehicles started moving, the headlights formed a wreath of lights,
which Gerda thought was more festive than an Advent crown
with its candles. The people on the truck started singing and
she joined in with her still childlike voice. They sang "Brunnen
vor dem Tor, Wo der Wildbach rauscht, Kein schöner Land":
songs in which romantic love merges with the love of the
Heimat. Gerda didn't know the words: she'd never sung in
chorus at a country festival. However, the melody took pre-
dictable, reassuring turns, and the notes resounded on the roof
of her mouth and deep in her throat, as though she had always
known them. The icy wind slammed in her face and she felt
happy, even though Peter hadn't told her why there were so
many people, or where they were going. For the first time in
her life, however, he bent down to his little sister and smiled.

Three hours later, when they reached their destination,
Gerda was asleep, her head in the lap of the woman who had
given her elderberry juice. The truck stopped with a tired
moan of the brakes and she opened her eyes.

She wondered if she was still dreaming. She had never seen
so many people at once. Not even at the *HerzJesu* procession,

or at the funeral of the local nobleman, when the funeral cart, pulled by four black horses, had proceeded along the Medieval street with people on either side. Peter lifted her off, his hands in her armpits, and put her down on the ground like a doll. Gerda was surrounded by people who squeezed her, pushed, halted and, like a river going in the wrong direction, flowed up the slope that rose from the Bolzano valley all the way up to the dilapidated ruins of Castel Firmiano. Gerda held Peter's hand tight, but she wasn't afraid. On the contrary, she felt as though the crowd was a single organism, a living entity of which she was a part, and whose emotions and waves she sensed before they became also hers. Something she felt she belonged to and which gave even her, a girl who wasn't quite twelve, meaning and dignity. She felt brave, enthusiastic, a believer even though she had no idea in what. Never again was Gerda to see such a crowd, except on television.

It was a mild day. It was mid-November but the sun was more like September and made people's eyes glisten as they smiled and greeted one another, even strangers, even if they came from different valleys. Peter was right: this festivity in Castel Firmiano, Sigmundskron in German, was something that had never been equaled before in the whole of South Tyrol.

There were banners, signs. On many of them, Gerda, read: *Volk in Not*, a nation in danger. The rally was surrounded by two rows of Carabinieri, black as tar, with red stripes down the legs, which made them look like strange insects, their hands on machine guns. They watched tensely as the crowd went up to the ruins of the castle. They were young, some very young. They were more afraid of all that crowd than the crowd was of them, and Gerda saw that as soon as she caught the eyes of one of them. He was only a little older than her: eighteen, nineteen at most. He kept his eyes on hers as though finding comfort in them. Gerda had already realized that "they" were not a part of that thing she and Peter and all the others belonged to. On the contrary they represented exactly the "danger" her "people" were in. However, the boy in uniform, with his hat lowered too far down on his forehead, kept looking at her as though clinging to the grace of that little girl with dress that was too tight, in order to be able to bear his fear more easily. Gerda couldn't help but smile at him. The red handkerchief she was wearing around her neck got untied and fell to the ground. Instinctively, the Carabiniere made to bend down, and the hand that wasn't on the machine gun reached out to pick up the handkerchief.

The comrade in arms next to him turned abruptly and stared at him. He gave him a hard look, one that promised he would be reported to his superiors, or worse. The young Carabiniere's smile stiffened into a mask tenser than before. He hesitated, then his trunk became rigid and straight again, and his hand returned parallel to his hip. Gerda looked away. She picked up the handkerchief by herself and carried on walking. Peter didn't notice anything. The crowd was already pushing them ahead, to the top of the hill.

Bunches of people were hanging from the trees. They were gathered in the castle clearing, on the high ground around, on the battlements of the dilapidated bastions. It looked to Gerda that this field of people had germinated from the soil like gigantic grass made of flesh, clothes, hats, faces: you couldn't see the ground in between the people. Only on the overhanging rocks, from which the ruins sprang like fairytale excrescences, could you get a glimpse of the blood-red porphyry in between people's bodies.

There was a man on stage at the foot of the castle tower. Gerda couldn't decide which looked more stripped of flesh— him or the crutches on which he was leaning. He wasn't old, but he looked ill and very fragile. Gerda had seen many veterans who carried in their bodies the memory of the war that had ended just twelve years earlier: she immediately recognized the thinness of disabled people, those who had lost a leg, like this man who was now talking to the crowd, or a hand, or an arm. The part of them that no longer existed was in constant pain, which radiated and sucked the life out of what remained of the body, draining it like a vampire. The same man really looked as though he was prey to this phantom parasite: he spoke in a brooding, metallic voice that had nothing of the orator about it. Yet the crowd was listening to him in absolute silence. Only when he mentioned the then Minister of the Interior Tambroni did he have to interrupt his speech because of the hisses and boos. He did not lose his composure but waited, calmly, without betraying signs of impatience, and let the crowd boo the representative of the Italian government to its heart's content.

A minute passed. The catcalls continued.

Two minutes. The soldiers and Carabinieri forming a cordon at the foot of the stage began to exchange looks, as though wondering if they should do something.

Three minutes. The hissing directed at the government minister to whom they answered gave no sign of subsiding. Gerda picked a blade of grass, dusty and trampled on by the thousands of feet that had walked on it. She raised it to her lips which the same gesture John Gallagher, from Leeds, United Kingdom, had seen at the hut. She blew and produced a very high-pitched whistling sound. For the second and last time in her whole life, Peter turned to her and gave her a pleased smile.

Four minutes. The hands of the younger Carabinieri were beginning to leave sweat halos on the machine gun handles. The man up on the stage calmly looked at the tens of thousands of people catcalling. He was in no rush to resume his speech. He was taking advantage of the interruption to calculate the turnout to the demonstration he had organized. He was pleased. There, before him, Silvius Magnano, on that 17

November 1957, at Castel Firmiano, there were at least thirty, forty thousand people. Seeing that the total population of South Tyrol was scarcely three hundred thousand, that meant at least one tenth, possibly more, was there. Like Gerda and Peter, they had left in the middle of the night on trucks, buses, cars, motorcycles, tractors. They came from the outskirts of Bolzano, Oltreadige, but also from valleys farther away: Ahrntal, Schlanders, Passeier, Martell, Gsies, Vinschgau. From places where, in dialect, you count *oans, zwoa* . . . and also those where you say *aans, zwa* . . . And so they continued to hiss and boo, as though they never wanted to stop.

Five minutes. The Carabinieri looked at their superiors.

The skinny man onstage caught his breath and opened his mouth as though to resume his speech. Silence returned at once.

Silvius Magnago reminded the crowd of Canon Gamper di Bressanone. The clergyman, who had been persecuted by the Nazis, had launched an appeal a few months earlier: *"Es ist ein Todesmarsch!"* A death march was what South Tyrol was heading for, if things carried on like this: with forced immigration from Southern Italy, jobs being denied to the natives, the growing poverty and emigration. South Tyroleans would soon become a minority in their own land, before being finally swept out of History.

What he would fight for, promised Magnago, the head of the *Südtiroler Volkspartei*, the German-speaking South Tyrolean party, was an autonomous province that wouldn't be attached to another Italian-speaking province, like Trento. A true autonomy that would allow South Tyroleans to take back control of their own land.

He ended his speech by shouting once, twice, many times: *"Los von Trient!"*—Away from Trento! Away from that region with an Italian majority where, once again, Germans were in a minority and unprotected. The crowd cheered, and seemed never to want to stop.

Suddenly, the sound of a sheet being beaten came from the keep of the dilapidated tower. Everybody looked up. Two young men had penetrated the ruins and now, leaning out of one of the slits, had deployed a long, red and white flag. Displaying the Tyrolean flag was still forbidden by Italian law: one of the many Fascist laws no one had bothered to repeal. A small group of Carabinieri started to run toward the tower. Before they were arrested, the two young men began to shout, "*Los von Rom!*"

Peter and the others, mainly young men, joined them. "*Los von Rom!*' cried a small part of the crowd.

In other words: No to the autonomy of politicians, of diplomacy, of compromise. It's not enough just to leave Trento. Leave Rome. Leave Italy.

Magnago pursed his lips as the activists were being taken away by the Carabinieri.

Just over a year later, the monument to the Alpine troops in the town where the Hubers lived was targeted once more. This time, there was no red and white paint, no student-like provocations, but an explosive device blew up the pedestal. However, Wastl, little Johnny made of stone, was not destroyed: the charge was faulty.

That day, Peter was in a nearby valley, helping his father with a load of timber. After a quarter of a century driving trucks, Hermann was starting to have back problems. His son's help became necessary, even though that meant giving up the extra money Peter could have brought home from other work. In the evening, when they came back home, Johanna did not comment on what had happened to Wastl that morning. She felt sufficiently relieved that, this time, it hadn't been her son.

One June day a couple of years later, a man from Merano came to see the Hubers. He was *Daitsch* but swore in Italian.

All the South Tyroleans were now swearing in Italian everywhere, even in the privacy of their own homes. During Fascism, so many of them, like Hermann, had had to endure disapproval and even blows if ever they let exclamations slip in German dialect. So the entire population was therefore convinced that perhaps it would be better to swear in Italian even at home, just to get used to it. However, nobody can tell for sure if there wasn't perhaps also the hope that the *daitcher Gott*, the German good Lord, might not be that well versed in foreign languages: perhaps He wouldn't have entirely understood a *walsche* swear word, and would therefore have been less offended. Whichever way you decide to interpret this, the unanimous adoption of Italian swearing on the part of German speakers turned out to be, of all the Italianization imposed by Fascism, the only success story. But a lasting one.

The man from Merano had come to tell Hermann that he wanted his younger daughter to work in the kitchens of a large hotel. Tourists had only recently started coming back to Alto Adige after the war, so anyone looking for a job could now find one in tourism's new frontier: the Dolomite valleys. The large pre-war hotels in the health resorts in the Adige valley were therefore short on staff. The man was offering a good salary, free bed and board, and an apprenticeship in a steady profession: cooking.

Maybe if Hermann hadn't been a frightened little *Knecht* who wetted himself out of sadness; if he hadn't spread excrement over the doors of the masi during the dark months of the Option; if he'd chosen a woman to marry out of love and not powerlessness; if he hadn't done and seen things on the Eastern Front that nobody could talk about; in other words if Hermann hadn't lost love a long time ago, too long ago, then maybe he would have taken into consideration the fact that the hard times were over, that his family was no longer grindingly poor, that his truck kept his children fed and clothed, nothing more than that, but at least that, and that everyone knew from many stories what awaited his daughter if she went (there was a reason they called young female cooks *Matratzen*: matresses).

And he would have said to the man: *Wort a mol*, wait a moment. He would have said *Des madl will i net weggian lossn*, I am not letting this little girl go. Her cheeks are still round like a child's but she already has a woman's shape, and slender legs, she is beautiful, very beautiful, she is exactly like her grandmother, but she doesn't know it yet so I have to protect her, which is something only I can do, and must do, as her father. I will take her to dance the polka at the *Kirschta'* in the summer, to show all the young men how desirable she is but also how protective and careful her father is and that he will never allow anyone to hurt her. So, no, I will not let you take her to hotels for foreigners so she can be called a *Matratze*.

Instead, Hermann said, *"Passt."* All right.

Gerda was sixteen. She left.

The journey to the health resort wasn't long but it was complicated. When she arrived at the train station in Bolzano, she was taken aback: she could hear only Italian spoken around her andcould see only dark complexions. This was, after all, the same city where, a few years ago, Peter had seen immigrants arrive from the South.

She was supposed to catch the bus to Merano, but she couldn't see any. There was a wide, tree-lined avenue in front of the stairs to the station. She went there clutching the ticket on which the man had written the name of the hotel where she was going. The flowers of the chestnut trees on the avenue gave off a powerful scent. The man from Merano had told her to walk halfway up then turn left. Gerda walked, uncertain, intoxicated by the scent of the clusters of flowers above her, clutching the handle of the small suitcase containing her few possessions. The bus station was there. Gerda approached the driver but didn't dare ask him for information: she was embarrassed to speak Italian.

"*Schnell! Der Bus Richtung Meran fährt jetzt!*"[7] she heard a couple of elderly German tourists. She ran after them to a bus with the engine already started, and got on. She was lucky: just a few seconds later the driver closed the doors and drove off.

[7] Quick! The bus for Merano is leaving now!

I call my mother and tell her that I'm not coming to Easter lunch. I won't be eating the delicacies she and my *Patin* Ruthi have been preparing for the past week. She won't be able to show me off in front of the tribe of relatives, or get the usual compliments on how beautiful and clever her daughter is, but such a shame she never married (I'm greatly relieved they now say "never" when they used to say "not yet"—turning forty brought with it that achievement).

"I must go away," I say to her, "it's something urgent."

I've never missed a festive meal with her. Therefore, this exception can only be something important. As a matter of fact she doesn't demand an explanation. She simply asks, "Do I know him?"

Does she have any doubts that this urgency might not be connected with a man? No, none whatsoever.

I look at the glaciers in the distance, or at least at what global warming has left of them.

"You might do," I say, and she doesn't persist.

It's impossible to find a plane to Calabria the day before Easter. I call all the airlines, and then the airports of Bolzano, Verona, Venice, Milan, Munich, Innsbruck and Brescia. I try for hours on the Internet. Nothing. The first seat on a flight to Reggio Calabria is in three days' time, after Easter Monday. That could be too late for Vito. There's just one other option: a sleeper train to Roma Termini, and from there another train to Calabria. It will take a long time. Italy is a long country. And so, here I am on the local train that's taking me to Fortezza/Franzenfeste. High up at the other end of the carriage, there's a poster of the *Deutsches Kultur-und Familienamt*, the local government's family and culture department for the German-speaking population—strictly distinct and separate from its Italian counterpart. It's publicizing training courses for adults in the Bolzano area. There's a picture of a man in blue overalls sitting in what we imagine is his workshop. He must be a mechanic, an electrician or a welder. With his large worker's hands and the expression of an attentive child, he's folding a pink sheet of paper carefully and turning it into a delicate origami.

There's a caption at the bottom of the picture: *Wer Lebt, Lernt.* Those who live, learn.

Did I ever think about Vito while I was growing up? I'm not sure. He exited our lives so suddenly. So unexpectedly, at least for me. Not for my mother, of course, but no one explained anything to me. Vito left just when I was thinking that he would now always be part of my world, and we of his. I was his daughter now, and Gerda Huber his woman. He was there. Then, suddenly, he was gone.

No, I haven't thought of Vito very much.

Fortezza/Franzenfeste is so narrow! The steep slopes of Val d'Isarco come so close together here that they barely leave room for the bottom of the valley, which they enclose like a bite. I always wonder how anyone can live here. What could the railroad men Mussolini brought here from Rovigo, Caserta, Bisceglie, Sulmona have thought when they saw that this valley is so narrow that to see the sky you don't just have to look up but also bend your neck back? Rumor has it, when the Nazis were fleeing to Brenner, they hid the gold stolen from Italians in the dark fortress the town is named after, and, every so often, someone starts shifting a few stones and digging beneath the bastions. I suspect it's just a legend invented to give a meaning, however absurd, to such a claustrophobic place.

I'd better have dinner here. The connection to Bolzano is over an hour away.

The pizza restaurant next to the station doesn't seem to have updated its menu for twenty years: *Knödel, Wiener Schnitzel,* steak, salad, spaghetti with tomato or meat sauce. There's nothing else. The pizzas, though, include the Hawaiian, with pineapple, and the Treasure Hunt (*Schatzsuche*): cherry tomatoes, anchovies and olives stuffed with capers. Could they be the treasure?

As I eat a cutlet that's not particularly tender, I look around. In the bar mirror opposite my table I can see my head against the light. I immediately look away, startled. High up among the bottles of liquor no one ever orders, I've seen three of those damned targets. I really hate them.

They're hand-painted wooden circles. At the center of two of them there's a capercaillie holding a coat of arms in its beak, while on the third one there's a pheasant. High up on the edge there's a different date on each: 9/8/84, 12/5/88, 3/10/93. And three names: Kurt, Moritz, Lara. Dates of birth and names, just like those my uncle had written on the target dedicated to the newborn Ulli. Here too there are tiny holes in the center, in the picture of the animal. The owner of this restaurant is obviously a hunter, just like Peter, and like him, he and his friends celebrated his becoming a father by shooting (my God, shooting!) at the names of the newborn children. But he was a better shot than my uncle, or perhaps he had drunk less: because instead of the picture in the middle, Peter hit his own son's name.

The last time I saw it—that horrid target even Ulli had always hated—it was being lowered with him into his grave. It was easy to believe that being such a bad shot, his father, the uncle Peter I never knew, had riddled with bullets not just his son's name, but also his life. Yes, I remember it now. That day I missed Vito terribly. The day Ulli's coffin was lowered into the grave.

"We've lost a friend, a wonderful person," someone said to me. I was so angry I clenched my fists in my coat pockets. I hadn't lost anyone! I hadn't gone to the supermarket with Ulli and suddenly turned around and not found him like it happens with children. I hadn't put him in a drawer and then couldn't remember which one. I hadn't left him on the bench like a newspaper or my cellphone. Or in somebody's house, like an umbrella. Or on the train, like a suitcase. I hadn't lost Ulli. Ulli had killed himself. And there were many people there who could have spared him a few reasons to do it. My anger rose and dropped like a wave, then all I felt was great tiredness. That's when I missed Vito.

I felt the need to rest my head on his shoulder—on his belly, in fact, because even though Vito wasn't tall, the last time I'd seen him I was a little girl—his little girl. That's how I remembered him at that moment: strong arms wrapped around my chest from behind, me barely leaning my head back and brushing his breastbone with the back of my neck, reclining against him with all my weight, certain that he would support me. Standing by Ulli's grave, I suddenly felt such an explosion of longing for Vito that for an instant it even covered the pain I felt for the death of my cousin, my playmate and confidant, more than my brother, my friend, perhaps my one and only love.

That was the moment when Lukas, the old sacristan, started his astounding speech. And only from Vito would I have accepted to hear, later: you see, Ulli didn't die in vain. Except that Vito wasn't there at the cemetery.

It's time to pay my bill and go. The train from Innsbruck that will take me to Bolzano is about to arrive.

1961 - 1963

When, at the headquarters of the Italian Armed Forces, they heard that Gerda had gone to work in a large hotel in Merano, they immediately decided to send about a thousand soldiers to Alto Adige. The army requisitioned her hotel, occupying all its rooms, as well as other major hotels in the renowned health resort. When the new and very young *Matratze* arrived at the hotel to begin her apprenticeship, she found over a hundred Alpini waiting for her. The soldiers saw the perfectly developed sixteen-year-old come in through the tradesman's entrance, wearing her Sunday dirndl, the knuckles of her right hand so tight around the handle of her suitcase that they were white. The troops expressed gratitude and enthusiasm for the decision made by their generals: they were finally seeing the reason for a mission in that land of Krauts where all they could understand were the swear words.

But no, that's not how it happened.

The reason for the arrival of all those soldiers wasn't Gerda, but high-voltage pylons. Forty-three of them, all blown up at the same time: *Feuernacht*, the Night of Fires. The spectacular action staged in a precise, meticulous, patient—this time you simply have to say it—German manner.

The *Befreiungsausschuss Südtirol*[8] claimed responsibility for the attacks. Their objective, as stated by their cyclostiled leaflets, was not the administrative autonomy strived for by the

[8] Committee for the Liberation of South Tyrol.

SVP of Silvius Magnago, the thin, charismatic orator of Castel Firmiano: they considered that to be a petty political compromise. They insisted that only the Volk, the people, had a right to decide with whom to stay: be it with the Italian government that had been occupying South Tyrol like a colony for the last forty years, or with Austria, from which they had been snatched away by force through a historical abuse of power. They wanted a referendum on self-determination and were convinced that the outcome would be a majority vote in favor of returning to the motherland. Fifteen years after the end of Fascism, the Italy of the Christian Democratic Party was shilly-shallying, ignoring the problem, and hoping that it would resolve itself by magic. So the attackers decided to strike.

For their most spectacular blow they chose the June night when Tyroleans light thousands of fires on top of the hills to commemorate the courage and unity with which their people halted Napoleon's advance. Every Tyrolean child knows about the exploits, studies the life, and imitates the words and actions in school plays, of Andreas Hofer. By knocking down about fifty pylons on that special night, the attackers were sending a very clear message: South Tyroleans did not feel Italian. They were not Italian, and they never would be.

The dailies informed readers in Rome, Milan, Palermo and Turin, of the existence of a South Tyrolean issue. Until then nobody had ever heard of it.

That first summer in the hotel was therefore a baptism of fire, and not just for Gerda. The health resort was besieged like the whole of South Tyrol, which had suddenly become a war zone. Roadblocks, curfews, mass requisitions. Fifteen thousand men were deployed, including police, soldiers, Carabinieri, and customs police.

With them came jeeps, motorbikes, and dogs. Few of them were professional soldiers. They were conscripts, boys. They arrived carrying large, torpedo-shaped shoulder bags, side caps on their heads, and binoculars around their necks. They had the Arabic profiles of Sicilians, pale Etruscan eyes, protruding ears from Bergamo. And all of them looked at Gerda.

She, too, however, looked at them. Some of them didn't seem all that different from the men in the town where she had grown up, from her cousins or her schoolmates. Some Alpini from Friuli, for example, walked in the slightly stiff way people from places of stones, forests and slopes once did: that was exactly how her father Hermann walked, and Peter, too. She had also seen the taut lips, beneath eyes from which an almost childlike light escapes: when emotions become difficult, mountain people purse their lips but, higher up, their clear eyes seem to beg to be saved from all that silence. Other, more Southern faces, however, were new for Gerda. A certain almost feminine softness in the hips, a lack of rigidity in some of the wrists, a way of smiling that didn't take anything, especially not oneself, too seriously: these things didn't exist among the adult males of her people. She'd also never seen two men walking close to each other with that familiarity between male bodies which some of the Southern pairs on patrol had. And then there were the compliments! These were soldiers sent on a mission to a place where they feared a full-blown attack on the government, armed from top to toe, and certainly also frightened; and yet they still had something light about them, or perhaps they were reckless enough to tell a blond girl wearing a *dirndl*, so clearly German, "You're beautiful!" and manage to make her smile in spite of everything. Their eyes were like velvet, and their eyelashes long like little girls', and even with their uniforms and weapons, they just couldn't manage to be totally military.

Not all of them, however, were like that. In a hotel not far from the one where Gerda worked, an entire battalion of the new special branch of the police created by Mario Scelba were quartered: the *Celere*. Their compliments were frightening.

They looked at the population with the expression of those who've come to bring back order to things which had very clearly run amok with the end of Fascism. Those who were certain that every Tyrolean was a terrorist by virtue of the mere fact of speaking German, those who—had they known about the Option (but they didn't, no Italian knew about it)—would have considered it an excellent idea: Alto Adige is Italian, and anyone who doesn't like Italy can leave.

Still, most of them were young men far more interested in good food and lovemaking than in shooting. One day, at a road block, Gerda saw a cameraman documenting the commitment of the Armed Forces to the defense of the nation. Seeing he was being filmed, a soldier stopped controlling the documents, lifted his arm, the same arm which was holding the semi-automatic machine gun, and waved "ciao" with his hand. Gerda found that gesture very revealing.

Even though tourists did not show up that season, the large hotels were not left idle. That entire summer, in the kitchens, hundreds of pounds of spaghetti, macaroni and polenta were cooked and stirred every day. The streets filled with the warm smell of fried onions, the slightly sour scent of tomatoes, and even the pungent aroma of raw garlic, which even the bravest of skilled local housewives had never used until then. Gerda's apprenticeship in international hotel cuisine (*tournedos, coq au vin, pâtes feuilletées*) was postponed. Instead, she learned a lot about the preferences and flavors of the South: a large chunk of the latest generation of young Italian males had arrived in South Tyrol, and they had a healthy appetite.

However, none of these soldiers, who called the braid twisted around the local girls' heads a "spare wheel," none of the officers lodged in the requisitioned hotels with balconies covered with cascading geraniums, none of them knew that, a few weeks earlier, the commander of the 4th Army Corps,

General Aldo Beolchini, had communicated to the heads of the army that there was the risk of an unprecedented wave of violence. He had reported to his superiors that trusted informers had warned him that infrastructures, electricity pylons in particular, would be targeted.

The heads of the military did not follow up on the general's warning. He was, in fact, immediately transferred far from Alto Adige. Shortly afterwards, the explosions of the *Feuernacht* took place.

The comprehensiveness of the attack created panic in Rome. According to the news, the attackers were determined to strike at the unity of the government. No deployment of means against them was considered excessive. They were said to be cold as killers, sneaky as spies, immoral as hardened criminals. And extremely dangerous.

It was therefore a disappointment when, just over a month later, almost all of them were caught and discovered to be, in fact, ordinary people: small traders, mechanics, blacksmiths, peasants. Except for Sundays and when asleep, the conspirators always wore the blue work apron, the *Bauernschurtz*, symbol of the Tyrolean work ethic. Their hands were callused from wood, soil and engine oil. They had courted their wives at *Kirschta'* dances, married young, and had many children. Many among them, or their fathers, had been persecuted as *Dableiber* during the Option: they hadn't wanted to leave their land but neither had they wished to pretend they were Italian. A few of them had been sent to Dachau for dodging the SS draft. They cared little or nothing about Communism: it had no bearing on their peasant, Catholic reality. They were all believers, some of them deeply religious, and had vowed not to endanger human lives. When the road worker Giovanni Postal was blown up because of a faulty fuse, many of them wept in their homes: the death of an innocent man was the worst thing that could have happened to them, both personally and to their cause.

For years, they'd had gatherings, though not, as Italian journalists insinuated, in secret underground lairs or foreign consulates, but in the timber *Stuben* of their houses, and in taverns. They had been collecting explosives for years, carrying them through the Brenner Pass and the old smuggler trails; they'd hidden them in haylofts, in workshops, buried them in manure. They'd practiced with explosives on minor but symbolic targets: for example, the equestrian statue of the Duce at the hydro-electric plant in Ponte Gardena, which was still standing sixteen years after Mussolini's death.

When they had started to prepare the great Night of Fires, each one of them was entrusted with the task of identifying targets in the area he knew best, in other words, near his own house. After stuffing the pylons with explosives they would take precautions so that when the pylons fell they would neither claim human victims, nor damage the neighbors' orchards. They were men who understood what hard work meant, and for whom an act of protest wasn't worth destroying a vine or ruining a peasant.

Contrary to what Italian newspapers wrote, the components of that first generation of bombers were not members of the secret service, nor veterans in search of action fifteen years after the end of the war, nor anti-Communist idealogues. They were not pan-German, or Neo-Nazis, or paramilitaries. All this did come, but later. It came along with the Neo-Fascists, the secret service, the corrupt Carabinieri of General De Lorenzo, and brought bloody attacks against barracks and customs houses, and people killed, but this time not by error. At that point, though, the first generation of bombers—the *Bumser*, as they were subsequently called almost affectionately—these people who had been careful about preserving orchards, were all already dead or in prison.

The *Bumser* were down-to-earth people but, when it came down to it, they trusted in human beings. The conspiracy strategy was simple: if someone was arrested he could simply keep quiet and not mention any names. In other words all you had to do was respond to the interrogators with silence and the organization would be saved. It wasn't hard.

Before that, none of them could have imagined those interrogations. Before that, none of them could have imagined the blows, the deprivation, the fluorescent lights straight in the eyes, the scalp naked because hair had been forcefully pulled out by the handful, fingernails wrenched out, teeth falling out, cigarettes extinguished on the skin, salt water down the nose, electric shocks to the genitals. Before that, none of them had heard of the "hot box," a technique perfected by the OAS in Algeria, and which Italians were now applying diligently, always with successful results. Before that, none of them could have imagined that uniformed representatives of the Democratic and Republican government would reduce them to a "subhuman, subconscious state in which you would do and say anything just to make whatever it is they're doing stop, and you're no longer a person but just a thing," as one of them said after he was freed.

Some prisoners managed to let people on the outside know about the torture they were enduring, by means of notes written on toilet paper. The Minister of the Interior, Scelba, inventor of that special police corps that frightened Gerda, was asked to comment.

"Police everywhere, all over the world, beat people up," he replied.

The conspirators talked. All of them. The network of attackers of the Night of Fires was dissolved in less than a month. Two of them were tortured to death in jail. Some time later, the carabinieri who tortured them were tried for cruel and unusual treatment and all were acquitted.

There was a full-page headline in huge characters on the front page of the newspaper Alto Adige on 23 June 1961:

BOLZANO IS AN INTEGRAL PART
OF THE ITALIAN STATE.
IT WOULD BE BEST IF EVERYBODY
ACKNOWLEDGED THIS REALITY.

"The bombs are driving tourists away."

That's what the people in the town were saying when Gerda went home at the end of the season.

Meanwhile, Peter had managed to get married. Leni, a small, dark girl like Johanna, but who liked dancing, had gone to live with the Hubers, and was now expecting a child. Gerda's sister Anne-Marie, too, had got married a couple of years earlier, and joined her husband in Vorarlberg. Since then, her parents hadn't seen her: going to visit her would have been a journey/hike.

"The bombs are driving tourists away." It was especially the members of the new Consortium and its president, Paul Staggl, who were saying it.

The poorest among Hermann's schoolmates, the one who would join him and Sepp Schwingshackl on the way to school, had become a man with reddish hair, pale, reptilian eyelids, a rough voice, the wide-set legs of someone who owes his success solely to his own abilities. Out of the steep, shady land that had kept his family in grinding poverty for generations, he had made his fortune. At the end of the 1920s, while Hermann was being taught to drive a truck as a reward for becoming a Fascist, young Staggl had built a rudimentary pulley on his land. The adventurous skiers who would climb up to the pastures above the town, armed with long skis and seal skins, would attach themselves to it so as to be taken uphill, and save time and effort. In the beginning, the pulley was operated by his father's large draft horse, but soon enough Paul earned enough from the toll paid by the skiers to be able to afford a generator.

When his father died, during those troubled 1930s when Hermann had become first a Fascist then a Nazi, Paul had convinced his mother and two still unmarried sisters to rent out the rooms of their maso to those same skiers who were using the rudimentary ski lift. What could be better for German sportsmen than to wake up early in the morning and be already at the foot of a ski slope, and on the right side of the Alps, the south side, at that? Soon, business was going so well that Paul was able to invest in enlarging the house next to the barn. Its most sensational novelty was the creation of a real toilet, and not in the courtyard but—an unheard-of luxury—inside the house: so when nature called on a winter's night you wouldn't have to go out in the open anymore. Paul invited the entire neighborhood to the inauguration party. He behaved with great generosity: not only did he show his neighbors the immaculate *Wasser Klosètt*, but insisted they try it in person. To make sure the exceptional occasion was exploited to the full by everyone, adults and children alike, he got his mother and sisters to prepare large quantities of *Zwetschgnknödel*— prune dumplings.

The *Wasser Klosètt* was tested by the neighbors time and again. The waste outlet didn't get blocked. It was a memorable party and people were to talk about it for many years to come.

At the time of the Option, Paul Staggl had kept a low profile. He had avoided taking dangerous stands, opting to be transferred according to the wishes of the authorities. Good businessman that he was, however, he had taken into account the fact that the imminent war would postpone, prolong, perhaps even interrupt everything. It turned out to be one of his many accurate predictions: the only ones who left in time were wretched people who had nothing to lose, or fanatics like Hermann. He also had a stroke of luck: his property on the steep side of the valley was untouched by Allied bombs, which destroyed so many houses at the bottom of the valley.

And so, just a few years after the war, instead of the old *maso* with its very steep field that had broken the backs of generations of Staggls, there was a large hotel, and the wide view from its rooms over the glaciers soon attracted an international clientele. Paul had built three other pulleys on as many neighboring fields. Even those who would never have agreed to pay the ascetic toll of effort and sweat in order to climb up for just a few minutes of exhilaration, could now be skiers. Every winter, tourists flocked in increasing numbers.

At the beginning of the 1960s, Paul Staggl wasn't yet one of the richest men in town, but he intended to be. There really was no place for bombs in his plans. As for the South Tyrolean issue Peter and other angry young men were so passionate about, Paul refused to express his opinion: Italians, Germans or Austrians, it was all the same to him, as long as they left their money in the hotel owners' coffers. Money, Paul realized much earlier than many of his contemporaries, not only has no stench but also no ethnicity. *Das Geld, l'argent, the dough, la plata*, has no *Sprachgruppenzugehörigkeit*,[9] and never will.

Paul had married the eldest daughter of a wealthy family trading in textiles, whose four eldest daughters had been educated in Switzerland, far from the valley and its frugal peasant ways: they needed to polish in the girls that care for the inessential, so necessary for accessing middle-class circles. The plan had worked and now Paul frequented only the town's polite society. Shortly before the war, he finally had a son, without whom the creation of his wealth from nothing would have been an incomplete success.

[9] Belonging to a language group.

At the time of the Night of Fires, Hannes Staggl was just over twenty. He had his father's Celtic complexion, almost transparent eyelids, and the pungent scent of a redhead. What he lacked, however, was his father's solid, grounded presence, his kind but determined smile, and the ruthless willpower you sensed behind his politeness. In other words, those very characteristics that had allowed Paul to rise.

Hannes would speed down the roads of the valley in his cream-colored convertible Mercedes 190 with a vanity that smacked of despair. He would change gears abruptly and, with his daring choice of trajectory, scare whichever girl happened to be sitting next to him at the time. He got drunk on speed. The wind slapping his face, the portable record player spitting out sexual Negro music, a soundtrack to his reckless driving— he imagined he was in an American movie. Except that the highway along the valley was not Route 66, he was not Rock Hudson, nor heading toward an epic destiny, but toward Bolzano at most. Above all, it wasn't he but his father who had accomplished the spectacular escape from the darkest of prisons: poverty.

Paul Staggl almost never came across Hermann Huber, his old school mate. If they ever happened to meet on the street in town, both adhered to a tacit agreement: they would be seized by a sudden curiosity for a shop window, or bend down to tie their shoelaces, or feel the urgent need to check if a button was fastened. Nobody could have attributed their lack of greeting to rudeness or embarrassment, let alone to Paul's arrogance or Hermann's envy. Their eyes failed to meet every time only through a series of fortuitous circumstances, which were minimal but objective, real, for which reason neither of them was responsible. It had been this way for decades and there was no reason to change. Consequently, their children had never met, either.

One day, though, as he was coming back from a ride in the car, more irritated than usual at how easily girls agreed to get into his cream-colored Mercedes, Hannes saw Gerda.

He didn't know she was his father's old schoolmate's daughter. He didn't know that, as a child, Gerda had spent her summers in a mountain hut and her winters in service. He didn't know that, for the past couple of years, she had only come to town during that couple of months when hotels were shut: a month between All Saints and Saint Nicholas, and a few weeks between Easter and Pentecost. He didn't know that, so when he saw her he just wondered: how come I haven't noticed her until now? Where has she been hiding, when was she born, this blond girl with oblong eyes, lips like tulips, a long but soft stride—not like the other women in the valley, who, although they have long muscles in their legs, also move harshly, like their men? Where has this girl with a woman's body, a woman's bust, a woman's bearing, and even a woman's ears, been until now?

Gerda was walking along the highway, in a little green coat that was somewhat threadbare and too short: she had inherited it from her much shorter married sister. It left exposed her straight legs, her feet in the flat, comfortable shoes of a hard-working girl, her fine wrists swaying in a barely pronounced movement as she walked. Desire rushed up from Hannes' groin so violently that he slammed the brakes and the wheels locked. The dark-haired girl sitting next to him hit her forehead on the dashboard of the Mercedes.

"What happened?" she asked.

He looked at her, suddenly surprised to see her there, on the crimson leather seat next to him. She was a pretty girl, and the scarf tied around the throat highlighted her sharp profile and fair skin. She was massaging her bruised forehead with her tapered fingers, her young breasts pleasingly round under the leather sports jacket. However, Hannes wasn't even interested in this girl's name anymore, now that he had seen Gerda walking down the road.

Who was she?

Gerda had been a *Matratze* for a year.

The *Matratzen* were the unloved. The orphans, the illegitimate, the lonely. Gerda was neither orphaned nor illegitimate. She was a *Matratze* because her father Hermann had let her go.

In the kitchen hierarchy, the *Matratzen* were down there with the scullery boys, except that they were worse and lower than them, because scullery boys at least, even if alcoholics and poor, were men. They were women, and even if they were assistant cooks or, in rare cases, cooks, they would always remain *Matratzen* because, as everybody knows, a woman in the kitchen is only respectable if it's the kitchen in her own home.

The kitchens where the *Matratzen* toiled, on the other hand, were in large seasonal hotels, huge rooms full of smoke and steam that had nothing in common with the domestic hearth, with the quiet, healthy atmosphere where children do their homework and mothers darn clothes while waiting for the soup to boil. The kitchens where the *Matratzen* worked were noisy and overheated caves full of shouting, swearing, and sweating, steeped in penetrating smells and sticky fumes, so that the only way you could survive was by becoming insensitive.

The *Matratzen* were called that name by the scullery boys, the cooks, the chefs who managed the kitchens and, albeit never openly, also by the hotel managers. They were made for just one thing, it was said, unlike the mattresses they were named after, on which, if you wished, you could also sleep.

Theoretically, Gerda too was a *Matratze*. However, nobody could use coarse language with her, not even the drunkest scullery boy. She had long legs, high breasts and, especially, eyes that never looked down. The desire she triggered was too real and intense, and men would have felt they would be exposed in their very essence if they had made to her the coarse insinuations they made to all the others. Of course, it would have been better to have sex with the other women than not to have it at all: none of the cooks, not to mention those wretched scullery boys who couldn't even spare a penny for the *Nutten*[10] on the highway, did it very much, hardly at all, in fact. But they really would have liked to do it with Gerda. They would have liked to slide their tongues into the groove between her breasts. They would have liked to slip their fingers into parts of her body which, just imagining them, put you at risk of cutting yourself because you lost your grip on the meat cleaver, and your blood drained from your head and descended elsewhere, lower down. They would have liked— and how could they confess that to the other men in the kitchen?—to watch her smile at the moment of pleasure. No, you couldn't make coarse jokes about Gerda. Nobody could.

What did Gerda think about the desire she triggered, and had triggered ever since she was a child, in the males around her? Actually, not much. It's not that she didn't notice. Even when she slept in the hay next to Simon and Michl, she'd noticed the brief, suffocated breaths, the strange rhythmic oscillations of the wood beams followed by strangled moans like little insults and then, suddenly, the embarrassed silence. She couldn't understand those goings-on very well, but already felt that they had something to do with her. Ever since she was a child she'd been used to having upon her the eyes of all the men she crossed in the street, always, especially in the summer when thin dresses emphasized her figure. John Gallagher from Leeds, United Kingdom, had merely been the first. She learned to recognize those looks, both predatory and confused, vulgar and adoring, but they washed over her without

10 Prostitutes.

permeating her; they told her nothing about herself. That desire corroded only them, the men who felt it, not her; just like caustic soda corrodes only the fingers that handle it and not the cake pans that are scoured with it.

In reality, ever since she had been a small child, Gerda had felt destined for something which, she was sure, she would recognize when it appeared before her, and which she would certainly be able to tell apart from those looks. This something resounded within her like the longing she experienced when listening to certain songs, or when the thaw diffused the first fragrance of resin in the air that still smelled of snow, or in the middle of her menstrual cycle, when her breasts would harden and something, like a call, grew between her legs. It protected her from coarse jokes like a cloak. So the men looked at her with dismay and rapture, like a force of nature outside their control, and ended up desiring her even more, but from a distance.

So Gerda became the first *Matratze* in the history of Alto Adige hotels to be respected by the men working beside her. She would not be the last, nor the only one; at one point, more or less at the time when the pop singer Mina retired from the stage, they even stopped being called *Matratzen*. But she was the first.

As was only right, Gerda started from the very bottom: washing dishes.

When she would walk into the kitchen at around six-thirty, there wasn't anybody there yet. Every morning, it was up to her, as the latest arrival, to light the oil burner that fueled the stoves. She was skillful and fast, she had been handling fire and flammable material while still half asleep ever since she was a child, and it came easily to her. The oil burner would take over an hour to warm up and, by eight o'clock, you had to be ready to serve coffee to the guests—no one in South Tyrol had heard of Neapolitan-style espresso yet—and boiled milk. As it switched itself on, the burner produced a dense, pungent, bituminous smoke. A black cloud would spread through the still deserted kitchen, and there was always a moment when her breath would catch in her throat. That balmy air smelling of pine needles and hay, which the guests of the large hotel came especially to fill their lungs with, seemed, inside there, like a treasure lost forever. When the burner would start pulling, the kitchen would become alive with the arrival of cooks, assistant cooks and scullery boys, and Gerda would start her day at the marble sink. Dishwashing machines didn't exist yet: everything, from the huge braising pots to the tea-spoons, was washed by hand.

Some encrusted pans had to be scoured and rubbed for over half an hour: at the end of the day, Gerda's arms and shoulders were so sore that she would take off her apron slowly, like an old woman. The worst thing was the soap. It was made there in the kitchen, boiled on a stove slightly apart from the others in huge pans full of caustic soda and pig fat. The result was a kind of sticky cream which Gerda then spread on a wide board, like polenta. Once it had cooled and hardened, she'd cut it into blocks. Soda soap burns your skin; after a month the tips of her fingers were stripped to the flesh. But if she'd put on gloves she would have been considered "deli-cate," an insult almost worse than *Matratze*.

If the extractor hood wasn't washed every seven days, the accumulated grease would start dripping down on the food. Once a week, on a Friday, Gerda and the scullery boys would boil it in a tub full of soda, and scrub all the kitchen tiles thoroughly. On those days, Gerda had to skip the *Zimmerstunde*, the hour of break in her room between the lunch and dinner shifts.

Her final task of the day was to sterilize the wooden board used for meat and fish. In the evening, once the kitchen was closed, she would pour alcohol over it, then set it ablaze. Gerda's day began and ended with fire.

Herr Neumann, the head cook, was a fat, ruddy man with puffy eyelids like ravioli and a small, Cupid-like mouth. He never used spatulas or forks. He said that the consistency of food accounted for half of its flavor, and a cook who doesn't touch it has no idea of what he's cooking. For this reason, he always used his bare hands, sticking his surprisingly tapered fingers into pots and skillets. He didn't even use a ladle for trying sauces. He'd dip a finger in then lick it: a quick, childlike gesture, like a little boy being caught stealing. And yet he never burned himself.

When the almost two hundred places had filled up with hungry guests, urgent orders would start coming in thick and fast. Waiters would practically skate in from the dining room and read out their notes, screaming, before stacking them up beside the serving hatch:

"*Gerstesuppe, neu!*"
"*Filet au poivre, neu!*"
"*Lammrippen aux herbes, neu!*"
"*Rollade, neu!*"

They would swipe the dishes the cooks had laid out on the serving hatch, stack them up on their arms and forearms as many as six at a time, then set off again, skating on the marble floor to the dining hall.

The cooks never talked among themselves, or at least not during rush hour: they were too busy cooking, stirring, trying not to scorch themselves, garnishing. Some conveyed their rush with abrupt gestures, like nervous birds. Like Hubert, the cook in charge of the counter for starters and cooked vegetables, who would dance among the rings on stiff legs that looked about to snap like dry spaghetti. Herr Neumann did everything with equal speed, but calmly. Sometimes, the cooks' paths would cross and then, with large, elegant air gestures, they would stop the burning pans from hitting people's backs. It was a frenzied, urgent dance which nevertheless had an essence of quiet concentration.

As far as waiters and commis coming from the dining hall were concerned, however, any delay, even a few seconds in the limbo between the steamy kitchen and the dining hall full of impatient guests, became an obstacle for which to blame someone. This would often result in insults between them and the cooks.

Countless ready dishes would appear and disappear swiftly from the serving hatch counter, like raindrops on a window during a storm. The executed order notes were speared by Herr Neumann onto a spike next to the serving hatch. At particularly hectic times, with a slight grunting effort and satisfaction, he would sometimes push down twenty notes at once. Woe to anyone who, through inexperience or absent-mindedness, dared to replace him in this task: only the head cook could sanction that an order had been executed to perfection, delivered and, therefore, archived. Once, a young, recently hired Ladino man thought a slip of paper containing an order that had already been delivered had been forgotten on the counter, so he dared spear it onto the spike. Herr Neumann said nothing. He simply grabbed the assistant cook by the wrist and flattened his hand on the serving hatch counter. Then he took the spike and, with the hard, swift and precise blows he used to pound escalopes, he stuck the iron tip into the wood of the counter in the spaces between two of the young man's fingers. "Next time, it won't be between your fingers," he said.

After that, nobody ever touched the order slips.

The waiters emptied the dirty plates into a bin next to the

door, then placed them on a rack for the dish washer. When Gerda washed a plate, she immediately knew who had brought it back from the dining room. With male waiters, you were lucky enough if they removed the largest leftovers, like chicken bones and ribs. The plates they put on the rack were full of leftover food. Their message was crystal clear: theirs was a superior job, so it was up to her to clean the plates. The women, on the other hand, would throw the leftovers into the bucket, carefully scrape the plates with cutlery and, if they had the time, would even drain excess sauce: the dishes they placed on the rack were much easier to clean. Some of the plates almost looked as if you just needed to wipe them with a cloth and put them away: like the ones brought back by Nina, a waitress from Egna, who was about thirty. The first few times, Gerda had thanked her, but Nina had stood before her, staring with her dark eyes, slightly too close together, ready to carry out the four dishes balanced on her forearms, her feet swollen in orthopedic shoes. "*Lass es*," she had replied: don't mention it. In other words: better dispense with courtesies here. I come in and out of that door a hundred times a day, so if on top of that I had to thank the cooks for every dish then this would really be hell.

Gerda stopped thanking her. However, Nina's dirty plates still remained the cleanest ones.

The staff had lunch at eleven, while the final basic concoctions were being made on the rings, just before the customers arrived in the dining hall. They ate in a dark little room in the basement under the kitchen, next to the stockroom, waiters on one side and cooks on the other. Herr Neumann cooked for them. He insisted that the staff eat well, and was always improvising something with the leftovers. With leftover roast he would make meatballs with sauce; boiled meats he would shred and stir-fry with potatoes, onion and bay leaves, making a fragrant *Greastl*; mix macaroni with meat sauce with cheese and béchamel, and bake it in the oven; with broth, leftover vegetables and a sprinkle of chives, he would create a risotto. Even so, he did not lunch with them: a chef never leaves his kitchen unattended.

Gerda ate quickly, practically on her feet, three mouthfuls at a time, then rushed upstairs. She didn't enjoy eating and not only because it's hard to work up an appetite when you're constantly surrounded by the smell of food. It's something she never enjoyed, not even when she became a great cook, and not even when she retired—that was also something Eva was to inherit from her. But there was another reason for Gerda to eat so quickly: she wanted to have time to watch what Herr Neumann was doing.

The head cook had noticed how attentively Gerda would observe the stages of food preparation in the various departments. She never asked for explanations but, on the rare occasions when there was a break, she would stare with her pale, elongated eyes at what was happening at the salad and starters counter and the first course and dessert counter and, sometimes, she had the incredible cheek even to watch the meat counter, Herr Neumann's kingdom. Consequently, he decided to check whether this girl who was too shapely and whose gait was too slinky to guarantee a modicum of calm in his kitchen, was wasting time that would be better employed scrubbing plates and glasses, or whether she would learn something. And so, against all the rules, after as little as a year, Herr Neumann promoted Gerda to assistant cook. Hubert muttered heavy hints under his breath about the true reason for this promotion but he didn't have the courage to say anything in front of her, let alone in front of the chef.

Being an assistant cook was hard work, especially in the summer, when the kitchen was hotter than a tropical forest, and even steamier. Everybody, not only overweight apoplectics like Herr Neumann but also skinny poles like Hubert, sweated buckets. The first course and side vegetables cook always had at the end of his already long arms, like metal offshoots, pots or pans with contents that needed to be tossed in the air, but never out: penne to coat in game sauce, potatoes to smear in butter, mushrooms to fry with garlic and herbs. Sweat would run down their premature wrinkles and sometimes even drip off their chins. Sometimes, even Gerda couldn't work out if her sweat was coming from her or from the thick fumes in which she was immersed. Down her temples, on either side of her nose and behind the ears, sweat would make sores as deep on her skin as streams on Dolomite limestone. Every evening after having a shower, Gerda would smear Nivea cream on the furrows on her face and neck, but even so by the end of the season her flesh was raw. The only way to dull the burning of salty sweat on your sores was to smoke, and soon Gerda, like everybody else, started to have always a cigarette between her fingers during breaks.

There were no mixers, slicers or blenders: only the arms of scullery boys and assistant cooks. Gerda would remain in the kitchen until midnight to prepare the raw materials which the cooks would use the morning after. She would peel and slice the vegetables that would then be kept in drawers under the cooked side dish counter; she would stretch the pasta for tagliatelle, prepare the sponge, make the cakes and the puff pastry for the house specialty, Strudel, without which a holiday in South Tyrol can't be called such. Every evening there were therefore dozens of kilos of apples to peel, slice, cover in lemon juice and store under a wet cloth, ready for the pastry cook to put into the dough the following morning. In the evening, Gerda would also put into the oven, which was turned off but still hot, the long stems of rhubarb, lime green with purple streaks, and the sugar. By the following morning they would turn into a stew ready for blending with cream, gelatin, and more sugar, then served chilled in pudding bowls.

Next, Gerda had to prepare the eggs. She would whip the whites to a stiff snow in large copper pots, to make meringues; mix the yolks with sugar and milk in white ceramic mixing bowls, to be used for cakes. Often, she had over fifty eggs to beat and there were evenings when her right arm was so sore that she had to ask Elmar for help with untying her apron.

All the scullery boys in all the restaurants and all the large hotels—and Elmar was no exception despite being barely sixteen years old—were alcoholics. Even so, without them, the kitchens wouldn't have lasted more than a few hours. They were generally the youngest sons of the poorest peasants, who'd had to choose between dying of the cold by becoming *Knechten* in the wealthier *masi*, or dying of the heat in the large hotels. For Elmar, the decision had been easy: he'd had more than his share of the cold, just like his father, his grandfather and his ancestors, for too many generations. Besides, anything seemed preferable to him to the loneliness of the *masi* in his Val Martello. Now that Herr Neumann had promoted Gerda to assistant cook, it was up to this boy with a long face and large ears, the one at the very bottom of the kitchen hierarchy, to stay behind and scour the cast-iron gridiron shelf after everyone had gone to bed. On the evenings when Elmar had untied Gerda's apron strings, his grazed, scalded adolescent fingers would tremble. Later, lying on his iron bed, the memory of close contact with the hollow above Gerda's backside stopped him from sleeping for hours on end.

"Good cooking doesn't take place in the kitchen but on the market and in the stock room."

The art of choosing, putting away and preserving foods was at the root of everything for Herr Neumann. Under his guidance, Gerda learned to select everything that was the best.

The fish arrived from Chioggia at dawn on Fridays, in wooden crates covered with ice: mullets, pilchards, sea bass, clams. Herr Neumann used their Italian names, as he did with fruit and vegetables, and especially salads: *radicchio, lattuga, valeriana, rucola, portaluca, crescione*. Radicchio, lettuce, rocket, valerian, purslane, watercress. On the other hand, he used German for meat: *Rindfilet, Lammrippen, Schienbein*, and also for desserts: *Mohnstrudel, Rollade, Linzertorte, Spitzbuben*. This culinary bilingualism was shared by all the staff, as an obligation. The only exception to the rule, almost an involuntary homage to Italian and German stereotypes, were potatoes: although they were classified as vegetables, or at least tubers, everyone always called them *Kartoffeln*. However, when fried, they would transcend South Tyrolean ethnic tensions and acquire international status, becoming *Pommes Frites*.

The refrigerating cells were two actual rooms. One for dairy products and the other, the larger one, for meat. It was a kind of furnished room, not with but with hooks from which were suspended quarters of beef, lamb halves, whole chickens and turkeys. It was closed by a heavy wooden door outside of which hung two thick woolen greatcoats on a hook. The first time Herr Neumann took Gerda into the refrigerated cell, he picked one and put it on. She looked at him, puzzled.

"It's colder in here than at the top of Mount Ortler in January. Have you ever been there?"

She shook her head.

"Neither have I. If you don't want to die young, wrap up well before coming in here all sweaty."

From the first time Gerda went back home during the low season, when the hotel was closed, no one ever asked her anything. Neither her mother nor her father enquired what her duties were, whether she had enough food and sleep, or if she got on well with the rest of the staff.

When he wasn't driving around on his truck, transporting timber, Hermann would sit at the *Stammtisch*, the table at the tavern reserved for regular customers, and be poked fun at by those made more talkative—not more silent than usual like him—by wine. Johanna had not only given up talking to her husband but also looking at him straight in the face. The last few times she had tried he had stared at her as if she had caused him an unforgivable offense, and she had understood that the offense was the affection Johanna insisted on feeling, in spite of everything, for the man with whom she had been sharing a bed for thirty years.

* * *

Peter's wife, Leni, had had a child. On the moldy wall of the damp house in Shanghai hung a wooden target with his name painted on it, Ulrich, pierced by the shots fired by Peter and the *Schützen* of his garrison on the day of the christening. As though the birth of his first child had been a lucky hunt for Peter, he had placed it among his trophies: stag skulls with ramified antlers, steinbock that looked like the close relatives of unicorns, a royal eagle nailed to the wall with its wings spread out. Every so often, Peter would vanish for days on end without warning his parents or his wife, and gave no explanation when he returned. And so, together with little Ulli, Leni became hostage to the darkness of that house. One night, with her baby in her arms in the fir wood marriage bed, Leni dreamed of the scary day when, as a child, she had gotten lost in the forest during a storm. In the dream, lightning struck just a few yards from her feet, making the earth shake. Leni woke up with a start and opened her eyes. Next to her, Peter had thrown himself on the bed with his clothes still on. His hair, skin and clothes, everything had the acrid, sulfurous smell of lightning. As usual, Leni didn't manage to ask for an explanation: within seconds, her husband had fallen asleep. Ulli, however, had woken up. Leni couldn't calm him down immediately so she had to get up. With the crying child in her arms, she walked for over an hour on the grayed wooden beams of the *Stube*. After a while, numb with cold, she put over her shoulders the coat her husband had left on the chair before throwing himself on the bed. She slipped a hand in one of the pockets and when she took it out, it was covered with a thin layer of slightly greasy powder, of the color of bread paper and smelling of sulfur. Leni couldn't have known that it was an explosive. She wanted to talk to Peter about it the following day but barely an hour after Ulli had finally fallen asleep, and Leni with him, he had gone out. Leni then told Johanna about that strange powder and the smell of sulfur that impregnated her husband's hair and clothes. Her mother-in-law listened but remained silent. She didn't tell her about the time, many years earlier, she herself had found traces of red paint on her son's coat, the very night the granite Wastl had been soiled by unknown persons. Johanna didn't look at Leni. She remained on her knees in front of the wood stove, and carried on rubbing its enameled doors and steel handles with water and ammonia. When Leni realized that she wouldn't get a reply, she left the kitchen and the house with Ulli in her arms.

Only then did Johanna turn to the point on the floor where until a moment ago her daughter-in-law's feet had been. Her left arm, with which she had kept the stove door still in order to rub it better, had all of a sudden become numb, and an unexpected cold sweat beaded her forehead. She suddenly felt nausea, as well as a sense of impending threat. She shouldn't let herself be frightened like this by what Leni had said, she told herself, after all nothing irreparable had happened. In truth, the disaster was already taking place but inside her body, in the ebb and flow of the blood in her veins and arteries which, ever since she had been born, had been supplying organs and tissues with a silent, regular swish. For some time now, unbeknown to her, her left coronary artery had been partially blocked and was making it hard for the blood to go up to the front wall of her heart. Johanna didn't know it but there and then, kneeling on the wooden floor covered in drops of soapy water, she was having a mild heart attack.

After spending months in the heat, the shouting and the smells of the large kitchen, the silence that had invaded her parents' house seemed to Gerda, whenever she went back there, as dense as mud dried after a downpour. Every word that was not strictly necessary, every comment, question, exclamation, adverb and adjective had been buried in it. All that remained were imperative verbs (take this; carry this; go out; wash it; eat this) and the names of things: *tello*, the bowl you reached out with so that soup could be ladled into it; *foiozoig*, the lighter to hand her father for his evening pipe; *holz*, the timber to stack up next to the stove. These surviving words would spring out of the silence the same way objects of a life that has been swept away emerge through a gap in the mud that covers a village buried by a landslide. Things like the back of a chair, a pan with no handles, an odd shoe.

* * *

The first time Hannes spoke to Gerda, he asked, "*Wo worschin bis iatz?*"

Where had she been until then? How was it possible that he'd never met her before in the streets of the town? She told him that for over a year now she had been spending most of her time in Merano, working in the kitchen. While she was speaking, Gerda noticed in Hannes's eyes that same look of defenseless astonishment her father had given her that morning, so many years earlier, when he had called her *Mamme*.

Now that she saw it, it was clear to her: this was what she'd been waiting for all these years without knowing it.

The cable car that would unload dozens of skiers on the top of the mountain, opening the doors to prosperity for the town and its residents, had now been completed by the Consortium. Half of the forest of larches, pines and spruces which covered the north side of the mountain, and which had been cursed by Paul Staggl's ancestors because it was steep and without sunlight, had disappeared. Now it had been plowed down by the winding paths of ski tracks, and the almost straight line that connected the pylons of the new ski lift. A few weeks later, its inauguration would take place. The red cabin with room for thirty, hanging from a heavy steel cable, would stand out against the blue sky and, flying above the heads of the band, all the gathered citizens, the mayor, and especially Paul Staggl, the visionary capitalist responsible for its creation, would show everyone the bright future awaiting the valley.

In view of the inauguration, last-minute safety tests and rescue drills in case of a power cut were taking place. Hannes persuaded his father's workmen to use him and Gerda as the victims of a pretend accident. They would act the parts of skiers on holiday trapped in the cabin because of a power outage, and the workmen would come and save them.

When Gerda walked into the lower station of the cable car, she thought it looked like a cave large enough for giants rather than humans. The huge wheels suspended from the roof were dragging a fake steel cable from which dangled a red cabin attached by a black clamp—like a cloth fixed with a gigantic peg to an enormous washing line. However, when it completed the tour around the pylon and drew near with the door open, Gerda thought it looked more like a squat, square tourist coach than something suitable for staying up in the air: it was both scary and ridiculous at the same time. Hannes noticed her hesitation. He held her by the arm and helped her walk into the cabin. The doors closed behind them, the large wheels continued to turn with the roar of a furnace, there was a sudden increase in speed, almost a change of state, the cabin got off the ground and began its suspended journey.

There was a sudden silence. What made Gerda's heart leap into her throat more than the growing distance between her feet and the ground, more than the treetops she was seeing from above for the first time, more than the horizon of glaciers and faraway peaks that spread before her, was the silence, which was interrupted only by light gusts of wind. It wasn't the silence of her childhood pastures, of windless, moonless nights when she huddled up with Michl, Simon and little Wastl in the hay, while telling stories of witches. Those nights, through the cracks of the mountain hut beams, an infinite, enveloping space resounded all around, and everything was a part of it—the four children, the starry sky, the screams of night birds, and the cracking sound of the mountain. That silence that echoed a thousand presences, and from which nothing and nobody was separate from it.

Here, however, the glass of the cabin was separating Gerda and Hannes from the noise of the world, from the rustle of the tallest fir tree branches, from the calls of the crows that were flying parallel to the cable, curious about that strange flying object, from the increasingly distant voices coming from the tiny houses at their feet.

When the cable passed through the small wheels of the pylons, it produced for a few seconds a metallic screech which then made the silence that followed even more intense. It was a silence reserved for just the two of them. Gerda looked up at Hannes. This was the moment he seemed to be waiting for: he bent over her and kissed her.

At that moment, the cabin suddenly stopped and started swaying in the void. But Gerda wasn't scared. That swinging over the abyss, which tourists jammed in a cable car would always find scary, and which would provoke screams, fainting, and scenes of panic, was for her a sign: the first kiss of her life had to be precisely here, right now, with Hannes. It was written, it was fate. It was what she had always been waiting for. And now, finally, she knew it.

A few weeks later, when Gerda went back to the hotel for the winter season, she got Nina to read her fortune with cards. Gerda wanted them to say that Hannes loved her, that he thought of her every single instant just as she thought of him. She wanted to hear about his love and wanted an opportunity to say his name out loud: Hannes!

Nina had a wide face with dark eyes that were a little too close together, a beautiful straight mouth and almost all her teeth. She looked at Gerda without smiling. "He's rich, isn't he?" It was as though she was asking confirmation of a diagnosis.

"*Isch mir Wurst*," Gerda replied. I don't care about that. It wasn't wealth but love that was important for her. Her love for Hannes, and his for her. Nina shook her head, displeased. She laid out on the table seven Watten cards, face down.

"Turn over one card. Don't think about it."

Gerda didn't think and turned over the first card on the left. "Seven of acorns."

Nina stared at the card with the bitter satisfaction of someone who has foreseen the worst and it is coming true.

She looked up at Gerda and said, "You're pregnant. And better give up any idea of his marrying you."

KILOMETERS 35 – 230

On the Fortezza-Bolzano train there are two girls sitting opposite me, probably about sixteen. One is blond, the other dark. They look like the kind of scantily-clad young women you see on Italian TV, like the soubrettes in the programs my mother claims not to know because she watches only the Austrian ORF channels, but which she actually sits and gulps down for hours on end. They're dressed identically: black jacket with gray fur collar, black trousers worn very low on the waist, slid into black boots. They look like they're wearing a uniform. They get off at Bressanone, where Max, the largest discotheque in the area is situated: Easter Saturday or not, they're going dancing.

South Tyrol discotheques used to be closed on Easter Saturday. In fact there weren't any. Max didn't use to hold a gay night every third Thursday of the month. No South Tyrol hotel would have written "gay-friendly" in their brochure (but only in the English-language ones aimed at an Anglo-Saxon clientele, not in the German or Italian ones). In the snow bulletin issued by the pistes and the pharmacy opening times on the Internet, you didn't use to see a list of places where you could go cruising (in my town it's the toilets of the bus station and the parking lot by the river).

My land has changed a lot. And Ulli bears witness to that.

There's more waiting at Bolzano station, since the Rome sleeper leaves at midnight. I have a coffee. The barman is polite and speaks good Italian as well as German, with a distinct Bolzano accent, but his face, skin and body language are North African. I wonder which box he ticked on the *Sprachgruppenzugehörigkeitserklärung* form of the census, that heap of syllables and consonants, which intimidated even Signor Song.

Finally, it's nearly midnight. I go to the platform and the train is already there. In the distance, beyond the freight trains on dead-end tracks, beyond the electric lines, beyond the rooftops and the cleft of Val d'Isarco, illuminated by the moon, the mountain peaks, called *Catinaccio* in Italian and the *Rosengarten* in German. More than simply two different names, it's really about two different ways of living in nature. As a loudspeaker announces arriving and departing trains, the distant, pale presence of the Dolomitian needles seems to occupy, as well as another space, another time. Seen from the station, they look magical and unreachable.

The Neapolitan couchette attendant is about thirty, overweight, and has no wedding ring: it seems that the holiday shifts fall to the bachelors. He takes my ticket. "I'll keep it and give it back to you in the morning. This way the ticket inspector will wake me up and not you."

He's protecting my sleep but, for a moment, the thought of being without my ticket makes me feel at his mercy.

"You're all alone in the carriage," he adds. That's exactly what he says: "all alone"—and his tone is formal. It's true that I'm all alone: all the other compartment doors are bolted, except for mine. It's Easter Saturday, after all. Anyone gone to see their relatives for Easter has already arrived, and anyone who's taken two weeks' holiday is already in the southern seas. I too would be at my mother's now if I weren't here on a train, going to see Vito. Consequently, I have the compartment all to myself. The light is on and, neatly folded, the blanket with the embossed logo of the *Ferrovie dello Stato*, the towel and the sponge slippers, are waiting for me. With a creaking sound, the train departs.

"Would you like a nice coffee when you wake up?"

The couchette attendant comes knocking several more times, always for a different reason. After asking about the coffee he wants to make sure I lock myself in properly. He shows me how to arrange the ladder for the top bunks as an anti-burglar device: you have to jam it in the handle in such a way that if anyone tries to open the door, it'll fall with a crash. He wants me to arrange it as he says, so that he can prove that if you want to force the handle from outside (he does it), the ladder would make quite a racket (it's true) and I would wake up (that's assuming I manage to get any sleep, I think, doubtfully). He keeps repeating, "It's just the two of us in the entire carriage."

Then he goes back to his compartment at the end of the carriage. But he hasn't finished with me yet, and shouts, "What do you think, shall we turn down the heating?"

He's gone from addressing me as "you" to referring to "we."

As a matter of fact, it's too warm, and my throat is beginning to feel dry.

"Absolutely!" I also shout back to make myself heard—there are at least four compartments between his and mine.

"Perhaps I'll turn it up again before dawn when it's colder!" he yells.

"All right!" I yell back.

We keep shouting like that from one compartment to the other but it's something very intimate and confidential, like a husband and wife would talk to each other loudly from one room to the other in their home. (My mother's always doing this when she comes to stay. She begins to cook and starts yelling a long speech about Ruthi from the kitchen, while I could be on the phone to a client. I've never managed to tell her just how annoying it is.) Well, at least, as Carlo would say, the couchette attendant didn't decide to talk to me about his unhappy marriage. Perhaps because he's a bachelor, even though I have a creeping suspicion that he might take off his wedding ring when he's on night shifts—you never know if you might find yourself with a lady, "all alone." Or perhaps because he's tired, poor man.

I lie down on the bunk, facing the window. It's almost one o'clock in the morning and I switch off the light. Since I'm lying down, it's only when the train tilts on the curves that I can see the streetlights. Otherwise all I can see is their reddish glow reflected on the pale rocks of Val d'Adige, which consequently look as though they are bathed in their own light.

HAPPY EASTER OF THE RESURRECTION!

HAPPY HOLIDAY BUT ONLY TO BEAUTIFUL PEOPLE!

TAKE CARE, MY FRIEND.

HAPPY EASTER!

It's late, but not all my friends lead the kind of lives where this is an important factor; besides, some of them live in different time zones. That's why I keep receiving text messages wishing me a happy Easter: secular ones, religious, jokey, affectionate ones. The screen of the cellphone I'm holding lights up every time and for a couple of seconds, my face, illuminated by its blue light, is reflected in the window in front of me.

HAPPY EASTER, MY LOVE.

Carlo. I keep my finger on the keypad so the display doesn't go off and I remain illuminated for a long time. My somewhat ghostly reflection is superimposed on the nocturnal landscape rushing past outside the train, with vertical, luminescent rocks and the star-studded darkness. My face flies over churches, over many castles on rocks, each and every one of them a cultural jewel of which I don't even know the name (except for those where I have organized memorable PR events).

Suddenly, the lights and racket of the tunnel: we're cutting straight under the Prealps and leaving Val d'Adige.

In a few minutes time we'll be in Val Padana. *Aussi*. I'm coming out.

1962 - 1963

Paul Staggl was a businessman, so it was important for him to have his finger on the pulse of the world. He read *Dolomiten* but also *Süddeutsche Zeitung* and *Corriere della Sera*. When people talked about his homeland, more often than not, they did so in terms of "the South Tyrolean issue," "attacks," "bombs," and he didn't like that. It was not a good thing that Italians heard so much about Alto Adige in this worst possible light. In addition to his other worries, the winter didn't look promising: it was already late December and there had been very little snow. Now that the new cable car had been inaugurated, the pistes were full of stones and desolate patches of brown. For some time now Paul had been thinking about the possibility of pistes that were no longer dependent on snowfall. He'd heard of Swiss research on the creation of artificial snow but the technique was still in its early stages and the results had been disappointing. However, Paul's belief in technology was equaled only by his belief in himself. The matter was still futuristic and experimental but, of this he was certain, it was the future.

Paul also knew all about that girl his *Trottel* of a son was fooling around with. The cable car workers had told him and it all was very clear to him. Of everyone in the valley, Gerda's father was the last man Paul wanted to be related to. Not because Hermann was a *Rückkehrer*, a Shanghai resident, or because his terrible temper had now turned him, even though he wasn't even sixty yet, into one of the many characters in provincial towns: Hermann, the abrupt, silent type, the one you couldn't get a smile out of even if you paid him. (Once, at the tavern *Stammtisch*, as a bet, a joker had offered him a nice little sum of money if he would only lift the corners of his mouth, but no one could tell if Hermann was offended by that or not: the dark, universally disgusted expression with which he had reacted was his usual one.) No, Hermann's only true fault was to have been Paul's schoolmate at a time when the land on the steep, north facing side, hadn't yet become synonymous with skiing slopes, tourists cable cars, wealth—just with abject poverty.

Paul decided that his son's professional training had been delayed enough. He sent him on a long educational tour of Engandin, Carinzia, Bavaria, and even Colorado: it had become imperative for him to study the management models of the most reputable ski resorts. Gerda never found out what Hannes thought of all this. When she called him from the hotel to tell him about her pregnancy, he had already gone. His father's polite voice advised her to call back after at least six months.

Gerda spent a few days in a state of shock. It's not that she became inattentive in her work. She cleaned, cut, sliced, beat, grated, kneaded, stirred, whipped and chopped as she had always done. She was no less careful than usual. She didn't burn the sauces, overcook the pasta, didn't slice julienne-style the vegetables she was supposed to slice *à la brunoise*, or vice-versa. As usual, she left her workstation clean and tidy at the end of the day, which is something that couldn't be said of her male colleagues. She had convinced herself that if she ignored what had happened to her, it would go away without a trace, just as you ignored a burn caused by a splash of boiling oil and it left a small scar. Nevertheless, persevering in her belief required an effort of concentration, so she had to eliminate any superfluous mental activity: talking to other assistant cooks, saying hello, responding to non-essential requests.

Even so, despite the intensity, the determination of her belief, her already full breasts were growing and swelling under her apron. It was as though she didn't just have one pregnancy, and not just in her belly that was still flat, but also in each of her breasts.

More than once a day, especially in the morning, she had to run and vomit in the staff bathroom. She would return to the kitchen with blue shadows under her eyes, pale lips, her cheeks still moist from the icy water she had splashed herself with, and resume her work with a neutral expression. Her silence stopped any comments or nosy looks on the part of scullery boys, cooks and waiters. And yet despite all this self-discipline and determination to deny reality, Hannes didn't call to tell her that he loved her and would marry her soon, nor did her pregnancy vanish. Gerda realized that cultivating the certainty that it would go away was no longer enough.

One evening, at the end of the shift, when even Elmar, the scullery boy, had gone to sleep, and the guests of the large hotel were having their nightcap on the terrace overlooking the mountains, Gerda went from the deserted kitchen to the vegetable store room. There were crates of Rovigo asparagus, Treviso radicchio, and lettuce from local peasants, all lined up methodically so the contents wouldn't get bruised. Gerda reached out for a bunch of green leaves in the corner reserved for aromatic herbs. It wasn't chives, sage or even marjoram. She took a whole handful, then another, until her arms were full and carried it up to the kitchen. She put it on the board and started eating one leaf after another. Her lips turned green, the leaves got stuck in her teeth, but she kept tearing more from the slender twigs and stuffing them in her mouth, chewing like one of the cows she used to look after during those dis-

tant, happy summers. Soon, there was a halo around her
mouth, and she wiped it with the same gesture of the wrist her
father used when wiping his lips after drinking milk as a child.
Except that her mustache wasn't ivory but green, just like the
leaves which, twig after twig, one handful after another, she
chewed and swallowed.

Elmar, the scullery boy, returned to the kitchen. As he often
did, he was coming to steal a drop of brandy or marsala or any
other liquor from the spice and seasoning shelf. He looked at
her, guilty at first then puzzled, his face too long between the
protruding ears, like an eggplant.

"*Wos tuaschn?*"

"I'm making green sauce," Gerda said, her lips appropriately green. The absurdity of her lie didn't make her cast down
her eyes and in the end, as usual, it was Elmar who had to look
down.

At night, lying in her cot in the large attic where she slept
with the rest of the female staff, Gerda held onto her stomach,
suffering terrible pain. She got a fever, diarrhoea, vomiting,
then a couple of uterine contractions which gave her great
hope. But nothing else.

The parsley didn't work, so Gerda tried with the pine wood
stairs. They led to the attic where she slept, the only non-refur-
bished part of the hotel, unchanged from the time when this
was still the southern stretch of the Austro-Hungarian Empire
and the Viennese middle classes would come and spend the
winter.

To avoid cushioning the blows, Gerda kept her legs
straight. She would push herself off with her elbows and throw
herself down the stairs, hitting every step, which meant fifteen
hard knocks. Knocks to her hips, which was fine, but also to
her ribs and shoulders which was useless, however. When she
reached the bottom, for a few moments light and dark would

swap places: the lights that coming in from the narrow window would become black and sticky like tar, while the shadows would light up with a supernatural glow. Then, she would stagger back upstairs.

There were fifteen steep, narrow steps made of pine wood time had turned gray, slumping in the middle after centuries of use. The ridges and depressions of the grain were in relief and the knots were like dark, oblong spirals, like miniature galaxies. But Gerda wasn't admiring the perfection of the old wood: she would climb back up to the top, sit and throw herself down again.

She hurled herself down the stairs twice, five, ten times. Twenty times. She lost count. Her coccyx hit the steps with a nice full sound, like a musical instrument: the stairs were like a xylophone and she, the mallet. After a while she thought she would go on like this forever: throwing herself down these steps all her life, then go back up with more and more bruises, to play that rhythmic composition of wood, anger and determination, hollow, without thought, simple, almost pleasant. At the bottom of the stairs, sprawled on the ground like a disjointed puppet, Gerda closed her eyes. The shadows were throbbing, fluorescent, and there was almost no light anymore. On all fours, she climbed the stairs again.

To Eva, a tiny little lump, the knocks were cushioned: out there, things had boundaries that could hit one another, slam into one other violently, and get hurt. But that couldn't happen to her. Those knocks were no more than little waves in the boundless ocean that contained her.

Finally, Gerda lay almost unconscious at the bottom of the stairs. She looked up. Outside the narrow attic window, clouds were rushing over the mountains: tall, incessant, implacable. She stared at them for a long time without focusing. The dark shadows of the nimbus clouds brushed the wooded slopes and pasture against the grain, scraped the bare rocks of the crags, and she thought she heard the rustling sound of this outsized caress. She remained like that for a long time, her body aching, her mind a blank. Then she slowly got up. Supporting herself against the wall she went down the corridor to the staff sleeping quarters that gave on to the narrow corridor.

She had failed.

Eva's eyes were just two dark bulbs, huge compared to the rest of her body. They had no eyelids or lashes, and still couldn't close. But Eva slept the sleep of fetuses, that of creature and creator joined as one, the sleep of a god who dreams the beginning of time: his own.

Fifteen minutes' walk from my nice, elegant apartment, as you leave the Medieval city, following an ascending path, you get to a wide clearing where corn and potatoes grow. In the middle of the field there's a small chapel. From there, the slopes of our valley open up and the sky grows very broad. People come and sit on the bench along the low wall of the little church, and enjoy the sunset and the view over the glaciers.

My mother used to bring me here on her visits when I was a child. I didn't dare tell her that I would have preferred to spend my precious time with her going to the pond on the other side of the fields, and giving pieces of dry bread to the ducks who had hard, voracious beaks; or else slipping between the bushes along the path and picking raspberries until our faces and fingers were red, and perhaps even taking some back home in a glass jar. I didn't say a word about my wishes, and would run after her with my short legs, clutching her hand. All I had to do was feel how tight she held my hand to realize that she was distracted and wasn't thinking about me—and yet her hand was always wrapped around my fingers.

It was only a few months ago, coming back from a weekend in Paris, that I realized where she had taken me during all those years. Countless times, even as an adult, I have sat on that bench, looking at the sky, gone into that chapel, and looked up at the fresco decorating the small apse. Staring into space, Mary is about to tread on a little dog who, poor thing, is standing up on its hind legs, trying to show affection. I've never paid attention to the sign the Tourist Board put outside the chapel a few years ago but that day, for some reason, as I was reading it, that my mother must have always known the story of that chapel, just as she had known, ever since she was a child, the story about the bearded female saint in the little church among the *masi* where I grew up.

The chapel was built by a local nobleman who had led a dissolute life as a young man. He was punished, after a marriage that sanctioned his return to sobriety, with the birth of a son with the body of a dog (the sign states as fact the direct relation between his previous depraved behavior and the monster: "and so a son was born that . . . "). The man made a vow to the Blessed Virgin that he would build a chapel in her honor if she would show him the grace of making the child die. Judging from the fresco of the poor little dog about to be squashed by Mary, the nobleman's prayers to the Virgin were granted. In fact, the sign above the altar, in high German, says: IN PRAISE OF GOD AND WITH CHRISTIAN THOUGHTS THIS CHAPEL WAS BUILT IN 1682 A.D. As I was reading it, I thought: my mother would never have done that. Even if she had had the necessary means to make a vow of an entire chapel, she would never have asked for my death.

My mother never told me I ruined her existence. On the contrary. When I was a little girl she would cling to me like a small raft and I was proud of that, I wanted to be able to take her to safety beyond the rough waters of her life. But I didn't save anybody. Not myself and not her.

As a young adult I tried to run away from my inability to make her happy. I remember the day of Ulli's funeral, I decided to leave our luminous mountains, with the air fragrant with hay, the balconies full of flowers. Suddenly, all this beauty seemed to me like a cruel farce that could no longer cover up the narrow-mindedness that had killed him. I could afford to do it. I was twenty-five years old, with no children (all my life I've taken great care not to get pregnant). I'd already been working for several years and had put some money aside. I was planning to go to Australia and look for work there. I wanted to get away, away from Alto Adige/Südtirol, and from its obsession with itself, away to a new life in the Antipodes!

When I communicated these intentions to my mother, she replied, "I've always wanted to see kangaroos, and now I'll finally get the opportunity."

I couldn't get anything else out of her.

I didn't go to live in Australia in the end. When all's said and done, I am a *Dableiber*.

Lying on the bunk, rocked by the motion of the train, I can't get any deep sleep, only shreds of dreams. The Po Valley flashing past us outside the window penetrates the side of the carriage, the blanket provided by the train company, and my skin. Its monotony, no less absolute just because it's invisible in the darkness beyond the glass, takes possession of me, and my mind becomes flat and without relief. Even so, every time my consciousness starts to forget itself and finally dissolves into sleep, the clatter of a high-speed train bursts in on me. A metallic, linear, daytime ego self that wakes me with a start. Once, startled, I prop myself up on my elbows, lift myself up and look out. We're standing still in a small, deserted station. The blue sign with white lettering says: POGGIO RUSCO, a name that evokes countryside, tractors, home-cured pork without polyphosphates. For some reason the train stops there for almost half an hour. The Po Valley air is so thick with the juices of the soil that the cones of orange light projected from the tall lamp posts look like jelly. I try opening the window. It's jammed. If I wanted to call the attendant from one compartment to the other in that intimate, almost conjugal way, he'd rush straight away, his eyes puffy with sleep. He would clumsily try to conceal the excitement triggered by the unhoped-for night call, unblock the window lock with a spanner, watch me as I inhale that greasy humidity smelling of manure and recently plowed fields, then ask, "Why aren't you sleeping?" And I would have to explain to him that I am already an insomniac as a rule, let alone today that I'm traveling the entire length of Italy, rushing to Vito's bedside.

Vito. Why did he call me and not my mother? She was his long lost love, whereas I was just a child when he last saw me.

"I always think about you," he said on the phone with that tired voice of his. What does the word "always" mean?

Once again I lie down on the bunk. As if this was the secret signal it was waiting for, the train starts again.

1963

Gerda lost both mother and father in less than an hour. She had returned home after over three months' absence, her belly already stretched. She revealed her state to Johanna, who put a hand on her chest, her face twisted with retching. A gush of transparent vomit came out of her purple lips, splashing Gerda's shoes, then she fell off the chair. This is what Hermann saw when he came back home: his wife's body lying on the floor, nothing more than a thing now; Gerda's belly next to her, throbbing and swollen with life; his daughter's suitcase leaning against the *Stube*. For a moment he remained motionless and silent, slightly bow-legged. Then, with an odd kind of efficiency, as though he had practiced this gesture all his life, Hermann picked up Gerda's suitcase and, tracing an elegant arc with his arm, hurled it through the front door, which had remained wide open. The suitcase rose very high, struck the lamp post outside the house, and opened in mid-air. Gerda's clothes flew out, colorful and fluttering like migrating birds. Hermann and Gerda watched their ocean crossing in silence. The continent on which they landed was the patch of dirt track between the Shanghai houses. And once they were lying there on that dark, damp stretch of suburb where the sun shone only in the summer, their wretched inanimate nature was obvious once again.

Hermann didn't look his daughter in the face. He pointed with his finger at the area outside the door, now covered in clothes that had been bought at the Wednesday market, clean but overused underwear, knitted sweaters.

"*Aussi*," he said.

So Gerda left.

With a quiet but nonetheless definitive sound, the front door closed behind her. Gerda bent down to pick up her scattered clothes, stuffing them back into the leather suitcase as well as she could. She picked from the ground her best outfit, a green-and-white shirt-dress she had made herself from a sewing pattern. It was tailored at the waist and she hadn't been able to wear it for months. She carefully dusted it before putting it back in the suitcase.

From inside the house which she would never re-enter, Gerda heard the man who until just a few moments ago had been her father strike hard blows on the walls, or perhaps the floor or the table, without emitting a single lament.

The building of the National Organization for Mothers and Children was on the outskirts of Bolzano, near the steelworks where Peter hadn't been hired. It was a triumph of rational dimensions, solid and ultra-Fascist; even the garden hedges had pedantic lines. The river Talfer ran nearby but you couldn't see it because of the high wall that separated the garden from the street. When Gerda walked in, the janitor nun closed the iron gates behind her in a way that left no doubt: you didn't come here out of free choice, but necessity. Then she led her through wide corridors to the large empty dormitory, where there lingered a smell of boiled vegetables and chicken stock: lunch was being served in the refectory.

Her suitcase closed as well as it could be—after the knock one of the clasps wasn't working anymore—Gerda had arrived two weeks before she was due. However, Eva, who from the start was a child who caused very little trouble, sped things up: Gerda was still finishing putting her clothes in the small iron cupboard when she felt a violent clawing in her gut. Surprised, she looked beyond the tall windows, as though looking for a reason in the garden.

The janitor nun, who was explaining the rules and timetable of the place, noticed immediately. It was the same with all these girls: when the moment arrived they always looked astounded, as though until then they hadn't really believed it. At the second spasm, Gerda didn't look out but down on the floor, between her shoes, and a soft moan came out of her lips.

"You're complaining now, but you enjoyed it before," the nun said, but without any acrimony or moral judgment— rather, like a fact she had observed over her long years of experience, something it was as pointless denying as it was trying to stop labor.

The midwife's eyes were the color of water in a thick glass; a sweaty blond lock of hair escaped from her cap, even though it wasn't she who was giving birth. She had a Star of Goodness medal pinned to her white coat, above her large bosom: it had been conferred on her just a few months earlier for services rendered, on Mother and Child Day. During the ceremony one hundred and forty gift packages were handed out to as many unmarried mothers and their children.

"Push," she said.

Gerda didn't react, she was drowning in the pain. The other woman, a nurse nun, clicked her tongue. She was small and black like a watermelon seed. She had a starched white coronet, and you could just about see the dark roots of her hair on the back of her neck. She said contemptuously to the midwife, "This one doesn't even understand when you say 'push'."

Gerda waited for the pain to subside, then stared at the nun and said, "I do undershtand."

The nurse nun made a grimace of disbelief. "Undershtand . . . " She repeated, aping Gerda's German accent. She burst out laughing. "Undershtand . . . " She laughed, her bony shoulders shaking, unable to stop.

The midwife and Gerda stared at her, motionless.

"Undershtand . . . " the nun kept repeating as she left the room. Her laughter echoed down the entire corridor, until she went beyond the glass door that sealed off the ward.

The midwife nun looked at Gerda. She raised a shoulder and protruded her lower lip. She half closed her eyes deliberately, as though inviting her to do the same.

"Pay no attention to her. She's from the south that one—a *Terrona*."

Terrona. Gerda, a young *Daitsch*, who had known few Italians, knew nothing of the differences among the *Walschen*, and how important it was for them not to be confused with one another. She made a mental note to learn this new word. *Terrona*: "A stupid, rude person who laughs inappropriately."

Meanwhile, however, she had another surge of pain.

It was a perfect pain, of blinding beauty. A galaxy of suffering-inflicting stars that throb, tear, pierce. In the middle they came thick and fast, unbearable. In the thin spiral arms spiraling outward/that spiraled out , however, they were rarer.

The galaxy was spinning on itself, majestic and relentless. Nothing could have stopped it, neither Gerda's screams, nor terror, nor exhaustion. In the rare moments of pause the long tentacles of pain stretched out, transporting Gerda to their very tips, and then for a moment she would look out onto a quiet stillness, a vibrant infinite silence which encompasses everything, including itself.

Here, Gerda breathed.

But soon the tentacle of pain would contract again with an animal shudder, violently calling her back. And, once again, Gerda would fall into the incandescent heart of the pain.

It was as though she had been there for thousands of years

but it had only been a couple of hours. Her wide hips had been made especially to make the passage of a new life easier. And now, after one last burning explosion between her legs, Eva was born.

She had fair skin. Her upper lip, like a shell, promised that she would have full lips, like her mother. Her bald skull looked like a map of the world: the network of tiny purple veins caused by the effort of being born traced rivers, chains of mountains and continents of a new planet. The little hair she had was very blond, almost white. There was no hint of red, something that made Gerda very relieved: this yet unknown newborn looked only like her.

By the time the midwife brought her back all washed and dressed in the regulation little outfit of the Organization, Gerda's breasts were already huge and painful, streaked with green veins, and the rise of milk had wet her nightgown. She received the newborn's hungry mouth around her dark nipples like a blessing. Eva's head started bobbing up and down on her breast, like a strong, efficient little pump. The midwife with the Star of Goodness stood watching her with her transparent eyes, then proclaimed, "This one won't ever give you any trouble."

Almost as though she heard herself being mentioned, Eva opened her eyes and fixed them on her mother's. As though it was she who wanted to get to know her, and not the other way around.

The janitor nun was right: until this moment Gerda didn't think it would really happen. Only now was she beginning to realize that she had a daughter.

It was the first thing in the world Gerda could call her own.

Many girls remained at the Organization way beyond the regulation three months. Many had nowhere to go. The nuns of the house gave them little jobs in the kitchens, in the creche, or cleaning. If they were lucky, they would find them piece-work with local craftspeople: embroidery, knitting, sewing, then they could become independent and start looking for rooms to rent. However, sometimes months or even years would pass before that became possible. When, with the nuns' help, they managed to find a job and went back into the world, they would linger at the gates and turn to look back with a mixture of regret and relief—but only those who had kept their children. Those who departed alone, whose children were left behind in the orphans' wing, which was separate from the one for the women who had just given birth, would leave as quickly as they could; no sooner were they able to walk after delivery than they would exit through the iron gate. When the janitor nun closed the gate behind them, none of them turned to look back.

In the bed next to Gerda's, in the dormitory with tall, arched windows, which she shared with seven other unmarried mothers, an obese woman stayed for a couple of days. They called her Anni. It was impossible to tell her age, at night she snored and during the day she kept the tip of her index finger pressed against the corner of her mouth even when she ate. Gerda heard that Anni had already been through here five other times. She was never able to say who the father of her newborn was. Some nuns suspected Anni wasn't even aware of the connection between the children that came out with extraordinary ease from between her huge thighs, and the things men did to her under tavern stairs while clinging to her enormous body, amid cans of beer and buckets full of sawdust. Every time, she looked perplexed at the sight of the newborn covered in blood and meconium coming from her, and hand him over to the midwife or one of the nurses. When she was attending to women like Anni, certain thoughts about abortion and contraceptive methods would come to the midwife's mind, which, if they had been heard by the authorities of the National Organization for Mothers and Children, would have cost her Star of Goodness. Consequently, she kept them to herself.

Gerda watched Anni as she would an inhabitant of the Amazon jungle, dressed only in pearls and feathers, whom reliable sources had told her was a distant relative of hers: with dismay, disbelief and suspicion, but also with uncontrollable curiosity to discover if they had any characteristics in common. She did not discover any. Certainly not the fact of giving children up for adoption: that was a possibility that hadn't even crossed Gerda's mind. In any case, whether or not Anni ever had any sadness or regret nobody knew. The morning after every one of her brief stays, her bed was already vacant.

The days drifted by, all alike, punctuated by the rhythm of feeding times and weighing times, meals and sleep. The surrounding wall that had seemed to Gerda like that of the prison was now beginning to feel like protection: from that world which, judging from the way things had turned out till now, didn't promise to welcome her back very warmly once she had left here.

Only fragmentary echoes reached her from that world. After dinner, Gerda would sit with Eva in her arms in the television room. The legs of the uncomfortable iron chairs had carved countless, perfect little circles on the green linoleum on which were reflected the black-and-white images of the bulky television in the wooden chest. Every evening, albeit without particular interest, she watched the news.

SCIENTISTS AGREE: ALGAE WILL BE HUMANITY'S FOOD OF THE FUTURE. IT IS INEXHAUSTIBLE AND NUTRITIOUS.

THE DISAPPEARANCE OF A HAIR OF PROPHET MOHAMMED'S HAT, KEPT IN THE HAZRATBAL SANCTUARY OF SRINAGAR, HAS CAUSED PROTESTS AND DEATHS ACROSS INDIA.

THE UN IS DISCUSSING THE PROPOSAL TO MAKE THE YEAR ACROSS THE WORLD START ON A SUNDAY AND END ON A SATURDAY. THEY ARE WAITING FOR THE POPE'S APPROVAL.

They were also announcing Mina's return to television. The singer had been banished for over a year after having a child with her married lover—the announcer managed to convey the news without using the world "banished," "lover" or "married" even once.

That evening, the unmarried mothers crowded the television room. The program was called "La fiera dei sogni" and Mina was singing È l'uomo per me. She had the nose, eyes and mouth of an Egyptian queen, and arm and hip gestures that ruled out any contrition with regard to her own immorality. Many girls grew almost tearful with the unexpected hope that this both daring and gentle voice gave them, apologizing for nothing and to no one.

"Maybe one day it won't be so bad to have children without being married," a dark girl the same age as Gerda said to her softly. She was never very clean and had a look in her eyes that was akin to hunger. She hadn't yet learned to hold her dark, wrinkled newborn, who was always crying.

"It will always be bad," Gerda said without turning around.

Mina carried on singing, her face more luminous than the rhinestones on her low-cut dress.

The janitor nun hadn't yet dared confess to her spiritual father the business with the tweezers. It wasn't exactly theft.

Their owner, an unnatural blond with underwear that was a little too well cared for, had left the institute over a month earlier, leaving behind an extra orphan for whom they had struggled to find a family. Finding the chrome steel tweezers at the bottom of the empty cupboard couldn't be considered a sin, and perhaps nor could not handing them immediately to the Mother Superior. The fact was that once the pointless period pains which she had suffered for over thirty years had ceased—thank God!—a few hairs as tough as barbed wire had started to grow on the sister's chin. When nobody could see her, she would furtively look for them, holding her hand like a claw, and, with a decisive grip of her thumb and index finger, she would tear them out. The tweezers had been an epiphany.

Now, however, she feared the moment when she would find the strength to confess that sin of vanity, not just because of the shame and contrition that awaited her, but because she would then be ordered to hand the tweezers over to the Mother Superior once and for all. And so she would have to do without their neat, accurate pull, which was so much more pleasant and elegant than the angry gesture with her fingers. And so she was intent on tweezing tufts of very tough hair, still telling herself that it was the last time, though not really believing it because she had had this resolution for days without acting on it when, in the porters lodge that was her kingdom, the gate bell rang. To serve in that Institute was probably the charitable activity least likely to make a nun regret taking the vow of chastity. The sadness, disorientation and fear of the girls who found here a brief refuge was nothing to envy. "You're complaining now, but you enjoyed it before," the janitor nun had said to Gerda when her labor had begun, which could have seemed like acrimonious jealousy. Instead, in that sentence that was not original but which she used with almost all the girls giving birth as a distilled point of view based on her experience, a question was especially implicit. Since they had enjoyed the before so much that they were ready to ignore the serious consequences they were suffering now, exactly what was so pleasurable about this before?

For over twenty years, the janitor nun had been watching lonely, depressed young women crowding the dormitories, clinging to their children like buoys after they'd seen their lives sink before their very eyes. Every so often, the very men who hadn't married them would turn up at the iron gates: boys with a shudder of regret or other women's husbands who, after all, felt affection for the mothers of their bastards. They were all so universally inadequate to the drama being lived by the women they had made pregnant that the porter nun couldn't bring herself to cast too severe a judgment upon those failed fathers. To her they looked like spoiled children unequipped to understand the harsh destiny awaiting their lovers. They would insist that the nun deliver cheap jewelry to girls who, instead, had to be watched so they wouldn't commit suicide; they would propose romantic trips to remote little hotels, taking advantage of wives who were conveniently away, to women who were suffering from mastitis because they had just given their newborn up for adoption. And these weren't the worst ones: they, at least, got in contact. They'd peep through the gates, looking awkward, wearing their best suits; the janitor nun knew they would have given anything to obtain from her a word or a look that would state that their choice not to acknowledge those children and marry their mothers was inevitable, understandable and right. The more of these men she saw, the less she understood what was so attractive about them as to lead these women to such disasters. It was a mystery to her, and meeting Hannes Staggl certainly did not shed any more light on the question.

When she pulled the heavy wrought iron bolt she noticed the cream-colored Mercedes 190 outside the institute gates. The janitor nun saw a large white bird on the chrome mudguards: her own reflection. It's only when she looked up that she noticed Hannes. He was behind the car: standing in the middle of the empty road, he was looking at the windows beyond the top of the surrounding wall. The nuns were not so naive as to lodge the girls in rooms overlooking the street, or they would have spent entire days checking for themselves whether the miracle that would save them was coming. The windows through which Hannes was trying to catch a glimpse of the girl he had gotten pregnant belonged to the staff.

She was struck by the young man's almost orange hair, his transparent skin and freckled hands. Hannes asked after Gerda Huber and the child she had given birth to, and the janitor nun found herself breathing a sigh of relief. She'd seen too many bastards forever condemned to carry around the faces of the fathers who'd abandoned them. Luckily for her, Gerda's daughter looked entirely like her mother.

"It's a girl. She's healthy. Her mom is well too."

He started blinking with those opalescent eyelids: the word "mom" had struck him with the force of reality.

"What's her name?"

"Eva."

He looked at the Mercedes for a moment. "It's a beautiful name."

"Yes, it's beautiful."

Again Hannes raised his eyes to the windows of the building, and squinted. Was it to glimpse the interior beyond the sky on the glass panes, to stall, to get used to this beautiful name?

Here we go, the janitor nun thought, he's about to ask. He is not holding packages or flowers but it's a rich man's car and when a girl ends up here because of a man with money there's not much point in fooling oneself.

"Can I see her? The little girl."

The janitor nun tucked her chin into her throat and looked at him from below. "Yes, if you give her your surname."

He lowered his eyes to his well-made shoes. He remained like this for a long time. The hazel irises of the janitor nun had lost their definition with age and blended into the cornea with the gray halo; but her pupils were still clear and black. Her expression was not severe but rather objective, patient, resigned; it did not express condemnation, but not his yearned-for absolution either. She knew he would leave without a word, his head down so as to avoid seeing the windows behind which he thought there was the daughter he did not acknowledge whereas, instead, there was the bursar nun examining the invoices of the suppliers, and the cook deciding on the dinner menu.

As the Mercedes vanished beyond the crossroads, the janitor nun wondered once again what the pleasure was that made all this worthwhile. She really couldn't imagine it.

Gerda was informed, however, of the other visit she received.

When the janitor nun opened the bolt and found Herr Neumann standing before her, what she noticed were the puffy eyelids, the large belly that pushed against the buttons of his cloth jacket, and especially his age. She felt relief that the blond, solid girl who said little but was so helpful in the kitchen and whose gait everyone found attractive, even the nun, hadn't been made pregnant by this man. Then Herr Neumann explained that he only wanted one thing from Gerda: that she should come back to work. Nobody would say anything offensive to her about what had happened, he guaranteed it. The janitor nun was sorry for having misjudged this generous man from his exterior look. As if the hairs on her chin truly revealed who she was! She mentally slapped her fingers and ordered herself to report her superficial arrogance to the father confessor.

When Gerda came out of the building, Herr Neumann's breath caught in his chest and the buttons of his cloth jacket nearly exploded because of this extra pressure. Never in his life had he seen a more beautiful woman. It's what he had thought the first time Gerda had walked into his kitchen wearing the scullery maid apron, but he never thought of it again in order not to make working next to her unbearable. Herr Neumann had been not unhappily married for almost thirty years, had grown children who had already made him a grandfather and, besides, he had promised to keep Gerda safe from insults. So he just said to her, "*Gerda gibs lai oane*": there's only one Gerda.

She packed her suitcase and got into the pistachio-green Fiat 1300 with the white top, for which Herr Neumann had already payed half the installments. Leaving the National Organization for Mothers and Children forever, Gerda took two things away with her: a five-month-old daughter who never cried, and significant progress in mastering the Italian language. One thing, though, she left behind: the certainty that absolute love existed and that she was destined for it.

Once the Fiat 1300 vanished at the crossroads, the nuns, the Star of Goodness midwife, the *Terrona* nurse and the rest of the staff were on the sidewalk, saying goodbye, happy that Gerda—at least she—had somewhere to go. The following day, the janitor nun waited for her weekly interview with the spiritual father. She confessed all her sins. Then, with relief and regret, she handed the tweezers to the Mother Superior.

KILOMETERS 295-715

A year after the 1980 Bologna massacre, in the summer of my high school graduation, I was on my way to the Tremiti Islands with a school mate. I didn't care for him but he fancied me so had persuaded his parents, rich shopkeepers in Bolzano, to pay for my travel and camping too. Until then I'd only ever seen the sea at Cesenatico, opposite the square buildings of the ex-Fascist colonies: the only travel agent my mother could afford was Caritas. Sea holidays for me meant the rancid smell of tomato sauce, the stench of too many badly washed children in a single dormitory, sand thrown into the eyes of the weaker children by older ones, abused by teachers angry with exhaustion.

It was before the days of the Italian Eurostar with compulsory bookings, and our carriage seemed full of war evacuees. Holiday makers going to the sea in August were bursting out of compartments as though from crammed cupboards that won't close anymore, they sat on the foldaway corridor seats, on each other's laps, on the floor, on the steps outside closed doors, inside the toilets (especially those traveling without a ticket, and there were quite a few of those). The boy ready to pay and I, like so many others, were overloaded with heavy backpacks made of thick, coarse fabric, with aluminum frames that were supposed to distribute the load on your back but just dug into your ribs. We smelled of feet, cannabis, strawberry-flavored Del Ponte chewing gum, and especially smoke: we always had a cigarette in our hand, you still could then. When we arrived at Bologna, our train stopped on the first platform and I saw right outside my window the tear in the wall, emphasized by the glass which even today commemorates the exact location of the explosion, and the clock fixed at that time: 10:25.

I grew up in the South Tyrol of bombs and attacks, and I was already old enough to have formed a definite opinion about Uncle Peter's death; but even I, the child of a land of terrorists and roadblocks couldn't—can't—fully imagine the extent of the Bologna massacre. Eighty-five dead, hundreds of injured: a massacre that belonged to horror on a different scale. When the train started again, I tried talking about it with the boy. He didn't reply, skated over the issue, and changed the subject as soon as he could, so that I had to keep my confused dismay to myself. I added this obvious lack of sensitivity to the many other factors indicating that he was unworthy of my love. The fact that he had paid for my trip didn't seem relevant in evaluating the issue.

I spent the holidays allowing other people to come on to me before his eyes. In the evening, around the bonfire on the beach, I let other boys with sleeping bags or young residents of the island touch me, but then I always searched his eyes. He never protested. He paid for everything until the last day. It was only many years later, after I'd lost touch with him for a while, that I heard from mutual acquaintances that one of his relatives from Val Passiria had been among the Bologna dead. He had been very fond of her, they said.

Now, in the middle of the night on a train, we come into Bologna station. We're at platform four and you can't see the gutted wall from my window.

There is nobody beneath the drably-lit platform roofs. The loudspeaker announces the rare arrivals and departures like a voice in the desert: an invisible prophet with a thick Emilia accent. His hermitage isn't made of mystical rocks but of marble benches, drink dispensers, tracks. His tiny community of followers is made up of me, the Neapolitan attendant, and the engine driver whose presence I've been sensing for hours as the train slowed and accelerated.

The prophet hurls his invectives at us: "The night InterCity train 780 'Freccia Salentina' from Bari and bound for Milan Central, is about to depart from platform . . . "

"The train 1940 'del Sole' from Villa San Giovanni and bound for Turin Porta Nuova . . . "

The train departs again while the voice carries on preaching in vain.

We exit the old-fashioned station light and dive once again into the darkness of the countryside, the great obscurity of natural night time which is neither hostile nor friendly, but simply different from us.

That's exactly how it was when I kept Ulli company while he spent the whole night combing the ski pistes on Marlene, his snowcat that was more comfortable and personalized than a truck: the zebra seat upholstery, the heating turned up to maximum so you could sit in a T-shirt, the stereo light flickering to the rhythm of Queen or The Clash with dozens of luminous LEDs, still a novelty back then in the Eighties. Outside, the throbbing winter sky and the wind at 2,000 meters. And us going up and down the pistes, making the snow a perfect white velvet for the skiers, which the factory would churn out the following morning.

It was on one of those nights that Ulli told me he was no longer afraid of being a *Schwul*. He used that very word. Not *gay* or *homosexuell*, but the term used by pontificating retirees in the tavern *Stammtisch*, the one Ulli had heard uttered behind his back by his peers, by the neighbors' children, by his younger brother Sigi, ever since, at the age of eleven, he no longer wanted to play football or ice hockey, but only spend time with me.

A month earlier, Ulli had been to London. There, his homo-sexuality hadn't ensured him original status in the least. On the contrary, he'd been treated almost as someone quite ordinary. He'd liked that. It was also on one of those nights that I'd told him of my lightning marriage, celebrated and soon afterwards annulled, in Reno, to Lesley—or was it Wesley? I pretended not even to remember the name of that two-week husband. Naturally, Ulli didn't buy it and laughed. Afterwards, however, he'd fallen silent and looked at me with that sad, tender expression he often had.

"I wonder what Vito would say."

I sniffed hard. There we were again, Ulli and I, on the same wavelength. Every time it came as a surprise and yet it was almost taken for granted: at that moment I was also thinking about Vito. And yet he hadn't been mentioned by anyone for years, either by Ulli or me. And especially not by my mother. What would that duty-bound Carabiniere from the South have said about me and that lightning marriage? I wasn't sure I wanted to know.

To prevent the snowcat from overturning on the steep slope, a cable secured/hooked to its front was attached to a winch at the station above. It shone like a precious necklace in the headlights. I remained silent, watching it tighten.

I began telling Ulli about how I'd met his brother Sigi at the *Altstadtfest*[11] wine bars the previous summer. Along with the stench of beer and Currywurst, these words had come out of his mouth: "If I ever read in the paper that you've ended up badly because of a man, I'll be sorry but not surprised."

Ulli had continued to maneuver Marlene in silence, staring at the cone of light from the headlights on the snow ahead of him. He had long-term experience of Sigi's brutal and obscene way of speaking. Many times he'd asked me to help him under-

---

[11] Town celebration.

stand just when exactly, and why, his little gentian-eyed brother, whose shoe laces he had tied for years, had turned out . . . like that. Now Ulli's eyes suddenly opened wide as he turned to look at me. In the dim light of the cabin his eyes glowed with indignation. "He wants to fuck you! Even Sigi wants to fuck you!"

"Why are you so surprised?"

"I don't want to fuck you."

"You don't count; you're a *Schwul*."

Ulli stopped the snowcat and jumped out, closing the door behind him. I was afraid I'd offended him, even though he'd used the word *Schwul* about himself earlier. But it wasn't that. He was picking something up he'd seen in the snow. Lit up like a rock star in the middle of the huge stage of the entire mountain, Ulli lifted his arm to show me what he'd found: a strange pink animal with two heads, no body and a long string of a tail. Only when he came back into the cabin, bringing in with him the night frost, I saw what it was: a lace bra.

We spent the rest of the night up and down the mountain's immensity inside our heated microcosm, wondering how it could have ended up there. During that harsh December which had made the stream in the middle of town freeze over, who—and especially why—had someone felt like peeling off, like an onion, the complex layers of ski wear in order to slip off the bra? And why on that particular track, the black slope where champions of the special slalom trained?

We talked about it all night without finding an explanation.

When I met Carlo, I decided for the first time in my life that I would be faithful to him. Carlo should never know that, of course, but it was a great relief to me, and still is, eleven years later. No one can deny that for me this was progress.

We're now between Bologna and Florence. The darkness outside the window has lost the deep breath of the night sky, but is now black, narrow and noisy: we go in and out of tunnels beneath the Apennines, just as I go in and out of my thoughts. What would Vito have said about me? If he'd been there, he would have said . . .

But he wasn't there.

Did he ever think about me? I'm sure he thought about my mother. Why didn't he phone her?

Vito called me. And now it's me rushing to him. Carlo knows nothing about Vito. I've never mentioned him. Realizing this is like one of the dams Ulli and I used to build as children: it stops the flow of my thoughts just as we would stop, albeit briefly, the streams. With splashes and hollow thuds, like a drum, we used to drop the largest stones we could find into the water: porphyry the color of black pudding, gray-green granite, salmon-streaked pale dolomite, schist glowing like cat's-eye. Our arms hurt from the effort and our hands, after soaking for hours, would become white and wrinkled like blind creatures from the abyss. When we managed to disrupt the water's course, it would start flowing in strange ways: it would dig furrows through the emerald moss hairs on the shore, form unexpected bogs in the grass, and start spinning in whirls in front of certain streaked rocks which up to then we hadn't considered as part of the stream but of the undergrowth. Still, it didn't matter how tall the pebble barrier we built was, or how much moss and bark cement we used to plug all the leaks: in the end, and always, the water found its way.

I have never told Carlo about Vito.

That "never" is like a slab of rock thrown into the flow of my thoughts. They stop for a moment. When they start flowing again their nature is altered and they have become something halfway between sleep and waking, something different, just like the secret water of a bog is different than the fast and gurgling water of a stream.

In this half-sleep I see myself as a little girl. I'm about to fall asleep in the furnished room where I lived with my mother during the low season. There's an Italian Eurostar train standing still next to the bed she and I share. There are passengers looking at me through the windows. They have the expression of people who have already spent a long time staring at the passing panorama: a neutral expression untouched by the landscape rushing past them for hours. Some don't even look up from the newspapers they're reading. Only then do I realize something: they're all men. And I notice that, lying next to me, there's my mother Gerda as a young woman. She is supporting her head with her hand, her elbow digging into the mattress, her heavy, full breast falling on one side of her slip. She's more beautiful than I will ever be. The train conductor whistles, the fast train starts again and crosses our room like a station. A man strains his neck so he can see the bed from his window for as long as he can. She puts a finger to her mouth and, addressing the train, murmurs suggestively, "Eva is asleep . . . "

"No, she's not!" Vito's cheerful, musical voice breaks in. "My *Sisiduzza* is still awake."

He appears next to me, with his laughing, loving eyes. To fall asleep more easily, I hold his hand tight. However, the Eurostar passes next to the head of the bed and wakes me up completely with its loud rattle . . .

An insistent metallic din wakes me up. The ladder the Neapolitan couchette attendant has taught me to use as an anti-burglar device is rattling against the handle next to my head.

"We arrive in Rome in twenty minutes!" says a male voice from the corridor.

I have no recollection of Florence Station, I must have dozed off in the Apennines. My eyes are puffy and my hands are clumsy from waking up suddenly; only after messing about and knocking metal do I manage to free myself from the prison of the anti-burglar ladder. Even before I open the door completely I can smell coffee. The couchette attendant hands me a plastic cup with a contrite air.

"It's cold. I'll make you another one . . . "

"Oh, no, please don't worry . . . " I reply, taking it.

He also gives me a sachet of sugar and the little white plastic spatula that acts as a spoon.

"Thank you . . . "

I drink the coffee in one sip and wipe my lips with my wrist. "The same gesture as your mother," Ulli once said to me and once again I promised myself from then on to use my fingers, like everybody else, except that I never remember until it's too late.

I stare at the Neapolitan couchette attendant with my hands still in front of my mouth, like a Muslim veil.

He's also looking at me, with a serious expression. His forehead is a little low but he has the wavy mouth of the Southern seas. I also notice his neck, which emerges decisively from the light blue uniform shirt, his shoulders broad, just as I like them, the skillful hands of a man familiar with engines, minor home repairs and a woman's body. I'm a lot taller than him. Neither of us has looked away from the other one yet. His eyes have clouded over as though with a sudden sadness. Or is it desire? My breathing has gotten deeper, and so has his.

And I find myself thinking: I've been faithful for eleven years—not to Carlo but to his wife. So why not betray her with an attentive couchette attendant who hasn't taken advantage of the situation and is ready to make me another coffee if this one gets cold?

"Thank you . . . " I say, returning the empty cup. He takes it, careful not to brush my fingers. I'm about to go back into my compartment. "I'm going to tidy myself up."

"You don't need to." His beautiful, pearl-fisher mouth hints at a smile.

"Thank you," I say for the third time and close the door behind me.

The train is already running next to the fork in the motorway past the Fiano Romano signal box. It'll soon go past the ring road and we'll be in Rome.

It's six-thirty in the morning when we arrive at Rome Tiburtina, but it hasn't been daylight for long: it's already daylight saving time so the sun rises late. A middle-aged woman is watching our train as it stops at the platform. She has two commas of silvery eyeshadow beneath her plucked eyebrows, a purple coat that opens on a black sheath dress too short for her age, and gold leather shoes. She looks like the survivor of a night that has fallen short of her expectations. Behind her, there is a plaque on the wall commemorating the passage of armored trains carrying the Roman Jews rounded up in 1943. In order to send them to Auschwitz, the Nazis made them go up Italy along the same rail track I have just travelled on.

The couchette attendant brings my suitcase down from the train. He hops off the footboard with an agility that betrays his youth. However, he's all grown-up and earnest as he holds out his hand.

"My name's Nino."

"I'm Eva," I reply, shaking his hand.

"A beautiful name, almost like you . . . "

Driving my trolley suitcase, I walk away cheerfully: nothing puts a spring in a woman's step more than a compliment. Something my mother knows very well.

1963 -1964

The pact between Frau Mayer and Herr Neumann was clear. If he really wanted to have back in his kitchen that assistant cook who'd gotten herself in trouble and whose trouble, as it happened, was already two months old, with fat pink cheeks and her mother's transparent eyes, then she wouldn't stop him. For years, the chef had filled her esteemed guests' bellies with Tyrolean specialties which, if they were not fancy then at least were perfectly produced, and thus contributed to their return season after season. So now she had no plan to deny him this favor.

Frau Mayer was a woman of about fifty who could have been described (and, in fact, was at one time described) as a "classical Aryan beauty": slim, with athletic legs, a bosom not large but emphasized by the low-cut bodice of the *dirndl* and a thick blond plait twisted around her head from which no one had ever seen a hair stray. She spoke good Italian with an almost elegant turn of phrase, being a former pupil of a Fascist period school, but it was when she spoke *Hochdeutsch* with tourists that she revealed her deep love of correct language.

Everything about Frau Mayer was controlled, except for her blue-green eyes. Frightening yet beautiful, they suggested that, instead of spending her life bestowing dignified smiles upon her guests, she could just as well have lived a life of wild excess. It wasn't impossible to picture her as a temptress in a *Kabarett* who drives men to the brink of suicide, a barbarian female warrior with dragon blood on her dagger, a prophesying poetess in touch with the underworld.

Perhaps it was that talent for the absolute which shone from her eyes that had led Frau Mayer to give up the chance of a family and devote herself to the well-being of her guests like the worship of one god. Despite the large number of staff upstairs, in the dining room, and in the kitchen, not a single detail of the hotel management escaped her. The correct plumping up of the goose feather pillows in the birch bedrooms; the supply of sacks of sawdust to throw on the kitchen floor; the decorations made of dried flowers and the threads of plaited hay that embellished the dining room; the boiler repairs: everything had to be approved by her. Even the choice of music played by the small orchestra on the terrace during warm summer evenings relied on her taste, which was based on a very simple premise: always—always—favor sad love songs! Those guests who were lonely and melancholic would feel understood and in harmony with the atmosphere, those happily accompanied would generously take part in the wide range of human emotions, and everybody would have more drinks.

The only detail that sometimes escaped her control was death. Almost all her guests were there because of the town's spa, whose waters were renowned for being beneficial to a wide spectrum of ailments. Therefore, many of them were of an advanced age and unfortunately this carried a corollary: every so often, they died. Moreover, with little consideration for Frau Mayer, sometimes they even did so in the rooms of her hotel.

Frau Mayer didn't think of herself but rather of her guests (the live ones, that is). For them, witnessing the transfer of the dead body of someone their age just as they were searching for relief from their own ailments wouldn't have been pleasant. For that reason Frau Mayer had agreed on a special service with the local undertaker. The corpses were not taken away in traditional coffins but in single-door wardrobes made of good, ancient walnut, thus giving the impression of a house move rather than a funeral. So the only guest whose holiday was disturbed was the one who—peace be with him—would not be having any more of them.

The Mayer family had owned the hotel ever since the noble families of *Felix Austria* would come to take the waters here, in this southern outpost of the Empire, where the sun shines for two thirds of the year. The Kaiser, coming down to Tyrol in person to check on the emplacements of the Great War, had spent the night here. Frau Mayer retained a vague impression of an imperial hand, gloved and splendid, being placed on her blond curls. Was it an actual memory or a story someone had told her when she was three, and which had been repeated countless times? She didn't wish to know with certainty.

The hotel was destined for the eldest son, while Irmgard, the third of six children and the only girl, would give up any claim on her father's estate by getting married. History, however, had not treated the Mayer family plans with much consideration.

Julius, the eldest brother, had died in Montenegro as early as the first year of the second world massacre.

Karl, the second son, had been captured near El Alamein and spent the rest of the war in a prison camp in Texas. There, although he had never had any Nazi sympathies, he had refused to renege on his oath of loyalty to the general staff of the Wehrmacht, something required by the Americans of German officers in order to free them. He returned home almost three years after the end of the war, gravely ill. His fellow townsfolk shunned him as an ex-Nazi—especially those who really had worn the brown uniform of the SS. He passed away shortly afterwards because of "general deterioration" as the family doctor wrote on the death certificate.

Anton, the fourth son, who at the age of twenty had gone to seek his fortune in Brazil in the 1930s, had found it in a coffee fazenda, a mulatto wife, many lovers of various ethnicities, and a dozen children. That he would come back and manage the family hotel was out of the question.

Stefan, the fifth son, had died at the age of three in the Spanish flu epidemic of 1919.

Josef, the youngest, had been hit right in the forehead by a Russian sniper at Kalitva, on the loop of the river Don, southeast of Stalingrad, in 1943.

There was only she, little Irmgard, left to help the parents broken by grief. The profession of faith to the god of hotel hospitality, which marked Frau Mayer's entire life, was, in other words, the result of a dynastic accident.

The only employee who dared escape Frau Mayer's total control was Herr Neumann. It was he who made up the menu every day, who decided on the orders of the raw materials and who paid the suppliers. It was he who managed the kitchen personnel. This exception had been agreed on by Herr Neumann and Frau Mayer ever since he had first been employed, just a few years after the end of the war.

"Chef means boss, you don't need to speak French to know that. You tell me how much I can spend and I'll make sure the dishes reach the dining room. If the guests are unhappy you can fire me. But you can't tell me what to do. I'm not working in a kitchen where I'm not the one in charge. Take it or leave it."

Frau Mayer had taken it and had had no regrets for almost twenty years.

Now that Herr Neumann was asking her to employ Gerda again, she had no reason to refuse. Of course, even she could see that she was a beautiful girl and her suspicion that this somehow accounted for Herr Neumann's stubbornness did not make her happy. However, she dismissed the thought: the chef had never tolerated anyone who didn't work hard in his kitchen and, until her belly had started knocking against the food counters, Gerda had been no exception. Besides, there wasn't exactly an abundance of good assistant cooks around to whom you didn't always have to explain everything, and that also had to be taken into account. However, she laid out very clear conditions: the baby was not to be seen or heard. And the possibility that she could disturb guests in the dining room wasn't even worth mentioning. No point in considering the inadmissible.

The day she returned to the kitchen, Gerda took an apple crate made of compact smooth wood and no prickles. She lined it with cushions and towels, placed it in a corner where it wouldn't be in the way, and put Eva inside it. Then she went back to work at Herr Neumann's side as though she'd never been away.

Even now that Gerda had gotten herself into the kind of mess that perfectly defines the *Matratze*—getting herself pregnant without making a man marry her—none of the other scullery boys, or assistant cooks, or waiters showed her disrespect. Perhaps it was Eva, in her apple crate in a corner of the kitchen, who made that impossible. Her presence diverted attention from the activity that is the usual subject of coarse jokes to what the aforementioned activity can produce: irresistible, pink, chubby babies. Nobody made any comments even when, several times a day, Gerda would untie her apron and, without taking it off, turn it to one side, unbutton her blouse and give Eva her breast. Of course, everybody looked. Waiters looked, while passing through the kitchen, shouting, "*Spinatspatzlan, neu!*." Cooks looked, while frying, stirring and tasting. Elmar looked, while dropping leftover food from plates into the garbage buckets. That white roundness with blue veins and a dark nipple that glistened with milk that would appear and disappear into the little mouth was the focus of all the eyes in the kitchen. While in the sudden silence all that could be heard was the powerful sucking and clicking of the baby feeding, everybody contemplated, speechless, that part of Gerda about which they had always fantasized but which, now that it was performing its primary task, silenced them.

However, there were also difficult hours. When bitterness gained a specific flavor through the incessant rhythm of the daily actions and tasks, just as the bitter taste of radicchio suddenly explodes in your mouth after hiding among the other ingredients of a salad.

In the evening, before going to sleep, Gerda would give Eva her breast one last time in her bed in the attic dormitory she shared with the rest of the female staff. The little one suckled expertly, then both would fall into a deep sleep, the daughter huddled in the crook of her mother's arm, both enveloped by the smell of milk and diapers. On the first night they were back at the hotel, Eva woke up after just a few hours and began searching for the breast. Gerda's fingers, numbed by sleep, took a long time to unbutton her nightgown. At first, Eva emitted breathless little moans, then cried increasingly loudly. Protestations, huffs and half-accusations rose from the beds of her dormitory fellow-occupants, which ceased only when Eva found the nipple and quieted down.

The following night, Gerda gave her the breast straight-away to prevent any protest. However, after the feed, Eva began to cry. Gerda lifted the baby from the bed and started walking up and down the dormitory, patting her on the back with the palm of her hand, as the Star of Goodness had taught her. Once again, sleepy voices commanded silence. Gerda was able to go back to bed only when a nice big curdled-milk-smelling burp put an end to Eva's crying.

There was a repeat of this for a few nights, always in the

darkest hours before dawn, when anyone waking up has to fight their own ghosts before they can fall asleep again, and doesn't necessarily succeed. After a week, her roommates gave Gerda a brief, not impolite but direct speech: if she wanted to carry on sleeping there with her daughter, she couldn't disturb their sleep anymore.

Gerda could understand them. Like them, she knew the tiredness at the end of the working day, limbs hard as stone, joints on fire, a foggy brain: only sleep can, at least in part, make the idea of starting all over again the next day bearable. The protests were fair: you can't run around all day from the dining room to the kitchen, your arms loaded with plates, or tidy up dozens of rooms and leave them as new even if they've been used by vandals, or wash the floors of a four-story hotel as well as an outbuilding, if you haven't had enough sleep. Nor could you stir, slice and cook in the overheated kitchen, for that matter, but that baby was her daughter, not theirs. It was therefore her problem. They made a deal: Gerda could stay in the room until the feed before dawn. Then she'd have to go out.

For weeks, Gerda spent the final hours of the night strolling in the corridor with her baby on her neck. Exhaustion and fatigue separated her from the rest of the world like the walls of a prison: she couldn't imagine ever escaping. Sometimes she fell asleep on the very steps from which, a few months earlier, she had thrown herself precisely so she wouldn't have to hold a fatherless child in her arms. But Eva was here now, and would let her little blond head down on her shoulder, in a pose of total trust. Gerda had never felt so alone.

Sometimes, during the day, she would fall asleep for an instant while standing at the work table or between steps as she went to fetch ingredients from the store room. Once, she was suddenly overwhelmed by sleep while inside the meat freezer. She had put on the heavy, coarse wool greatcoat, and couldn't resist lying down on the ground among the quarters of beef and the kid halves covered in brine. If Herr Neumann hadn't come down immediately after her to fetch a turkey for roasting, she would have frozen to death.

That day Nina, the waitress from Egna, offered to mind the little girl during the *Zimmerstunde*.

"It won't do you any harm to get a couple of hours' sleep," she said, taking Eva from her arms. Gerda looked into her disillusioned eyes that were too close together. She felt gratitude take over her body, like wind before a storm, and she burst into tears. She calmed down only when she was in her bed. However, sleep was waiting to ambush her and grabbed her suddenly, the way you capture a prisoner.

Ever since a grenade had torn off his leg, Silvius Magnago hadn't slept well. The physical pain in the phantom limb had been his secret companion for over twenty years. Only to it did he feel he could reveal his true nature: his strength, his anger, his tenacity and despair, his resentment toward healthy people who don't know what it is to live with the suffering of the flesh, but also his ability to focus on what's essential. Ever since Magnago had received those pieces of rough toilet paper purloined from the jail in Bolzano, however, the pain in his leg seemed like nothing in comparison with his other pain: that of not having done anything for those who had placed their last hope in him.

The clothes returned to the wives of those imprisoned after *Feuernacht*, some time after the arrests, were covered in blood, vomit and excrement. However, the *Bumser* of the BAS were, after all, simple men. In spite of everything, they trusted the fact that if the world had known about the inhuman treatment they were suffering in Bolzano prison, it would have done everything to save them. They'd done all they could to communicate information outside the prison about the torture they'd been subjected to. A few notes were intercepted and their senders punished, but others managed to evade censorship. The obvious addressee of their request to help had been him, Silvius Magnago, the most authoritative political voice in South Tyrol.

Magnago had received those wretched pieces of paper in late 1961. And he, who knew physical pain only too well, had felt the spasms of lactic acid in arms kept raised for hours as if they'd been his own; the tissue torn by fists and the sinister clicking of shattered bones; the retching of incredulous horror of someone forced to eat his own excrement; the lungs bursting because your head is kept under water; the delirium of sleep deprivation. He'd read the notes almost without breathing. He'd wept in the silence of his pale, wood-paneled studio overlooking an exclusive Bolzano street. Episodes he'd witnessed as a young *Gebirgsjägerleutnant*[12] at war had flashed before his eyes, images he'd hoped never to have to remember again. He'd directed his gaze outside the window, at his beloved chimonantus tree that was now bare; the yellow flowers that announced the spring with their scent of vanilla hadn't blossomed yet. They couldn't comfort him either.

The *Südtiroler Volkspartei*, the party he led, couldn't afford to be associated, even from a distance, with the *Bumser*. The process of acquiring true autonomy for South Tyrol was still too fragile. The biblical timing of politics, the dance of talks, of promises and threats on the part of a government that had denied the problem so long it had allowed it to fester, and was beginning to realize that a plan for this province was necessary only now that it had become a ticking bomb—all that had to be taken into account.

Magnago had started to weave a fine and delicate canvas of negotiations and compromise in order to obtain that provincial

---

[12] Lieutenant in the German Alpine Infantry

autonomy (*"Los von Trient!"*) which alone could resolve the South Tyrol deadlock and prevent the worst possible scenario: an ethnic war. He knew very well that the strong German accent with which he spoke otherwiseimpeccable Italian convinced his Rome interlocutors a priori of his fundamental, encysted hatred toward them. He knew how much diplomacy, patience, and deliberate deafness to jokes was necessary even just to explain the starting point of the negotiations: South Tyroleans did not hate Italians but rather the colonization they had endured on the part of the Italian government. He knew that he couldn't take the risk of being painted with the same brush as those who had resorted to bombs even simply against infrastructures.

However, there was another reason for anxiety, which wasn't linked to considerations of political opportunities but rather an existential one, in those little sheets of paper which were written on literally with the blood of tortured men. At his Bologna alma mater, from where he'd graduated in Law, Magnago had become convinced that only dialogue, the search for a compromise, the hard but honest meeting between positions, no matter how different, were tools superior to any—any—form of violence. Whoever gives up on verbal discussion and resorts to destructive action against people or things, no matter how justified the reason, automatically gets on the side of the wrong: that was Silvius Magnago's one and only political creed. Never had he been seduced by any of the ideologies of this fire and arms century. He'd reached adulthood just before the start of the world massacre, and had seen only too clearly what is achieved when politics gives way to violence: a planet in flames. He felt in his own amputated flesh and the pain it radiated every second the duty to safeguard bodies, always. Not just the bodies of the people of his *Heimatland*, those who'd charged him with a mandate to represent them; but also the bodies of his opponents, of the ignorant politicians in Rome, even those of the administrators who from their positions of small, obtuse power made his people's lives difficult. His duty was as follows: to separate, always, political struggle from physical destruction, even that of electricity pylons. He had carefully folded up the sheets of paper, placed them in an envelope, and put them where only he knew. Later on, people found out about the torture in Bolzano prison, but it wasn't Silvius Magnago who reported it.

In the two years that followed, two BAS men had died in prison from beatings and their consequences. Many had suffered permanent damage. Torture left the indelible mark of suffering on their bodies, just as the war had done on the body of *Gebirgsjägerleutnant* Magnago. The Carabinieri guilty of mistreatment were tried, and their defenders claimed that, to the contrary, the prisoners' wounds were self-inflicted— despite dozens of medical certificates documenting otherwise—with the sole purpose of discrediting Italy. The theory was accepted, the defendants acquitted and, as the verdict was read out, they walked out of the court free, celebrating with their relatives. All were officially praised by the chief of the Carabinieri, General De Lorenzo. Their victims, the prisoners they'd reduced to the state of broken, weeping creatures, were sent back to prison in handcuffs.

Silvius Magnago never revealed what his decision not to act on the *Bumser's* desperate request for help cost him. Or if their martyrdom brought nightmares to his already scarce sleep at night.

Bodies. To safeguard bodies. He hadn't been able to do it for them.

In autumn 1963, a young girl dressed in white, holding bunch of flowers, smiled from the posters that papered the streets of Milan. A Mediterranean version of Gerda: full breasts, soft lips, high cheekbones, but dark-haired. It was the Christian Democrat party's way of projecting a more youthful image, and to do so it had turned to Ernest Dichter, the American guru of motivational research in advertising—creator of the famous dried Californian prunes campaign. It was he who had coined the slogan that appeared under the beautiful girl:

THE CHRISTIAN DEMOCRATIC PARTY IS TWENTY!

From Domodossola to Siracusa, from Udine to Bari, on posters throughout the entire peninsula, anonymous hands added a note underneath, in felt tip pen:

TIME TO FUCK HER!

That was something Mr Dichter had not foreseen.

The incitement to do to the twenty-year-old Christian Democratic party what every Latin male would have liked to do to its flesh-and-blood contemporaries was followed by many: in the 1963 elections the Italian Communist Party obtained, for the first time in its history, over a quarter of the votes. The absolute hegemony of the Christian Democrats had been broken.

Under the leadership of Aldo Moro, the first center-left government in Republican Italy was formed. Once the votes had been counted somebody delivered a large box of dried prunes to the headquarters of the Christian Democratic party in Piazza del Gesù.

Nobody laughed. This was a disaster for the Yalta equilibrium. Secret services on both sides of the Atlantic agreed that it was necessary to start playing a different game than the one that had been played up to then. Once again Gladio—the secret paramilitary organization formed in Italy in the 1950s by the CIA in order to counter the advance of the Left—proved useful. The so-called "Solo Plan" was devised. It had three objectives: a military coup that would bring down the newly-formed government, the institution of a "public security" government led by right-wing members of parliament and the military, the murder of Prime Minister Aldo Moro.

The Solo Plan was never carried out, and only the last of the three objectives was achieved, albeit with a belated operation—fifteen years later—and by a third party. However, a secret new game, much dirtier and more violent than before, had begun. Italy was about to enter a season of bloodshed.

On 9 December 1963, four days after the Moro government was formed, the biggest political trial since the end of the war started at the Palace of Justice in Milan: the trial of the Feuernacht attackers. There were ninety-one defendants, twenty-three of them on the run.

Up to then, Italians had being totally ignorant about Alto Adige. Almost nobody knew that German was being spoken on a stretch of the national territory. It was only by following the trial in Milan in the newspapers that they began to discover the existence and the character of this borderline province. About a month after the hearing started, on a cold January morning, the doors of the High Court opened its session before an unusually colorful audience. The rows of chairs behind the wives and relatives of the defendants were occupied by dozens of men wearing Lederhosen, red waistcoats, boiled woolen jackets, little felt hats with feathers: Schützen. Among them, with his garrison almost all made up of hunters like himself, was Peter Huber. Just like the wives of the defendants, who'd shared the trouble and expense of the journey by Tränenbus, the so-called Bus of Tears, the Schützen had also hired a bus to arrive en masse at the Milan courthouse. They could only attend a few sessions, no more than a couple of days—they all had jobs and families to get back to—but they felt it was important to show the "BAS Heroes" the support

Silvius Magnago had always denied them. Still, the attackers of the Night of Fires continued to disappoint the expectations of those who wanted to see exceptional figures: be they heroes or murderers. Their moral leader was the owner of a small shop in Frangarto, just outside Bolzano. Sepp Kerschbaumer's body was marked by torture. He was a small man with a gaunt face, an absurd 1920s haircut, and the rather sad eyes of someone who feels more comfortable in the world of ideals than that of commerce where, however, he has to earn his living. For years he'd forced his wife to chase after poor debtors while he recited the Lord's Prayer several times a day and forgave them their debts. His intelligent, fervent idealism, and his determination to explain the human reasons behind the BAS actions before the historical ones, inspired real respect from the jury in Milan. Kerschbaumer expressed simple concepts which everyone could understand. He talked about the humiliation of going into a government office and not being understood by the staff, about not being able to fill out the forms in Italian, about doctors in hospitals who demanded that the patients—no matter how ill or wounded—should express themselves in a language they didn't speak, about the lack of prospects for a German-speaking South Tyrolean looking for work outside his own maso. In the heaving courtroom, the crowd of Italians listened to Kerschbaumer's quiet eloquence, and didn't find his arguments unfounded.

During the hearing, in order to illustrate the abuse suffered by the South Tyroleans, another defendant said, "My mother-in-law hasn't received her pension for over six years."

There were titters of laughter in the courtroom, murmurs of approval. Also, clearly sympathetic shouts from the audience:

"Neither has my mother!"

"Neither have I!"

It took a long time to restore order.

That's how, thanks to the sessions in the Milan courtroom,

Italians discovered not only Alto Adige but also the meticulous mechanics, peasants and small craftsmen of the BAS, and many South Tyroleans became aquainted with an Italy beyond the straits of Salorno, that oblong boot of which their *Heimat*, whether they liked it or not, was now a part. They too began to realize that also in Lecce, Rome, Novara,, and even Milan, the Italian government treated its citizens carelessly, and that the slowness and convoluted nature of public administration was therefore not a form of ethnic discrimination. In other words, the pachydermic inefficiency of Italian public administration had nothing personal against South Tyroleans—or at least not them alone.

Peter looked at the faces of the audience in the heaving courtroom. These were not the Italians he'd seen arrive at Bolzano Station almost ten years earlier. They didn't have the gaunt faces of people running away from poverty, eyes blank from hunger, hope and fear, the dirty fingernails of people who, the night before leaving for the factories of the North, had brought their goats back to the stone fold for the last time. These Italians could call the cities where they were living "home." There were beautiful Milanese girls with their hair in beehives; young men with thick black-rimmed glasses bending over their notebooks; housewives with swollen ankles but shrewdness in their eyes, accustomed to tackling the prices at the market every morning and often having a laugh with their friends; metalworkers who would come to the courthouse on their way home after an overnight shift to see the faces of the peasant Krauts who had proved to have such rebellious organizational skills that they might even be able to teach the workers' movement a thing or two.

There, next to citizens of boom time Italy, sat a company of Schützen in 19th-century costumes. Peter wore the capercaillie feather on his hat, the waistcoat with crossed straps like the one worn by Andreas Hofer when he was pushing back

Napoleon's army, patent shoes with silver buckles over white cotton socks. Maybe it was precisely because of the incongruous clothes he was wearing that the Milan trial had a different effect on him—the opposite effect—than it did on the majority of South Tyroleans. He became convinced that the protest actions against electricity pylons carried out by the *Bumser* sitting there in the defendant's dock, were no longer enough. It was time to step up the game.

When Peter came back home after a few days in Milan, over the course of which once again he hadn't taken the trouble to send news of himself, he found that his wife had gone: Leni had returned to her parents' house. She was two months pregnant with her second child, but she no longer wanted to live in that house of absence and silence.

Eva was growing. Week after week she slept a little longer without interruption. After a while, Gerda stopped falling asleep on her feet: her daughter no longer cried at night. From the crate, she watched, wide-eyed, the red sauce being poured into pots, the clouds of steam rising from uncovered saucepans, the long, springy legs of Hubert, as he drained Schlutzkrapfen with one hand and browned sage in butter with the other. Eva's eyes, very long and transparent like Gerda's, didn't possess her mother's haughty expression but gave and yearned for affection. The expression in other people's eyes had never meant anything to Gerda; but to Eva it seemed to mean everything.

They'd put tiny pieces of carrot, slivers of fennel, flakes of Grana Padano into her hand. They laughed at the seriousness with which she would lick them, suck them, nibble them with her toothless gums, testing their consistency like a scientist, her face scrunched up when she discovered that the yellow half-moon they had handed her was a segment of lemon. Like parents proud of their offspring, the kitchen workers sought one another's eyes in order to enjoy her irresistible baby deeds together. During the months when Eva quietly occupied the apple crate there were almost no screams and insults between cooks and waiters.

Gerda had begun to laugh again. Her full lips would stretch to reveal white teeth that were still very young in spite of everything, especially when she was looking at her daughter. And then all the men around her, cooks, waiters, Elmar the scullery boy, felt something stir inside them. As for Herr Neumann, when Gerda laughed, he would wipe his forehead with his apron to hide his face.

Gerda had changed: she was now aware of men's looks. And she didn't pretend not to like it.

Months went by. The apple crate was no longer large enough for Eva. Elmar helped Gerda build a kind of cage by nailing different crates together. They put it under the dessert counter, safe from splashes of boiling oil, large meat knives, bottles of detergent. Occasionally, flour and sugar fell on her head, making it comically white. Die letze, the little one, was a braves Schneckile, a well-behaved little snail who did her best not to cause any bother. She'd lie there in her spot, looking around hesitantly as though asking: I'm doing alright, aren't I? Nobody refused her the smile she asked, but it was clear that she couldn't stay there forever.

"What are you going to do when she starts walking?" Nina asked one night in the attic dormitory.

After a day imprisoned under the dessert counter, Eva was swimming on the wooden floor of the dormitory, propelling herself with her arms and legs, her bottom puffed up with a diaper and held high like a flag. She'd reached one of the beds at the end of the room and now, gripping the iron bedpost with her fat hands, had managed to raise herself on her feet. With a triumphant gurgle she searched for her mother's eyes to share her victory. She couldn't find it: Gerda's head was bowed and her eyes downcast. She had no answer to Nina's question.

Everybody feared Eva's eviction from the kitchen but nobody was surprised when it came. One day, cooks, scullery boys, and assistant cooks were in the dark little room next to the store room, eating the lunch prepared by Herr Neumann. Gerda had stayed behind in the kitchen to warm up the baby bottle. When she approached the dessert counter, she noticed that one of the bars on the cage had been moved. Eva wasn't there. The hot baby bottle in her hand, Gerda rushed around the kitchen. On the meat counter, heavy, sharp knives were less than an inch from the edge, ready to fall off like axes. There were burning hot metal handles on the lit oven right at the level of the baby's hands. Even a child bigger than Eva could have drowned in the pail of dirty water next to the sink. Gerda didn't find her daughter sliced, scalded, or drowned, but each new relief soon became deeper panic: her daughter wasn't there. She came out of the kitchen.

In over two years of working at the hotel, Gerda had gone through the swing door that separated Herr Neumann's kingdom from the dining room only once. On the morning of her first day at work, before the guests had come down for breakfast, and Frau Mayer had shown her the arched windows overlooking the mountains, the tables with the flower decorations in the center of linen tablecloths, the Murano glass chandeliers. Then she had informed her that it was the last time Gerda would ever be setting foot there.

Gerda lingered on the doorstep. The first guests were about to sit at the tables. There were couples, single men, and elderly people. With formal gallantry, the men pulled the chairs out for the ladies, who sat down, casting benevolent looks at the panorama as though it was their property. Gerda was stunned by the contrast between these serene gestures and the anxiety squeezing her chest. None of them was looking for a daughter had with a man who hadn't wanted to know, and who was now too big for a cage made of fruit crates; a child she had no idea where to put anymore because her job in the kitchen was the only thing she had left and if she lost that too she would end up in the street like all the other girls who'd had no Herr Neumann to come and take them back despite everything, and who left through the gate opened by the nun with a mustache, a child in one arm and only despair in the other.

Then she saw her.

Eva was crawling efficiently toward a specific target: the legs of a middle-aged man sitting alone at a table by the large windows. Her round face was lit up with a satisfied smile that told the world: you can't but think I'm wonderful, and in fact I am.

Gerda crossed the dining room and scooped her daughter off the floor like soup from a pan. Eva was not pleased to have her plan sabotaged. She began to scream, reaching out with her arms to the gentleman at the table who, surprised but not annoyed, was staring at Gerda with raised eyebrows.

He wasn't the only one. All the men in the dining room were looking at her. Her breasts, swollen after the last feed, pushing out of her apron, her blonde curls escaping from under her assistant cook's cap, her cheeks flushed with agitation, her mouth made especially for indescribable delights, her lively legs peering out from the hem of her work skirt that was too short, and that pink little girl in her arms who made her look both younger and more feminine. Even the women couldn't help looking at her, though they were trying to focus on the grease stains on her apron, the sawdust stuck on the soles of her work clogs, the sweat that glistened in the space between her nose and her lip. Even so, nothing changed the fact that the woman who'd just walked into the dining room was more beautiful than any of them.

"Sie haben unser Abkommen gebrochen."

Frau Mayer had suddenly appeared next to her like a Germanic goddess invoked by a spell. Her voice was calm, disappointed rather than annoyed. You have broken our agreement.

Two days. That's all Herr Neumann could do. Two days off in order to make arrangements for Eva. After that, if Gerda hadn't made any, he would be forced to fire her.

The bus journey from the main town to Gerda's birthplace was slow, which gave her a lot of time to think. With whom could she leave her daughter? After Johanna's funeral, which had taken place while Gerda was pregnant, her sister Annemarie had written her a letter in her schoolgirl handwriting. She said she held her responsible for their mother's death, made her opinion of Gerda clear with various adjectives, and ended the letter with a wish never to see her again. This request wasn't hard to grant: ever since Annemarie had moved to Voralberg, she and Gerda had only met twice: at Peter's wedding, and at Ulli's christening.

After over three hours on the road, when the bus halted at the town station with a huff, Gerda still had no idea what to do. Holding Eva in her arms, she started walking in a daze, aimlessly; her directionless feet then took the most familiar road. Less than half an hour later she found herself a couple of miles out of the town center, near a group of houses on the slope in the shadow of the Medieval castle. She'd reached Shanghai.

The house, built of plaster and river stones, was in the same dark, humid corner. The door was shut.

There was no smoke coming from the chimney. It was still daylight and impossible to see through the dirty windows if there was anyone inside. Gerda stopped on the spot where, in a distant time when Eva hadn't been born, her father had hurled a suitcase into the air. She looked at the lamp post against which it had been knocked and she thought of somewhere to go.

She began walking fast. Besides Eva, Gerda had with her only a small shopping bag with a few changes of baby clothes and diapers. She picked up the pace. In less than half an hour she'd reached her destination, a little out of breath because of the climb.

It was the end of the summer; the steep meadows that had broken the backs of generations of Hubers were ready to be harvested for the second and last time of the year. In the distance, she could see the men of the household scything away. The cows sent to pasture hadn't returned yet, and in the sheds there were only those with newborn calves. The air smelled of hay, smoke, manure, and freshly baked bread. High on the door jamb, the slightly faded letters C, M and B were written in chalk, spaced out with 19 and 64. On New Year's Day, the children, dressed as the three wise men—Caspar, Melchior and Balthasar—had wished health and luck for 1964, in exchange for a few coins. Gerda knocked. Uncle Hans, Hermann's eldest brother and the only heir of the closed maso, had died a couple of years earlier. It was the young wife of Michl, the eldest of the cousins with whom Gerda has spent her summers in the pastures as a little girl, who opened the door.

Gerda showed her Eva, and explained.

The young woman, who was only slightly older than Gerda, stared. Neither her husband Michl, nor her brother-in-law Simon (who was now living in Switzerland) mentioned their cousin very often, but when they did it made their eyes glint in a way that made the wife uneasy. Gerda hadn't come to her own mother's funeral, and then they'd found out that she was pregnant: without knowing her, the young bride felt no sympathy for her.

Sweaty from work, her husband's youngest brother came

back from the fields. It was that same Sebastian, nicknamed Wastl, who had been cuddled in the hay like a doll by Gerda and his older brothers. He'd grown into a handsome fourteen-year-old boy, tall and strong, with a straight nose, dark blonde hair cut in a brush, and a joyful expression in his eyes. He hugged his cousin warmly. When he became aware of the situation he said to his sister-in-law, "We'll keep this letze."

The young bride looked at him in disbelief.

"It's not as though you're the one who's going to look after her."

Michl arrived too. When he saw Gerda his eyes opened wide and his arms started to spread in a hug, but then he glanced shamefully at his wife and stopped himself. The unbestowed hug lingered in the air, heavy and charged with meaning, while the young bride watched her husband with suspicion. Wastl told his elder brother about Eva, while his sister-in-law's lips narrowed, and they started to argue. Gerda looked at their mouths but couldn't keep up with the words, as though they'd started speaking an unknown language. After a while, Michl's wife said she had a lot to do, that dinner was on the stove and would get burned, and disappeared inside the house. Michl invited Gerda in. She declined. He gave her a sad, guilty look, then went in after his wife.

Wastl also went in but soon came back out with a glass of milk for the little girl, and some Speck and cheese for Gerda. He stood there while Eva drank the milk with small, thoughtful sips, her blue eyes fixed on the hens that were scratching about between the house and the barn. Gerda thanked him and put the food in her bag. Wastl hugged his cousin again. She was so beautiful, and so unlucky. He stroked the soft cheek of that little girl who never cried, then went in for dinner, closing the door behind him.

Even though the way back was downhill, it took Gerda longer to go back to the town than going up. Her legs felt heavy and not because of tiredness. The sun was low and would soon disappear behind the mountain peaks that framed the valley. When she reached the center of town, the shops were closed, the streets deserted. It was the time of day when the earth is already dark but the sky is still luminous, when the mothers have called back home the children playing outside, when dinner is ready, and anyone who has no home longs for one even more.

Gerda went to the Ursuline convent. When she reached the gate next to the steps, she pulled on the iron cord that was attached to a large bell. After a while, a small, elderly nun appeared. She let her in without too many questions—if a young woman alone with a baby knocks on the door, questions are not necessary.

The nuns gave her a cup of broth, then made their proposition. They would keep the little girl, send her to their school and, when she was grown up, teach her a profession; Gerda could come and visit her and even take her for a walk sometimes. Gerda insisted: perhaps she hadn't been clear, she hadn't given her daughter for adoption and had no intention of doing so now. During the low season she didn't work, so she would find a furnished room and for two whole months of the year, she wanted to keep Eva with her. The nuns said that wasn't possible. Either she left her there or not. There was no other option.

They gave her a camp bed in a room behind the kitchen. Gerda lay down on it, her eyes staring blankly at the high stone ceiling. In less than twenty-four hours she had to be back at the hotel without Eva, or she would lose her job. Still, the sleep of a twenty-year-old was stronger than worry: she curled up on her side, enveloped Eva in the crook between her chest and arms, locked her feet by sliding her big toe in the gap between the index and the left big toe, and fell asleep.

Gerda left the convent before dawn. Eva slumbered in her arms, her head dangling.

Leni opened the door still in her dressing gown, with little Sigi in her arms. Ulli stood next to her, a hand on his mother's leg as though to make sure that at least this parent didn't suddenly vanish away, like the other one always did. He looked up at Eva with his brown eyes and long eyelashes, and stared at her attentively but without hostility.

Leni was sorry for Gerda, who'd been kicked out of the dark house from which she, on the other hand, had run away. However, she wasn't sure that it would be better for her sister-in-law to live there alone with that black-hearted father. As for her, she was uncertain, embittered. She hadn't seen her husband for three months, didn't know where he was or what he was doing. There were strange, nasty rumors around, but she didn't believe them—everybody knows people talk nonsense. The head of Peter's Schützen company had come to tell her that sacrifices for the *Heimat*, no matter how hard, are always worth it. Leni hadn't liked to hear those words but hadn't known what to say in return. Until recently, when he disappeared for weeks, Peter would leave her some money, but not any longer.

A few months earlier, a large British company had opened a factory for mechanical parts on the outskirts of the town: the largest foreign industrial complex anyone had ever seen in Alto Adige. It required a workforce of almost five hundred workers, which was huge in proportion to the local population. Moreover, there were a few Italians in the town, and those were all civil servants, so finally they started hiring South Tyroleans. Leni had taken part in the euphoria that had invaded the valley. It would be the end of hard times for her family, and hadn't Peter wanted to be a factory worker ever since he was a boy? However, when she had shown him the flyer with the address and hiring times, her husband hadn't even looked at it. That same day, he had left and not been seen since.

So now, she told Gerda, she and her two children were dependent on her parents, not like a married woman but a girl with a child out of wedlock.

She suddenly stopped herself. Embarrassed, she looked at Gerda, who narrowed her eyes and lifted a shoulder as though to say: never mind.

Although much lower down, they were on the same mountain slope where the Hubers' old maso stood, and where Gerda had gone the day before, as well as Paul Staggl's four-star hotel. Not very far from there, there was another maso, linked to that of Leni's parents by a short dead-end alley. On the doorstep, over which there was a wooden arch that connected the house to the barn there was a nine-year-old girl. She hadn't budged from there ever since Gerda had arrived with Eva in her arms, and kept staring at her.

The bus to Bolzano was leaving in less than two hours, and if Gerda wanted to be back at the hotel by evening, as she had promised Herr Neumann, she couldn't miss it. Gerda said goodbye to Leni calmly, as though she had all the time in the world, and went to the neighbors' maso.

The little girl on the doorstep was wearing a faded dress that was too long, evidently handed down by more than one older sister. Her sockless legs stuck out like pale little branches from black rubber boots; she had two thin, badly braided plaits that framed the pointy face, and eyelashes that were almost white. Gerda asked her who was at home. The girl shook her head. They were all out collecting the hay, and she had been left alone to look after her little siblings and make barley soup. Her name was Ruthi and she was nine years old. She asked if she could hold the baby and Gerda handed Eva to her. The baby let herself slide calmly from one pair of hands to the other with a quizzical smile.

Ruthi cuddled and cooed, which Eva enjoyed, then she put her on the ground. Holding her by her forearms and not her wrists, like a careful mother, she held her up for a couple of steps. Eva turned to look at her with satisfaction. Ruthi smiled at her with encouragement, thus confirming that she was admiring her expertise.

Gerda watched her daughter's arms held tight by that little girl's hands which were already so expert. She looked at the fields behind the maso where, in the distance, looking like dark dots against a green background, peasants were sickling the hay. Then she stared into Ruthi's eyes.

Gerda was already on the bus back to the hotel when Ruthi's grandparents, parents, and older brothers realized that a baby girl not even a year old had been added to their large family. Leni was called from the neighboring maso, and told them who that blonde young woman who had left Eva as a gift, like a doll, was. The father threatened to whip Ruthi, but her grandfather stopped him. Sepp Schwingshackl wasn't sixty yet but his hands were shaking, he couldn't hear very well, and a coarse, white scar cut across his eyebrows: the signs left by Hermann Huber when he had beaten him until he bled almost thirty years earlier. However, he also had the clear eyes of someone who has nothing to hide and the sweet smile of an old man who understands children. In Ruthi's arms, Eva looked around anxiously. Still, she wasn't crying, as though at least one thing was clear: whoever these strangers were, it was obvious they were going to look after her. Sepp gently took her from his granddaughter's arms and put her on his lap.

"God has brought her to us, and we're going to keep her," he said.

It's not God but the Nutte daughter of a bad man, thought his son, but kept that to himself.

It's not God, but she's like my sister Eloise, only more beautiful, thought Ruthi, but kept that to herself.

It is God, or rather Her, but where is She? thought Eva but, since she couldn't talk, she kept that to herself. If she could have, she would have also said, "I shan't sleep until She's back."

However, tiredness and disorientation were starting to weigh heavily on her eyes. The soft little body relaxed against Sepp's hard one, which smelled of wood, soap and sweat. Eva fell asleep.

And so that was the beginning of what Eva's life would be for many years: ten months a year in the Schwingshackl house and, during the two months a year of low season, in a furnished room with her mother.

Meanwhile, on the bus, Gerda was crying. She cried all the way through the long valley of which her birthplace was the main town, she cried as they turned onto the highway, she cried as they arrived in Bolzano. There, crying, she changed buses, and she cried as she walked from the bus station to the hotel. However, when she walked into the dormitory she shared with the other female workers, somebody had turned on the radio, and Gerda suddenly realized a few things. She no longer had a little girl to look after all day long. She no longer had a reputation to protect. She wasn't yet twenty. She felt a sudden desire to sway her hips and arms to the rhythm of swing and, like Mina, to look straight into the eye of anyone who had any objection.

KILOMETER 715

I'm planning on taking the Metro from Tiburtina station to Termini, where the 7:15 train from Rome to Reggio Calabria is waiting for me. I don't have much baggage so it will be easy.

Mistake. It would be easy if I had a ticket. But I don't have one. I don't even have a one-euro coin, and in any case all the ticket machines are out of order. Only a child, a madman or a German could hope for a ticket window open at 6:38 in the morning on Easter Sunday. I may be ethnically Germanic but my region has been part of Italy for too long for me to harbor that illusion.

I go up from the Metro to the floor above and look for a newsagent. The first one I come across is open but has run out of tickets, the second one is closed because, as we said, it's now 6:43 on Easter morning, and the third one is at least a mile away, as I am told by the sleepy Ukrainian behind the counter of a café.

Never mind, I'll take a taxi. I come out of the station as the Roman sky starts to assume a thousand different colors, and stop to look at it. Impalpable swooshes of orange, grey, acid green and pink expand against a turquoise background. Delicate, dreamy colors you wouldn't expect to see above this cruelly ugly part of the city, with its overpass as high as the windows of the third-floor dining rooms and kitchens. And yet even above this flaky gray, even I, accustomed to mountain sunsets, am struck by the magnificence of the Roman sky. Then I look down again and go on my way.

Next to the sign that says TAXI, whose only aim is to fool the masses, there's a dozen or so passengers, survivors of sleeper trains, disheveled and dazed, scowling at one another. Because, despite an almost sleepless night, it's not hard to estimate the waiting time: at a twelve passengers to zero taxi rate, it's not going to be short.

Welcome to Rome.

When I manage to get to Termini, the train to Calabria must already be near Latina. The next one is at eleven something. I've got almost four hours to wait.

It's no longer dawn and the station is animated as though it were a weekday. Flat screens all over the place are broadcasting ads, the same ones over and over again. A woman of indefinable age, with thin gray curls like rat tails stuck to her head, stops me with a friendly smile. She asks me where the supermarket is. I can't tell her and apologize. She thanks me as though I've just saved her life. I go to the ATM, buy a newspaper, and see her again. She is now leaning over a baby in a carriage, and is making a coin appear and disappear before his eyes, except that the trick doesn't work very well. The baby and his young mother, both with smooth black hair and features from the Andes, neither encourage her nor send her away: they look at her silently and patiently, waiting for her to stop. Once she's finished her trick, the woman says goodbye and leaves with the contented smile of someone who has a place in the world. The mother and child don't even look at her.

I sit in a café. Coffee, croissant, fruit juice for the vitamins that keep your skin young, newspaper. I peruse everything from beginning to end, even the page about Rome, the letters from readers complaining about the potholes in the roads, the complaints about illegal parking, the real estate section. I decide to take a walk in that large shopping mall that Termini station has turned into. Even though it's Easter, many shops are open, especially the many lingerie boutiques: there seems to be one on every corner. I loaf around, trying to kill time. I'm traveling to see a man whose absence marked my life and my mother's, I'm not here to shop. Then I hear someone singing.

On the deepest underground level of the shopping mall, outside the umpteenth male-female lingerie shop, there's something that looks like the door to a car mechanic's. The inside glass doors are open on what leads to a kind of long, narrow garage, without windows, illuminated by a graceless neon light. At the end, there's a table covered with a white cloth and a large bronze crucifix on top of it. A group of people are singing together, led by a man dressed in white. It's neither a store room nor a garage. It's a church.

I used to like going to church when I was a girl.

I remember Christmas masses in the *Pfarrkirche*.[13] My mother wasn't there: the holidays were right in the middle of the hotel high season. As a child, I always spent Christmas with Sepp and Maria. It was they who explained to me that Jesus was a very good person, the best person that ever existed, who left a wonderful, faraway place to come here and teach us to love one another. I believed in this message, especially since it was passed onto me by my almost adoptive grandparents who really looked like they loved everyone.

The entire, huge Schwingshackl family attended the mass that celebrated the birth of this person who was so good: thirteen children, countless sons and daughters-in-law, hordes of grandchildren, as well as an appendix without a specific label—me. There were also the Hubers, my mother's cousins. Uncle Wastl played the clarinet in the *Musikkapelle*.[14] Dressed

[13] Parish church.
[14] Country band.

like that, in the satin waistcoat he wore for official concerts, he looked more beautiful than the trumpet-playing angels on the hut. When it was time for his solo, I don't know how he did it, but even with a clarinet in his mouth and his cheeks full of air, he always managed to smile only at me. Christmas Mass was beautiful.

Then there was the question of Jesus's daddy. It really wasn't clear to me if his real father was the Holy Ghost, the Angel, or God, but in any case it was Joseph who held the Child in his arms when Mary was tired, told him stories before he went to sleep, and protected him from Herod's fury. When Vito came into our lives, as I stood between him and my mother, I felt as though I was baby Jesus's secret little sister.

Easter was a little more difficult to understand. There was that cross and all that blood, then three days of death and darkness, and finally the resurrection: very complicated for a little girl. What I couldn't understand in particular was why, when Jesus was resurrected, he didn't want to be hugged by all those who had cried over him and were now obviously happy to see him alive again. It seemed somewhat strange and impolite, coming from a person who was so good and kind, but I didn't dare ask for explanations. In any case, I liked the bells that announced the triumph of life over death, and even I understood that was a beautiful thing.

The last time I recited the Lord's Prayer was on the day of my confirmation. Vito had just left us and my mother had started attending church again: she was no longer living *more uxorio*, so no longer in sin. In honor of my sacrament, she was wearing her most beautiful dress, one of many Vito had given her. A navy shirtwaist with white lapels. She'd had to take it in at the waist with safety pins: she practically hadn't eaten anything for weeks. She had a scarf over her head to conceal the bald patches she still had after her illness, and two purple rings under her eyes. She'd stopped crying, but for me her dry eyes were even more terrible than when they were all red and swollen. I would have done anything to put an end to her pain, but I couldn't.

The parish priest stood smiling at the door to the church, congratulating her on her life that was over. And so never again did I pray to that merciless God who allowed Gerda Huber back into His house on condition that she arrive ravaged.

I'm sitting on one of the polished wooden benches of the garage-church. We're in Rome, the city of a thousand churches, a hundred basilicas, each of them a treasury of art, history and beauty. This one must be the ugliest of them all. Standing before the altar is a thin, no longer young priest. He has the face of an ant: wide at the top, narrower at the bottom, eyes that are already large made huge by thick glasses to correct his myopia. He has very long fingers and large rubber-soled shoes that squeak with every step. He's right in the middle of his sermon and is speaking with great passion, in his audience there are many women—Filipino, South American, Polish—elderly people alone, homeless, the odd traveler with a suitcase leaning against the wall, African street vendors. There's also the elderly lady from before, the one with hair like rat's tails. There are forty of us at most but we take up almost all the seats.

"Christ is truly risen," the priest says, underlining every word with hands that are almost too elegant. He walks up and down the aisle between the benches, his shoes squeaking at every step: squeak, squeak. He's commenting on the section in the gospel where they find the empty tomb. He explains in detail how the corpse was wrapped, of what kind of fabric the bandages were made, and how long they were. He mimes, squeaks, waves his hands.

It's important for him that his audience follows him.

"Are you following?" he asks the faithful, staring into their faces.

They nod, so he carries on squeaking, looking them in the

eyes one by one, every so often closing his own to concentrate better. He talks about John.

"He saw and believed (squeak, squeak). But do you understand what it means?!"

Well, from what he says it's pretty obvious that he really believes. The priest with a strange insect head puts forward the density of the faith, powerful and without frills, of a man who has soiled his hands with true charity. That's what this dull chapel in the underground of Termini Station seems to me: a mission church in the heart of Rome, devoted to the city's forsaken.

He ends the sermon by talking about La Pira. "The greatest mayor we've ever had in Italy." I look around. Among these foreign workers, elderly people on a minimum pension, passing American tourists, Romanian care workers, does anyone know who La Pira is? Perhaps the elderly woman who walks around the station annoying strangers' children with silly little games? Or that illegal Senegalese vendor with a large parcel next to the bench and the motionless, focused, griot profile? I, too, strain to remember a vague notion: a Florentine Christian Democrat in the 1950s? But the ant-like priest considers none of them, of us, to be beneath this historic character and, first half-closing his eyes to convey his respect, the rounded tips of his fingers raised on his shoulders and spread open, he tells us about a session in the council hall of Palazzo della Signoria many decades ago:

"During a fierce discussion between Communists and Christian Democrats, at the end of which both parties were attacking him, screaming and shouting, La Pira closed his eyes and remained silent for a long time, thus forcing everyone to be equally silent . . . And so they said nothing, waiting to hear what he would say."

The priest pauses, and looks his audience in the eyes. Nobody breathes. Homecare workers, sellers of pirate DVDs, homeless who haven't washed for months, everybody is anxiously waiting to know: during the faraway years of the Cold

War, in the middle of diatribes between Catholics and Stalinists, what did the mayor of the city where many of them will never set foot say? What did he say? The priest shifts his weight from one leg to the other (squeak), lowers his voice, and starts speaking in the present tense.

"La Pira continues to say nothing, his eyes shut. Then, finally, still without opening them, he says softly: 'What does all this matter, seeing that Christ has risen?'"

The ant-like priest raises his enormous eyes behind the glasses, looks at us and repeats, announces, with a joyful smile: "Yes! Christ is truly risen!"

And, to my great astonishment, for a moment, I also feel joy. When it's time for the Lord's Prayer, I look around. Everyone around me has their palms joined together, and a collected expression. And I also find myself, after who knows how many years, muttering the first words of the most child-appropriate prayer there is:

"Vater unser in Himmel, geheiligt werde dein Name. Dein Reich . . . "

I clam up, I don't know why. After a moment's hesitation, I start again. But this time in Italian, Vito's language:

"Padre nostro che sei nei cieli,
sia santificato il tuo nome.
Venga il tuo regno,
sia fatta la tua volontà . . . "

"Our Father who art in Heaven,
Hallowed be Thy name,
Thy Kingdom come,
Thy will be done . . . "

It's not that I've unexpectedly discovered I'm a believer. I haven't suddenly found again a faith I haven't been longing for, not even thanks to this very human, inspired priest. It's just that it comes naturally to me to join those around me, here in this ugly chapel. They all seem like me, children of an unknown father.

After mass, I stop by the bulletin board at the church door. There are the usual missionary magazines, leaflets from religious orders, the program of a trip to Lourdes, the times of masses and extra services for Easter Sunday and Monday, and a checked sheet of paper with, handwritten: on the Tuesday after Easter the Italian rail company chaplain will give a blessing to all the Termini shops.

I can just picture the ant-like priest entering the lingerie shops with his squeaky shoes, walking among dummies with tits and asses covered only by baby-dolls and tangas. He will not lose his composure, he will bless everyone with his wide smile, sprinkle holy water with his long fingers over see-through push-up bras, look with benevolence from behind his thick glasses at sales assistants with too much make-up piously bowing their heads.

It's almost time for the train. I buy water, some fruit, no sandwiches because there simply has to be a restaurant car on a train journey of seven hundred kilometers, right? An eighteen-year-old Romany in a colorful skirt is sitting on one of the black, fake leather couches scattered around the station; she has a baby in her arms, plus a girl who looks about two and a slightly older, snotty-nosed boy on either side. They're staring intently at one of the flat screens constantly recycling advertising, paying no attention to the bustle around them. They're relaxed and at ease like any family watching television on their living room sofa. When I get on the escalator to the platform, they vanish from my sight.

1964

T he situation was as follows.
The hayloft of a very old maso, at the end of the summer. The harvest has been good, it hasn't rained too much or too little, the hay is stacked up to the ceiling. The chute through which the peasant is going to lower it down to the cowshed and into the troughs is made of very old wood; the floor, walls and beams supporting the roof, the tiles, everything is made of very old fir. There's a lit candle on the floor; it crackles, smokes, devours its wick. The wind is blowing through the cracks between the wall planks, agitating the flame. A stronger gust and the candle will be knocked over into the hay.

That summer of 1964, just about everybody had come to blow on the flames of Alto Adige.

First, it was started by the BAS who were in hiding, and who had dissociated themselves from the methods of the other *Bumser*, which they considered too soft. Enough attacking electricity pylons, they said. What was needed to free the *Heimat Südtirol* was action by armed guerrillas, and if blood flowed, then so be it.

Then Austrian Neo-Nazis had arrived. Self-styled intellectuals of the NDP, born of the Nazi party, pan-Germans who missed *Deutschland über Alles*. Italian Neo-Fascists. Far-right Austrian university confraternities. The KGB, which, from its Soviet diplomatic residence in Vienna, had made contact with the most extreme terrorists. Agents from the Italian, American, Austrian, German secret services, and even the odd Belgian one. It was understandable: any Flemish agent provocateur with an ounce of professional dignity would have wanted to emigrate to the troubled South Tyrol of the 1960s, which was far richer in career opportunities than Flanders. Finally, De Lorenzo arrived, the commanding general of the Carabinieri, as well as the recent head of the SIFAR secret service, and the man the CIA trusted to create Gladio, with his Carabinieri.

They were all there, in the fields fragrant with newly-cut hay, the rosy peaks, rocky slopes inflamed with rhododendrons in July, the sparkle of glaciers on the border and the cable cars teeming with skiers intoxicated by their athletic feats, all there to stage the dress rehearsal of something that didn't yet have a name, but which would subsequently be called, like an after-dinner game, "the strategy of tension." The players: blood-thirsty, earnest extremists, agents provocateurs geared toward raising the level of the conflict, and government repression almost as harsh as under Mussolini.

All you needed was to light the fire.

Peter had only a very vague idea of all this. Yes, he'd taken part in secret meetings in Alpine huts just over the border, where he'd met people who were very different from what he was used to. Students with thick glasses, for example, who recited passages from *The Robbers* as though Schiller had written it just for them, who would fill their lungs with the sharp air of a night in the Alps, like someone living a heroic moment and wanting to fix it in his memory. A young university assistant from Innsbruck, with thick lips and fat fingers, eloquent despite the shortness of breath he owed to his weight, convinced he hadn't been born too late to still live the dream of the Thousand-Year Reich. A Bavarian chemist who'd taught Peter to put together a bomb, whose hands hovered over explosives and detonators with the light precision of butterflies over flowers in the field. None of them ever mentioned the fact that in order to gain a public office certificate in his own land, Peter had to speak a language that wasn't his, or that he hadn't found work in a factory because he belonged to the wrong ethnic group. They were concerned with other issues: the struggle for national liberation, the holy soil, *Bedrohtes Grenzlanddeutschtum*[15], *Volksund Kulturgemeinschaft*[16], the expansion of the German people in their rightful *Lebensraum*[17].

Peter knew nothing about them but asked no questions. He didn't know that they had already taken their explosives right into the heart of Italy with secret plans bearing names straight out of a photo-romances: *Operation Sophia Loren*, a series of explosions in Bolzano cinemas frequented by soldiers stationed there (the project was aborted before being executed); *Operation Panic*, against public transport in some large Italian cities (many were wounded on a tram in Rome, the car of one of the attackers was blown up by mistake); *Operation Terror on Trains*: a high-potential bomb at Verona Station (about twenty injured and, finally, after trying such a long time, the first dead).

The only thing that interested them about Peter was that ever since he was a *Bub*[18] he'd walked up and down the border passes with a shotgun across his body. He knew better than the wrinkles on his mother's face the tracks of deer and on both sides of the border between Austria and Italy, slight lines of moved soil carved between mountain pines and gravel. He could therefore point them out to someone carrying sticks of dynamite under his shirt, someone who needed to avoid a

[15] Threatened border Germans.
[16] Community of people and cultures.
[17] Vital space.
[18] A little boy.

guard post in order to take Italian soldiers by surprise, or someone on the run after an attack. And, finally, what these men, who were so much more educated than Peter, were interested in was the fact that Peter didn't feel squeamish about killing—and not just trophy animals.

What turns a man into a murderer? At which moment does anger over a historical injustice blend into another resentment that's more ancient, private, shameful because nobody else shares it, and make this man put his hand on a detonator? When does his desire to obtain what he considers the general Good become indifference to specific Evil committed in the name of that same Good? What makes him capable of breaking the most important of prohibitions which, like a wall, divides the human consortium into those who have killed even just once, and those who haven't? What that man needs above all else is absolute conviction, or rather a state of mind that has become cold, silent and motionless like a winter lake, in which pity no longer flows except downwards, downwards in dark and invisible eddies which may barely stir the light pebbles at the bottom, but not the icy slate on the surface. Peter never explained it to anyone, let alone himself.

Gerda's brother, whose eyes were so dark they didn't reflect the light, had only ever seen his son Sigi a few times, and just for a couple of hours. Unlike what he had done with Ulli, Peter didn't shoot at any target with "Siegfried" written above it in Gothic lettering: he wasn't there for his second child's christening.

For some time now, Leni had stopped waiting for her husband. Her parents had taken her and the two children back with them to their maso not far from the town. On the rare occasions Peter would reappear, fleeting visits and mostly at night, after weeks of absence, nobody asked any questions; not only because they wouldn't have gotten a reply, but especially so as not to query their own opinion about the state of affairs.

Officially, Leni was still Peter's wife, but she knew now that her husband's true family was no longer Ulli and the newborn Sigi, but unknown people who didn't share his bed or the warmth of the *Stube*, but weapons, explosives, mines, wicks, detonators, plans of escape, forged documents, border crossings along smugglers' paths, and the avoidance of roadblocks.

On 27 August 1964, the *Musikkapelle* of a nearby town staged a special concert on the peak of the mountain where Staggl and other members of the Consortium were building, at amazing speed, a splendid ski carousel. The event had been organized in order to contradict those who had already started to call it "the Factory": a mountain that had now been ruined by the steel of the cable cars, no longer suitable for real nature lovers. Staggl wanted to prove to his fellow citizens and some guests who, despite the chair- and ski lifts, the refreshment spots, the poles of the cable cars (soon they would occupy three sides of the mountain), the restaurants with the innovative self-service formula copied from the soldiers' mess, the three-star hotel built at about 6,500 feet altitude, that in spite of all that, nature still reigned supreme up on the peak and the beauty of the *Heimat*, with a view that spanned three hundred and sixty degrees from the glaciers on the border to the faraway Dolomites, was still the ultimate winner. The city tourists, after all, didn't come here just to ski, now a compulsory sport for the middle classes of the economic boom, but also to enjoy all this majestic splendor.

And nothing could highlight this better than a concert performed right at the summit by musicians dressed in the costumes of their ancestors. The program included the first performance of a composition by the director of the *Musikkapelle*, called "An meinen Berg," To My Mountain.

On that day, the cable car tested out by Gerda and Hannes took a lot of money: tourists and town residents went up en masse. Leni brought the children and her parents. The new-born Sigi, inebriated by the rarefied 6,500-foot air, didn't wake up once, not even when his baby carriage kept knocking against the stones concealed in the tall grass. Ulli was holding his maternal grandmother's hand tight, his forehead rounded like that of a roebuck, his eyes with their long dark lashes open wide in that expression of anxious anticipation he would so often have during his brief lifetime.

The public finished settling on the folding chairs arranged in the field and silence fell, punctuated only by the intelligent caws of the crows. The conductor lifted the golden baton with which he beat the tempo of marches during parades: and one, and two, and—a bang.

On the highway at the foot of the mountain, a couple of miles east and 6,500 feet lower down, a Carabinieri jeep had exploded on an anti-tank mine. Nobody died, but there were four injured, all of them seriously.

At the beginning of September, a Carabiniere was killed in a neighboring valley with a shot to the head through the window of his barracks. The death was attributed to terrorists, but apparently it was a settling of private scores.

In the night between the sixth and seventh of September, in an isolated Alpine hut, a Secret Service infiltrator executed in his sleep Luis Amplatz, one of the two BAS *Schützen* in hiding who had decided to embrace armed struggle. His funeral had more resonance and attendance than a state funeral: even the South Tyroleans who didn't share the armed struggle considered Amplatz's death an execution by the regime.

A few days later, near the town where the Hubers and Staggls lived, another military jeep was blown up, this time by a remotely controlled bomb. Six Carabinieri were injured, four of them seriously. One of them lost an eye, the other, a leg.

The cows are sniffing anxiously the acrid smell of the candle. Soon, the flame will reach the hay. It's hard to imagine who could save the hayloft at this stage.

Once a month, a boy would deliver to Frau Mayer whatever was necessary for making sweets: flour, sugar, pine nuts, raisins, candied fruit, confetti made of colored icing, silver beads, cocoa powder. He was from Trento, and had a surname ending in "nin," like a child's nickname, but everybody called him *Zuckerbub*: sugar boy, or sugary. The latter interpretation was owing to the glances, sweeter than his merchandise, that he would shoot toward every woman without exception. When they announced his arrival from the kitchens, even Frau Mayer would check herself in the wall mirror behind the bar.

The hotel owner did not interfere with Herr Neumann's management, and let him supervise the sacks being unloaded from the van. However, when the *Zuckerbub* arrived, she always found a way of going to the spot at the back of the kitchen; she'd ask for details of an old invoice, send her regards to the boy's boss—her old school mate—or give the general duties man instructions on how to dispose of certain barrels: anything, just so she could show herself, even briefly, to those eyes that would wrap around a woman's figure like silk. Frau Mayer spent the rest of the day when the *Zuckerbub* made his deliveries in a state of vague anticipation, of trusting melancholy, in the blurred memory of something all-consuming but which she wouldn't have been able to name.

Frau Mayer's feelings were as unspecific and rarefied as the young man's precision and determination toward Gerda: he would come to pick her up on her first evening off, and take her dancing.

For all his experience as an Italian male with a smile like honey, even the *Zuckerbub* wasn't used to stepping into a nightclub with a woman who caused everyone's pupils to dilate: men's from desire, women's from comparison.

Gerda had never been taken out like this either. With Hannes, she hadn't been out in public. When they'd met, they'd always been on their own, not only on that suspenseful—appropriately so—day in the cable car, but on other occasions too. Hannes would drive his Mercedes, with her sitting next to him, as far as the bends of the passes and there, in the secluded, windy fields, they would make love. Once, he had taken her to Cadore, to a hotel like the one where she worked ten months a year, albeit smaller. Gerda was spared the embarrassment she felt toward the staff, people like those with whom she worked and sweated every day: they didn't leave their room for two days, and ordered food and drinks to be left outside the door.

Gerda had experienced this secluded love as proof of its absoluteness. It never occurred to her that Hannes might have been motivated by embarrassment or different intentions. Be that as it may, Gerda had never been out in public with a man.

There was a juke box.

"Which song do you like?" the *Zuckerbub* asked.

"Mina."

He slipped in a coin, and she selected a 45: "È l'uomo per me." Then he put his arm around her waist and pulled her toward him. Gerda thought of the singer's Egyptian eyes, of the thousand implications in her expression, and smiled: now she too, Gerda Huber, Hermann and Johanna's daughter, was dancing.

They spent the night making love amid the sacks of sugar and flour in his van. There were silver beads, chocolate flakes, and colored sugar sticks tangled in Gerda's hair. Thanks to the Zuckerbub's cheerful and expert touch, she returned to the hotel feeling as creamy, soft and light as a Carnival cake.

A few hours later, Frau Mayer appeared in the kitchen tight-lipped. Herr Neumann wondered if any of the guests in the dining room had made a complaint. With a gesture as hard as stale bread, she indicated Gerda who was cutting up radishes into flower shapes for garnishes on the salad counter. All the kitchen staff had the same thought: she was jealous. With cutting politeness, she said, *"Zwei Soldaten fragen nach Ihnen."*[19]

Gerda looked up at her chef. Herr Neumann tucked his chin into his fat neck in a sign of agreement. Less than twenty minutes later, Gerda was at the barracks at the end of the road. There were two soldiers behind the desk in front of her. One was sitting down and she thought he had a higher rank, even though she knew nothing about medals or decorations. The other one was standing, his mouth half open, as though unable to decide whether to view her as a citizen, a stunning-looking woman, or a suspect. The one who was sitting spoke.

"Is Peter Huber your brother?"

"Yes."

"What do you know about his activities?"

"What activities?"

"When did you last see him?"

"When my mother died."

"When was that?"

"A year and a half ago."

"Are you very close?"

She blinked. "He's my brother."

"Your brother stands accused of attacks against infrastructures of the Italian state."

"What does that mean?"

The officer sucked the air in through his teeth in contempt. "Yes, of course. You people here don't even know what the Italian state is."

"No . . . 'infra . . . '?"

---

[19] Two soldiers are asking for you.

The soldier who was standing looked away from Gerda for the first time and, even more submissively than required, said to his superior, "'Infrastructures' is the word she doesn't . . . "

He was silenced by the other man's irritated look. The soldier cast down his eyes then raised them again at Gerda and resumed his astonished silence. The tone with which the sitting officer addressed Gerda contained gratings, handcuffs, harsh but fair sentences:

"It means bridges, Signorina. Roads, electricity pylons . . . And especially soldiers struck down while doing their duty."

It didn't take them long to realize that Gerda knew nothing about her brother. They kept her a little longer than necessary but just for form and not out of any particular cruelty. Gerda felt quite indifferent to all this: if she could enjoy a couple of hours of unexpected rest, then she certainly wasn't about to complain about it. Still, she was upset: what was Peter doing? Why were these soldiers asking about him? She felt sorry picturing Leni's disorientated face, her two children. Then she thought of Eva and her arms felt empty. She had placed her daughter on the large Schwingshackl family like a pebble atop a *Mandl*, a stone cairn along a path—a path from which you should never stray or you risk roaming blindly in a blizzard, amid pine trees and quarries: her life.

The lower rank soldier escorted her to the barracks exit. He stepped over the threshold that separated the Fascist buildings from the sidewalk and thus, free from architecture-bound constrictions, asked if he could see her again.

He'd already arrested her once, Gerda said, so he could always do it again.

The young soldier gave a silly laugh but she didn't care. It's not as though she had to marry him, have a child with him, exchange promises of eternal love. All she had to do with him, on her next evening off, was to sway her hips against the gritty velvet of Mina's voice.

*

It was a mixture of mold, rot, stale alcohol, and urine. It hung over the scent of cut hay that spread from the fields around the town, weighing over the breeze on that clear September night, and, slippery, filtering in through the nostrils like a poisoned tentacle. This smell greeted the four Carabinieri who knocked on the door of the Shanghai house just before dawn. Its residents couldn't have been sleeping very soundly: as soon as Marshal Scanu, the highest ranking officer, lifted his arm to knock again, the peeling door turned on its hinges. The air that came out from inside the house triggered in him an archaic terror, like a curse.

The corporal and the two Carabinieri with him also came from the South and the islands, and all four were almost half a head shorter than the man who opened the door. Only the hats with the peaks evened out the proportions. Some had been posted to Alto Adige just few months earlier, some years, but they all missed home very much. One thing, though, couldn't be denied about South Tyrol residents: these people were precise, clean, and valued tidiness very highly. These people didn't ask you, "Everything all right?" but *"Alles in Ordnung?."*[20] Therefore, they had never seen a house like this.

The *Stube* that led to the front door was covered in piles of wood, dirty clothes, loose engine parts. On the shelf of the wooden stove, there were saucepans and plates covered in old dirt mixed with the crumbs and leftovers of food in a single smelly slush. Various pails more or less full of dirty water cluttered the floor over which were scattered dozens of empty bottles. Until a year and a half ago, the house had been lived in, even though it was dark and damp, but it was now reduced to a dump, a junk dealer's storeroom, a trash can. The man who had opened the door was wearing a yellowed

---

[20] "Is everything in order?"

undershirt, old pants covered in crusts, and had an unkempt beard.

Standing there in the middle, they questioned him. They were looking for his son. He said he hadn't seen him for a long time. Did he know where he was? No. Where he was living? He had no idea, even his daughter-in-law had left. The Marshal made a show of not believing him and threatened him with serious consequences for lying. The man remained silent. The two Carabinieri started searching the house. When people have their house searched they always follow and make sure that nothing is broken, put everything immediately back in its place, rush to open every lock to avoid it being broken or even just to speed up the process. But not this man. He stood motionless in the middle of the room, lit up by a single bulb, silent, as though the coming and going of the soldiers did not concern him.

He didn't ask the reason they were looking for his son, not because he already knew it but because, in this old man—who wasn't even sixty yet—there were no more questions left.

Scanu looked at Hermann Huber's face and thought of a cemetery.

Raids, searches, military incursions into the homes of civilians aren't carried out when the sun is up, when people have washed faces and their bellies are warm with caffelatte, when the humors used by the body to express itself to itself in the pagan intimacy of sleep have been washed away with water, soap, work clothes. Nor are raids conducted when the soup is simmering on the stove, when the welcoming smell of translucent onion wafts out of a cast-iron pan into which potatoes and cumin seeds will also soon be poured, and the bread is on the board, ready to be sliced. If the peasants are in the fields and so are their women, when low, black, late summer clouds menace cut hay, and every arm is needed to make sure it's safe in the hayloft before the first crack of thunder, then that's not a good time for raids either. Nor is it a good time when the earth is already black but the sky still opalescent and, inside the *Stube*, babies have already fallen asleep in the arms of their older sisters, women are darning holes in socks, and men are talking about the stretch of road that slid down during the most recent thunderstorm. Raids, arrests, searches: they, too, like all human activities, have a correct and appropriate moment which, since the dawn of time, has only ever been the darkest hour before sunrise.

When nocturnal animals are back in their dens, with a moribund bit of fur or feathers in their mouths, and the day-time ones haven't yet emerged; when humans have stopped running and flying with the eternally agile body of dreams, but haven't yet been remembered by their earthly one, full of aches and pains; when the currents between the valley and the mountain are in harmony, when, for a moment, cold and warmth no longer stir and mix as usual and the air is still; there: that dark, silent and motionless brief space of time when nothing happens is the time when people expect soldiers to arrive, complete with jeeps and boots, and abrupt shouts not aimed at being understood but at terrorizing, with that primeval power that the man who has a weapon in his hand possesses over the one who has not.

Instead, it was in full daylight, just before noon, that the soldiers arrived to the group of masi clinging to the slopes of the valley and gathered around the little church. It was an inter-forces operation involving Alpini, Carabinieri, police. There were almost a thousand of them, they had jeeps, armored vehicles, and even a tank. In other words it wasn't hard to notice their arrival. Shots were fired from behind a haystack. Was it Peter? If so, were the others who were responsible for the anti-tank bombs that had injured half a dozen soldiers a few days earlier, there with him? Were the people behind the haystack terrorists? If so, how many? Just one? More than one? No one ever found out. They'd fired from behind a makeshift shelter, like children playing at cowboys, but the weapons were real and a soldier was injured. Whoever they were, they ran away along the steep slopes behind them, along the hunters', then steinbocks' paths, then, like after every attack, dispersed in Austrian territory, leaving the residents of the group of masi to face the reprisals and frustration of Italian soldiers on their own. Suddenly, the tolling of bells filled the cool September air, as though sounding the alarm.

It was Lukas, the elderly sacristan with thin, often disheveled hair, arms that were short but muscular from decades spent pulling the bell rope. The fact that the village was surrounded by armed soldiers didn't seem to him a good enough reason to fail in his daily task: toll the bell twelve times to mark noon. The soldiers, however, didn't know Lukas or how zealous he was: they were sure this was a signal for terrorists to attack from above, so they mounted an assault against the group of masi, as though storming a fortress.

They kicked doors down, barked orders as though the war wasn't over and Italians and Nazis were still allied, they fired at panic-stricken hens around their boots, turning them into motionless heaps of blood and dirty feathers. They forced everyone out of their houses, men, women, old people and children. A soldier burst into a *Stube* where a deaf old woman was spinning, shut away in the private silence that had enveloped her for decades. He was a young man from Niscemi, outside Caltanissetta, just two months in the army. He was eighteen, and was holding an assault rifle he barely knew how to use. When he saw the old woman motionless amid all the screams and shots, he was certain she was hiding something. He shot at her face. The bullet missed her and got stuck in the pine-coated wall right next to the gray plait twisted around the old woman's head; like a new knot in the old timber. Only then did the woman raise her head.

Two other soldiers burst into Leni's parents' house. When Ulli saw them, he ran across the kitchen and buried his face between his mother's legs: perhaps to blot out that unfathomable nightmare. Leni lowered the pan in which she was about to melt some butter and turned it sideways, placing it in front of his head like a shield. One of the soldiers remained on the doorstep; the other one went up to the little bed in the corner of the room and pointed the automatic rifle against the head of little Sigi, who was asleep, shouting at Leni to tell him where her husband was or he would shoot.

Leni didn't know where Peter was. She didn't know where he went, what he did, or why. She'd never known or asked. She wasn't even certain that the furtive man who had come in and out of her bed in the middle of the night a few hours earlier had been the same to whom a long time ago she had sworn to be faithful before God. She hadn't seen her husband's face in the daylight for months. All she knew was that the head of one of her children was sticking to her thighs with the frying pan shielding it, and that the other one, so soft and smelling of sleep, was in the firing line of the rifle on the opposite side of the kitchen. Her children's heads seemed farther apart than two continents; between them, like an ocean, stretched her powerlessness as a mother.

Leni and the soldier remained looking at each other in silence, as though searching for an answer neither of them knew. After a while, the soldier (aged twenty, born in Bucchianico, near Chieti, education level: elementary school) frowned and blinked like someone with a speck in his eye but who can't rub it because his hands are occupied. Then he lowered the rifle.

All the men and a few women had been assembled and handcuffed. Tied up like that, they were led to the stream behind the houses. Among them was also Sepp Schwingshackl and his elder sons. When the raid started, his wife Maria was in front of the hayloft with Eva in her arms. She barely had the time to put her down on the ground before they clipped the handcuffs around her wrists and took her away. Eva remained sitting amid chamomile flowers, her hands on the ground, spread open like fans. Her fingers weren't stepped on by spiked boots, her face wasn't burned by the incandescent barrels of automatic rifles, but nobody entirely knows why. As though saving Eva had become her destiny, Ruthi ran to her. She lifted her up against her protruding left hip, the way mothers do when they want to keep their right side free, and remained there, motionless, frozen by uncertainty and fear, amid hen feathers and the traffic of soldiers. One of these (born in Accettura, near Matera, age: eighteen, school qualification: three years of middle school), with forehead and cheeks covered in pimples, his upper lip with just the shadow of a velvet down, had started firing at the crossing point of the beams that were holding up the roof of the hayloft. Eva opened her eyes wide at every shot. She followed with her gaze as the cartridge cases splattered and fell on the ground like crazed insects, the cloud of smoke that surrounded the barrel like the steam from a pan cooling down. Tff! the BM59 made a noise, and Eva's eyes became two dark blue buttons, Tff! and Eva held her breath. T-Tff!

The men were kept standing by the stream for several hours. The soldiers fired at the walls of the houses, threw grenades into the haylofts, stole Speck, cheese, bread and beer. Four drunk Alpini grabbed Eloise, Ruthi's eldest sister, by the arms and dragged her behind a manure pit. They had already thrown her to the ground when the lieutenant-colonel commanded them to let her go. The girl was about to run home crying, but was put together with the group of people tied up the stream. When the sun began to set they were all still there, standing, supporting one another to avoid fainting.

The lieutenant-colonel of the Carabinieri didn't like the

way things were going. This was not the fight against terrorism he had in mind. He was here, in a village that looked like an idyllic vision in the golden September light, directing an operation that was tactically a failure, as any first-year military academy student could have seen. Moreover, it lacked any sense, both in its operational orders as in its means: could anybody please explain to him just what there was to gain with hunting down terrorists who would slip away up and down smugglers' paths between Austria and Italy in an M47 armored vehicle, an exasperating mass of caterpillars and iron which would stop after an hour even on a plain, let alone up here?

He hadn't even been able to pick the men he was now commanding. On the contrary, these troops seemed to have been selected precisely because of their inefficiency: drafted boys capable only of scorching their fingers on the barrels of the BM59s, people who'd been handed Berettas without any training . . . All you could do was close your eyes and not even think of the damage they could do with those sub-machine guns in their hands.

Still, what worried the lieutenant-colonel most were certain non-commissioned officers, people who said strange things and showed off too much historical knowledge of, and even nostalgia for, the Mussolini era. Sometime earlier, when he was still in Rome, the army commander General De Lorenzo had personally given the lieutenant-colonel a worrying order: to pick out the men willing to fire even on civilians, and add their names to a special list. The lieutenant-colonel could not refuse but, in the best military tradition of passive resistance to senseless orders, he had shilly-shallied, beaten about the bush, and stalled for time while awaiting developments. For as long as he had been commanding this motorized battalion in Alto Adige, nobody had mentioned the list of the "willing," as De Lorenzo called them, to him again. But now, seeing all these non-commissioned officers who weren't lifting a finger to stop their men from looting, getting drunk, and firing at random, the lieutenant-colonel wondered if that perverse selection hadn't already been implemented by someone else.

Marshal Scanu, for instance, a trusted non-commissioned officer for whom he had respect: the lieutenant-colonel had received the explicit order to exclude him from the operation. As though the human compassion, despite the official jargon, which Scanu had shown in his report on the living conditions of Hermann Huber, the father of the wanted man Peter Huber, had not been appreciated. The lieutenant-colonel was beginning to wonder if perhaps someone wanted to keep away from operational duties anyone who could build a bridge of understanding between the armed forces stationed in Alto Adige and its residents. Someone behind a desk in Bolzano or even in Rome, someone more interested in blowing on the flames of this land that was already on fire than in bringing moderation or soothing the violence. Someone who *wanted* the situation to come to a head. It wasn't a certainty but a feeling he couldn't share with anyone, let alone substantiate. But if it really was a matter of strategy, then what could be the reason? For whom would it be advantageous to trigger violence instead of soothing it? The lieutenant-colonel really couldn't understand, he just sensed that there was a lot, too much, that he didn't know. And, remembering with a lump in his throat the solemn moment when he had sworn loyalty to the Republic and the Constitution, it was a thought he didn't like. Not at all.

At that moment, in the lapis lazuli sky of almost autumnal high pressure, the helicopter appeared. It ruffled the tops of fir trees, grass, jacket lapels, with its spinning blades, and landed in the field. A colonel of the Alpini got out. He spoke quickly, abruptly, without looking the lieutenant-colonel in the eye.

"How many people have you arrested?" he asked.

"Fifteen."

"Good. Stand them against the wall and shoot them."

The lieutenant-colonel stared at the officer. The noise of the helicopter was impairing his hearing, he must have misunderstood. "Excuse me?"

"Stand them against the wall," the colonel articulated. "Every one."

The lieutenant-colonel stood motionless. He spoke softly, politely. "I'm here to deal with crimes and make arrests. I'm not a murderer."

The colonel started to shout. "You have to shoot them, do you understand? And then burn the village. Raze it to the ground!"

The lieutenant-colonel realized he was hungry, or rather his stomach contracted in a spasm and he remembered that he hadn't eaten for several hours. He felt a hungry man's anger explode inside him and also began to shout. "You're crazy!"

"It's an order!"

"It's a crazy order!"

"I'll report you for insubordination if you don't obey!"

"We're not Nazis!"

Men of every rank, both Alpini and Carabinieri, had drawn nearer. Not even the older ones had ever seen two officers screaming at each other like that in front of the troops. Jaws dropped, many men remained with their mouths open, forgetting themselves. The lieutenant-colonel took the colonel by the arm, dragged him to the helicopter, and threw him inside with a shove. Like a backpack, or an ammunition box.

"Take him away," he said to the pilot, more like a prayer than an order.

The pilot had watched the scene in silence without leaving the cabin. His mouth hadn't fallen open. On the contrary, he'd kept his lips so tight that all that remained in the middle of his face was a purple line. He started the engine, avoiding the lieutenant-colonel's eyes, like someone bound by the selfsame sense of shame. The engine began to stir the air, the soldiers all raised hands to their heads to stop their berets from flying off, and some of them started closing their mouths.

The helicopter flew up, metallic and animal-like, like a Medieval war fantasy. The lieutenant-colonel watched it grow distant, smaller, and finally disappear in the sky, which was beginning to have pink streaks across it. He felt overwhelmed by a warm flush of gratitude for that pilot who was now risking punishment at the very least, and whose name he didn't even know. He'd even already forgotten his face.

The consequences of the military operation that took place on that golden September day in 1964 were many and various.

No terrorist was arrested during the operation. All the men who'd been arrested were released within a few days as it was proved that they had nothing to do with the recent dynamite attacks. Only an old man who was hard of hearing, and who didn't manage to communicate with the investigators, was transferred to Venice where he was kept in custody for almost three months, until the following December.

Sigi was marked forever by that rifle barrel pointed at his baby head: he grew up to be a nostalgic devotee of Andreas Hofer, full of rage and exultation, and joined the Schützen. At least that was Ulli's version whenever he tried to find a reason for his brother becoming an obtuse, homophobic racist. However, this explanation circumvented the fact that if anyone was traumatized that day, then it was only Ulli and his mother: Sigi had slept through it all.

One night at home, after the auxiliary Carabiniere from Niscemi had been relieved of his draft duties, he dreamed of the moment when he'd fired at the deaf old woman. This time, however, after he'd pulled the trigger, the old woman's face disintegrated before him in an explosion of fire, blood and horror. The morning after, the young man ran to the church of Santa Maria Odigitria, where he prostrated himself fervently at the feet of the Madonna, who had already granted him most precious grace: poor aim.

The Italian newspapers didn't report the raid, only the local German-language ones did, and were then accused of propaganda against the government. A representative of the provincial council began collecting evidence from the village residents: he meant to present them at a memorial in support of a parliamentary investigation by the Südtiroler Volkspartei. He was working on his paper when, a couple of weeks after the events, he died in murky circumstances while rock climbing. They even said that the rope he was tied to had been sabotaged. In any case, the parliamentary investigation at the Chamber of Representatives on 25 September 1964 took place without the documentation, which the councillor hadn't had sufficient time to put together. Member of Parliament Almirante therefore had no trouble in describing as "Austrian-sympathizing propaganda" any allegation of abuse committed by the Italian Armed Forces. That's how he used to refer, in all his official appearances, to German-speaking South Tyroleans.

When he returned to base, the lieutenant-colonel immediately telephoned the army commander General De Lorenzo. He informed him of the crazy orders he'd received, and of his obvious refusal to implement them.

"Yes, they have already informed me that you refused to fight," the general replied.

The lieutenant-colonel's hairs stood up on his forearms, as though in the presence of a strange, incomprehensible phenomenon.

That very evening, an urgent dispatch arrived relieving him of his charge in Alto Adige and ordering him to transfer within twenty-four hours as assistant commander with the Legion in Udine. As is customary whenever there is a change of destination, his superiors gave him the usual report, an essential evaluation for advancing his rank. Ever since he'd entered the army he'd always obtained the maximum grade, "excellent," but now they only just gave him "average." This was an indelible stain on his career.

KILOMETERS 715-850

T he 11:28 from Rome to Reggio Calabria leaves on time. To my great relief, it's not one of those torpedo-style Italian Eurostars with over a hundred shouting, eating and especially phone-calling people, forced to share the same space for hours. This is a good old long-distance train with six-seat compartments, one of those where, if there's nobody opposite you, you can pull out the seats and lie down, and then if you close the curtains, nobody bothers you. Why don't they make them all like that anymore?

My compartment fellows are two twenty-year-old American women, one overweight, the other underweight, both in jeans and T-shirts, unassuming, with not particularly clean hair, and huge backpacks in the best tradition of Inter-Rail travel. The one belonging to the chubbier of the two is particularly dirty. It's covered in felt-tip pen scribblings and coats of arms of cities and countries sewn on, but something doesn't add up: the dates go from 1993 to 1999, when this woman must have been in middle school at most. Perhaps it's a hand-me-down from an older brother who used it to roam during his year off? It hasn't occurred to her to clean it, but she has added a personal touch: a soft pink teddy bear tied to the zipper upside down, swinging in a macabre way, as though from the gallows.

The line of the other girl's shoulders, however, is defined by sharp, unhealthy corners, her legs are like sticks wrapped in jeans. Despite being so thin, she has huge tits. They're like two balls added to a pole, and perhaps they are—added, I mean.

The fat girl lifts the backpacks and puts them on the baggage rack, filling the whole space between the seats with her outsized behind. She pants, puffs, stands on her toes, reaches up with her arms while two dark circles of sweat spread in her armpits, her T-shirt comes away from her low-waist jeans, baring her large stretch-marked hips. None of this prompts the skinny one to get up and give her a hand. She contents herself with watching her, detached, as though patiently waiting to see whether or not she's going to make it. I stand up to help but the fat girl places herself between me and the backpack she's lifting (the one belonging to the other girl), making it impossible for me. I sit back down, made slightly uneasy by her refusal. A moment later, I work out what happened: my gesture of kindness was something she simply didn't recognize. It's obviously something she's not used to.

We're barely out of Termini and already crossing an extraordinary landscape which, in any other part of the world, would merit a special journey: a countryside with the ruins of Roman aqueducts. But we're in Italy and nobody pays attention to these monumental vestiges of efficiency, grace, and longevity. Not even my fellow travelers, even though, after all, it should be their job as tourists to look at the view. They're both immersed in reading paperbacks, iPods in their ears. I'd like to say: Quick! Look up! Don't miss it! These aqueducts are one of the wonders of the world! But they just sit there. In fact, it's worse than that: when they first look up, it's when we're going past a graveyard of cars, the banal degradation of an urban suburb. One of them immediately goes back to reading. The other one, as though on purpose, looks back down just a second before the Roman chaos once more gives way to the countryside, with fragments of aqueduct standing out, slender and arcane. All around, there are sheep lying on the ground: sleepy, motionless, exhausted after Easter. They must be the mothers of the lambs Romans will have for lunch today. Maybe they miss their babies but don't know how to say it. It looks like a watercolor by a Grand Tour traveler with the title: Beneath ancient ruins, wistful sheep.

"Hallo? Hallo?"

From the compartment next door, a male voice with an unmistakable accent: Indian. After a brief pause, a female voice. It sounds mellow, with a tone suggestive of flesh and soil trampled on with bare feet—even though, in Italy, this Indian lady wears shoes. What about a sari? Who knows? This is another advantage of carriages with separate compartments: you can fantasize about what your neighbors look like from their voices. The concept expressed by the woman is not very different:

"Hallo? Hallo, hallo? O.K., O.K."

There's also a baby who emits low wails, but is immediately quietened down. By a breast, a bottle, an adult entertaining him with a game of grimaces?

On the right-hand side of the train stretches Agro Pontino, flat like only land snatched from marshes can be. An expanse of cultivated plots, with heaps of plastic boxes: an exclusively dark blue heap, in the field next door just a yellow heap, then a red, then a green one. They look like pieces of Lego sorted by color by a bored child. They're waiting for the next work day to be filled with vegetables. Here, the soil is the color of blood sausage, you feel like plunging your hands in and sniffing it, and even at a distance you know it's extremely fertile, a far cry from the gray soil of my valley where you're lucky if you can grow as much as potatoes. Far away, an elegant line of Mediterranean pines and then, beyond that, almost like a glow blending in with the light from the sky, is the first view of the sea.

On the left-hand side of the train, however, a different world is rushing past, a natural graduation of bare, arid hills covered in sparse Mediterranean woodland, and populated only by goats. Low, dry stone walls carve wretched little spaces for puny olive trees; here and there, the ruins of houses built with the same stones as the walls, which is actually what the hill is made of: stones on top of other stones, containing stones— that's how hard this soil is, such an extreme contrast to the fertile plain it looks over. Every now and then, the chain of Roman hills opens up and behind it tall mountains appear that are even darker and more desolate, enveloped by clouds, with no trace of human habitation. We're still almost at the gates of Rome, but it feels like we're penetrating into Italy's harsh belly, the land of wolves and brigands.

Then the train enters a tunnel, dark and very long, and you can't see anything anymore.

Wesley, the one lucky man I've ever called my husband, albeit for just two weeks, always claimed that the first time he saw me he noticed me because of the way I was looking at the landscape. Perhaps. Even though, it must be said, that day I was on a beach in Sri Lanka, among a dozen women in saris, and I was the only blonde, the only one with blue eyes, the only one who was almost five foot eleven tall. The only one in a bikini, too. I was twenty-two, it was the first exotic holiday I'd allowed myself with the proceeds of my work.

Still, Wesley was right, I do pay attention to landscapes.

Just a few hours after we met we had dinner together, and it was one of those tropical evenings manufactured especially to get Westerners to wind up in bed together: curried lobster served by a graceful woman wrapped in silk, the ancient cries of a faraway peacock, the black waves of the Indian Ocean illuminated by phosphorescent plankton, the exchange of childhood memories. I told Wesley about how Ulli and I would go and shout at the rocks of a landslide which, a couple of years earlier, had washed away a slope of the mountain under which we lived. We would stand with our legs spread over the edge of the new ravine, where the flood had eaten away a chunk of field like a mouthful of *Krapfen*, and shout at the pile of rocks beneath us. The rocks answered with voices like ours but not identical, as though the mountain used our words to express something else. But what? Wesley looked at me with the expression of a gold prospector who had finally found a nugget in his pan.

"You really do have a romantic soul, you know?" he exclaimed. He was assistant professor of English literature at the University of Indiana, and spoke like the English poets about whom he wrote books with titles like *Divine Manure: the Myth of Gea as Nostalgia in the Self-Conscious Narrative of Modern Intellect*—that there are people in circulation who dedicate essays to "Divine Manure" is one of the many things I really didn't know until I met Wesley.

The romantic soul, Wesley explained, is convinced that the landscape has something to tell it; that it's always about to reveal something the human beings who inhabit it don't know, or have forgotten, or consider irrelevant; that in reality geography is a book written in a language unknown to us, but whose significance will perhaps one day be revealed.

"'Call the world, if you please, "the vale of Soul-making." Then you will find out the use of the world.' Keats."

I raised my eyes from the lobster and looked at the waves. I wonder what Keats would have said about that phosphorescent plankton: it looked so poetic and artificial, like the anti-darkness stars in a child's bedroom.

Actually, what Ulli and I were shouting at the landscape in order to obtain a revelation of its soul, were, at most, insults against our enemies:

"Di Greti hot dreckige Untohosn!"
"Do Sigi isch an Orschloch!"

"Do Pato Christian figgt mit di Kia,
und mit di Hennen aa!"

Rocks would confirm that our fury and our contempt were
a good and righteous thing:
    Gretl has dirty knickers (*Untohosn . . . hosn . . . hosn . . .*).
    Sigi is an asshole (*Orschloch . . . schloch . . . loch . . .*).
    Father Christian shags cows (*mit di Kia . . . Kia . . .*) and
also hens (Hennen aa!).

But I didn't say that to Wesley.

That night, Wesley came into my bungalow on the beach,
and stayed for three days. Sexually, he wasn't as romantic as his
poets. He had the body of a WASP who's been practicing sport
since kindergarten: long, toned, covered in fine blonde down,
without an ounce of fat despite being over forty. With athletic
efficiency he provided me, as well as himself, with strictly
equivalent orgasms. When I took the initiative to give him
pleasure, he appreciated it but then reciprocated immediately,
as though it was very important to balance the double entry
between giving and receiving. In other words, an accountant's
sexuality, but when you're twenty-two, you're not looking for
subtlety. At least, I wasn't.

On the morning of the third day, I went for a solitary dive in
the ocean while Wesley was still asleep. When I returned to the
bungalow, I woke him up by covering him with my wet body.

"I know why you sleep so little, Eva," he said. "You don't
want to miss out on the secrets that the Archangel Michael
confides to Adam."

"What?"

"Milton, *Paradise Lost*, Book Eleven."

I must have looked at him with the expression of a gold
prospector who's finally found a Rubik's cube in her pan. He
caressed my thighs, which were still damp and salty, with the

patience of a lecturer who has to explain everything at length to ignorant, bikini-wearing students every single day—because, after all, somebody has to do it. "In the penultimate book of his masterpiece, Milton gets the Archangel Michael to speak with Adam. He shows him the future: Cain and Abel, the destruction of the Temple of Solomon, Kublai Khan, the Russian Tsar, Montezuma . . . "

"What's Adam got to do with Montezuma?"

"Nothing. Michael reveals to Adam the future history of man. That's why he gives Eve a sleeping potion: she mustn't hear, she's a woman. And so, while Adam learns the secrets of the times to come, Eve sleeps."

He slipped a hand into my bikini. "You're also a woman, Eva . . . " he started moving his fingers, " . . . but you stay awake, so you can hear."

A liquid warmth began to rise between my legs. "I'm not interested in knowing the future," I said. "That's a man's desire."

"And yet it's obvious you don't want to miss out on their secrets. That's why you refuse to sleep."

Something in Wesley's words rang true, but I didn't know what. Meanwhile, his fingers had found the center of me, and I couldn't think anymore.

We got married a few days later in Reno, Nevada. I'd changed my flight from Colombo to Frankfurt for a Los Angeles one. I'd sent my mother a telegram: *I gea heiratn*, I'm getting married.

The Reno marriage license office promises its public to issue a license within ten minutes at most. They gave us ours after eight. An employee with a pock-marked face and the aquiline nose of a Native American, asked our names, surnames, marital status, place of residence of our mothers (but, to my great relief, not our fathers) and fifty-five dollars in cash—the marriage license office must be the last place in the US not to accept credit cards.

Then we went into the office of the Commissioner for Marriages, half a mile away. It was a room covered in pink and orange carpeting. A black woman with monumental legs constricted in anti-varicose-vein pantyhose was standing in front of a chunky wooden desk. It was she who married us. Our witness was the cleaning man, a Mexican about my age. He had an upper lip like the baroque volute of a colonial church, and the eyes of a little girl. He'd just obtained his Green Card through a lottery, so the joy with which he added his signature at the bottom of our marriage certificate was very sincere.

When we came out of there, Wesley suggested we celebrate our wedding night with Joan and Elliot, a couple of friends of his who lived on Lake Tahoe. Now he was a married man, he said cheerfully, he'd be able to have sex with Joan: he had me to offer her husband.

I told you, his book keeping was precise.

I remembered what was written on the inside flap of the book about divine manure:

Before becoming Associate Professor at the University of Indiana, Wesley Munro was a shoe repairer, a member of youth gangs, a boy scout, a dish washer, a golf caddie, an undertaker, a coffin shiner, a hamburger maker, an engineering worker, an assistant plumber, a voluntary subject in medical experiments, a lab assistant in charge of cleaning hamsters' teeth, an organist in a Baptist church, a soap dialogue writer, a private tutor for wealthy teenagers, a translator, a truck driver.

He collects stamps.

Only then did I realize that "collects stamps" should have rung alarm bells.

"Pull up, please," I said, and got out of the car.

Our marriage lasted two weeks for the simple reason that it was only two weeks later that we were together again in the same room, that is, in the office of the Commissioner for Divorce.

It was identical to the other one, but with gray and green carpeting, colors more suitable to a failed marriage, in fact, than pink and orange. The two weeks between wedding and divorce, I spent with the Mexican cleaner cum witness, who shared with me his joy about his Green Card. As for Wesley, I have no idea. With no hard feelings, we signed the document which separated our fates for ever, left that green and gray room dazzled by the naked desert light, and never met again.

Over twenty years have passed since my brief and only taste of that legendary status: a married woman. Now, however, whenever I need to renew my identity card, I can put "divorced" on the marital status line. Not "single," as my mother has had to do all her life.

"What would Vito say?" had been Ulli's comment when I told him about my lightning marriage.

An impossible question, of course, which never got an answer. Now, however, there's another one: what will Vito say when he sees me? He's sure to ask me if I'm married, if I have children. Will I tell him about Wesley? I don't think so, not because I'm ashamed, but because we won't have any time to waste on what's irrelevant. And what about Carlo, who doesn't speak about his wife and children and after whom I don't enquire? If Vito were my real father, would I confide that in him? If Vito were my real father, would my life be like this?

My throat feels tight. I'd better go back to observing the landscape outside the window.

After Monte San Biagio, the mountains on the left of the train are triangular peaks, almost like pure geometrical forms, without a single human construction. However, toward the sea, the stretch of greenhouses on the plain continues. Once again the windows on the right and those on the left seem to give onto two opposite worlds, very distant from each other.

The skinny American girl, whose waist is narrower than one of the other girl's thighs, hands the latter a cookie. Her gesture is that of a tamer: she holds it in front of her but at a distance, denying it to her, expecting obedience. The fat girl has the expression of someone ready to do anything just to get that cookie; the skinny one, that of someone who knows it. Only after a while does she grant it to her with a smile that suggests power. Her companion grabs it quickly, immediately looking away from the one who is both the perpetrator and the witness of her humiliation and, chewing, returns to her book. The title is embossed in gold lettering, illegible, and I only manage to make out the subheading: *A true story.* I imagine it must be the story of a tormented life, complete with a difficult childhood, abuse, and an edifying final redemption.

Finally, after another tunnel, the sea. Close, infinite, luminous, sunny and, especially after the constriction of those ragged mountains, wide open. In the warm April sun, it's animated by sailboards, by the even lines of clam cultivations, by people celebrating Easter with their first trip to the beach. Formia Station is slightly uphill from the town, and it has such a wide view over the gulf that it makes you gasp. But not even now that the joyful light of the Mediterranean is flooding in through the window, that agaves, bougainvilleas, plumbagos, lemons, jasmines, hibiscuses, wisterias, and oleanders are hitting us in the face with their multicolored vitality, and that the sea is glistening like wrapping paper around the gift that is Italy, not even now do the two girls look up from their best-sellers. And so all this splendor is wasted before their eyes. I feel the same kind of disappointment as a proud hostess whose guests are too absent-minded to notice how beautiful her apartment is.

Hostess?

All of a sudden, a simple syllogism:

South Tyrol is my *Heimat.*

South Tyrol is in Italy.

Ergo

Italy is my . . .

How do you say *Heimat* in Italian? It's a word that has nothing to do with Italy, that feels too much like bread with cumin seeds, like a warm *Stube* when it's cold outside, like *Adventskalender*[21]. "Homeland" isn't right either because it feels like monuments made of granite, like borders traced by absent-minded chancellors, like poorly-equipped boys sent to their deaths by elderly generals. "Country?" Yes, right:

Italy is my country.

I'd never said it before. But perhaps today is not the right time to do so, now that I'm traveling down the whole of this long, long Italy, splendid, defaced, dressed in flowers, monuments, and unregulated buildings, in order to reach the only man who's ever made me feel at home. The man who hasn't been my father, but almost.

Vito.

---

[21] Advent calendar.

1965-1967

I t was always the same question.
"*Fo wem isch de letze?*" Whose little girl is this? It would
happen at the wedding of a great aunt's son. Or at a
nephew's christening, with the *Pate*[22] and *Patin*, the most
smartly dressed people there because it was their day. Or at the
collective first communions of the first, second, and third
cousins all turned twelve the same year, and who, that morning
in church, had been given the communion wafer by the priest's
hand in succession, like young battery hens. The result was
that every time there would be a crowd of people in their best
clothes—the women in dirndl but the men in jacket and tie so
they wouldn't look old-fashioned—gathered in the area
between the Schwingshackls's hayloft and house for a party
after the religious ceremony. Everybody was linked to almost
everyone else present by either blood or marriage: all were
grandchildren, uncles, nephews, grandparents, godparents,
brothers and sisters, sons and daughters, cousins, great-grand-
children, sons-in-law, mothers-in-law, and daughters-in-law of
one another. The relationships between them were woven with
invisible threads, a large quilt of belonging, perhaps threadbare in places where two brothers weren't speaking or because
of an obvious dislike between a mother- and daughter-in-law,
but which, nevertheless, was spread over everybody and from
which no one was excluded. No one, except Eva.

[22] Godfather/mother

Like a tiny, disorientated buoy, Eva floated in that sea of people, the only one without relatives—even though Sepp and his wife always treated her like one of their own. Thirteen pregnancies had rounded Maria's body until it had lost its shape. Even the color of her eyes was no longer well-defined, although they were still sharp and luminous like the diamonds on the peacock-shaped brooch she would pin to her dirndl on celebration days. She wore her hair twisted around her head like Frau Mayer, but while the hotel owner's plait was the product of care and perfection, Maria's looked like a work of nature, unavoidable and necessary like an ear of barley, a tree, a potato. Her hands were so rough that when they squeezed Eva's soft, fat fingers, they were almost scratchy, yet they also conveyed a calmness that erased every anxiety—almost. Nobody knew how Maria, with her thirteen living children and dozens of grandchildren, found the time to walk hand-in-hand with a girl that didn't even belong to her. But her religion had taught her that there is no limit to the love of one's neighbor and, like Sepp, she was a strong believer.

Even so, sooner or later, there was always some distant relative from a neighboring valley, a partially deaf great-aunt, the mother of a young bride who'd just become part of the family, who'd ask who that little girl was.

"*Fo wem isch de letze?*"

Maria, Sepp, Eloise, Ruthi had tried to explain. "It's the little Huber girl, not the ones in the maso above us, but the ones in Shanghai, the daughter, Gerda, got into trouble and . . . "

However, what the nosy parkers wanted to know wasn't Eva's story, with its difficult side plots (unmarried mother, terrorist uncle, and a grandfather who gave you the creeps when you so much as looked at him). All they wanted was to see the stitch that reassuringly darned the communal cloth of belonging. People like Sepp and Maria, generously tolerant of loose threads and frayings, are few and far between. Therefore, a different answer became commonplace:

"*Fo wem isch de letze?*"

"Fo niamandn."

Whose little girl is this?

Nobody's.

Until she turned thirteen, when she went to high school as a boarder in Bolzano, Eva lived with Maria, Sepp, Ruthi and the entire Schwingshackl family for ten months of the year, during the hotel's summer and winter seasons. In November and again soon after Easter, from the steep slope to which the maso clung, Eva would start scanning the cars driving on the highway down along the river like busy ants. She learned when she was very young that joy arrived on a blue bus with yellow letters. She soon grew able to differentiate it from other vehicles: cars, trucks, tractors, tourist buses, and vans. When the bus from Bolzano emerged from the bend at the bottom of the valley, her heart would leap in her chest like a grasshopper in a cage. She would start following it with her eyes as it turned at the intersection, tackled hairpin curves, disappeared in a thicket of fir trees, reappeared, then stopped, huffing, in the space in front of the little church.

Then Eva would let go of Maria's hand, stop playing with Ulli, disengage herself from Ruthi's arms, and would have even taken leave of herself if she could have, in order to run faster, and she never tripped over so she wouldn't waste silly time on getting back up. But for days on end she ran in vain: the bus doors would open like a promise but the people who got off were useless, and not her mother. Then, every time, in fall and spring, during all those years, just when a desolate hollow was beginning to grow in Eva's chest, and a grayness would extinguish her thoughts, then, lo and behold, a pair of long legs would appear on the steps of the bus, then a face that was astoundingly beautiful albeit familiar, two strong arms would lift her up and hold her tight, and the smell, the smell, the mammal smell of happiness. Gerda was back.

The tourists who stayed in the town while Gerda was working in Frau Mayer's hotel would all leave during the low season. There were plenty of vacant furnished rooms when she came to stay with Eva, and it wasn't hard to rent one. Gerda was now earning enough to provide for herself and her daughter without needing to ask anyone else for anything. Not that Gerda or the other members of staff were earning a fair wage. Yet nobody protested: everybody knew the story of the Trade Unionist, as she was still called.

It was Nina who had told her about the Italian waitress who had been kicked out a couple of years before Gerda's arrival. She was a young woman with more education than the rest of them: she had attended high school for at least two years. She was in the third year of her bookkeeping course when a two-hundred-pound hook had fallen on her father's skull—her father who wore himself out working overtime at the steelworks in order to give his daughter a qualification, and the possibility of a better life. Left with a widowed mother and three little siblings, she'd had to abandon her studies. After working in Frau Mayer's hotel for two years, she noticed in her work booklet that she had received only one month of employer's contributions per season, instead of five. She had protested. Not only that, but she also dared make another demand. The weekly day off started at three in the afternoon and lasted until eleven the following morning: she and the rest of the staff would have to be remunerated for the missing four hours off.

Fray Mayer fired her on the spot. She even took care to report the episode to all the young woman's future potential employers. Despite the demand for personnel caused by the tourism boom, the Trade Unionist, as everyone was now calling her, never managed to find work in the hotel industry again.

As she told Gerda the story, Nina's close-set eyes were impassive. She commented neither on Frau Mayer's behavior, nor on that of the young woman. She let Gerda make up her own mind.

And she did. She checked her own work booklet. And that's how she discovered that she had lived the recent years of her life on an eternal, careless vacation: only a handful of working days a year were recorded in the work booklet. She also saw that Frau Mayer knew how to time travel, from the present into the future, to steal the pension of the elderly Gerda.

Thief! she wanted to scream at her.

But Gerda had two things, and no more: a daughter and a job.

And Gerda knew only too well the terror of losing everything.

So Gerda said nothing.

Every day, Herr Neumann's legs hurt more and more, and he had to leave the kitchen increasingly often to urinate: his diabetes was getting worse. One spring day he was standing by his table and, trying to ignore the hollow throbbing of the poor circulation in his shins, he was cutting open, gutting and slicing a kid with expert fingers, the only remaining tapered part of his body. The carcass was losing all semblance of an animal and assuming that of biblical matter. When Herr Neumann had finished, he carefully arranged on his right hand side the dead meat which, soon, through the mystery of digestion, would become living flesh again, but made human: and on his left he put the insides that were now chaotic and deprived of any function.

From the salad counter, Gerda had been watching attentively, as usual. She approached the head chef and pointed at the liver, dark red like a carnivorous flower, with the small heart-shaped bulge attached to it like a uvula it could have been a creature apart from the rest of the carcass. Shyly, she asked if, instead of his throwing it away, she could use it.

For a second, Herr Neumann forgot the annoying throbbing inside his legs. He'd been expecting this moment for a long time: he'd always been certain that, sooner or later, Gerda would ask to experiment, invent, try something out. Trying not to show how pleased he was, he nodded. Gerda cut the liver into very thin strips, quickly fried it on the hotplate, seasoned it with thyme, marjoram, shallots, garlic, and lemon, poured it all into a bowl full of purslane and, finally, seasoned everything with a few drops of balsamic vinegar. With the understanding expression of a child showing the drawing she's proud of, she proffered him her invention. Herr Neumann stuck three bare fingers into the concoction, squeezed them like pliers and, while Gerda watched him, put a handful of salad and liver into his mouth. It was balanced, flavorsome, satisfactory. Just like Gerda: simple and very well put together.

From his first courses and cooked vegetables counter, Hubert had watched the scene with vague condescension. He handed Gerda a handful of chopped chives.

"*A bissl Schnittla aa . . .* [23]"

Herr Neumann gave a definitive shake of the head. Gerda's invention already had everything a successful dish needed: any further addition would have been too much.

Peeved, Hubert pirouetted on his long wiry legs without a word and went back to his first courses. He had just finished stirring a pot full of *Schlutzkrapfen* in browned butter. He took the handful of the snubbed chives and threw it in, as though hurling an insult.

One morning, when he woke up, Herr Neumann's legs were inert like undercooked chops. Urgently called by Frau

---

[23] Also a bit of chives . . .

Mayer, the doctor administered insulin and anticoagulants, then said that the kitchen would have to do without its chef for a few days.

The meat counter was only a couple of yards away from the first course counter but Herr Neumann's kingdom had always been inaccessible to Hubert—as it had been to everybody else. Hubert suggested standing in. "Temporarily," he said, but it was clear he was considering this, finally, to be his chance. He was wrong.

Herr Neumann had a wife and three children who lived in a respectable apartment with geraniums at the windows, at the far end of Val Venosta. Like the lowliest of scullery boys, like Gerda, like all the hotel staff, Herr Neumann returned to his family only during the low season closure. During the working months he stayed in one of the two single rooms reserved for the staff: besides him, only the maître enjoyed the privilege of not sharing with others the tiredness at the end of the day, the body smells and the indiscriminate, revealing sounds of sleep. Until the doctor arrived nobody had ever entered Herr Neumann's room except him. And now Gerda was there.

Ever since, at the age of sixteen, this beautiful, very beautiful woman, too beautiful for him, had walked into his kitchen, there had been one thing he'd wished to do more than anything else, and he was doing it now: initiating her into the secrets of meat.

It was Elmar who helped her carry a quarter of beef weighing eighty pounds to the little room in the attic, puffing and stopping halfway on the steep wooden stairs where Gerda had tried not to become a mother. They were both wearing the woolen greatcoats you used for entering the refrigerated cell and which were now protecting them from the blood and the grease. Gerda had set up a work table on Herr Neumann's desk, dragging it from the little window overlooking the mountains to the bed to which he was confined. She had retrieved all his knives from the meat counter: for carving, boning, filleting, the bone hatchet, the carving fork, the flintlock, knives forged into specific, unmistakable shapes for roasts, hams, cured pork and venison. Gerda could barely believe that she was able to touch their impeccable, functional forms: to hold them, use them, and even wash them was the head chef's exclusive privilege. Their cold, steel glow highlighted further the sad physicality of the sickroom.

Herr Neumann was neither embarrassed nor humiliated by the stale smell, the small window, the modesty of his quarters despite his status as head chef. There was joy in his heart and his legs were no longer throbbing, or at least he didn't notice: Gerda was there sitting next to him on the wooden bed and he was guiding her hand, showing her how to bone, slice, and scoop.

The huge quarter of beef, he explained, was like a block of marble in the hands of a great sculptor: all it required was for its true shape to be revealed. The long, fleshy cylinder of the fillet, the triangle of the rump, the deformed pyramid of the shank with that bone sticking out, so graceless but so full of flavor . . .

Querrippe, Entrecôte, Steak, Lende, Kugel, dickes Bugstück, Zungenstück, Hüfte, Hals, Zwerchfell, Schulter, Schulterspitze, Dünnung, Schenkel. The names of the meat cuts in German were precise and unambiguous, like everything else in that language of philosophers and mechanics.

The Venetian, Calabrian, and Sicilian workers of which the Bolzano slaughterhouse was now full, and where Herr Neumann bought his supplies, had also taught him the most florid words from the South: *filetto, sottofiletto, fesa, spalla, costata, piccione, cappello del prete, campanello, pesce, lacerto, piscione, lattughello, imperatore, manuzza . . .*

The cut was everything, Herr Neumann explained. No

amount of perfect timing, flavoring, stuffing, marinading, browning, or salting can save a poorly cut piece of meat. The frying pan, tin or pot where it's cooked is like the bed where the marriage between the meat and its cook is consummated; but the house where the couple lives more or less happily is the chopping board where it takes on its shape. If it's cut badly, in a rush, or carelessly, the meat will behave like a woman who's badly treated by day: however much her husband might flatter her at night in the bridal bed, she remains cold, unresponsive, depressed. When you handle her right, however—Herr Neumann was looking at Gerda, at her lips, the curve of her breasts pushing against the apron splashed with blood, the roundness of her behind digging a hollow in the mattress and almost brushing his deformed leg—meat is like a satisfied lover: it melts, becomes yielding and tender, and gives up its juices.

These, however, were thoughts Herr Neumann perhaps couldn't allow even to brush his mind.

By the time the chef returned to his kitchen, Gerda had been promoted to assistant cook at the meat counter and, whenever he had to go to his increasingly frequent medical appointments, his substitute. Hubert, never much of a talker, stopped speaking altogether. Naturally, Gerda paid no attention: ever since she was a child she'd known how dense the silence between two people can be. So it was she who made the *Wiener Schnitzel*, which had now become her specialty, for the prestigious guests who sat at Frau Mayer's tables on that Sunday in 1965.

The hotel owner had rushed into the kitchen, her turquoise eyes blank like those of a crazed clairvoyant, breathless from pride and excitement, to tell Herr Neumann that tomorrow he would be cooking for the *Obmann* of the *Südtiroler Volkspartei* and his guests, representatives of the Italian government. What with local and national politicians, lackeys and undersecretaries, there would be over fifty people eating.

Frau Mayer had no interest in Italian politics, but not because it was so convoluted and incomprehensible to the uninitiated. In her eyes, as in the eyes of almost all German-speaking South Tyroleans, the only noteworthy politician in the country whose citizenship they had was the figure leaning on a stick, with a hollow face and straight hair: Silvius Magnago. The residents of the rest of the peninsula were starting to get used to their politicians, like relatives to whom, no matter what, you're linked by fate; Frau Mayer, on the other hand, didn't even know their faces. Therefore, she didn't recognize Magnago's guests, nor did she feel any curiosity toward them. Only after an obscure master of ceremonies informed her did she realize that the Prime Minister himself (as well as interim Foreign Minister) would be sitting in her dining room, stopping in on his way to the Alpine hut between Alto Adige and Austria where he was to meet the Austrian Foreign Minister Bruno Kreisky. But this seemed a privilege less extraordinary than being able to serve at her Obmann's table.

Herr Neumann was requested to provide a menu of samples illustrating the Alto Adige gastronomic tradition to the guests from the capital city.

The head cook took the request to heart.

As a starter, he suggested top quality *Speck* and *Kaminwurz*[24], accompanied by *Schüttelbrot* from Val Venosta and apple horseradish; goat's cheese with herbs spread on *Breatl*[25]; little *Tirtlan* with sauerkraut, spinach and potatoes. These were served very hot and crisp straight after being fried, and the Roman lackeys asked for a double portion.

The same members of the political underworld, however,

[24] Smoked salami.
[25] Rye and wheat bread flavored with fennel, cumin seeds or coriander.

wondered if the second helping had been a good idea when, arriving on trays garnished like paintings by Paul Klee, various kinds of *Knödel* were served (with liver, *Speck*, cheese, spinach), *Spatzlan, Schlutzkrapfen* served on slices of *Graukäse* and red onion rings, and wine soup.

There followed the pièces de résistance, an appropriate word since many guests were beginning to feel as if they were on that frontline where exhausted gastric juices, heroic but desperate, put up resistance before advancing battalions of food: oven baked shank, lamb chops in herb crust, *Greastl* scented with bay leaves, venison shoulder on red cabbage and, finally, accompanied by blueberry sauce, Gerda's *Wiener Schnitzel.*

There were cooked vegetables to lighten the load: asparagus in vinaigrette sauce, young watercress salad with *Kohlrabi*[26], sauerkraut with juniper, and *Rösti*[27] with potatoes from Val Pusteria. When the desserts arrived, the members of the government, who had wanted to try everything for love of novelty, felt discouraged: the capacity of their stomachs had gone beyond all natural limits, and yet more dishes heaped with delights were coming their way. Assorted cakes (carrot cake, buckwheat cake, cake with berries, walnut cake), *Linzertorte, Buchteln*[28], apple fritters with vanilla cream and, to finish, hot slices of the unmissable *Strudel* with vanilla cream. Moreover, besides delighting the members of both delegations, Gerda's *Wiener Schnitzel* (her secret: before dipping the veal slices in flour, rolling them in breadcrumbs, and frying them in an abundance of lard, she had marinated them for half an hour in marjoram-flavored lemon juice) had triggered a discussion about history two tables away from the table of honor. Middle-ranking government representatives from the Bolzano

---

[26] Turnip.
[27] Pan-fried potatoes.
[28] Sourdough cake.

Christian Democrats and the *Südtiroler Volkspartei* were seated there. The South Tyroleans had surprised their interlocutors with their correct, albeit rigid, Italian; nobody among the government delegates in charge of solving the Alto Adige issue, however, had deemed it necessary to learn a single word of German. The discussion therefore took place in Italian, more or less as follows:

"The breaded cutlets, like so many good things in the North, were actually copied from Italy by the Austrians."

"We had nothing to copy, we've always breaded our meat. Like in the *Wiener Backhendl*[29], which is also called *poulet frit à la viennoise*."

"But it's a well known fact that it was Radetzky who took them to Vienna! He may have fired his cannons at the Milanese, but he certainly liked their cutlets."

"That's a myth! Both in Vienna and here in Tyrol, we'd already been eating them for centuries."

"*Cotoletta alla milanese* or *Wiener Schnitzel*, what's the difference? You're all Italians now!"

(No reply; the sound of chewing, embarrassed clearing of throats.)

The person who had less food than anyone else was the *Obmann* Magnago, sitting at the table of honor, but his guest the Prime Minister also ate with moderation. There's a singular man, Magnago thought, watching him toy unnervingly with his food before putting it in his mouth: closed, introverted, he never looked his interlocutor in the eye and when he laughed it seemed he did so under duress. He listened with heavy, half-closed eyes as though his mind was far away. He spoke very softly with sleepy, exasperating slowness, and his gestures and movements were limp, as though as a child he used to trip when he ran, slam drawers on his fingers, and forget to tie his

[29] Viennese fried chicken.

shoelaces. Everything about him seemed helpless, weak, certainly not a man of action but rather, the classicist Magnago thought, a *cunctator*. And yet, over the course of several personal meetings, the *Obmann* had had occasion to see that this inexpressive face concealed highly subtle political intelligence. Unlike so many other representatives of the Italian government, the man sitting next to him was an intellectual, as well as a high-ranking lawyer. Above all, he was a man out of whose mouth, no matter how tired or distracted he was, stock phrases would never come.

Magnago knew very well that the hard German accent with which he spoke, however perfectly, the language of Dante, and the fact that he had done his war service in the Wehrmacht made his interlocutors immediately associate him with Nazism. He knew how futile it would be to try and explain that not all German officers had been Nazis, and that he'd been drafted into the German army because the residents of his land had had to choose between . . . No, it was impossible: he couldn't forever inflict a compendium of South Tyrol's complicated history.

And so the word "Nazi" remained implicitly and powerfully unspoken between him and almost all those with whom he spoke on board the ocean liner that is the Italian Parliament, and something he was very much aware of. Every so often, the label would become explicit, especially on the part of certain right-wing leaders, particularly those who really had some explaining to do as to where they had been after September 8. They, of all people, weren't ashamed to call South Tyroleans of German ethnicity the name given to traitors during the Risorgimento: austriacanti. As though the Italianization of Alto Adige from Fascism onwards had been the Fifth War of Independence, as though here too Italians had been the oppressed and Austrians the invaders, instead of the other way around. Magnago had lived and studied in Bologna, where he still had many close friends from his university days; and because he knew them very well, he knew that when Italians are given the choice between identifying with the role of victim or that of the aggressor, they will always choose the former. Even in the face of historical truth, if necessary. "Self-pity," a concept that has no lexical equivalent in the language of Goethe, and which Magnago, even when he spoke German always used in Italian.

However, fortunately, the thought process of the man sitting next to him was not as lazy as that of so many of his fellow countrymen. Naturally, he wasn't the only intelligent Italian politician. Of course there was Andreotti, for example, though his subtlety and complexity, Magnago thought, sometimes verged on the abyss. Then there was the intellectual refinement of Fanfani, although somewhat corrupted by the envious nastiness typical in some people of small stature: Magnago knew that his own grenadier height triggered irremediable aversion in Fanfani which, he felt, would yield nothing worthwhile in their negotiations. No, the *Obmann* thought, the intelligence of this man who had allowed the waiter to pour his wine with absent-minded indolence but who had then muttered a submissive "thank you" was as refined as that of Andreotti and Fanfani, but much more humane. When he had met him for the first time after spending years in the baroque halls of Roman palaces, in order to bring to the government's attention the necessity of a negotiated solution in Alto Adige, years of absent-minded interviews lasting just a few minutes and with a quick handshake for the sole benefit of photographers, Magnago had asked him, "How long can you give me?"

And he had replied, "As long as it takes."

This interminable luncheon wasn't just celebrating the start of real talks on the future of South Tyrol, Magnago thought, dabbing his mouth with a linen napkin—picked out especially by Frau Mayer in the workshop of artist weavers in Val

Venosta. What was also worth celebrating was the fact that his interlocutor was none other than Aldo Moro.

After lunch, Herr Neumann, Gerda, Hubert, Elmar and the entire kitchen staff washed their hands, straightened the white canvas caps on their heads and, under the fiercely proud eyes of Frau Mayer, stood in a row in order to say goodbye to the illustrious guests.

Gerda didn't meet Aldo Moro's eye, and barely heard him say goodbye. Later, she wasn't even able to say whether his hand had brushed hers or not. However, when Silvius Magnago shook hands with her, she recognized the skinny man she had seen, as a little girl, direct the course of the crowd in Sigmundskro like a captain on a ship. He was barely ten years older now but already looked like an old man. And yet during that time, Gerda thought, the one who had been most transformed by life wasn't the *Obmann*: it was her. And the thought made her feel pride as sharp as the steel in Herr Neumann's knives.

The political reconciliation in South Tyrol that was beginning to be planned wasn't good news for everyone: there were those who did their best to sabotage it.

The newspapers became war bulletins.

23 MAY 1966: ATTACK ON THE FINANCE POLICE AT PASSO DIVIZZE. CUSTOMS OFFICER BRUNO BOLOGNESI IS KILLED.

24 JULY 1966: NIGHT ATTACK WITH MACHINE GUNS ON THREE CUSTOMS EMPLOYEES IN SAN MARTINO IN VAL CASIES. CUSTOMS OFFICERS SALVATORE GABITTA GIUSEPPE D'IGNOTI ARE KILLED. A THIRD, COSIMO GUZZO, IS SERIOUSLY INJURED.

3 AUGUST 1966: DYNAMITE ATTACK ON THE PALACE OF JUSTICE IN BOLZANO.

20 AUGUST 1966: DYNAMITE ATTACK ON ALITALIA OFFICES IN VIENNA.

SUMMER 1966: THOUSANDS OF DRAFTED AND REGULAR SOLDIERS, AND ANTI-TERRORISM UNITS ARE SENT TO ALTO ADIGE. ROAD BLOCKS, SEARCHES AND ARRESTS ARE A DAILY OCCURRENCE.

SEPTEMBER 1966: EIGHTEEN-YEAR-OLD PETER WIELAND FROM VALDAORA IS KILLED AT A ROAD BLOCK—HE HAD NOT STOPPED WHEN ASKED TO. MASS DEMONSTRATION OF MEN, WOMEN AND CHILDREN AT HIS FUNERAL.

It rained, it rained, it rained. In 1966, the sky never seemed to run out of its water reserve. As though it had stored it up for decades with the sole aim of pouring it out on human beings all in one go. Florence had been buried in mud, and the mountain slopes all over Italy were sliding downstream. Even the river that crossed Gerda's home town had burst its banks and filled houses with mud and detritus, taken chunks out of roads, washed away bridges, and killed people. The flood also invaded the chocolate and *Magenzucker*[30] (small digestive, aromatic sugar lumps red as rubies) factory. For days on end, aid workers shoveled mud that smelled of cinnamon, cloves, and bitter chocolate.

Then the snow came. It fell abundantly on the town, and then some more fell and didn't stop. Snowflakes continued to fall, lace hexagons fluttering in the air like butterflies. It was only the beginning of December, the beginning of Advent, and children were starting to think that it would never stop, that it would snow forever, till the end of time, and that the world would become a giant snowball, but then who would throw it?

[30] Sugar for the stomach.

A muffled silence had filled the space between sounds: the gravelly tone of discontented wives had softened, the crying of babies almost seemed a melodic call, and the insults shouted by drunkards as they came out of the *Kneipen*[31] had now acquired a faint elegance. Even the rattling of military vans on the motorway, with heavy chains wrapped around their wheels, had become vague, soft, almost evocative. However, the night of December 2 was torn apart by a specific, pure sound: the roar of an explosion.

Nobody had ever believed in the recycling of the monument to the Alpini into a symbol of reconciliation between South Tyrol and the Italian army—especially not now, with the ubiquitous presence of military columns, barracks in a state of high alert, road blocks, arrests, searches.

Neo-Nazi paramilitary explosives experts from beyond the border had been well-trained: this time the charges were placed perfectly. Not even a fragment remained of that poor, ugly, coarse granite Wastl, the hapless ambassador of Italian humanity and of its humble Alpini.

Things had changed since the last time it had been hit: nobody considered these to be childish actions any longer. The terrorist from the new bloodthirsty BAS who claimed responsibility for the attack was sentenced to seventeen years and called "government enemy number one." The verdict was pronounced in absentia, however, because he was on the run.

A life on the run was what Peter had been looking for ever since, as a boy, he would walk around the woods and glaciers, his soul stripped bare by solitude, like a shelled kernel,

That's what he'd always wanted, to find himself exposed to the non-human: the perfect Y-shaped tracks of a hare in the

---

[31] Taverns.

March snow; marmots blinking in the June sun, thin and bewildered after the long fast, the same ones which, in September, after a summer of eating their fill, with fat behinds like babies in diapers, whistle while doing clownish somersaults; needles that look gold in the October light, raining down from pine trees at the first gust of a northerly wind, messenger of winter; the horizontal pupils of an ibex, caught unawares a few yards away, its alien expression free of reproach, even toward the bullet seconds away from killing it. And now, in addition to all this, Peter also had a mission: the *Heimat* had called him and he had answered. It was his answer to every other question.

The equipment, the lifestyle, and the way his days panned out, weren't that different from when he was a hunter. Ankle boots, knee-high socks, binoculars around his neck, a peaked hat, a backpack, a rope, a shotgun. For a few weeks now, he and his companions had been calling home a rocky recess of green granite with black streaks from the humidity, its open side shielded by boughs. It was comfortable. They'd built themselves benches and a kind of low table with carved branches tied together. Nails in the walls acted as a wardrobe, the nearby stream as a bath, shower and sink. A trusted woman who understood them and shared their views, not like that silly Leni, climbed up from the bottom of the valley every so often. She would take winding paths so as not to be followed and bring blackened pans full of food, bags of provisions, bottles and cigarettes. But it was risky, so they mostly managed by themselves, crossing the border to Austria where there was no danger and they could even go to the shops.

Sometime earlier, the Bavarian chemist with fingers fluttering like butterflies had returned to the cave, panting from the effort of dragging his huge baby thighs all the way up there. He had topped up their supplies of raw materials—which was neither food, nor grappa, nor cigarettes. He had also brought along what would make that inert material alive and exciting: wire, fuses, detonators. He'd given final instructions but hadn't stayed long: he really didn't care for the life of an explorer. He was a civilized man! A city man! An intellectual! One day, the war would finally break out in Südtirol, he thought, and then these mountain people who stank like goats and hid in caves like in the Stone Age, would realize that only they, the pan-Germans from across the border, could lead them. Meanwhile, they might as well be useful.

And now, hidden in the ditch next to the motorway, on a night of the waning moon, Peter was fearlessly tinkering with sticks of dynamite and fuses. He didn't picture the faces of his future victims, the Carabinieri on duty who would be passing there a few hours later. If he really had to think about his targets—which he almost never did—he thought of uniforms, ranks, machine guns and, mostly, of sentences in a language with too many vowels that called for you to halt.

He was working, his fingers agile even in the dark. His opaque eyes had never needed much light, and the crescent moon over which clouds floated like the figures of a magic lantern was enough for him. The clover crushed by his boots gave off a fresh, sour smell.

He picked one and put it in his mouth. He felt an explosion of sharp, peppery taste which made him happier than he had ever been. Happier than that time when the Carabinieri had surrounded him but he had managed to escape. Happier than when he had entered Leni's body on their wedding night. Happier than when he had killed his first chamois. Happier than when his mother was nursing him and—at the age of twenty Johanna could still do it—smiling at him. Happier than before he was born, and the world was One.

The happiness Peter felt was blinding, luminous, total. Perhaps even eternal.

When her sixteen-year-old cousin Sebastian, known as Wastl, laughed, he sounded like a woodpecker digging a nest in a trunk: "T-t-t, t-t-t, t-t-t!." To Eva, it was the most cheerful sound in the world: whenever she heard it, she was shaken from top to toe by a laughter the reason for which was irrelevant. This, too, her cousin-uncle, who was almost a man, had taught her: that you could always find a reason to laugh, laugh, and then laugh some more, if you really wanted to.

In the field between the Hubers' maso and that of Leni's parents, Wastl was showing off an imitation of a distant relative who liked Schnaps a little too much. *"Madoja, oschpele, hardimitz'n"*[32] mumbled Wastl, swaying with the dignity of a drunkard, almost falling over his intertwined legs; there was no doubt he was about to end up on his face but no, he managed to stand up, then he would arch his back and almost fall backwards . . .

Eva watched with her mouth open, her eyes shining, breathless, her belly sore. She was laughing uncontrollably. Next to her, Ulli, her other cousin, a year older than her, was laughing a little because of Wastl, and a little because of Eva, who was now spread on the ground like a broken doll and couldn't stop giggling, not just at the drunken imitation, but because laughter had made her limbs limp and she was unable to stand up, and then because Wastl and Ulli had started laughing at her, and finally because, when the desire to laugh hasn't stopped yet and nothing can be done, you have to drink it up, until the last spasm in your solar plexus, until the last tickle in your throat.

When Leni appeared in the hayloft, they were still laughing, but no sooner had they seen her face than all three of them stopped abruptly.

Leni approached Wastl and said something to him. Eva, who

---

[32] Swear words.

was still only four, didn't understand much. She just understood that it had something to do with Ulli's *Tata*, the one who wasn't there. And now, judging from Leni's confused words, he would carry on not being there, but differently. For the first time in her life Eva noticed something: that there are many ways in which a father can be not there, but some are worse than others.

Gerda sat before the same officer who, sometime earlier, had called her in to request information about Peter. This time, it was he who imparted information: her brother had been blown up while preparing an attack. He was no longer outraged, but rather stiff with embarrassment. How do you express condolences to the sister of a man whose death has avoided the one he was planning for five of your fellow soldiers? Gerda thought she felt in her chest the explosion that had torn her brother to pieces. Her heart stopped. So did her breath, and the growth of her nails and hair.

The soldier standing next to the desk was also the same one as the previous time. He leaned toward her and with awkward concern asked if she had understood. Gerda half closed her eyes and this was correctly interpreted as a "Yes." He offered her a glass of water and she cocked her head: "No."

The officer reassured her: she didn't have to worry, his remains had already been identified by the wife of the deceased. Gerda wanted to stand up but didn't quite know where she had put her legs and hands, and yet she'd had them when she'd come in. When she found them again, she stood up without a word and left the room, supporting herself against the wall.

The soldier ran after her and, on the same spot on the sidewalk where the other time he'd asked her out to dance, he said, "My condolences."

She looked at him like someone searching for something. "He with me, once . . . an *Ausflug* . . . How do you say?"

The soldier spoke a few words of German but couldn't remember that one. He felt sorry for it. Gerda walked away, straight and stiff like a sentry box in the barracks. She knew only this: that if she didn't lower her head or curve her shoulders, if she could walk in a precise line, without smudging it with wayward steps, then she would be able to reach Frau Mayer's hotel. Only when she had disappeared behind the block did the soldier remember.

An outing.

Ausflug is an outing.

Peter was not buried in the town's largest cemetery but in the tiny village gathered around the bulb-shaped belfry on the northern side of the mountain.

The living had been generous to the dead: on that steep, vertical land, they had dedicated to the little cemetery, surrounded by a low lime wall, a precious plot of flat land which stretched out, like a minute soul, toward the imposing vastness of the glaciers. For centuries, it had been the Hubers' final resting place. Even the younger offspring, the ones who through the hard but necessary law of the maso were kicked out to go and seek their fortunes elsewhere, were welcomed back, in death, to the soil of their forbears. A cemetery is certainly not like a hayfield which, when parcelled out, drives everyone to poverty within a few generations; in a cemetery people cultivate memory and identity, facts decided by destiny that never diminish, not even if shared with others. This is where Hermann's parents were buried after the Spanish flu had swept them away, both on the same night. This is where Johanna rested and, next to her, there was space for her husband. This is where they buried Peter.

Crowded funerals for *Bumser* people were a thing of the past. Tens of thousands of South Tyroleans had taken part in the funeral procession of Sepp Kerschbaumer, the gentle idealist who'd died in prison after the conclusion of the Milan trial. However, nobody understood these new terrorists who not only struck at Fascist monuments or electricity pylons but also at people, even if those people wore uniforms. They killed and maimed then ran across the border, giving soldiers an excuse to make the lives of family members in the maso even harder, as had happened right there during that raid, just over two years earlier.

That day was still spoken of with terror, as well as with incredulity and relief: it really had happened *right there*, where the last noteworthy event had been the passage of a Russian prisoner who'd escaped during the Great War. And that helicopter! It had appeared in the sky like a *deus ex machina* in reverse, a dazzling incarnation of Evil which, however—as everybody knew because every line of the dialogue between the two officers had been repeated countless times—had been vanquished by an unlikely hero, the officer commanding the raid, the very man who until that moment had played the part of the bad guy. It therefore didn't seem strange that Peter, the search for whom had been the trigger behind the event, was buried there. The soldiers were welcome to come back and look for him now: they would find him, with no need for all that *Schweinerei*[33] again.

Now, the bells, whose noon tolling the soldiers on board their vans had once mistaken for a warning signal, were ringing for a funeral. Lukas, the sacristan, a little older now, the hairs on his sinewy forearms a little grayer, was pulling at the thick rope hanging from the belfry. The hollow sound seemed to be descending, as though weighed down by its own load, into the town, toward the highway from which, every so often, rose the isolated rumble of a car engine, toward the river that glistened in the July light at the bottom of the valley.

[33] Pigsty. Mess.

Besides his closest relatives, there was just a small group of *Schützen* there to pay homage to Peter, the comrades with whom he had boarded the Bus of Tears in order to attend the Milan trial. They hadn't followed him in his more extreme choices, hadn't gone to hide in the forest or ordered attacks; however, they had carried on with the parades for the redemption of the *Heimat* on *Herz-Jesu* day, the anniversary of the heroic resistance against Napoleon. Once, while peeling potatoes in her *Stube*, Maria had silently wondered what all that display of weapons, those marches, and those orders, screamed worse than at war, had to do with the heart of Our Lord. And Sepp had said that as far as he knew Napoleon hadn't bothered anyone for a century and a half, not even that poor devil buried in the soil, who now had a right to rest.

More and more people thought that way about the *Schützen*. As for those with their *Lederhosen*, their waistcoats with green and red straps, their white lace socks, and little shoes with silver buckles, they really looked as though they had remained stuck in the times when Napoleon was waging war on Europe. The *Schützen*, who were the last remaining terrorist sympathizers, would have liked to fire a few blank shots in Peter's honor, as befitting the memory of a hero; but, during that period of attacks and checkpoints, the authorities had suspended the Schützen their privilege of bearing arms, even those ridiculous trombone-shaped rifles that followed such inconsistent and random trajectories that it was a miracle you didn't shoot yourself in the face. Therefore, no salute, just a wreath of flowers and a scroll with Gothic lettering: *Im Schoß der Heimaterde*, in the womb of the native soil.

Leni stared at the coffin. She was the only one there who had seen its contents. Seeing with her own eyes the matter that had been her husband (she had identified him through a scar on a fragment of ankle) had left neither pain, nor repulsion, nor anger but rather a kind of cosmic perplexity. Ulli and Sigi hung from her arms like small, unripe fruits, a question on their uncertain little faces: would this incomprehensible storm leave them attached to the branch, or would it, sooner or later, knock them down to the ground?

Hermann was reasonably presentable. He had washed, shaved, and even his Sunday suit was clean, with just a moth hole here and there. The last hands to soap it, rinse it, hang it out to dry, then put it back in the drawer with bags of rice against the damp, had been Johanna's—whose funeral Hermann had attended in his work clothes, his truck loaded with timber parked outside the cemetery. However, as they lowered his son's coffin into the rectangular hole, the nakedness of his sorrow was almost obscene. His eyes looked like the genitals in a porn photo: as raw and impersonal as pure living flesh.

The bus from Bolzano got a flat tire on the way and Gerda arrived half an hour late. She'd also had to go and pick up Eva from the Schwingshackls. Trying to keep up with her mother's large strides, and clutching with her fat baby fingers her mother's now callous hand, Eva was ecstatic at this unexpected visit, but also worried. She was confused by her mother's drawn face, which hadn't smiled at her once, the expression with which she held her hand tight, and especially by the explanation she'd been given: Gerda had come to say a last goodbye to Uncle Peter. Not only did Eva have no memory of Uncle Peter, but what was a "last goodbye"? What if you say it to a person and then meet them again? Eva had asked Ulli to explain but even he didn't know what to answer. So they went together to Cousin Wastl, who had clarified everything once and for all.

"If, after you've said the 'last goodbye' to someone, you then meet them again and they say *Grüß Gott*[34], you must turn away and pretend you haven't heard. It's totally forbidden to

[34] A form of greeting.

use another greeting once you've said your 'last goodbye,' as the word implies."

It wasn't that difficult after all, Wastl had added, you just had to pay attention. You could still talk to the person, and even ask how they were doing, but you had to be very careful never to use any form of greeting, *griastl, servus, pfiati* and (definitely not) *fwiedersehaugn*. You especially must never say "see you soon" again.

By the time they reached the cemetery, the coffin was already in the ground. Gerda stood apart, watching the undertaker throwing shovelfuls of soil on the pine coffin. A *Schütze*, of about thirty, the same age as Peter, approached. "Your brother was a hero," he said softly. Not to her but to the cleavage that peered out of the white shirt under the black, mourning pinafore. Then he smiled at her as though everything was agreed between them, and Gerda did not lower her eyes.

Eva, however, was worried. Uncle Peter, to whom she had to say her last goodbye, had already gone and she hadn't been able to see his face. So now how would she recognize him if she met him? How could she be certain she wouldn't say goodbye to him again and inadvertently say, "see you soon"?

Later, as they were leaving the cemetery, Gerda said to Eva, "That man's your *Opa*[35]."

They'd just put a bunch of flowers in a pewter vase engraved with a heart around the letters Jhs on Johanna's grave. As they were walking away, a tall man who was too thin for his moth-eaten suit had approached the headstone.

Gerda had said it without looking back: obviously the blood link between her daughter and "that man" didn't concern her. Eva kept staring at the man. She saw him remove the flowers she and Gerda had put in the pewter vase and throw them into the alleys between the two graves, the no man's land

[35] Grandfather.

that separates the dead. The man looked up and met her gaze. She started walking, her face turned back so she could keep looking at him, her hand held tight by her mother, who was on her way to the iron gate, and tripped on a black marble headstone.

That's how Eva learned what an *Opa* was: a skinny old man who makes you feel sad to be alive if he looks you in the eye.

The owner of the small ground-floor room where Gerda lived when she wasn't working let her stay there with her little girl. Even though they were right in the middle of the summer season, there were few tourists during that year of bombs and attacks, and many rooms were vacant. Eva was lying on the bed next to her mother's body, in a slip. She demanded that body like when she was an unweaned baby.

She knew very well that four was too old to be given the breast, but on that unscheduled evening, Gerda was more patient than usual, and Eva intended to take advantage.

There was a knock at the door. Unpleasant things that have no reason to exist should be ignored, so Eva carried on trying to sneak under her mother's armpit, breathing in. But Gerda raised herself on her elbow and tensed up, listening. There was another knock, accompanied by a man's voice: "Gerda? *Bische do?*"[36]

Pulling her muslin slip down to her knees, Gerda went to open the door. It was the Schütze who, at the cemetery, had called Peter a hero. He was no longer in the uniform of the Andreas Hofer followers, but in normal peasant clothes. His eyes were sparkling with drink, but not a lot of drink, just enough to get his courage up.

"Is Eva asleep?" he asked, putting a hand on Gerda's bare shoulder.

She looked at Eva, who, from the bed, was staring at the

[36] "Gerda, are you in?"

intruder with silent dislike, then pushed the man's hand off her shoulder.

"No," she replied and closed the door in his face.

So that was something else Eva learned that day: not being asleep keeps you safe.

I can picture two travelers. They come from far away, perhaps from another continent, like the Indians in the compartment next door, who are constantly talking on their cellphones, or the American girls. One is looking at the Italy that runs past the window on the right, the other one on the left.

Two worlds. On the right-hand side of the train, the promontory of Gaeta springs like the mythical head of a cetacean from the waters of the Mediterranean. Descending toward the glistening sea are olive and citrus groves, yellow, fuchsia, and red fields. Colors of abundance, of generosity, of a good life. On the left-hand side, in the distance, there's a parade of rough, hard, grim inland mountains. Even though they're much lower than our glaciers, they're no less intimidating. Even the climates are different. A young, spring light is shining on the plain and the sea; inland, however the peaks are wrapped in gloomy, heavy clouds that seem to have been produced by the mountains themselves.

"What a sunny, fertile, cheerful country," says the first traveler.

"It's so desolate, harsh, hostile . . . " says the second.

When they tell each other what they've seen, nobody will believe that they've traveled along the same stretch of Italy.

On the four or, at most, five-hour journey between the Brenner and Bologna, there's always a restaurant car. There's bound to be one on the Rome-Reggio Calabria train. But no.

"There used to be one but they removed it," the train attendant says when he appears at the compartment doors, announced by the clanking of the refreshments trolley. He brings water, carbonated drinks, salted crackers, mass produced snacks. The reason why the only edible things on this train are all junk food is something I learned at school, and which has a ponderous, important name: the "South Question"

The American girls buy two bags of chips.

"And what would you like, Signorina?"

"Those." I indicate a box of chocolate cookies.

"Two euros ten. Do you have the right change, Signora?"

I count it out into the palm of his hand, the exact amount to the cent.

"Thank you, Signorina."

Signorina, Signora, Signorina. I'm used to it. My age, in strangers' estimations, sways like a cable car in a thunderstorm. I just smile, as though both forms of address were necessary.

The attendant is a handsome young man, almost exaggeratedly Southern: an open smile, eyebrows joining above his nose, the narrow hips of a dancer. The strategy of Trenitalia is crystal-clear: go ahead and remove the restaurant car, just keep the staff looking good. A shame that his movements leave no doubt that he's a homosexual. What a waste, I think.

Speak for yourself, Ulli replies. Just as if he were sitting next to me on this southbound train.

When I was a little girl I wondered: why is it that Ulli never paws me? All the boys of my age did it, or tried to, or waited to pluck up the courage to. But not him. Never. Was it because we'd grown up together? Because he was my cousin? You must be kidding. Getting your hands on your teenage cousins is a rite of passage, almost a social obligation. So that wasn't the problem. But then why not? I had no idea.

Ulli's puberty seemed to go on forever. By the time his voice began to break, the other boys had been looking at my neckline a lot more than into my eyes for a while. His peers were already dressing up their desperate urge for sex with vulgar casualness, while he still didn't have a single hair on his body. Then, one day, when he was almost twenty, Ulli told me he'd been with a woman. Following a well-established tradition, his sexual initiation had been undertaken by a German tourist.

"Was she beautiful?" I asked.

"She was skilled," he replied, and I knew I had nothing to fear. He talked about it as though it was a completed task, a milestone reached. There was nothing strange there: all young boys talk like that about the loss of virginity. But in their case, finding a girl who'd go *all the way*, and being able to cling to her precariously and clumsily at least once, was just a catalyst to do it again, and again, and again. Ulli, however, looked like a climber who had come back down after going up Mount Everest: now that he'd reached the peak, he didn't have to go back up any more.

When he confided in me his first relationship with a man, he was completely different: his eyes were dilated from the enormous discovery, its terror and excitement.

"This is what I am," he said, as though he'd found his own name after a long search. And never again did he mention that North European girl, his first and his last.

Only many years later, when he'd already heard people (men, never women, not even the most narrow-minded ones) say to him things like, "Hitler is what your sort need,"; when his mother had already assured him that, naturally, she still loved him, but that he should simply go to the doctor and that, nowadays, there was no disease that was incurable, so there was sure to be a medicine for this one too; only after he'd already been to Berlin and London, where he'd felt like a man among many—hooray!—a banal homosexual man; after I'd already lent him my bed several times so that he and his lovers wouldn't roam around the woods like cats on heat, after all that had already happened, only then did he confess that, in order to be able to penetrate the girl's long, blonde body, he'd had to close his eyes and imagine that she was a man.

As usual, we were in the warm cabin of Marlene. There had been little snow and the cannons for whitening the ski pistes even in the warmest winters weren't there yet. Every night, Ulli would struggle against the patches of brown that grew wider, like melanomas on the skin of the mountain, shoveling, distributing, and moving snow from the edges of the pistes to the center. He always told me everything, or so I thought. About the train station toilets; about his military service in Veneto ("not all soldiers go with women, you know? Least of all officers."); about meetings in public parks, almost faceless bodies, disembodied genitals. And yet he'd been so ashamed of the secret fantasies he needed in order to possess that only woman, he'd kept quiet about them for years. I couldn't understand this. So I asked him to explain.

Ulli was maneuvering the large shovel at the front of Marlene. He was sitting in profile, in his eyes the reflection of the snow lit up by the headlights.

"You've no idea how often it happens, to how many women. I know, because I know their husbands."

He used the lever next to the steering wheel to stop the shovel full of snow, which remained halfway up in the air. He turned to look at me. He still had the roebuck eyes from when he was a child, and eyelashes too long for an adult. "Eva, no woman deserves that kind of lie."

And he stroked my face. It was a brief, light, protective touch.

Question: if a man who loves men could love a woman, would this woman finally feel loved?

A useless question. Ulli is dead, so I'll never know.

The plain has grown wider, and now there's more space between the sea and the mountains. The contrast is now smoother: the soil of the plain is less red, shameless and fertile, and the mountains in the background less forbidding. We pass a tiny station and a blue sign runs outside the window. I read it quickly before it disappears: MINTURNO SCAURI.

Then, with a screech of the brakes, the train stops right in front of a huge industrial hangar emerging from the countryside like a spaceship. There's a sign in huge letters: MANULI FILM. Just outside my window, a billboard illustrates its activities. The train isn't leaving yet, so I have time to read it.

PRODUCTS: *Mineral water, other, carbonated drinks, cocoa, coffee, infusions, tea, sugar, meat and derivatives, tobacco industry, graphics/publishing industry, fresh pasta, dried pasta, rice, ready meals, baked products, sweets, fish, fruit and vegetables, frozen foods, cosmetics, sauces, dressings, seasonings, salt, soft drinks.*

PACKAGING: *Bag in box, plastic bottles, multifunction envelopes, envelopes, pillow packs, labels (sleeve, decorations, seals), plastic film joined together and co-extruded, mono-material plastic film, thermal retractable film, wrapping material, adhesive tape.*

A complete list, obviously. Shame, though, that the Manuli Film hangar should be empty, and that weeds should be sprouting from cracked cement forr, and that the windows have never been fitted. There's a whitish dog lying on the stretch of dirt track behind the billboard.

When the train starts again with a squeaking noise, the dog remains motionless, enjoying the sunshine.

Shortly after Sessa Aurunca, the American girls, while

munching their chips, stop reading and look outside. As luck would have it, at that very moment we enter a tunnel. And so their eyes can feast on one of Italy's most famous and renowned beauties that is the envy of all the world: the white strip that zigzags past in the darkness of the vaulted tunnel.

1967-1968

The old woman was about seventy, but ten or twenty years from now she wouldn't be all that different. Under the handkerchief tied beneath her chin, her cheeks were marked by intricate, purple capillaries. She was hunched over, one shoulder lower than the other, her hands leaning on the handle of the stick she held very straight in front of her legs. She was wearing a long skirt, like her grandmother had: the twentieth century, which was already two-thirds of the way through, had taken a lot away from her, but left enough fabric for making skirts. Above her skirt there was a forget-me-not-colored *Bauernschurtz*, boiled wool gray slippers with leather soles.

There were four coffins in front of her, covered with white cloth, tall candles, flowers. The picket Alpini were young men, the same as, until yesterday, those who were lying inside. They had their arms behind their backs in an alert at-ease position, and the sad, impartial expression one wears when everything has already happened and what is about to happen hasn't started yet.

A few hours earlier, Prime Minister Aldo Moro had paid his final respects to the four victims of the terrorists. He had stayed in the chapel of rest for a long time, hands linked in front of his body, shoulders low, embarrassed pity on his face. Next to him, the right-eye monocle of General De Lorenzo caught the photographers' flashes.

A charge of explosives had knocked down an electricity

pylon in Cima Vallona, Porzescharte in German, on the border between Eastern Tyrol and the region of Belluno. It was a trap: anti-personnel mines awaited the Italian soldiers who rushed to the location of the explosion. When the soldiers Armando Piva, Francesco Gentile, Mario Di Lecce, and Olivo Dordi, reached the fallen electricity pylon, they were blown up inside their van.

In addition to politicians and generals, thousands of people visited the resting chapel. German-speaking South Tyroleans, Italians from Alto Adige, from Comelico, from Cadore, soldiers, tourists. Any sympathy for the attackers' motivations had now run out. Nothing in the experience of the residents of San Candido, where the bodies were displayed, gave any meaning to this violence. A young peasant whose skin was already cooked by the sun, a navy-blue apron over his white shirt, stood by the bodies for a while, his head down. Then it was the turn of the old woman.

She didn't know the names of the four Alpini. Maybe they'd told her but they were Italian names, difficult to remember. They didn't matter to her: names are the least of anyone's worries. She stroked the coffins one by one. They were closed: an anti-personnel mine is not kind to the body that passes over it.

Over a quarter of a century earlier, the war had taken away from her four sons. They were more or less the age of the Alpini shut away in the four coffins, give or take a year. She hadn't been able to say goodbye to her sons, and all she had to mourn were the letters from the brigade headquarters. Their names, of course, were there, inscribed in the marble at the entrance to the cemetery, with the names of other fallen soldiers. But there's not a lot you can do with a name. A name doesn't reap the hay, doesn't fix the tiles on the roof. Names are the least of your worries.

The four young men were dead, just like her sons, what did it matter that their names were not Sepp, Gert, Manfred and

Hans, but Francesco, Mario, Olivo, Armando? The name of the place where they had fallen didn't matter either: Porzescharte, Cima Vallona, what was the difference? They were dead, her sons were dead, and all you can do for the dead is pray.

The old woman pulled a rosary out of her apron pocket, and began.

Silvius Magnago spread his elbows, bent his head forward, leaned his forehead on the interlaced hands over his desk. The shoulders of his suit, always too wide for his skinny frame, rose like wings on the back of his neck. His thick, black-rimmed glasses were in front of him, next to the pen, and the crutches were leaning parallel to the wood paneling on the wall.

He remained like this, hunched over, his forehead on his desk, his eyes shut. He was tired. In June, in Porzescharte, or Cima Vallona as the Italians called it, four soldiers had been killed in a horrific attack. In July, the Neo-Fascists had demonstrated in Bolzano in favor of "the fundamental Italian nature of Alto Adige." In September, at Trento Station, a bag had exploded in the hands of police officers Filippo Foti and Edoardo Martini, killing both on the spot. It was to be the last deadly attack by South Tyrolean terrorism, but Magnago had no way of knowing that. The TV news had broadcast one of his statements, issued right from that desk.

"The recent dynamite attacks have left a deep mark on the Alto Adige population, whatever their language. It is only with the tools of democracy that problems can be solved. We refuse to believe that they can be solved with violence."

He had delivered it in his impeccable Italian, but his German accent had come across as harder than usual. The Italian television caption had presented him as follows: Silvius Magnago, leader of Südtiroler Volkspartei, former Wehrmacht.

He hadn't felt this tired since the war years.

Besides, there was this heavy new atmosphere in the sleeper car. Now, when they traveled to Rome with him, the members of Parliament and senators of the Südtiroler Volkspartei— whose leader he still was, after all—no longer came to his compartment for a nightcap before bed: they'd wish him good night frostily then retire to their couchettes. Magnago knew what they said behind his back: that he'd sold out to the Italians; that they considered his attempts at bringing together the Italian government, the Austrian authorities, and representatives of Alto Adige Italians, as petty political bargaining; that they were muttering about the *Heimat* being sold off, about too much *Realpolitik*; that they uttered the word *Kompromiss* like the worst possible insult.

Yet he also knew that the only alternatives to Kompromiss are heroes and, from Andreas Hofer to Sepp Kerschbaumer, Südtirol had had its fill of heroes. Even those wicked bombers who carried on killing probably thought themselves to be heroes. Magnago knew he was the only one able to obtain from the Italian government those guarantees of linguistic and administrative control that his people had been waiting for for half a century, precisely because there was nothing of the hero about him.

He raised his hollow face. Before him, on the walnut desk, there was a stack of papers: the first draft of the Autonomy Statute of the future autonomous province of Bolzano. He would still need to take tiring trips to Rome, engage in exhausting negotiations, before it would assume its definitive form: one hundred and thirty-seven articles, thirty-one marginal notes. There was still a lot to do.

Silvius Magnago rubbed his eyes, put on his glasses, and picked up the first sheet of paper.

When they were together, Gerda would take Eva into her

large bed in the small ground-floor room. Eva would cling to her, her mother's body both the lifeboat and the ocean where she would lose herself. And Gerda let her.

Eva had started to notice that she didn't have a father like the other children. She wasn't the only one: Ulli and Sigi, for instance, didn't have one either. But they'd lost theirs, whereas she'd never had one. She wasn't sure what the difference was but there clearly was one.

Another thing Eva had never had: new shoes. She'd always inherited Ruthi's old ones or those of her sisters, and even Ulli's boy's shoes. However, Gerda had been promoted to cook, her salary had increased, so she had decided to buy her a pair. Now, sitting on the bench in the shop beneath the town porticos, Eva couldn't believe there was such beauty at the end of her shins. They were solid shoes, with rubber crepe soles, but to her they were more splendid than if they'd been made of black patent.

When they left the shop, Eva walked with her eyes down, not to miss the sight of the new shoes that followed her every step.

"That's your father."

Eva was reluctant to look away from her feet, but what her mother had just said wasn't something you heard every day. At the age of five, she had never yet heard it.

"The one in the dark suit."

Eva looked up. There was more than one man in a dark suit on the sidewalk and in the street.

"Which one?"

"The one looking at us."

Several men were looking at Gerda, but not because they were the father of her child.

"*Giamo*,"[37] Gerda said with a sudden impatience. She took

---

[37] "Let's go."

her by the hand and dragged her away with long strides. Eva carried on searching the passing men for a resemblance, a specific sign, a clear trace of belonging. But she couldn't find it: when he'd seen Gerda and that little girl, Hannes Staggl's face had turned the color of the geraniums on the balcony beneath which he was passing, and he'd already walked away. The young woman at his arm, elegant and slim, in a coat that Audrey Hepburn could have worn, asked, "Who was that woman?"

"What woman?"

"The one with the little girl."

"I didn't see a little girl," Hannes replied to his fiancée.

3:45 A.M.

At 3:45 A.M., while patrolling the guard stations, I was reaching station 6 North-West, which was assigned, as per—

The pen wasn't writing anymore. The ink must have dried up. He slipped it under his clothes, under his armpit, like a thermometer. It would take a couple of minutes to warm up enough to write again. He struggled to move his fingers despite the woolen gloves.

The staff sergeant had decided not to add wood to the stove. There was only a small heap piled up against the wall of the old finance police hut. Also, he would make too much noise going out and coming back in and he didn't want to deprive those asleep of even just one minute of the remaining fifteen minutes' sleep before the change of guard. Still, it was bitterly cold. The kind of cold you just can't imagine unless you've known it. How can you convey this kind of cold to someone from Reggio Calabria?

He'd tried to describe it the first time he'd been back home on leave (forty-eight hours on the train there and back, seventy-two with his family): "You feel your fingers, your feet, and your nose burning, not from the heat but from the cold."

"Burning?" his mother had repeated, perplexed.

It was pointless. The cold up there was like the sea, you couldn't describe it to someone who'd never been there. The night before, the thermometer had plummeted to minus twenty-three Celsius. But the worst time wasn't at night. Even then, with the wind hitting your face like a spiked shoe, and homesickness which always grows stronger in the dark, night time wasn't all that bad, with those stars as pure as gemstones and that all-enveloping silence like the dome of a basilica. It was dawn that was ugly, with its promise of sun and heat, which it betrayed with that humid, gray light that made your bones stiffen worse than before. It was horrible to force a nineteen-year-old auxiliary, grown incapable of thinking through solitude, to wash his face.

He was a non-commissioned officer, he'd gone to school and was prepared. But these conscripted boys who were born in Salemi, Sibari or Bisceglie, they just couldn't cope with being at 2,000 meters without going down into the valley for months on end.

Of course he'd also found it tough when he'd first arrived in Alto Adige.

He had enrolled at the German language course for non-commissioned officers of his own free will. He liked the idea of chewing on another language, even though he'd only spoken Calabrian at elementary school. In fact, he hadn't found it too hard, nor driven his teacher to despair, like that guy from Bari who, when asked *"Wie alt bist du?"*[38] always replied, "One meter sixty-three!"

Alto Adige was the right place for serving your country in danger, of that he was convinced, so after his two years of training, he took his oath and was proud to go.

His first disappointment was when he arrived at the bar-

---

[38] "How old are you?"

racks near Merano. Headquarters wasn't prepared for such a large dispatch of soldiers, and everything was provisional. The courtyard was full of weeds, the dormitories filthy and with peeling walls, so there were one hundred men cramped together in a single place with all their bodily smells, just a tent to separate him and the other Carabinieri from the Alpini. There was no kitchen, so meals were cooked on large camp stoves that stank of kerosene, and there wasn't even a mess, so you had to eat in the freezing courtyard from the same mess tins you then used for washing yourself.

And forget about the troops. These young conscripted and auxiliary Carabinieri had been selected of course, but not for their abilities. On the contrary: military service in Alto Adige was a punishment.

Many could barely read or write, and hardly had any sense of discipline or order. More than once, at 6 A.M., when it was his turn to do reveille, the staff sergeant had narrowly avoided being hit in the face with a shoe. The same boys who, after a month in the passes and screes, if asked the name of their hometown, would burst into tears like children.

And then there was the cold. What can a Calabrian possibly know about the cold? A Calabrian knows stifling heat and scirocco, he knows drought, he knows the cannibal sun that sinks its teeth into your head, and the wind that makes you mad, euphoric or unconscious; but a Calabrian certainly doesn't know this cold. The first time he'd experienced it was in the barracks courtyard, squatting like a beggar, eating soup that had frozen before he'd had the time to put his spoon into it. That was nothing compared to the freezing cold he was to suffer whilst patrolling the border crossings, but he didn't know that yet.

His only consolation, during those first months in Alto Adige, had been the pasta with chilies in a trattoria near Ponte Druso, owned by southerners, where he went with his comrades. And of course, there were the Fräulein.

He'd always pictured German women like the singing Kessler twins, with their never-ending long legs, glittering bodices, backcombed blonde hair. South Tyrolean women were not as elegant even though they were blondes, and didn't have toupees but plaits twisted around their heads like spare wheels. Still, you had to admit it: South Tyroleans legs were much more beautiful than Calabrian ones.

"These," the mad second lieutenant Genovese would say, "have a high center of gravity."

He'd spent the first year patrolling the border, the only Carabiniere among platoons of eighty or a hundred Alpini. Their mission: to stop terrorists from entering Italian soil. Or, better still, catch them so that he, who was on police duty, would hand them over to the law. They would hike up and down the passes beneath the peaks on the border between Italy and Austria—Passo Resia, Vetta d'Italia, Val Passiria. His backpack weighed over ninety pounds: weapons, machine guns, sleeping bag, tent and canvas, army meal supplies, mess tin with its little stove, shovel, pickax. All that on your back: the point was to go where no van could. They looked like tortoises, with all that stuff on their backs, except that nobody has ever ordered a tortoise to walk up to its waist in snow for hours on end.

They wouldn't return to the barracks for weeks.

By day, they walked along the watershed; at night they would make holes in the snow a couple of meters long, throw the tent canvas over it like a cover, camouflage it with some snow, then go to sleep inside. Two hours of sleep, two hours of watch. There was always a fierce wind blowing on the border—he came to realize that mountain passes are like open windows on both sides of the house, they compete. That's why they never put up the tents: if there was a snowstorm during the night, they wouldn't notice they were being blown away, they were so exhausted.

Already after the first week, some would start hallucinating. It was the cold, the lack of sleep, the tiredness. Those who were constipated would start hallucinating first, un-expelled toxins mixed with exhaustion going straight to the head. Every so often, someone would become delirious. Everyone, sooner or later, would start calling for his mom.

Sometimes, the staff sergeant wondered what the point of these operations was. A hundred soldiers clinging to a snow-covered slope are more visible than a line of armored cars, whereas the terrorists moved about skillfully, two or three at most, and knew every scree, every rock, every protrusion in these granite mountains, and would slip over the border and back beyond the boundary stones, like chamois, without leaving a trace.

As a matter of fact, they hadn't seen a single one.

However, the motto was, "Usi obbedir tacendo." Keep silent and obey. If he'd considered questioning orders he wouldn't have become a Carabiniere.

Another consolation was reaching the masi. There were some even at high altitude, especially in the neighboring valleys of Val Venosta, beneath the glaciers. It was normal to be welcomed by ten or even thirteen children. They were poor peasants with many children but they always had enough to eat. 50,000 lire was enough to produce a hot meal for the entire troop. The women would serve them then watched them eat, silently but without hostility. Not like some waiters in the town cafés, who pretended not to speak Italian and when he ordered a coffee, replied, *"Nichts verstehen"* or *"Wiederholen Sie auf Deutsch,"* so then he would enunciate with correct pronunciation, *"geben Sie mir bitte einen Kaffee,"* and then, Deutsch or not Deutsch, they had to bring him coffee. These mountain peasants, however, genuinely didn't speak Italian, and when he tried to communicate in German they didn't exactly smile but, well, almost. Then they would send their children up to the attic and give their eiderdowns to officers and non-commissioned officers, so that they could lie down on the tables of the *Stube*, in the warmth. He, however, would go into the hayloft with his men, without a single regret: lying in the fragrant hay, with the warm breath of the cows rising from the cowshed, you slept like a king.

Not so, here, in the hut abandoned by the customs police, where he couldn't sleep at night. During the day he'd lie on the camp bed for a couple of hours, and perhaps also have a snooze before evening. But never after dark. To keep awake, he would write. He brought along many notepads, the kind with the sheets bound together at the top, like the ones used by cartoon journalists. He also had pens, but now he realized he should get a supply of pencils instead: lead doesn't shrink in the cold like ink does. His handwriting was tidy, diligent and what he wrote was also precise: whether a magazine was jammed, how many tins of food had been used up, the sighting of a capercaillie. And, of course, the watch shifts.

He wrote on his rickety table, watching all those who slept and going out for a quick chat with those on watch. His hearing, which had always been sharp, had become even more so. He heard every sound in the night: the rustling of trees, the call of the night predators, the stones rumbling down the screes, the cracking of glaciers. Sometimes, he thought he could detect the buzzing of constellations that stood out with their sharp light from the cosmic blackness. That's when he knew he was really tired.

He was twenty-four years old while the eldest among his men was four years younger. He watched over them like a mother over sick children. After all, they were somewhat ill: with fear, isolation, cold, and homesickness. With silence, too. With that motionless, unknown mountain that gave birth to sons who could pop out of nowhere, massacre the bodies of fellow soldiers, then disappear again into her lap.

Right there, sometime earlier, terrorists had killed three customs officers. The border was less than ten meters away and, using a kind of zip wire, they'd run a bomb from Austrian territory to the windows of the hut. Three men had been blown up in their sleep and a fourth had been blinded. It was too dangerous for customs officers to remain there. And so, for almost three months, it had been the staff sergeant's lot to be there, in the hut in the pastures, and command a platoon of thirty men—well, men . . . it was hard to call these frightened boys that. They had dug out a dozen holes in the snow around the perimeter of the building, and when it was your turn to keep watch, you'd get into one of them, only your shoulders above ground like a pestle in a mortar. At night, he would place a soldier in every emplacement, but two or three were enough during the day. He'd put up a barricade of barbed wire all around and, as they used up the food supplies, they'd tie the empty sauce cans to it: all you had to do was touch a single point of the barbed wire and it would ring out like cow bells. Nobody would be able to approach the hut without making a racket.

A few yards beyond no man's land, there was an old Austrian customs house, much smaller than the Italian one. The zip wire that had killed the customs officers had been dispatched from there. He always kept an eye on it day and night. Was there anyone inside? Would they return and kill them from there? Sometimes, farther away, he could see two men with binoculars watching the horizon for hours. They never got close enough to be recognized. It was hard to resist the impulse to go check them out but the orders were quite definite: do not cross the border. The terrorists made relations between Italy and Austria tense enough as it was, the last thing they needed were skirmishes on the border.

He was a soldier, he wasn't in the business of politics. He used to think that Alto Adige folk, all of them, were ungrate-

ful traitors to the unity of the country. Then he had arrived in
Alto Adige. No sooner had he left the cities at the bottom of
the valley, with their factories full of southern workers, and
met the peasants, than he had immediately understood: there
was nothing Italian about the people here. However, terrorists
were bloodthirsty cowards who wouldn't even let you see their
faces.

Since the recent attacks on fellow soldiers, the atmosphere
in the barracks had become heavy. There was talk that an officer of the Alpini, a guy who used bombs and grenades as
paperweights and who, instead of the President of the
Republic, had a portrait of the Duce behind the desk, had
declared, "It's now the turn of a South Tyrolean."

The staff sergeant didn't want to hear such things, not even
as a joke. Then, a few days later, that young man from Val
Pusteria had been killed at a roadblock. The soldiers who shot
him were young conscripts, so it could only have been a tragic
error due to the tension. And yet, when it happened, he'd
remembered the officer's words and, for a moment, felt the
blood chill in his veins.

Now he had received an order: the Italian flag had to flut-
ter on the boundary stones. And so, every morning, the raising
of the flag was performed with pride by the soldier in charge.

However, there was another order to execute, which was no
less difficult because he'd given it to himself: to return every
one of these boys to his family.

There was a false alarm at least once every night. "I heard
someone cough," one of the men would say. Or else, "There's
a small light among the trees." And immediately, all the others
keeping watch would confirm that yes, they too had heard a
suspicious noise, seen a light, heard footsteps crunching in the
snow. They'd stir one another like pigeons. Or else he would
fire a reconnaissance flare with the Garand rifle, and in the
eight seconds between the shot and the little comets lighting

up in the sky, somebody would start screaming, terrified, "They're attacking!" and perhaps even start machine-gunning at random with the *Maschinengewehr*. In the morning, they would find larches and fir trees mown down, stone dead: no wonder they used to call the MG 42 "Hitler's saw." It was a miracle that there weren't any wounded among them yet. Thankfully, he didn't have to give his superiors an account of the ammunition.

Once when—by pure chance—the radio was working, he had begged for reinforcements: he'd explained to headquarters that the men were exhausted, that they couldn't take it anymore and, especially, that there weren't enough of them to take it in turns to keep watch. He could no longer guarantee the effectiveness of the service or the safety of his men. He'd even drafted an official report. *It has become necessary to replace the soldiers who have been here for over a month*—he had written. *I, the officer in charge can no longer answer for those who are in such an altered state of body and mind.* Then he had tied the envelope to the dangling wire attached to the belly of the helicopter that dropped supplies and ammunition.

Another month had passed. No reinforcements or replacements had arrived. And even the helicopter hadn't appeared for days because of the strong winds. They'd finished almost all the cans of food, and all they had left was a little flour. Those with a good aim had been given permission to go hunting, so they'd eaten the odd hare. But they were beginning to feel hungry. They'd spend the evening huddled around the radio, trying to make out the warm trace of human voices through the crackling. Like miners who go deeper into a dark and muddy gallery in search of rubies.

He took the pen from under his armpit. It gave out much more warmth than he felt inside. He read what he'd written up to then, and resumed his writing. The ink ran fluid once again.

3:45 A.M.

At 3:45 A.M., while patrolling the guard stations, I reached station 6 North-West, which was assigned, as per schedule of watch shifts, to the auxiliary Carabiniere Ciriello Salvatore until 4 A.M. I found it empty.

The staff sergeant paused. Then he crossed it out and corrected it.

I found it undefended.

When I got back inside, I went to the dormitory where, even though there were thirty-five minutes to go before the end of his approved watch shift, I found the above-mentioned auxiliary Carabiniere Ciriello Salvatore sleeping on his camp bed.

The staff sergeant re-read what he'd written. He took a deep sigh. He looked up at the peeling wall. He put the pen under his armpit: he wanted to take time to think without the ink freezing. But he didn't think for long. He resumed writing on his notepad in a hurry, with renewed urgency.

However, I finally decided not to write a report and not to punish the man responsible for the episode because he's just a boy who's dead tired and who hasn't slept properly for a month, and now he's also hungry and now this icy wind is making it impossible to keep your eyes open, so no wonder they're so exhausted and end up mad, but those people down there don't realize it, they really have no idea . . .

He stopped as though he'd been running: suddenly, with a residual thrust that almost made him fall over.

He never showed this personal notepad to anyone, certainly not to his superiors. Even so, just to be careful, the staff sergeant began to cover the words "Ciriello" and "Salvatore" with thick lines of the pen. The name of the guilty auxiliary Carabiniere vanished in a black patch.

You never know.

Instead, he put his own name at the bottom of the page. As though this page of the notebook were an official report, a document for whose contents he took full responsibility, as a soldier and a non-commissioned officer.

Then he signed: *Staff Sergeant Vito Anania.*

Kilometer 903 - 960

T he greenhouses of Villa Literno roll by in the distance: you can't see either the tomatoes or the foreign-born slaves without whom they would rot. A long tunnel takes us to Bagnoli, an uninterrupted series of industrial ruins. They're surrounded by tumbledown apartment. Blocks coated in peeling plaster of an unmistakable color, one we've always given a specific name: *fascistagrau*, or "Fascist gray." It's the color of the houses Fascism built in Alto Adige for all the employees it imported en masse in order to Italianize it: teachers, civil servants, road workers and especially rail workers. It's the color of an era and an ideology, but for me it's also an ensemble of smells. As a child, whenever I went past the houses next to the station, which bore the inscription ANNO IX EF under the cornice, I'd smell aromas unknown in the Schwingshackls' kitchen drifting out through the windows: the acidic smell of tomato passata, soup with Parmesan. Nice smells, but which I didn't stop to inhale: after all, I had nothing to do with the homes of the *Walschen*.

Relations between us, *Daitsch* children, and Italian kids were simple: they didn't exist. They were Walschen, precisely; we were "Krauts" or at most, "pylons" in homage to the electricity pylons our terrorists enjoyed blowing up so much. There were districts, areas of influence, territories. It was preferable for us to keep walking straight past the houses of the rail workers, and the same when we were among the social houses behind the barracks where the soldiers' families resided. The children who lived there seemed totally inscrutable and fierce to me, even though, if you thought about it, they were probably as frightened of us Germans: there were many more of us. In any case I didn't play with them. Never.

Then, when I went to high school as a boarder in Bolzano, I found myself rubbing shoulders with children who'd lived in *fascistagrau*-colored houses. Now they were grown up, there was nothing inscrutable about them. On the contrary. While my German peers would throw coarse remarks, prickly like timber, at the girls, the Italians searched me with velvet eyes. I need not say which I preferred.

Ulli agreed with me, wholeheartedly, in fact. When he went to do his military service, the soft sentiments of Italian boys were a revelation to him. And the sadness that grew within him, the sadness which took him away in the end, was also partly due to that: with us he only met men who had sex as a physical need, something which isn't good manners to mention in one's own life, and which is done in the dirtiest place in the house. Ulli, too, had done it that way for many years, but only because he hadn't found anything better. When he did fall in love, it was with a boy from the south, as it happens.

One night, when Marlene was combing the snow on the tracks with its caterpillars, Ulli said to me, "I'm in love."

His name was Costa, he was Greek, he had long hands and dark eyes, and worked in a pub in Innsbruck. When the winter season was over, he and Costa were going to live together. Ulli couldn't stop saying his name: Costa, Costa, Costa, Costa. He also said, "I am his, and he is mine."

Then, "When we're together I understand why I was born" and "Our love is bigger than we are."

Ulli had started to talk like fortune cookies.

I should have been very happy for him. But I wasn't. Not at

all. What was happening to Ulli was that thing everybody talks about, sings about, writes about. The only thing, they say, which, alone, makes life worth living, opens the doors to heaven, hell, and all the secrets next to which nothing else is important.

That night, it was as though my friend, almost my brother, had suddenly revealed that he was the secret son of an emperor, and the owner of boundless riches, palaces and servants, and that he'd been eating bread and onions with me until thenout of sheer curiosity.

That's how I felt: poor.

"How nice. I'm happy for you."

I couldn't expect Ulli to believe me, he knew me too well.

As a matter of fact, he stole a glance at me but didn't reply. Perhaps he appreciated the effort it took for me to lie to him, that first and only time.

There was a lot of snow that winter, not only in our mountains but also farther south. The television news showed pictures of a white St Peter's Square, with the fountains on either side of the obelisk embellished with ice patterns like lace. That year, the ski pistes were easy to beat, the skiers were enthusiastic, the hotels full. In other words it was an abundant year. But not for me.

And now, when I look out, I feel like one of two travelers sitting on different sides of the train, seeing two different landscapes from their windows. At least Ulli did once catch a glimpse from his window of the vast horizon of love. Just as my mother did from her window. Whereas I have been married, divorced, chased, I've had men waiting for just a sign from me; I've felt desire, esteem, affection—for example for Carlo. But I still remember clearly my mother with Vito, and Ulli's eyes as he said, "Costa! Costa!" and I can tell the difference.

I must have sat by the wrong window.

I met Carlo in a beautiful villa outside Bolzano. It was at the inauguration of a large private design studio, an event I had organized. It was the end of the evening and everything had gone well, the many guests had had a good time. I could finally relax a little. It's perhaps superfluous to mention that Carlo was without his wife. What I remember of that first conversation was that, at some point, he said, "The majority of Italian-speaking Alto Adige residents think that you German-speaking South Tyroleans are all Nazis."

I replied, "The majority of German-speaking South Tyroleans thinks that you Italian-speaking Alto Adige residents are all Fascists."

"They should form an alliance and wage war on the rest of the world. Except that I'm not a Fascist. Are you a Nazi?"

"No."

"I didn't think so. I'm the son of a rail worker from Isernia and a teacher from Salerno, but I was born and I live in Bolzano, the only place in the country where Italians actually feel like Italians, and not like Sicilians, Neapolitans, Venetians or Piedmontese. Unless they're actually Acitrezza residents— which is something completely different, so different in fact that you shouldn't ever confuse it with the people from Acireale."

"But at least," I said, "those who live from Verona down don't ask you the famous question."

"Let me guess what it is. 'May I take you out to dinner?'"

"No. It's 'Do you feel more Italian or more German?'"

"Do they really ask you that?"

"Always. Everybody."

"It must be really annoying. Look, I'd like to ask a question. Do you feel more Italian or German?"

" . . . "

"All right, then I'll ask another one: may I take you out to dinner?"

Napoli Campi Flegrei, then Napoli Mergellina. We've penetrated the belly of Naples, the city's intestines: we're going through the metro tunnels.

One after the other, we go without stopping through the underground stations of Piazza Amedeo, Montesanto, Piazza Cavour. They whizz past, separated by long, pitch-dark tunnels: they appear like lightning bolts imagined by a person whose eyes are closed. We're hurled onto the central rail track at great speed, while on the benches of the lateral tracksthe platforms people are waiting to go to work, to the dentist, to see a friend. In contrast with their everyday lives, our train looks like a supertanker on a river, a heavy truck on a cycle path. You get the impression of rattling your way into the city's intimacy. Almost like in my dream! Except that the roles are reversed. Now I am the passenger looking out of the train window into other people's bedrooms.

We stop at Piazza Garibaldi Station. It has light blue neon lights, tiles like a mortuary, deserted benches. It gives you the impression that if you got off here you could disappear into thin air and never be found again.

"Orangejuicemineralwatercocacolapizzassandwiches!"

They must have boarded in the rarefied silence of that Cold War-like station and now, to compensate, they're screaming with no thought for their vocal cords. They're dragging huge plastic bags and dark blue window-washer pails where they keep the drinks cool. They're young, elderly, children; there are no women. A dark man with the thick arms of an expectant mother looks into our compartment. The two American girls look at him, terrified as though he were a murderer, and the bag full of sandwiches a lethal weapon. I shake my head and the man walks past, an overfilled pail leaving a wet trail behind him.

One thing is for sure: The illegal vendors of food and drinks perform a fundamental service on a long-distance train where the restaurant car and the bar have been abolished. Since we're in Naples, a land where politics and shady business merge, you start toying with the idea that maybe the two things are not coincidental.

Finally, the sun once again. Naples has swallowed up the train, turned it over in its mouth, and spat it back out like an olive stone.

I can see the dark blue signs of Napoli Centrale but not the station. Right up against the tracks there are apartment blocks the color of human skin, cubic, square, graceless. Then the cranes in the harbor appear. Beneath, hundreds, thousands, tens of thousands of containers, almost all with huge writing like HANJIN or CHINA SHIPPING: you would think Italy has trade exchanges only with China.

Here we are, a few yards away from the sea, you can almost touch it from the window; we haven't been so close to it since we left Rome. Cliffs, waves glistening in the sun, fishermen with lines and pale hats, but also people wearing coats. Everyone interprets spring their own way. At Torre del Greco a wall acts as a vertical rubbish dump: a pile made of trash bags and other detritus climbs up it. Where there are gaps between the garbage, there are tender declarations: I'M SORRY, MY LOVE, I LOVE YOU PUPPY, I WANT YOU.

I've gone to the restroom and stolen a glance at the compartment of Indian telephone callers. It's four men and two women, one of whom has a little child curled up in her arms. Lying on the pulled-out seats, they're all asleep.

We're now south of Vesuvius, you can tell by its caldera. My mother has a dream: to visit Pompeii and Herculaneum, then spend a few days on the Amalfi coast. I really should take her—I did promise.

I don't know why I suddenly remember when I told her I

wanted to move to Australia and she replied that she would finally see kangaroos, that she'd always wanted to.

Wait a minute. I was the one going to Australia. Not her. And we're not the same thing, are we?

1968 - 1970

Cousin Wastl had gone to do his military service. Since he'd been playing the clarinet in the *Musikkapelle* for years, they'd taken him into the Alpini band in Rome. He liked the capital very much, and especially Roman women. When he came back on his first leave, at the end of June, he was in an excellent mood. The day after that, the umpteenth ceremony took place at the foot of the granite Alpino that bore his name. The monument had once again been rebuilt, identical to the one before.

They were strange times.

A handful of *Schützen* had gathered to protest against the inauguration. That wasn't unusual per se: the opposition of men in costumes against the symbols of the Italian government was commonplace. What was odd, however, was the group of youths that had gathered under the *Wastl* and wasn't just protesting against the monument, but also against the *Schützen*.

It was hard to understand, least of all for Eva and Ulli, who'd been brought here by their cousin in uniform to watch the ceremony.

The students were holding raised fists and were screaming slogans "against nationalism of any kind" in two languages. And that was something else nobody had ever seen before: a demonstration of Italian and German young people together.

Eva had never heard the word "nationalism." She looked up at Wastl, the flesh and blood one who was holding her by the hand. She was sad that some people considered it wrong to have a monument dedicated to him. People wanted to hear her dear uncle-cousin play even in Rome: she felt strongly that he definitely deserved a statue.

There wasn't a single white hair in Frau Mayer's blonde plait, gathered in a crown, even though she was approaching sixty. Every morning, she would spend almost half an hour on a single objective: to make her hairstyle identical to that of her mother, and her mother's mother. It was the rest of the world that had gone haywire.

A year had passed and now in fall 1969, spontaneous strikes at the Bolzano steelworks were gaining wide support. But they were not the only workers to speak out; pretty much all the workers, in every sector, had realized that they weren't alone. The unheard-of had suddenly become probable: that the scullery boys, assistant cooks, and cooks at a large hotel should strike together in order to obtain fair remuneration was no longer an outrageous hypothesis but a concrete possibility. Menacing or exciting, depending on your point of view.

All the kitchen staff had to do was threaten to strike. It was the end of December and the hotel was full. Frau Mayer capitulated within a few hours.

From that moment on, the pay contributions reflected the actual days worked; for everyone, even the lowliest scullery boy. And the four hours of extra work that were deducted from the day off started being remunerated. However, the contributions Frau Mayer hadn't paid during the previous years weren't recovered by anyone. When, at the age of sixty, after almost forty-five years of work, Gerda retired, whenever she returned from the post office at the end of the month, she would always calculate the difference between how much she had in her handbag and how much she would have had if Frau Mayer hadn't stolen from her old age all that time ago. Every time, after placing the envelope with the modest sum on the television doily, she would pull out of the sideboard the set of colored glasses that Eva had given her one Christmas, pour some of her favorite limoncello, and drink a toast to that young woman she'd never met: the only waitress who, when times were still hard, had dared to protest and been fired with the nickname of Trade Unionist pinned to her like an infamy.

Vito Anania had now been in Alto Adige for almost three years, mostly spent patrolling or supervising the border in extreme conditions. When he was promoted to sergeant, his superiors put him to work "in the warmth," as they said: they made him responsible for the provisioning of the barracks stationed in the plain. They thought they were doing him a favor, but they weren't. Vito soon discovered that the recollection of those moments spent in the rawness of nature, in animal communion with his men, was something he missed. But he was a Carabiniere, so he applied himself to executing his orders to the best of his ability, as he had always done.

The first day he went to see the suppliers, he thought: at least in the mountain masi, they'd say "*Grüß Gott*" to you.

"Buongiorno!" he called out with a bright smile as he entered the butcher's that had been supplying the barracks with meat for years. The butcher looked at his tense hand as though it were a bunch of offal, and replied, "How much meat?"

It was the same with the baker and the peasants who supplied the barracks with milk and butter; even the half-Trentine fruit seller didn't respond to his greeting. Vito was used to anti-Italian, not to mention anti-military, resentment. Later, however, he checked the accounts books and realized what was really happening.

For years, his predecessors, in provisioning, had skimmed some of the money intended for supplies. They'd accumulated debts with everybody and never paid anyone back. The situation was clear to these tradesmen: the *Walschen* are dishonest, with an arrogance that is typical of the military, they take advantage of their position not to pay. The butcher, the baker, the peasants, nobody could afford to refuse the barracks' custom. Four hundred and fifty pounds of meat a day, six hundred and fifty pounds of bread: nobody can turn down a customer like that. However, they weren't obliged to say hello.

Vito made a decision: to persuade each and every one of them that not all Italians were crooks. It's another way of serving your country, he thought.

For months he saved on the orders and managed to put aside some money which he used to start repaying his predecessors' debts. By spring, they would all be repaid, he hoped.

Now, when he walked in, the suppliers said hello.

The winds of change were also blowing beyond the barbed wire walls and into the barracks.

The lives of the Carabinieri stationed in Alto Adige had always been hard, even when they weren't patrolling the ridges on the border and had been assigned to duties in "the warmth" of the barracks. The weekly day off was an illusion: people talked about it but nobody had ever seen it. In the daybook of work shifts and leave, the commander wrote them down but only in homage to bureaucracy: you still had to go to work that day. If anyone complained he risked a poor evaluation.

But for some months now, Vito Anania, who had now been promoted to sergeant, enjoyed one real day off a week, like the rest of his colleagues. Even if it was just to catch up on some sleep: Vito hadn't slept nearly enough for years. The soldiers also obtained other new rights and contractual guarantees. It was Giorgio Almirante, the secretary of the MSI party, in particular, who fought to obtain them; when it came to voting, many soldiers would never forget that.

Vito considered these novelties in the life of a soldier very positive. Not other things, however.

"Sure, you'll get it when I'm done," he heard a sergeant say to an officer in the corridor one day. He knew that the two men had known each other for a long time, having attended military academy together. But the casual tone with which he was addressing his superior was something Vito considered inconceivable, and always would. More than shock or indignation, that "you'll get it when I'm done" made him feel deeply ashamed: for the officer, for the sergeant, and for himself.

Now that there was less work, Sergeant Anania sometimes got bored. He wasn't like Second Lieutenant Genovese, a Neapolitan constantly chasing after Fräulein and adventures. Genovese was good fun but it was better not to follow him all the way. On the occasion of the anniversary of the 1918 Italian victory over Austria-Hungary, he threw a party at the Marlinderhof Hotel, which he called a "non-commissioned officer party," as though they were in Cinecittà. He also invited commanders and officers as long as they arrived "in fair company," a category which, Genovese had firmly underlined, did not include wives or fiancées. In other words, they had to bring women who were unattached. And if their center of gravity was high up, then so much the better.

More than a hundred soldiers arrived with their female escorts. Vito, too, went: the butcher had allowed his daughter to be out until midnight. If you could trust a man who saves up in order to pay back other people's debts, he thought, then you could trust him to bring a girl back home on time. As a matter of fact, by eleven fifty-five, his daughter had already walked in through the front door. Vito went to bed, even though when they'd left the party things were just getting started. He had no regrets. He'd watched Genovese at work: as a master of ceremony he'd encouraged everybody to drink boundless amounts of grappa, while not drinking a single glass himself. Vito was certain that he had a plan. He knew him well enough and he preferred not to be there when the plan was put into action. It was fun hearing about the exploits of that second lieutenant whose hair was slightly too long, and whose buttons were a little too loosely fastened; but taking part in them wasn't his kind of thing.

Therefore, Vito wasn't there when Genovese, having made sure that the officers had drunk enough alcohol to disinfect a leper colony, began circulating through the party with, in his hand, neither a bottle of Schnaps, nor a young woman's wrist, but a camera with a built-in flash.

"Give Captain a kiss," he told one officer's "fair company," The young woman bent over the sweaty face of her escort and brushed his mouth with her lips, while Genovese pressed the shutter button like a trigger. Click.

"Give a kiss to the Major, the Lieutenant, the Colonel!"

The Fräulein would press their scarlet lips on the foreheads and cheeks of the officers and Genovese would take a photograph. Click. Click.

The next morning he printed the photographs.

He never showed them to his superiors. There was no need. All you had to do was let them know of their existence. From then onwards, Genovese had a very easy life in the barracks.

Gerda was in one of the photographs, too. She had accompanied a forty-something colonel determined to kiss her ear. She let him, high cheekbones reflecting the light like polished wood. Perhaps if Vito had seen that photograph, he would have fallen in love with her then and there. But he didn't see it, nor did anyone else, not even the colonel's wife. As a matter of fact, Genovese never had a reason to show it to her: his superior always treated him with consideration and respect.

When Herr Neumann retired early for health reasons, he had no concerns about finding a worthy replacement. Gerda smoked more than a faulty kerosene stove, and worked with more energy than a man. The scullery boys would have done anything for her, the assistant cooks a little less: they weren't used to being bossed around by a twenty-five-year-old ex-*Matratze*. Yet there was also something good about those strange times: unimaginable things were happening everywhere. After twelve hours working in the kitchen, in the evening, Gerda would go to the dance hall.

In her letters to her daughter, Gerda wrote about the "handsome young men" who took her dancing. Eva had learned to read and write from Ulli, and she was so bright, she was accepted at elementary school at the age of five.

In the evening, lying in the bed she shared with Ruthi, Eva would fantasize about her mother's nocturnal activities. As though she were sitting in the darkness of the parish cinema, watching a sped-up film of what she imagined Gerda doing with her escorts: eating pounds of ice cream, spending entire days at the fun fair without paying, throwing custard pies in each other's faces.

Teixel, ist das wenig!
That had been his second thought: good grief, is that all!
Silvius Magnago had been in the Kursaal of Merano for seventeen hours: from ten o'clock in the morning the day before, November 22, 1969, following an extraordinary plenary assembly of the Südtiroler Volkspartei. To the party delegates' credit, they had put up with those wooden reformatory chairs without a single complaint and now, in the middle of the night, they were even more numerous than in the afternoon. They were there before him, those in favor of the Package and those against, *Paketler* and *Anti-paketler*, and they were looking at him. How long had he been working on his draft? It felt like forever, to Magnago. It was only his war memories that stopped

him from believing that he hadn't done anything else all his life. It was precisely this extreme argument that he had used at his last appeal and declaration of vote.

"Ladies and gentlemen delegates, do you really believe that I would advise you to vote in favor of this agreement if I weren't convinced, after working on it for twenty years, that we cannot obtain more than this?"

For the umpteenth time, he had declared that if the delegates didn't approve of the Package—along with the measures with which the government guaranteed a large degree of autonomy to the province of Bolzano—it would be a disaster. He would resign as party *Obmann*, but his fate would be the better for it. On the other hand, those who were now saying he had sold out, calling him "Tolomei" and "digger of the *Heimat* grave," they would have to start negotiating with the Italians all over again from scratch, and he would have the bitter satisfaction of seeing them knock their heads against the fact that you can't get anywhere without the *Kompromiss*. Sooner or later, they would learn—they were neither stupid nor in bad faith—but, meanwhile, years, decades of work would be lost. With Italian governments falling and rising again like in a puppet show, there was no knowing when there would be one willing to take on the responsibility of a definitive agreement. And there was no knowing when they would find another interlocutor like Aldo Moro, who had inserted into article 14 the sentence according to which the defense of minorities was in the national interest, but without attracting too much attention on the part of his fellow party men because, as he explained to him in private, they would have repealed it if they had noticed it.

This was the day, or rather the night—since it was three in the morning—of judgment. If the Südtiroler Volkspartei approved the Package today, then the Italian government would take it up to Parliament where its approval was certain.

And then the foreign ministers of Italy and Austria would provide the signatures that would ratify peace in their land.

If, however, the Package was rejected by the party assembly, then . . . *Vogel, friss oder stirb!*—Eat or die, little bird! Magnago could not explain it to the delegates any more clearly.

And now, he was exhausted. He had a lot more resistance than his emaciated appearance suggested—without it, he would have already collapsed. That's what they always say, don't they? It's the skinny ones that are tough. And Magnago was no exception. The more the hours passed, the longer the debate lasted, the more he was on the war path. He knew that his people had many doubts: the Italians had been "ripping them off," as they put it, for fifty years, and the delegates were terrified by the idea of not doing the right thing for the *Heimat*. He had to conquer their votes one by one.

At this point, however, he couldn't bear it any longer. A little earlier he had said: "Enough, it's past two-thirty, let's vote."

The decisive ones had already slipped their piece of paper into the urn. The only ones still clutching theirs were the ones who had wanted to listen to all the orators before making up their minds.

The delegates from Schnals, Unteretsch, Gsies, Pfitschtal. From Sexten, Bruneck, Wolkenstein, Latsch, Kasern, Burgum. People who at this time were normally awake at the maso, not because they had been up all night, but because they were already milking their cows. On them depended the outcome of the vote. Eat, little birds, eat.

One by one, they slipped their crumpled pieces of paper into the urn. From there, they were extracted and counted.

And marked on the register.

The president of the assembly read out the results.

"Total votes: one thousand one hundred and four.

Votes in favor of Mr Magnago's resolution: five hundred and eighty-three.

Votes against Mr Magnago's resolution: four hundred and ninety-two.

Unmarked or spoiled ballot papers: nineteen.

Mr Magnago's resolution is hereby approved with 52.8 percent of the votes."

52.8 percent.

Teixel, ist das wenig! That had been his second thought: good grief, that's not much!

But his first one had been: *Du hast es geschafft.* You did it.

Paul Staggl, too, would have liked the bikini-wearing model.

Or rather: he would have liked the photo of the bikini-wearing model. Or even better: he would have liked the bikini-wearing model, too, but would have liked the photo even more. Or the other way around.

Anyway.

If only the Consortium he managed were able to host the skiing World Cup like Val Gardena! The publicity shot in Time Magazine had deeply angered his associates, but not him. Paul Staggl had been born to extreme poverty, in a sunless maso: if he'd wasted time and energy envying other people's good fortune he wouldn't have gotten this far. His thoughts spun like the wheel of a downhill cable car station: well oiled, constant, and with the sole aim of carrying it up high.

That's why he had paid great attention to the photo of the beautiful girl wearing nothing but panties, bra, ankle socks and ski boots, with one ski on the ground and the other stuck vertically in the snow in front of her, against the background of snow-covered Dolomites. And not just because some things are always a pleasure to look at, but because, as he was studying it, he'd had several thoughts. The first, and most obvious one, was that his town was not in the middle of the Dolomites. In the 1930s, somebody had tried to draw postcards with the pink needles of Monti Pallidi standing out behind the profile of the Medieval castle. A famous geographical forgery that was still possible in the prehistoric times of mountain tourism, but which nowadays was out of the question. Tourists watched television now, were informed, and couldn't be swindled like that.

The top of his home mountain, which was dominated by cable car pylons, built seven years before by his Consortium, definitely had a splendid three-hundred-and-sixty-degree view, but it was a far cry from the Dolomites. The whole world was in love with those coral-colored mountains, and the hoteliers of the Ladin valleys already had all their marketing done for them thanks to the location. No. Because there were no Dolomites here, there was another way of attracting hordes of British, Dutch, and Swedish skiers, the new tourism frontier, now that German and Italian—and perhaps even American—ones had been secured. And it was very clear in his mind. "His" mountain had to be turned into such an extended and diversified skiing area that it would have something to offer everyone. Staggl stared at the beautiful girl's naked belly and her pleasant curves for a long time.

Were they called "carousels"? Well, then, this was his vision: a network of ski lifts spreading in every direction in a sunburst pattern. So large that a keen sportsman would be able to ski for days on end without ever going over the same piste. There would be more modern lift technology, cutting-edge track maintenance, an investment plan worthy of a big enterprise. All this would allow his creature always to be state-of-the-art, as his colleagues from Colorado put it.

All his life, Paul Staggl had thought big. He didn't intend to stop just because he was past sixty. There was wealth in winter tourism. For him, his family, his valley, Alto Adige, the Alps. He was certain of it: the future was as brilliant as a snow-covered piste at dawn. And now even Hannes, who was approaching thirty, had made up his mind to get married, and perhaps he would finally give him some grandchildren. Of course those born to daughters are also a joy, but when they are born to your only son, everybody knows it's a special occasion for a grandfather.

There was wealth in winter tourism.

Paul Staggl was not the only one to have worked that out. Besides Gerda, many peasants were buying new shoes for their children for the first time that year. However, in return, these children had to sleep in the basement or under the stairs both in the winter and in the summer. Their rooms had become like gold dust: renting them to tourists for the few weeks of high season brought more money than a whole year milking cows. The bombings and attacks were over, and there were an increasing number of Italian tourists. Their rapport with the local population wasn't always straightforward. They often mistook for hostility the dour lack of ceremony of certain landlords who were used to peasant manners. When a reply in Italian came too slowly, or there was a menu written only in German, the Italian tourists would protest, "We're in Italy!"

On the other hand some bus drivers displayed all their indignation at the unfair transfer of South Tyrol to Italy in 1919 by addressing rude grunts to passengers who said "Buongiorno."

Actually, Italians were wrong when they thought they were the only ones to be treated with coarseness by some South Tyroleans: as it happened, Bavarians were also derided because they were drunkards, Viennese because they were condescending, Prussians because they were arrogant. But one fact remained, and it was the only one that counted: tourists brought money and money has no language, no frontiers, no history.

And no traditional costume either. Many new Italian guests

had gotten into the habit of wearing and, especially, dressing their children in typical Tyrolean costumes. Platoons of mothers and daughters from Rome, Vercelli and Florence showed off identical *dirndl* with flower-patterned aprons, with a more uniform effect than the *Musikkapelle*. Miniature *Bauernschürtze*—the navy peasant aprons for which Hermann was beaten up during the Fascist era—were put around Milanese babies' necks as bibs.

At first, South Tyroleans were perplexed by this kind of masquerade (except for shopkeepers who made a lot of money selling *Trachtmode*[39]), but then they got used to it. Those who saw it, however, never forgot the Neapolitan family—mother, father and four children from three to sixteen—who, one August day, were seen walking down the main street in town, shouting and calling one another at the top of their lungs, twelve thighs fed on sartù and pasticcio di maccheroni coming out of their *Lederhosen*.

Ulli, too, had to sleep in the attic: his and Sigi's room was let to tourists during high season. With the money she made, Leni bought her parents a new kitchen with a Formica top, like the ones you saw on TV. While she was at it, she also got rid of a lot of old furniture. A man from Bolzano offered to take it away, and even gave her money in return. Leni really couldn't understand what he saw in that old stove that had been in the kitchen for generations, or in that chunky painted cupboard that made the *Stube* dark. You could tell it was falling apart by the date under the decoration in the middle: 1773. Even so, she took the man's money: it wasn't her fault if some people just didn't know how to do business.

Among the Italian guests that came year after year, there was a family from Milan with three children. They had grown

[39] Traditional fashion.

fond of the beautiful view over the glaciers enjoyed from the maso, as well as the hospitality offered by Leni and her parents. The landlords may not have been very talkative, with their caricature Italian, but they were honest, sincere and, in their way, even affectionate. From the way she treated them, never would the Milanese family have ever guessed that the young widow's husband had been blown up while trying to attack representatives of the Italian government.

Their youngest daughter was the same age as Eva, with black frizzy curls around her head like an electric halo. She showed a disconcerting indifference to her condition as a city girl and had gotten along with Eva and Ulli so naturally that they could do nothing but accept her. Ulli and Eva would never have dived into the hay with their Italian peers who lived in the town, or dams in the stream in the wood; but they did with that little girl from Milan. Besides, as everybody knows, you must beware of your neighbors but it's all right to be curious about the inhabitants of other galaxies. Eva and Ulli would have been very surprised if she had said she was a friend: a friend doesn't vanish down a black hole eleven months of the year. But she was an intelligent girl, so she never did so.

As for Ulli, he'd always been Eva's friend.

Or perhaps he was also just a playmate until the day when, in the churchyard after mass, a child of the same age said that Ulli's father deserved to be dead because he was a *Verbrecher*, a criminal, and that Eva's father was alive but didn't want her. Like so many other times to come in his life, the words to defend himself remained stuck in Ulli's throat, rotting inside and infecting only him.

So Eva stuck the index and middle finger of her right hand in the little boy's eyes. Ulli and Eva became inseparable.

Sigi, on the other hand, was never Eva's friend, and she always considered him one of those unpleasant facts of life that you cannot eliminate or solve, but only ignore: a wood splinter that's too deep to be extracted, a wobbly tooth that won't fall, a father who's never been there. And if Eva had ever risked feeling any kind of affection for Sigi, the danger was averted forever the day when, at the age of five, he started making trophies.

It was Eva and Ulli, while Leni was in the cowshed, who found him sitting on the wooden floor of the *Stube*. Around him, there were a kitchen knife, nails, a hammer, pieces of wood, and the decapitated bodies of various stuffed animals: a red and white duck, a brown teddy bear with a red scarf around his neck, a hound with long black ears. The severed head of every cuddly toy had been nailed to a wooden plank.

Eva and Ulli looked at the scene in silence: it was too strange to trigger a reaction. Not even Leni asked Sigi for an explanation when she came in and saw all those poor stuffed animals reduced to hunting trophies. All she did was raise her eyes to the larch wall. There, fixed onto wooden shields, hung the only remaining traces, besides her two children, of her husband's passage on earth: the heads of deer, ibexes, chamois, their antlers as sharp as the day Peter had killed them.

Every so often the *Schützen* went to ask the widow of their former comrade-in-arms if she needed any help.

Leni would reply, "No, thank you," and her face relaxed with relief when they left.

Ulli never stayed long in the *Stube* when they came.

"Your father gave his life for you," the men said to him, and these words triggered in Ulli a mixture of hunger, nausea and questions without answers. How could he ever repay such a disproportionate gift?

Sigi, though, would follow them onto the street after they

left: he thought they were beautiful. Soon, before he even started school, they began taking him along on their drills. They said, "Your father gave his life for you" to Sigi, too, but what he felt was the void without memories his father had left in his stomach finally start to fill up.

Leni wasn't happy about Sigi spending time with the *Schützen*, but what could she do about it? The Schwingshackls agreed with her. Eva's adoptive parents felt sorry for Leni and the children, and also for that sick soul that was Hermann, who had lost his only son and disowned his daughter. But the fact that Peter was a hero was something they did not agree with. There are so many ways in which you can be useful to others, some of which require courage and sacrifice, but what was heroic about blowing up Christian folk and yourself was something Sepp and Maria would never understand.

Then the Open Air Concert arrived. Even saying the name tasted like the future.

It wasn't music. It was something solid that wrapped around you, which you didn't listen to with your ears but with your feet, your stomach, your hair. It would make your hairs stand up on your arms, grab you by the knees, and make you say yes to anything. And that rhythm! Who had ever heard such rhythm? The drummer shook his hair, long like a woman's, like snakes, spraying sweat all around: it was impossible to believe that the instrument on which he'd let himself go in a crazy solo could be a relative of the snare drum of the *Musikkapelle*. And in fact it wasn't. Nothing was the same. Even the castle, up on the hill over the town, where Eva, Ulli, Ruthi and Wastl were now, wasn't the same as before. Not even during Medieval assaults had those ancient bastions ever been shaken to their foundations by anything like this: a rock concert.

There had never been so many people like that, on the grass

and under the larches around its ancient walls: girls with bare legs and long hair tied with leather strips, boys with colorful T-shirts and handkerchiefs on their heads, entangled couples touching each other everywhere and kissing on the mouth. And, around and above everything, like thick liquid in which Eva, her cousins, young people in love, and the castle all floated, there was that divine devil music. Eva did not have the eyes, nor the ears, nor the skin for what was happening around her.

Ruthi, however, was sad. The little girl who had welcomed Eva like the present of a gift doll had become a girl of fifteen. She was still very blonde and a little too thin, but beneath her white lashes her eyes were so interested in others that everybody liked her company. Wastl, too. Very much. And she was beginning to realize that she found his company not just pleasant but almost indispensable. However, Wastl had just told her that after he finished his military service, he would save some money with the Val d'Adige harvest and that he'd then go to Morocco.

Morocco. It was the name of a place very far away, Eva thought, perhaps near America? Yes, that's right. Not so long ago, on Ulli's new television, they were talking about its capital: Morocco City. How did you get there? On the same bus that took her mother away? Perhaps Morocco City was in the same direction as the kitchen where she worked, only a little farther.

No bus, Wastl was saying. He'd be hitchhiking to Morocco. But he didn't ask Ruthi to go with him. The girl tried not to cry but the group on the stage, ineffably called The We, didn't make things any easier: they'd just started singing a slow, very sad song,with the electric guitar screaming in pain like a wounded animal.

Hitchhiking.

Another beautiful, cheerful-sounding word. Eva wasn't sure she knew what it meant but she said to herself: I'll do that too when I grow up.

Once again we're far away from the sea, with the mountainous mass of the Sorrento peninsula between us. From Angri downwards, whenever the train slows down, there's a terrible smell of burning rubber. I imagine it must be the brakes.

The farther south we go, the farther ahead we are in the season. Here, the fruit trees have no blossoms but already young green leaves. In the middle of the highway intersection, there stands an incongruous wrought iron and delicate glass Art Nouveau gazebo, like the pavilion of an Italianate garden. A little temple to beauty in the middle of nowhere.

All the rail tracks of Salerno Station are white with disinfectant, or perhaps lime. The impression is that here they're very keen on neutralizing those impolite people who go to the toilet when the train is stationary. The hill beyond the platform roofs is covered in identical buildings, really identical, identical in every detail without the slightest variation.

But they certainly do have quite a view of the sea.

The two American girls get off, presumably to go to the Amalfi coast. Once again it's the chubby one who pulls down both backpacks, while the other one just sits and watches her, impassive and sullen. This time I don't get up to give a hand, either, I don't know why. The stout girl puffs under the weight of her backpack with the pink teddy bear.

I feel like saying, turn the teddy bear over, you can't go around with a cuddly toy hanging head down! But I don't have the courage. It's unpleasant, and it's not a nice way of communicating, remember you're traveling, you need the kindness of strangers . . .

Perhaps, ever since Sigi, I've been too sensitive to the subject of "cuddly toys being used inappropriately." The two girls have already left the compartment without saying goodbye. We travelled together for almost three hours and didn't exchange a single word.

"One of these days you should really hurl the backpack right at that anorexic tyrant."

Before the train leaves again, a couple in their sixties and a young woman of twenty-five, thirty at most, with slightly pimply skin she clearly feels embarrassed about, the beautiful long eyes of a gypsy, T-shirt and jeans, come and sit across from me. The lady, her mother, I think, is right opposite me. She's holding her handbag, jacket, and a large plastic shopping bag, and doesn't look like she's going to make herself more comfortable. She doesn't put anything down even though there are two empty seats next to her.

There's loud snoring coming from the Indians in the compartment next door, as expressive as the recent, "Hallo? Hallo?"

From Battipaglia onwards, once again, greenhouses, greenhouses, greenhouses. Purple ones (curly lettuce), bright green (round lettuce), and red (tomatoes)—extend as far as some apartment blocks. There are even lemon groves in the midst of the buildings. The fallow field is covered in yellow, fuchsia, purple, blue flowers and, next to it, a field of brilliant green wheat. So many colors in this country.

On the other hand, the elegant spans of the decommissioned old railroad bridge are made of vermilion brick. It has a very narrow gauge, and the tracks look like those of a toy train set. I wonder if it dates back to the Bourbons, when Naples was one of the most modern cities in the world.

We cross a pair of small valleys with no houses and only after we've crossed Vallo di Lucania do the bricks of the ancient railroad reappear. Another bridge of that beautiful warm color launches itself over a gorge. The winding ballast carries on until it ends up against a house! Does it continue inside? Who knows? Perhaps it's like some houses in Rome, built around aqueducts: a span that, two thousand years ago, carried water to the Eternal City, and now acts as an architrave. It must be something, I think, to have a historic railroad going through your living room.

Some things happen only in Italy.

Now, whenever the train brakes, a sharp smell of dioxin penetrates my nose.

"What a stench!" the lady opposite me says.

Even though she boarded the train almost an hour ago, she still hasn't let go of anything: handbag, shopping bag and jacket, she keeps it all close to her chest as though we were on an overcrowded Indian train and not in a half-empty carriage over Easter. She even has the train tickets in her hand, ready to show the guard. After the usual Signora/Signorina ballet, we've started chatting.

They're from Messina. The husband is a retired policeman, as I should have guessed from the salt-and-pepper mustache and the formerly athletic physique. The daughter has a degree in ancient literature and is training to be a teacher. She is outraged.

"Even people with behavioral problems are admitted to the program, people who shouldn't ever be in contact with children. Or stupid people who have never studied but who know the right people."

They ask where I come from. I tell them.

The mother has been listening attentively from behind her barrier of possessions. Her arms must be aching by now and perhaps that's why she's raised her heels and is on her toes: in order to hold on to everything better so it doesn't fall off.

"Once, we went on holiday to Ortisei. When the kids were still little. Alpe di Siusi, it's so beautiful, isn't it, Mario?"

"Yes, very beautiful. A paradise."

Wife and husband smile at each other. Perhaps they're remembering a special moment they spent at Seiser Alm.

"You really do have regional autonomy! Not like us in Sicily, where we're autonomous from the Italian government but subjects of the Mafia. If I were to start my profession all over again, I'd move to the North and raise my children there. Without all those people with recommendations."

The wife looks at me and catches me by surprise: "Sorry to ask but . . . Do you feel more German or more Italian?"

And she didn't even put down her bags before asking me! I catch my breath. Naturally, my answer is well rehearsed. "I have an Italian passport but my language is German, my land is the Southern part of Tyrol, other parts of which, however, like North Tyrol and East Tyrol, are in Austria. We call it Südtirol but in Italian it's Alto Adige, since the difference has always been where you're looking from: from above or below."

My answer silences her. She looks at her husband.

"But didn't they speak Ladin in Ortisei?" she asks him.

"Yes."

"Which is actually a different Ladin from the one they speak in Val Badia," I say.

"What a complicated place!"

"Yes, it is."

Until a few years ago, when you said you were a German speaker from Alto Adige, they thought you were a terrorist. At the very least they'd ask: but why do you people hate Italians so much?

Then things changed. In the weekly supplement of the

newspaper, a few months ago, the front cover was devoted to separatist ethnic movements in Europe. It mentioned:
Corsica
Slovakia
Scotland
Catalonia
the Basque Country
Kosovo
Montenegro
Slovenia
Croatia
Bosnia
and
the Po Valley.
The Po Valley!
No sign of Alto Adige.

Once, when I took Zhou home after she'd been at my place, I met Signor Song, who was at home. A rare event since he's always out on his business, which is spread throughout the North-east of Italy. He asked me in and opened for me the box for fighting crickets, the only possession he took away from China. Inside, there were two miniature plates, one for water and one for food, finely decorated in enamel; the microscopic wedding cage where thoroughbred fighters are made to mate with the most fertile females; tiny scales for weighing the crickets in order to organize equal sides in terms of bulk and strength; a kind of small brush with a single horse hair at the end which, Song explained, was necessary to spur the crickets on before the battle and make them more aggressive. In that kind of tiny dollhouse the absence of the cricket, any cricket, evoked exile.

"Why don't you catch two crickets from our fields and try and make them fight?" I asked.

Signor Song looked at me with polite eyes. Without a hint of impatience, he replied, "Only a Chinese cricket can fight in a Chinese way."

I remember feeling it was a sentence full of great wisdom, so I kept quiet.

However, now I wonder, is that true?

In 1981, Ulli and I went to shut ourselves in iron cages on a Bolzano bridge with many other young people. We were protesting against the ethnic census included in the new autonomy statute.

It was seven years before his, well, let's call it accident at work. Ulli was nearly twenty, he could already vote and I would also soon be eighteen. Every Alto Adige adult had to state whether he or she was German, Ladin or Italian.

Those who refused to fill in the statement wouldn't be able to teach, claim state benefits, or work as civil servants. Above all you could not describe yourself as multi-ethnic. It was the *Sprachgruppenzugehörigkeitserklärung* so longed for by the old Magnago. He, of all people, the son of a German mother and an Italian father, had started saying, "*Nicht Knödel mit Spaghetti mischen*," you shouldn't mix Knödel and spaghetti. Schools, libraries, local authorities, cultural centers: in this vision everything had to be separate.

My mother claimed she was convinced this was the right solution.

"A marriage between an Italian man and a German woman could never work," she claimed.

It was already eight years since Vito had left.

In any case, my mother has always worshipped Magnago. As a little girl, she too was at Castel Firmiano, and she never tired of telling how she had shaken the hand of the Father of Autonomy in the hotel where she worked. We young people, however, didn't like him that much. The Greens had organized the demonstration. They were led by Alexander Langer, a visionary elf with rabbit teeth who, for our now autonomous *Heimat*, entertained dreams of a larger soul, less petty, and not such a narrow-minded mountain apartheid. That's why so many good South Tyroleans hated him, and so did Magnago, more than anyone else. On each of the two iron cages on the Talvera bridge there was a sign. DEUTSCHE, was written on one, and ITALIANI on the other. Anyone walking over the bridge was invited to come into the one corresponding to his or her ethnicity. Once you were shut behind the iron bars you could no longer communicate with the occupants of other cage. Exactly what the heads of the SVP hoped would happen between *Daitsche* and *Walsche*.

It was a warm sunny day and the bodies of the demonstrators all crammed together in the *Daitsche* cage smelled of wool and sweat. That's when Ulli said to me, "I've been living in a cage like this since I was born."

I couldn't turn around because we were too tight.

"What do you mean?" I asked.

He answered, "Ever since the midwife told my mother: it's a boy."

We're still crossing a timeless landscape: streams of limpid water, forsythias set alight by the sun, prickly pears clotted together like coral colonies, olive trees with manes wide enough for a whole family to fit underneath. Sitting under an almond tree in blossom, a young woman is breastfeeding her child. And once again, high above the gorge, the arch of a bridge of an ancient, vermillion brick ballast. That's the only place where the ancient railroad has been preserved: where it passes through the air and doesn't steal land from anyone, or where it has been incorporated into a new building.

Maybe the same is true for one's own identity, that very fundamental human fixation: either it remains unchanged outside History, or it gets transformed, or dies.

We emerge from tunnels to a view over the sea, then more tunnels, and more again. After Policastro, with its grey Medieval walls right over the sea, we're about to leave Campania.

White veil, long white dress, white scapular down to the ribcage: except for her little girl size, Eva looked like a novice.

But not Gerda.

She was wearing a chiffon outfit with aquamarine patterns, not as short as the ones she wore to go dancing, but almost. That "almost" had caused her much concern. She had carefully considered the amount of thigh she could show on the occasion of her daughter's first communion. Not too much, in order not to offend. Not too little, so no one would think she was trying to camouflage herself. Gerda fully intended everyone to know: she wasn't ashamed of being a free woman. She didn't need to ask anyone for the money to buy bread and milk for herself and her daughter; therefore, she was the one to decide whom she let into her bed and whom she didn't.

Even so.

Gerda had to concentrate very hard so that nobody would notice, especially not herself, that among all the mothers of the communicants, she was the only one unmarried. Therefore, for the whole duration of the mass, she kept her eyes on the stained glass that illuminated the ugly 19th-century frescoes, the depictions of the hapless bearded female saint. She would occasionally lower them and only once or twice looked at the children, her daughter among them, who were sitting on the bench in front of the altar while waiting for the sacrament—the girls dressed as nuns or brides, the boys like little masters of ceremonies, white shirts under satin waistcoats, clean but often threadbare because they had been handed down by more than one older brother. Above all, Gerda never turned to the rest of the congregation.

Eva, on the other hand, always remembered the day of her first communion because of the skis.

Coming back home after the service, she'd found them propped against the front door of the furnished room where she lived with Gerda during the low season. They were taller than her, lemon yellow, very heavy to lift. She tried immediately, still dressed like a sexto decimo nun, but barely managed it. She was particularly struck by the grips: the metal double bites, even though she hadn't put her feet in them yet, gave her an oppressive sense of constriction.

When she saw the skis, Gerda grew wary. The furnished room was on the ground floor of a new building several stories high, each of them a tourist apartment: now, in May, they were all empty. It was on the outskirts of the town, not far from the slope leading to the little church and to Ulli's, Wastl's, Sepp and Maria's masi. Opposite the apartment block there was a potato field left fallow that year, crossed by a white gravel road bordered with lilacs. The white, pink and lilac flowers spread their fragrance in the air. The cream-colored Mercedes 190 was parked there. Hannes was leaning against the trunk, his legs crossed, with the eyes of someone who had been staring at the same thing for a while: Gerda.

She didn't look down. She just slightly moved her focus so that her gaze flew over the head of her child's father, drifted serenely beyond the shape she wasn't noticing, and rested, detached, on the line of glaciers on the horizon.

Eva immediately understood who he was.

Hannes came up to them. Gerda lit a cigarette and began

smoking, holding her elbow in her cupped hand, her gaze lost in the distant infinity,

"Do you like them?" the man with orange hair asked.

"They're heavy," Eva replied.

"Because they're good quality. With these you'll be able to ski like Gustav Thoeni."

"I can't ski."

There was a silence. The daughter of the son of the winter carousel king had never worn a pair of skis; this discovery seemed to disconcert Hannes Staggl.

"I'm a cook, not a lady, I have no money to waste."

Gerda's voice, although it came from her mouth, less than a yard away from Eva, seemed to come from a faraway place. Hannes didn't turn to look at the woman—still very beautiful—he had impregnated not so many years earlier, and kept his face down toward the miniature white nun. "If your mother had wanted to marry me, she wouldn't be working in a hotel like a slave now. She would own a hotel."

Gerda dragged on the cigarette and kept the smoke in her mouth for what seemed to Eva like an eternity. Then she let out perfect blue rings that floated toward the flowering lilacs like small, brave spaceships. But their epic crossing failed: they all dissolved in space before landing.

"Nobody asked me to marry them when I was pregnant."

The cigarette wasn't finished but Gerda let it drop on the ground and crushed it with her heel. Then she took Eva by the wrist, walked with her through the front door, and closed it behind them. Gently, however.

It soon became evident that Hannes's present was incomplete: it didn't include ski boots. After trying to slide her rubber boots into the grips, Eva gave up.

It was Sepp who found a solution. He built two wooden stools and nailed one on each ski, which he had sawed a yard from the point, and to which he had also fixed a kind of handlebar. When winter came, Ulli and Eva came down the long slope behind the hayloft on their two *Böckl*[40] hundreds, thousands of times, without ever tiring. Gustav Thoeni would also have enjoyed it.

A few months later, Genovese invited Gerda several times to be his "fair company." The soldier had noticed her at the non-commissioned officer party, but he was already busy with other female attendees, almost too many even for him: it was impossible to add another one. The last one, not long before, had taken her leave after throwing an iced drink in his face in the lobby of the Greif Hotel in Bolzano. Genovese had appreciated this gesture: his reputation was important to him. Only now, over a year later, was he free to go with Gerda.

She quite liked going out with that Neapolitan who came up to her shoulder and never shut up. At the dance hall, the difference in height wasn't a big deal: nowadays it was no longer necessary for the woman's waistline to be lower than the man's. The Tuca Tuca, a dance that consisted in stretching out your hands and feeling your partner to the rhythm of the music was very suitable for non-commissioned officer Genovese, so much so that he might as well have invented it, and not the singer Raffaella Carrà. Even in sex, he came straight to the point and couldn't be described as a generous lover. But that was nothing new for Gerda. Afterwards, however, he was relaxed and pleasant. He would tell her about his wonderful city illuminated by the moon in the Bay of Naples, his agitated ferret eyes would soften, and he'd say, "One day I'll take you there."

She wasn't supposed to believe it but she appreciated the fact that he felt the need to tell her this lie. Above all, he made her laugh.

[40] Mono-ski sled.

"Si accussì bella ca si faciss' nu pireto m' 'o zucass'!" he told her one day while getting dressed again next to the bed.

Lying on her side, her smooth and voluptuous body on top of the sheets like an all-consuming letter S, she had looked at him without understanding. From under Genovese's shirt sprang his pendulous sex; short legs covered in black curly hairs, ending in the socks he would never take off, one of which had a hole in it. He spread his shoulders, straightened his back, lifted his chin, and declaimed in the accent of an Italian language academic, the translation in Italian: "You are so beautiful that if you farted, I'd suck it."

She asked him what "farted" meant. He explained it. She burst out laughing and didn't stop, even long after he'd gone.

That was why Genovese hadn't yet been stabbed by jealous husbands or trampled by the many fellow soldiers from whom he'd swiped their Fräulein, or demoted by all the superiors to whom he was forever supplying a new reason for doing so: for all his vulgarity, his lies, his betrayals and his idleness, he cheered you up. Therefore, that day, knowing that Genovese would come in the evening and pick her up in his Cinquecento, a car more suited to the length of his legs than hers, she was singing the Tuca Tuca song, with a hint of swing in her hips and shoulders as she came down the steps to the pantry. She threw the woolen greatcoat over her shoulders, walked into the refrigerated cell and, still singing, took off the hook the half torso of lamb she would be using to prepare the *plat du jour*: ribs with fine herbs.

In the frost of the freezer the rhythm of her song became visible, every syllable a puff of condensation in front of her mouth.

Yes, Gerda was in an excellent mood today.

At that precise moment, in a corridor of the barracks, Genovese was talking to Vito. He had a date that evening, he said, but something new had also arrived, something called Waltraud, and he didn't feel like turning it down.

"Do you want to go instead of me? Gerda is a very beautiful Fräulein, you're bound to thank me afterwards."

Vito didn't feel like going out that evening. The following morning he was due to go on patrol before dawn. Still, Genovese insisted, it's not nice—practically a mortal sin—to leave a beautiful blonde girl without an escort, and so, almost out of duty, Vito agreed.

Subsequently, when Gerda and Vito remembered the first time they saw each other, and compared their first impressions, they realized they'd been very different.

When Vito saw her, he considered running away. He could have done it: she hadn't yet made him out as the Neapolitan's substitute. In fact, she didn't even know someone else was coming. She's too beautiful for me, he thought. Not beautiful like any other healthy girl with a good body and a face without flaws. But so beautiful you felt pain, you felt longing even while she was right in front of you, so beautiful you wanted to hold her in the circumference of your arms and never let anyone or anything hurt her.

When Gerda, on the other hand, saw a Carabiniere in uniform waiting for her outside the staff entrance, her stomach seized up. What new terrible, unexpected event, was that Carabiniere about to inform her of? Was it to do with Peter? No, Peter was dead. Eva, then?

Meanwhile, Vito hadn't run away. He told her that Second Lieutenant Genovese sent his heartfelt apologies but had been prevented from keeping his date. However, if she was happy with the substitute for an evening's entertainment, then he was respectfully at her disposal. The language of an official report at the same time as a jungle inside his chest: as he spoke, his heart beat in his rib cage like a bird of paradise that's just been caught.

Only then did Gerda manage to see in Vito traits other than

the fact, predominant up till then, that he wasn't Genovese. He was the same physical type as the Neapolitan. He too was short, dark, with the pronounced nose of ancient seafaring people. But as far as his personality went, he might as well have come from a different continent: as noisy and over the top as the other man was, this one was silent and serious. A man who, moreover, looked straight into Gerda's eyes, and not at her hips, where her dress was a little tight, or at her breasts.

Gerda wasn't too disappointed. It was almost part of the deal that Genovese would one day disappear, and, as it was, their acquaintance had lasted longer than expected. Ruining her evening wasn't her style, so she accepted Vito as her escort.

Subsequently, even their memories of that first evening didn't match. Vito claimed he had taken her to dinner at the Trattoria near Ponte Druso; she was certain they'd gone straight to dance. In reality, Gerda didn't have many images of those first hours together. She didn't remember what music the small orchestra played, or their first dance. He probably stepped on her toes, though that wasn't a memory but rather deduction: Vito never was a skilled dancer. Gerda did not keep a particular memory of what the Carabiniere said or did. She was much more struck by what he didn't do.

The hands with which he held her by the waist during the slow dances didn't start to inch down her back and toward her buttocks. He didn't try to touch her breast after the third beer. In fact, he didn't even drink a third beer, but stuck to one. When he took her back home, Gerda expected a kiss, but he stood there, his arms hanging down his sides, stiff as a sentry. Moreover, for the entire evening, Vito's body had been that of a sentinel: it was the only way he'd managed to stop himself from making love to her on the dance hall floor.

Gerda went back to her room in the attic and undressed, a little disappointed. Clearly, Sergeant Anania really didn't like her.

The following day, Vito went looking for Genovese. It wasn't an easy enterprise. The Neapolitan went to his office as often as one visits distant relatives: only on special occasions and never for long. When he found him, he asked: would he mind if he, Vito, saw the woman he'd taken to dance instead of him, again?

"Absolutely not!" Genovese said. "I knew you'd get stuck on her."

He stared at him. There was something in Vito's expression which, for a rare moment, made him remain silent. Genovese had seen faces like that, head over heels in love, many times, and had formed a specific opinion on the subject: it was never good news.

"You know her brother was a terrorist?"

"Was?"

"The stupid delinquent blew himself up."

Vito's face darkened.

Genovese looked at him with his small eyes as sharp as a tailor's pins. "Anania, you're not like me. You're a serious man, so be careful. She's an unmarried mother, good for a fuck and nothing else. Remember that."

But Genovese knew that talking like this to a man in love was as pointless as taking roses to a brothel. Guys who got that face, kept it. Life wiped it off them soon enough. That's why he, Genovese, devoted his own existence to avoid getting it for himself.

The second time Vito met Gerda, he said, "Your eyes are beautiful and sad."

Those same beautiful eyes widened with astonishment.

Men had always said to Gerda: you're so cheerful, you're so lively, you really know how to have a good time. But not sad. That's something no one had ever said to her.

Only now that Vito mentioned her sadness did Gerda think

about it. Yes, there was a part of her that had been sad for years, but she hadn't noticed. So how did he know?

The first night they spent together, he did not penetrate her. When he saw her naked body, he was so overwhelmed with emotion that his sex had remained inert. With any other woman, this would have made him feel diminished. But not with Gerda. He felt an inexplicable trust that everything was going the way it should, and that there was no rush. She fell asleep and he held her in his arms until dawn, not believing his luck.

The next time they saw each other, he said, "You cross your big toes."

They were in a bar. He leaned his elbows on the table, raised his hands with his palms toward her, and slid one thumb into the nook of the other.

"Like this. When you sleep on your side."

Gerda had to think about it. She wriggled her big toes in her shoes to help her body remember and, yes, it was true: when she lay down on her side, she always slid her big toe into the space between the other one and the index. That's another thing she'd always done, without ever noticing. Who was this man who seemed to have known her since she was a child?

That night, Vito plunged into her like a deep-sea diver, and discovered treasures submerged in pleasure. Nobody had ever told Gerda that they were all there, at the bottom of her sea.

W e're going through Sapri station. In the compartment next door the following conversation is taking place:
1st Indian man: "Sabri?"
2nd Indian man: "Sapi."
3rd Indian man (stressing the R): "SapRi."
1st Indian man (stressing the I): "Saprì?"
3rd Indian man (stressing the A): "Sàpri."
Indian woman: "Sapri."
All (satisfied): "Sapri."

The wife of the ex-policeman opposite me still has all her things in her arms: the jacket, the handbag, the shopping bag, the tickets. She's holding on to them tight without letting go, resting her head on them, slumbering. When she opens her eyes, her husband says to her, and none too soon either, "Let go of this stuff."

She looks surprised as though it's an option worth considering even though it's odd. She reminds me of those women at the long tables during the Grillfest[41], who spend all their time pouring beer, serving Würstel, slicing bread, wiping children's noses; they never rest, never sit down, never stop even for a minute to have something to eat and enjoy the company. Not because it's always necessary, not because they're irreplaceable,

[41] Country celebrations.

294 · FRANCESCA MELANDRI

but simply because remaining even one second without making themselves useful isn't something they consider possible.

Finally, the lady lets go of all the stuff she's holding, the husband puts it on the racks, and I too feel relieved.

* * *

We keep gliding in and out of tunnels. In the short hiatus between two tunnels, a clear stream meanders through a field starred with blossoming almond trees. No human being, only a black bull. It's an image of almost subliminal brevity but of absolute presence: a large, dark, powerful animal, amid the white petals bursting around.

When we go back into the dark tunnel, my retina retains the imprint of the bull-shaped luminescent spot: its negative.

When Ulli took Costa to meet his family, Sigi said: don't come in to soil our mother's house with your shit if you want to take it up the ass then do it in the public toilets, you're disgusting and your friend even more than you you're two *Schwuchtl*[42] two *Warme Brüder*[43] two *schwule Sauen*[44].

He couldn't have found filthier words. He must have been mulling them over in his mouth for months, years, like poison, to then spit them out all at once.

Leni said: what's the problem? It's an illness you can treat it the parish priest said there's a doctor in Val Sarentina who knows how to do it if you want I'll give the address to your friend as well I'm sure he'll want to go nobody wants to remain sick and unhappy if there's a medicine for it.

Sigi said: people like you should have their heads stuck

---

[42] A vulgar term for a homosexual.
[43] As above.
[44] As above.

down the toilet, and he took Costa, who was much smaller than him, dragged him to the latrine and did it.

Ulli said: let go of him, and Sigi let go of him but first he flushed the toilet.

Costa said: leave me alone, and didn't let Ulli put his arms around him, or help him get up, pushed his fist against the ground and stood up by himself without looking him in the eye, his hair dirty with urine.

Leni said: I don't know why you're always arguing like this and why we can't just all be together in peace.

* * *

Ulli had been with Costa for almost two years. The first time I met him, I thought: Ulli has now found his true brother.

Sigi wasn't just a Nazi in his thinking but also in his coloring, which was like mine: blue eyes, yellow hair, pink skin. Costa, on the other hand, had soft brown eyes, like Ulli and his mother, and the same amber skin. A Mediterranean coloring bequeathed to our valleys by some passing Roman legionary, a Hispanic mercenary on the payroll of emperors, a Levantine merchant on his way to the capitals of the North. Ulli and Costa looked like each other, as often happens in well matched couples, seeing them next to each other you could easily imagine them together for a whole lifetime.

Ulli had wanted to introduce him to his mother for months. In Innsbruck, where they lived together seven months of the year, they didn't have to hide. But things were different during the winter season, when Ulli had to beat the ski pistes and live in our town. Costa had come a couple of times but found it suffocating. Too clean, too perfect the geraniums in the windows, too few the avowed homosexuals—actually, to be precise, not one. Ulli hadn't insisted but found it painful. Costa wanted to move to Berlin, which Ulli liked, he'd been there;

but he couldn't imagine living so far away from his mountains. Leni had stopped asking him about girls years earlier, but this silent agreement wasn't enough for Ulli anymore.

For a long time he'd had a dream: to come out to her and introduce Costa to her. He'd explain to Leni that this was the love of his life and she would not only accept it but would even be happy about it. What mother doesn't wish for her children to love and be loved?

However, I thought it was a bad idea to take Costa all the way up there, to that maso. I knew Leni, and especially Sigi. I should have told Ulli. But there was a problem. I was so ashamed of the jealousy I felt for his happiness that I acted like envious people always do when they have a fair criticism: they keep quiet because they're afraid of being seen through. So I listened to Ulli without saying anything, without sharing my reservations.

So it was Costa who told him what I should have told him. Costa, the man with whom he wanted to share his life, who made him realize why he had been born, but he did so while also telling him to go away, while walking out of his life forever: "You shouldn't have taken me there."

Ulli repeated that to himself while lying on my sofa, seeking refuge in my home.

"I should never have taken him home."

I had to lean over him to make out his words. I'd covered him with an eiderdown but he wouldn't stop shaking.

"It's not your fault," I said.

Sometimes we know our words are useless even as they're coming out of our mouths.

Sometimes not. I found out exactly ten days later.

I cannot get this out of my mind: when I stopped talking to Ulli openly, I too began to kill him.

At Belvedere Marittimo there's an enormous papier mâché mozzarella hanging from a rope in front of a food shop. It's like the teddy bear hanged by the American girl. Now it's the woman in the compartment next door speaking loudly on the cellphone in Hindi, with rounded Rs, and Ds soft as chapati. These Indians must be spending a fortune on the cellphone. Actually, they probably have one of those subscriptions where it costs less to talk to New Delhi than to Rome.

"Hallo, hallo!" she shouts at increasing speed, then bursts out laughing. As a rule, only cheerful sounds come out of their compartment: the child's gurgling, happy voices, contented snoring. Suddenly, the woman starts speaking in perfect Italian: "Where are you? We'll be there in an hour."

She laughs again then hangs up. Then the cell phone rings again. This time, it's mine. I take it out of my bag and look at the screen while it keeps ringing: CARLO. He must have found a way to absent himself for a minute from Easter lunch with his relatives. I let it ring. I can feel the eyes of the lady from Messina boring into me with curiosity, obviously wondering why I don't answer. And I think she may be guessing correctly: a man. The ringing finally stops and I put the cellphone back in my bag.

At Cetraro, the railroad passes near an intersection and you can read the blue signs on the highway. The one that indicates the direction from which we come tells us that Salerno is two hundred and twenty kilometers away. Others point to locations inland, with names that evoke defended rocks, people in flight, incursions from sea plunderers: Castrovillari, Spezzano Albanese, Saracena.

The arrow that points South, however, is a promise:

REGGIO CALABRIA 254

1971-1972

In off-season, when the hotel wasn't full, Gerda sometimes asked Frau Mayer for a couple of days off in order to go to see Eva, who waited for her visits like a devout person waits for a miracle: with faith, but no certainty. She'd follow the ascent of the blue bus from Bolzano along the curves, until it reached the space outside the little church. Ulli wasn't with her: the meeting between Eva and her mother wasn't his thing, he knew that now, and it was the only time he kept away from her. Eva would place herself in front of the doors, forcing the passengers to parade past her like a little honor guard, examine them one by one as they got off, and feel contempt for them because they weren't her mother. When Gerda finally appeared, like a vision at the top of the steps, happiness and anxiety would explode in Eva's chest: now, all she had to wait for was the forthcoming, certain separation.

That day, the brakes of the bus were still huffing painfully when all of the passengers had gotten off. None of them was Gerda. Eva looked up at the driver. He shrugged, his shoulders strong because of all the bends on the mountain along which he'd turned the steering wheel. He was sorry for her, truly, but he had to keep to a timetable; he pushed a button and the doors closed. In the glass, Eva saw her own reflection which then ran along the blue side of the bus until all she had left before her, against a backdrop of glaciers in the distance, was the square. A tan Fiat 600 was maneuvering there.

Eva seemed like the same blonde girl of a minute ago but,

in reality, what was left of her was just an outline with her features: inside, there was a void. She felt neither sadness nor disappointment, only perhaps a vague hint of relief. Because, now that the threat that had always been hanging over her had come to pass, she could finally stop worrying: her mother would never come back to her. That's why, when the woman got out of the Fiat 600, she didn't notice her. Nor did she pay attention to the man in black uniform walking up to her. Only when the woman called Eva by name and the man came close to look straight into her eyes did she begin to notice that something strange and wonderful was happening.

None of the men Gerda had known had ever acted like Vito.

While Gerda was cooking *Schlutzkrapfen*, Vito and Eva did a crossword in Italian. Eva had never done one before, neither in Italian, nor in German, nor in Chinese.

While Gerda served the food, Vito asked Eva about school, her favorite subjects, the girl who sat next to her.

While Gerda did the dishes, Vito reminded Eva to clean her teeth.

When Gerda was about to put Eva into the small bed, Vito protested. "Absolutely not. This Sisiduzza was here before me."

So Eva was able to stay in the large bed, just like when she was alone with her Mommy.

Gerda lay down next to her, and Vito lay down on the other side. She saw them through her eyelashes: two dark, trembling figures, like at the bottom of a glass of blackcurrant juice. Vito read to Eva the adventures of Sandokan, Yanez and the Tigers of Malaysia. Gerda had never read a book out loud to her before sleeping, let alone in Italian. Eva couldn't understand all the words of that language made of soft sounds and vowels but it didn't matter. She lay there listening to him, still, her eyes half closed, the blonde hairs of her forearms on end because of the caress of his voice.

"What does 'Sisiduzza' mean?" she finally asked.

"Tiny little spark," Vito replied.

So, framed by their arched bodies like the cockles of a shell, she felt more luminous than the Pearl of Labuan. Rocked by Vito's voice, her eyelids grew heavy until they closed completely.

"Eva is asleep," her mother said.

Only then did Vito lift her and put her delicately into the little bed.

Eva slept more soundly then than she had done since she was a baby.

Genovese had lent Vito his camera. There were many pictures taken over those two days.

Gerda in front of the little church, wearing a midnight blue shirtwaist. Gerda sitting on a wooden bench outside the hayloft. Gerda and Eva in a field covered in dandelions.

One picture was taken by Eva, who'd quickly learned to look through the viewfinder and press the shutter button: Vito and Gerda looking into each other's eyes, smiling, with her bending her knees so as not to be taller than him.

Another picture was taken by a passerby to whom Vito'd handed the camera: Eva between Gerda and Vito, against the backdrop of glaciers, all smiling like a family on holiday.

When Gerda took him to meet Maria, Sepp and their whole numerous family, Vito said as he entered the *Stube*, "*Griastenk!*"[45]

For over half a century, soldiers, office workers, civil servants, and teachers had addressed the two elderly peasants in Italian, demanding that they reply in Italian, and laughing at

---

[45] "Hello!"

their poor command of the language. Now a Carabiniere who said hello in South Tyrolean dialect with a Calabrian accent— that was something they'd never come across. Vito asked them if, that evening, they felt like trying the artichokes he'd brought back from his village, and Gerda invited them to eat with them in the furnished room.

When Eva picked one up, it seemed to her more like a flower than a vegetable: an enormous bud, prickly on top and with a heavy stem. You just had to look at it to know it came from a land of abundance. You never saw vegetables like this on the hard, vertical land of masi, for instance. Vito cooked the artichokes with herbs from the south. Sepp and Maria tried them without saying a word, concentrating, as though trying to discover their secret. When Vito offered them a second helping, they both said yes.

It was the first time Gerda had entertained in the small furnished room. Real guests to give food to and have a conversation with, while breaking bread and dropping crumbs on the tablecloth. And she, a real hostess, with her man at her side.

Before the guests arrived, Vito had brought a plank of wood into the room. He wanted to put it on the only little table in order to make it longer and for everyone to fit around it. Eva was drawing and didn't reply when Gerda asked her to clear away her papers and pencils.

"Eva, do as your mother says right away," Vito said in a voice that wasn't harsh but did not brook objections.

Eva looked up from her drawing and stared at Vito with wide-open eyes.

He was chiding her! Vito was neither the school teacher, nor the parish priest, nor Sepp (who never raised his voice at anyone anyway), and yet he was chiding her. Eva got up and removed the pencils from the table, her eyes downcast. She didn't want it to be noticed that she was sulking, of course, but only in order not to show how happy she was.

302 · FRANCESCA MELANDRI

Over dinner, Sepp told Vito about the two years he'd spent as a prisoner of war. The beating Hermann had given him at the time of the Option hadn't managed to convince him to abandon his *maso*, so, like all the other *Dableiber*, he'd been drafted into the Italian army. When the British captured him in the African desert, he asked to be transferred to the German camp so that he could at least speak his mother tongue with his fellow prisoners. However, as far as the camp commanders were concerned, Sepp was a soldier from the province of Bolzano, Italy, so he had to stay with Italians.

"It was a stroke of luck for me," Sepp told Vito.

The potatoes given to the Germans were rotten, he said, the bread had worms, there was cardboard in the soup. The potatoes and bread for the Italians, however, were almost wholesome and there were real cabbage leaves floating in the broth. Sepp said that the British knew Italians: they may be docile as prisoners, but don't you dare give them food that's too disgusting, or you risk a rebellion.

Vito served more artichokes. As he took the lid off the pan, a fragrance of garlic, mint and wild fennel drifted out. That aroma was for Eva like Vito's presence: something enveloping and intense, which you've never tried before, but which you can immediately get used to.

After two days off, Gerda returned to the hotel. There was something about her that even Elmar, the scullery boy, had never seen. It wasn't the cheerfulness of when she was about to go out with Genovese, but a quiet, fulfilled contentedness.

The consumption of alcohol that had carved a large purple nose on his old baby face had prevented Elmar's career from progressing beyond washing pots. Even so, he felt no resentment toward Gerda, on the contrary, he kept laying his eyes on her whenever he could. That day, however, watching her beating steaks on the board with new tenderness, he observed her, puzzled. She noticed, looked up and smiled at him. It took Elmar's breath away. Gerda's love for Vito was so plentiful that there was even some left over for him, a wretched alcoholic scullery boy.

At Lamezia Terme, the Indians next door, the enthusiastic cellphone users, walk past the door of our compartment in order to get off. The woman with a deep voice is wearing jeans, white socks and flip-flops covered in little pearls, the men have bellies like billiard balls over skinny legs. Two enormous dark eyes marked with kohl peep over the shoulder of one of the men. Clearly not an Italian child—for one thing he hasn't cried once in over five hours. I smile at him. At first he doesn't reciprocate, then suddenly he reveals little baby shark teeth, and his eyes light up like sparks.

A Sisiduzza.

They're met by an Italian woman who welcomes them with much laughter. The Indians also look pleased to see her, and unload their suitcases cheerfully. There are many of them, large, with sticky white bands that say FCO, for Fiumicino Airport. They must have just landed there from India, but despite their long journey they haven't lost their good cheer. They go to the underground passage with their Italian friend, and their laughter echoes long after they're out of my sight. I look at my three compartment fellows. It's only us Italian citizens left now. Without American tourists and non-Europeans, this Easter train is really empty.

Shortly after we depart, the ex-policeman exclaims, "You can see Sicily!"

There's tenderness in his voice. I go out into the corridor

and, yes, it's true: we're near the tip of Italy, and with the sun already halfway down the horizon, you can make out the dark outline of Sicily. Looking north, however, the golden coastline is so curved in on itself that you can see Calabria and, higher up, Basilicata, as well as a large chunk of Campania. You can almost see it all—the elegant boot shape drawn between Naples and Sicily. In the mountains, the light is made of air and wind, as the frost is hurled down from the heights like a sharp dart; this light, however, is liquid, dense, as though it doesn't color things but mingles their humors.

Between the coast, where we are, and the island, the luminous sea is crossed by a long dark shape: perhaps it's an oil tanker, or a large freighter that will unload thousands of Chinese containers in Naples. It glides like an apparition. On board, the sailors must be deafened by the racket of the engine but, seen from here, distant and silent, it emanates the grandiose fatality of intercontinental routes.

At moments like these, I miss Ulli so much.

The night he died, Costa had been gone a few days; Ulli had spent the first three on my sofa, trembling. I'd insisted he stay at home a little longer but he'd gone back to work a week earlier. I persuaded myself that being on Marlene, taking charge of a mechanical power, would do him good. That night I wasn't with him. These twenty years I still don't know why I didn't go with him to beat the pistes. Was I with a man? Did he ask me not to go with him? I rule out this possibility because I would have been suspicious and wouldn't have left him alone. But why wasn't I with him? I have no idea. I only remember that when the phone call came, I was in my bed, and without company.

Ulli didn't want to go to live in Berlin, London, or Vienna, like everyone was telling him to. He didn't want to be the *schwul* son of the hero who'd given his life for him. He didn't want to be a mother's obedient son, whose brain gets fried by electric shocks while they're showing him pornography—no doubt the therapy devised by that doctor in Val Sarentina so that he himself could watch images of homosexual intercourse to his heart's content. He didn't want to marry a woman, manage to have children with her only by closing his eyes and imagining she was a man, then make believe that he had a lover and, instead, go to the toilets in train stations. He only wanted to be himself where he was born and to love the person he loved.

He wanted the one impossible thing.

He went with the snowcat up the steepest piste, the one used for World Cup training, sixty percent of uninterrupted gradient. The caterpillars bit the snow while the safety cable dragged him up. When he reached the top, he unfastened the cable, turned the front of the snowcat toward the valley, stepped on the gas, and let go of the brake. That's how I've always imagined it, Marlene, the snowcat Ulli loved like a truck driver loves his truck, like a cowboy loves his horse: it slides elegantly along the piste, gets underway, a stack of snow makes it tilt to the side but the top-quality caterpillars keep it in line, it descends down the piste, acquiring speed without grazing the snow any more, flies and bounces like a child skier, crashes against a tree on the edge of the piste, then into another and another, until it ends up going over the cliff.

Marlene was red, vigorous and almost unstoppable, just like the blood pumped by the muscle we have in our chests. It deforested an entire slope before it stopped. Larches, spruces, pines, broad-leaved trees, it swiped them all like toothpicks.

The death notices in *Dolomiten* are in code, and you need to know how to interpret them, especially with regard to the cause of death of the people you're mourning.

"After a long, painful illness" means cancer.

"In a tragic road accident"—if it took place on a Friday or Saturday, it means drink driving.

When a young person suddenly dies, the family—to prevent confusion with one of too many peers who hang themselves every year in our *Heimat*—takes care to clarify the cause of death, which is generally the second one.

If the cause of death isn't stated but there's only an adverb ("unexpectedly" or "suddenly"), it's undoubtedly suicide.

In Ulli's case, the wording was "an accident at work."

1972

A ny idiot would have noticed. And Mariangela Anania, née Mollica, was no idiot. Besides, a mother knows these things.

She'd started to get an idea a year earlier, when Vito had come down on leave and told her he'd be staying up there a little longer, eating sour cabbage and balls of bread. She quickly put two and two together. If, after five years of honorable service in that land at the very top of Italy, his superiors weren't sending him back to his mother, then there could only be one reason: he'd asked to stay on.

So she really wasn't a fool, but not a whiner, either. She didn't ask him anything, she wasn't offended, she said, "Oh, really?" and didn't mention it again.

Then there was the picnic on the beach on Easter Monday, with the neighbors and their daughter Sabrina, you really couldn't say she was beautiful but she was well put together with everything in the right place and even in abundance, two beautiful, shiny green eyes, and she was even qualified. You could see a mile away that Vito wasn't interested in her, so Signora Anania and the girl's parents had exchanged looks as if to say: let's leave these young people alone, if they start talking and getting to know each other without us butting in, it's no bad thing. But, instead, every time that poor girl came anywhere near Vito, he got up, found a coffee pot to move, a glass to fill . . . anyway, it was obvious he was doing everything just so he wouldn't be alone with her. Now this isn't normal for a young man whose heart is free. On the other hand, if it's taken . . .

Then, a few months earlier, Auntie Giovanna, the one famous for always saying things other people think but don't dare say—something which had earned her universal—albeit peeved—respect, asked him, "So when are you going to get married, then?" Vito hadn't giggled like a donkey, the way young men do when what's on their mind is just easy-to-bed women, and that there's plenty of time to find the woman who'll sleep in just one bed for ever, but you can't say this to an elderly relative so they just giggle slyly, all cocky and embarrassed. No, Vito had looked down at his shoes and not raised his eyes for a good half hour, and that's something you do when you have a secret, and a very particular secret—one with a name and a surname.

In other words, Gerda Huber.

It took her ages to work out that you say Gherda and not Gierda. Not to mention the surname, I mean, how can a word start with an H and end in a consonant? Yes, it can, Vito said, and in fact, there's even one in Italian: "hotel." And then, Vito said, this isn't even as bad as some surnames, surnames you just can't pronounce, not even he after all those years, and he listed them. She didn't understand a word so, to entertain her, he wrote them down on a sheet of paper.

Schwingshackl. Niederwolfsgruber. Tschurtschenthaler.

She didn't find them funny but, on the contrary, they annoyed her, there wasn't even one vowel, all consonants, and not even normal consonants but Ks, and Hs, and Ws. What kind of names were they, anyway? Besides, they reminded her a bit too much of the days back in 1943, in Reggio, when her son was in her belly and her husband in a mass grave in Greece, though she didn't know that yet, and the Germans went from one house to another, banging on doors and screaming, "*sheenél actoon ràus capùt*" and it was a miracle she didn't miscarry from fear. But she didn't say that to Vito because once he'd told her, "Look, Mom, just because they're Germans doesn't mean they're all Nazis." So she figured it was better to drop it, because luckily he'd never had to hear those voices that sounded like machine guns, by the time he was born the Americans were already there.

In any case, since Vito had explained everything to her, she was reassured.

Because, it must be admitted, at a certain point she'd started to fear the worst.

If the woman he'd met was a good, patient girl, then he wouldn't be the first soldier who goes and marries a foreigner where he's stationed, but why keep it a secret from everybody for over a year?

She started to worry again. What if, behind all that looking down at the tips of his shoes, there was some problem, some lie, some dishonor? Her son Vito was a dependable kind, he'd never acted on a whim, even as a child. When he was six years old she'd send him to get the bread and give him extra money on purpose, to see if he came back with the change, but he wasn't just the future Carabiniere, he was like a finance police-man, one of those who check the accounts books, giving/taking all nice and precise: he'd come back clutching in his hand the little lire coins all counted, the five-lire ones with the little fish and the ten-lire ones with the ear of wheat and the plow, never any mistakes, he didn't even buy candy without permission. But then everybody knows sometimes it's the straightest sticks that end up in the fire.

But now he'd reassured her. He'd shown her a picture. Sure, she was beautiful, no doubt about that. Almost too beautiful, she thought, but didn't say it. And Vito was looking at the photo of that piece of blonde woman with a blank expression, so imagine how he must have devoured her with his eyes when she was there. Of course, besides being too beautiful, she was also almost too German but, oh well: a mom needs to know how to accept things, and she'd always disliked those mothers-in-law who make the lives of their sons' wives impossible just because they don't correspond exactly to their idea of how a daughter-in-law should be. Mariangela Anania, née Mollica, a war widow with a newborn son, knew how hard life can be for women, and while she was looking at the photo she was already thinking: if this is really the one Vito is going to bring home, I'm going to teach her to cook swordfish and eggplant with almonds and walnuts, I'll comfort her when she's home-sick for her land, I'll treat her like the daughter I never had.

But the thread of her thoughts got tangled up and snapped on something Vito said: "Except that there's a problem."

She felt cold inside. Something tight. And the certainty: here we go, now he's going to tell me about the lie, he's going to tell me the problem and the dishonor. She instinctively tight-ened her mouth and also the other orifices, those low down, like you do when you don't want trouble and pain to enter your life and especially that of your adored son. But she also knew that when you keep the doors of your body firmly shut, it means that troubles and pain are already inside.

And yet.

"She has a . . . she's much taller than me," Vito had said.

She had felt relief warm her whole being like a good broth on a winter's night. But since she was his mother, she saw it: a thing, a little thing that remained without a name or a surname, deep in her son's eyes. But she wasn't an idiot, and since Vito wasn't telling her, she also knew this: whatever this little thing he wasn't mentioning was, it wouldn't be up to her to fight it. It was her son, alone, who would see to eliminating it.

"So what?" she therefore said. "Your father wasn't much taller than me. Take her a piece of 'nduja to try."

Eva and Ulli spent their afternoons after school on top of the

Himalayas, on Nanga Parbat, to be precise. They had named their refuge at the top of the hayloft, the wooden balcony where the architrave meets the oblique beams of the roof, in honor of Reinhold Messner, the climber who tackled the twenty-six thousand feet with nothing but the power of his lungs, without tanks of oxygen. They would also climb their Nanga Parbat without artificial help and especially without Sigi: Ulli's little brother was forbidden from accessing the peak. The only time he tried to join them they named him the Yeti, but Sigi didn't like being abominable so he never came back.

Eva had stopped ignoring her cousin during Gerda's visits. Now she gave him permission to join her, her mother, and Vito. Sergeant Anania had extended his affection not only to Gerda and Eva but also to all those they loved: Maria, Sepp, Wastl. And naturally, Ulli. To Eva, her mother's presence had always been a synonym of scarcity: to see her arrive was already to fear losing her. Whereas Vito had brought along abundance: he had enough warmth for everybody.

Eva particularly liked hearing them talk about her, just like a couple of parents. Once, when they thought she was asleep, they'd even almost argued.

Gerda was saying that after middle school she'd be sending Eva to catering college: with all the new hotels being built she'd never starve. And especially, she wouldn't start working as she had, not knowing how to do anything except get her fingers corroded by caustic soda, or break her back over dirty pots. No, Eva would arrive at her first job with a diploma, a qualification, and skills. Perhaps she wouldn't start as head cook but at least as assistant cook.

"No! Eva must go to high school!" Vito had rebelled. "And then afterwards perhaps even university. She's too clever not to study."

Gerda had flown off the handle. University?! The children of ladies and gentlemen go to university, people who have money in the bank and saints in heaven. Whereas she only had two hands and was proud of them, and if he thought being a cook was a job for . . .

She'd stopped abruptly. In bed with her eyes shut, Eva had heard the silence, then the liquid sound of the lips searching each other, and Vito's gentle voice whispering, "you are to me . . . " and finally some indistinct murmuring. And even if she couldn't see her mother's face, she could imagine it, she'd seen it when Vito told her sentences that started with "you." She would become so beautiful that even Eva almost didn't recognize her.

One day, at school, the teacher came to stand next to Eva's desk. Instead of listening to the lesson she was drawing.

"And who's this?" she asked, pointing at the paper.

It was the picture of a man with dark hair and eyes, wearing a cap with a peak and black pants with a red stripe. He was holding, like a bunch of roses, a huge green and purple artichoke.

"*Mein Tata*," Eva said. My daddy.

His leave was over.

Vito looked out of the window but saw only himself: the night train had just left Reggio and outside, on the side of the sea, there was only darkness.

He'd promised Gerda before leaving: I'll tell my mother about you two. Gerda's face had stiffened as though in pain, it was actually joy. She had never been introduced to a future mother-in-law.

Next time I go on leave, I'll tell her about Eva.

He'd show his mother Eva's exercise books, how good she was at school. I can't wait to meet her, his mother would say. And also: I'll buy her lots of presents, I'll teach her our songs.

Without honor, contemptible, false. That's how Vito felt.

He was in a carriage that went as far as Germany, it was the train of the *Fremdarbeiter*, the immigrants who were going back after a holiday in their villages. They were occupying entire compartments with their caciocavallo cheese, tomatoes in oil, demijohns of wine. They were talking to Vito about homesickness, about how hard it is to live far from your land. "It's like a part of you is missing," they were saying. They always envied him when they saw him getting off on this side of the Brenner. They didn't know that, yes, it was still Italy, but just in name.

The train started and the long ride back along Italy began. At one end, the place Gerda called home; at the other, the one he called home.

Vito had been back a long time when he opened the door of the kitchen range and saw the 'nduja. It had been there for several days. It was a present for Gerda from his mother, she'd given it to his fiancée. But she hadn't been able to eat it. It was too spicy, too strong, too different than the flavors she was familiar with. And when Vito had left, she'd thrown it into the furnace of the wood stove. Now half of it was covered in ashes. It was gray, it stank.

Gerda went and clung to him. "I just couldn't eat it."

"Never mind."

But then he went to the window, the one overlooking the glaciers, and his lip quivered. He'd never felt so much sadness, and even he couldn't tell why. His eyes grew red.

Gerda was looking at him, scared. Why would anyone cry for a sausage? He straightened up, put an arm around her waist.

"I'm sorry," he said, "I'm a little tired."

He held her close, shut his eyes, searched for her skin. He only wanted one thing at that moment: to be blind, deaf, without a future.

Weeks passed, then months. Nothing had changed between Vito and Gerda.

They continued to visit Eva together, she lived with Sepp and Maria, went to school the rest of the time, and spent every free moment with her Ulli. Gerda worked in the kitchen, Vito at the barracks. They made love every time they had the opportunity. On the other hand, they didn't go dancing anymore: they'd realized that neither of them really enjoyed it.

Leni had built next to her parents' maso a new construction with three small apartments for tourists. She hadn't found it easy to obtain all the authorizations, but she had finally managed it. Her children caused her no problems at school, her elderly parents enjoyed reasonable health, she didn't consider herself an unhappy woman.

Wastl had moved to Munich, where he was teaching music and playing the clarinet in a jazz band. Ruthi had joined him, tried to show him that she was indispensable to him, hadn't convinced him, had come back home and, soon afterwards, had married the eldest son of a maso on the opposite side of the valley. Now, not even eighteen, she was expecting her first child.

Paul Staggl had finally become the grandfather of a grandson. His daughter-in-law had turned out to be an excellent mother; she was raising her children with a firm hand, even the three that followed. So as to spend as little time as possible with her or them, Hannes spent his days in his father's office. This had considerably increased his knowledge of cable cars, ski pistes, and of that new technological frontier: artificial snow. He still had his cream convertible Mercedes 190, but he almost always kept it in the garage. He went to the office on foot.

Hermann's house was demolished with the rest of Shanghai, and residential buildings were erected in its place, according to a new town planning scheme. At the age of sixty-four, Hermann became the youngest resident of the *Altersheim*, the home for the town elderly. The staff didn't find him to be a difficult guest. When he wasn't eating or sleeping, he spent his time modeling figurines with the soft part of the bread; some of them were even displayed in the Nativity scene that was set up in the entrance hall at Christmas. He never had any visitors in the retirement home.

When the winter season at Frau Mayer's hotel ended, Vito said to Gerda, "I'm taking you to Venice."

Eva would have run after the pigeons in St Mark's Square for hours but there were so many other things to see. Especially the streets made of water, gondolas like black fish, houses that looked made of lace and not bricks, and people. The city seemed like a single, permanent open air concert: tourists had long hair, either very short or very long skirts, almond-shaped or blue eyes, milky, amber or leather-colored skin.

There wasn't such a variety of people where she was born. In comparison, the tourists that filled her town during high season all seemed related to one another. Whereas here, there were Americans, Asians, Scandinavians, and even the odd African. Their skin was such a wonderful color. Why did they call them "black," anyway, when they should have called them "brown"? And how did Japanese women manage to see through those eyes as narrow as slits? Eva would squeeze her eyes to try to find out and discovered, in fact, that you couldn't see anything above or below but only to the side. And yet, and that was what was so strange, they didn't move their heads to look up; but then perhaps the Japanese weren't interested in the sky. While a passerby was taking a photo of her, Gerda and Vito together, she saw a woman wearing a tablecloth and a man in pajamas.

"Indians," Vito explained, but Eva was still astounded: she'd always imagined Indians with feathers on their heads, plaits and moccasins. This variety wasn't just fascinating to watch, but also a kind of calling: if the whole world came to visit Venice it meant that Eva, too, some day, would be able to visit the world.

Vito and Gerda walked with her in the middle, went up and down bridges, and along calli; when these were too narrow, they'd walk in line and take larger strides until once again there was room to be close to one another. They were staying in a little pensione behind San Stae. The owner had two purple rings under his eyes because of years of sleep interrupted by nocturnal patrons to whom he had to go and open the door. When they'd arrived at reception he'd said "Signora" and "your husband" to Gerda, and "your little girl" to Vito. Then he'd read the surnames on the documents and had grasped the situation. For the two days of their stay he managed to avoid addressing Gerda directly (at that point, "Signorina" would have been offensive), or specifying whose daughter Eva was. It certainly wasn't the first time this had happened: too many couples without wedding bands on the fingers had been there, and then, over the past few years, he'd seen all sorts of things, so he certainly wasn't shocked. Gerda, however, lit up a cigarette as the hotel owner was handing them the key, and Vito handed Eva the bronze bell on the counter, and said, "Look." But she knew: when her mother stared like that into space, taking puffs of smoke with indifference, it was never a good thing.

Apart from this brief moment of unease, Gerda was happy. She was in Venice! With Vito! And Eva! She felt as though she was living a song, a photo love story, a movie. In the movies, lovers in Venice kiss in a gondola and Vito had rented one. Leaning back on the red velvet couch, Gerda half closed her eyes.

"Will you take me to the Amalfi Coast on our honeymoon?"

Vito stroked her hair and held her tight, and Gerda didn't understand that it was so he wouldn't look her in the eyes. But then he said to her, "I would like to marry you."

"Would like" is similar to "want" but not the same, so she straightened up to look at him. That's when Vito confessed: he'd told his mother about Gerda. Not about Eva.

Sitting on the foldaway seat at the prow, Eva did not turn around.

Vito spoke softly, so he wouldn't be heard. "I'll tell her on my next leave. It's a promise."

Eva continued to stare at the oar with which the gondolier was slicing through the putrid water.

Vito kissed Gerda's face. She let him.

Eva looked at the little arched bridge going overhead and thought: if it breaks and falls on me I'll go underwater, swim, swim without breathing and get to the shore.

KILOMETERS 1303 - 1383

After Vibo Valentia, the view of the vast golden arch of the Calabrian coast line is interspersed with noisy darkness: one tunnel after another. It looks like a film projected so slowly that you can see the black strips between the frames. Then the sea disappears, we're inland, and between one tunnel and another round hills and monumental olive groves appear. We're now passing under the Aspromonte: a tunnel that never seems to end, as dark as despair.

Ulli's coffin was about to be lowered into its hole when an old man with hands deformed by decades of pulling the bell rope came forward. "I'd like to say something," he said.

It was Lukas, the sacristan. In church he hadn't gone up to the lectern next to the altar, like Sigi and the others, to carefully and vocally ignore the reason for Ulli's death. I hadn't done it either, or gotten up to take communion. I hadn't taken it since the day when, after Vito had gone, the parish priest had welcomed my mother back into the flock, but more as a broken lamb then a lost one. Lukas had been the sacristan of the little church facing the glaciers for almost forty years but nobody was accustomed to hearing his voice. At first it trembled, then he gathered his courage.

"I would like to tell everybody what Ulli gave me."

Surprisingly, there was a sudden, perfect silence, as though the most authoritative orator had taken the stand.

"But if my Anna were still alive I wouldn't do it."

The shock had turned into anxious curiosity, which, in Leni's case, had become panic. Terrible revelations she hadn't asked for had already first taken away a husband, then a son; she was now staring at the sacristan as though imploring to be spared.

But Lukas continued. Over sixty years ago, he said, when he was a child, there was a forbidden word, more than forbidden, in fact—unknown: *Homosexualität*. A clinical, almost academic word: it was astounding, hearing it spoken by this modest man who for decades had been arranging breviaries on lecterns, spreading incense on bigots reciting the rosary, rewarding with non-consecrated wafers children who'd been well-behaved during catechism. Truly strange.

"There was Fascism, but that was a word we didn't even know in Italian."

Lukas continued his story. When he was young he'd start sweating when he approached certain young men; but that never happened to him with women. At night, Lukas had strange dreams and confessed them to the priest who would tell him, "Say three Hail Marys and four Our Fathers and you'll have normal dreams again."

In forty years of marriage, Lukas had only ever been able to get close to his wife if he shut his eyes and imagined her to be a man. Anna didn't blame him for anything, but she could sense something. She didn't know that word either, however. Lukas was sure he was the only person in the world with that twist in him.

Lukas was the loneliest man who ever lived.

Only when Ulli had openly declared his own homosexuality had Lukas understood. *Ein Homosexueller*. So that's what he was. And he was no longer alone since there were at least two of them in the world. Lukas was an old man, his earthly existence was almost over, his good, blameless wife Anna had gone. And so he had decided: nobody else should have to spend an entire life in loneliness, ignorance, and confusion, as he had done. He had to speak out. And now Lukas wanted to say it: without Ulli he would never have known who he was. And even though Ulli had lost heart and gone the way he had, he, Lukas, was certain that now the good Lord—with whom he felt he had an excellent rapport since he'd always kept His house clean—would welcome him kindly.

Around the open grave, nobody spoke. Lukas, too, fell silent. He'd finished. He threw a handful of light-colored soil on the wooden coffin about to be lowered into the grave. On top of it was placed the target with Ulli's name, the one his father had riddled with bullets at his birth, like a gloomy prophecy. The sacristan walked away, his gray hair ruffled by the wind, with small, hesitant steps, perhaps not just because of arthritis. The undertaker looked around as though to ask if we'd finished. There was no answer, so he started his job. Little by little everybody left except Leni and Sigi, and I.

Beyond the graveyard wall, the glaciers had never seemed so near.

Sigi hadn't said to Lukas, the sacristan, the filthy words that had killed Ulli. He stood with his head down, his wide hunter shoulders unable to bear this kind of load. I'd never have thought it possible, and yet I felt sorry for him

However, Vito wasn't there to support me as I leaned against him, and say: you see, Ulli's life wasn't in vain. Vito hadn't been there for many years, and wouldn't be there for many more: but that was the day when, more than any other time before or afterwards, his absence was unbearable to me.

And finally, suddenly, it's the end of the tunnels and the last knotty mountain at the tip of the boot, and we're once again by the sea. We've really arrived: the train is running just a few yards from the water. Even though the ballast of the rails is protected by a stone breakwater, I'm sure splashes of saltwater must reach the windows at high tide.

The tiny station of Favazzina is squeezed against houses, neglected, dirty, covered in graffiti among which, in huge lettering: WELCOME TO FAVAZZINA HILL. Immediately afterwards, we go past another station just as small and helpless, but with a more evocative name: Scilla. And finally, there's the red and white lighthouse of Villa San Giovanni, which states: the continent ends here.

1973

Odontometer, tweezers, magnifying glasses. Bent over his desk, Silvius Magnago was examining a perforation gauge.

He'd never been a big traveler. The furthest he'd been was the never-ending plain of Nikopol, in Ukraine, and his left leg was still there. He'd often been to Vienna, visited a few European capitals and, going up and down between Rome and Bolzano, had covered more miles than if he'd gone around the globe. But seeing the world for pleasure was something he'd never done. His way of traveling was to collect stamps from every country. After so many years, it was a blessing to have a little time to devote to them.

With the approval of the Package, the attacks, the bombs, and the deaths had stopped. Three years later, a few months ago now, it had come into effect. Now it was a question of passing the laws for implementing the individual processes. Taxes, education, responsibility for road planning and facilitated construction: the whole administrative autonomy of Alto Adige had to find its rules of application. A long, bureaucratic, pedantic job. Magnago had never minded the search for concrete, detailed solutions, so the enterprise, tackled along with commissions led by people he respected, such as the Christian Democrat Berloffa, didn't alarm him. You needed to be meticulous, concrete, attentive to detail, and precise: the characteristics of a stamp collector, which he was. It was going to be a demanding but not difficult task.

Even the atmosphere in the *Heimat* was good. Tourism was bringing a sense of wellbeing nobody would have thought remotely possible ten years earlier. At the recent elections, his party had been rewarded with two thirds of the votes by an electorate pleased with the historical mission accomplished. Above all, he no longer received phone calls in the middle of the night, telling him that a soldier had been blown up, that a young man had been killed at a roadblock, that the wick of the explosive charge that was threatening to blow up the entire province was getting shorter and shorter.

With advancing age, his leg, the one that had stayed behind in Nikopol, was having increasingly frequent conversations with the rest of his body in the secret language of suffering, a language he couldn't share with anyone, not even his Sofia. However, the frightening, exciting years that had led from the Castel Firmiano rally to the agreement with Rome were over. Now, every so often, he could even spend time with his stamps. And yet, whenever Silvius Magnago watched the events of the country of which, by signing the Package, his land had agreed to be a part of, he couldn't feel calm. What was happening sounded familiar, like a recurring melody, but if at first it had been whispered by only a few in a small, peripheral area like South Tyrol, it was now being played by an entire orchestra: Italy.

Bombs. Massacres. Attacks. Terrorists. Roadblocks. Planned coups. Cover-ups. Rumors about the involvement of secret services in dark deeds. And, above all, the dead. Too many dead. In the streets, in banks, in police stations from which questioned people emerged dead, in crowded squares. It wasn't a happy tune.

Sometime ago, with Sofia, he'd seen a documentary about tornadoes and typhoons on television. It was then that he thought of South Tyrol like one of those areas in the middle of the ocean, unknown to the majority, crossed by few, but where hurricanes originate. Microscopic areas of low pressure seldom signaled by world radars, marginal on the global canvas, but where winds sometimes start spinning, waters bubbling, clouds gathering, until what starts as a little whirlwind turns into a cyclone ready to sweep the coast of continents, and does so, but only after it has departed forever from the insignificant place on the globe where it had started to take shape.

Here we are. The rumble of thunder, the tempest, the blizzards that had agitated his land in those years of fire between 1957 and 1969, seen from there they just looked like the first signs of something much larger and widespread, something— Magnago shuddered at the mere thought—*which had had its dress rehearsal right here, it was here that they had learned how to do it.*

Magnago was possibly the only Italian politician to enjoy, so to speak, double status. Terrorists and more extreme factions such as the *Schützen* viewed him as a political hack who betrayed ideals and kowtowed to the state's position; the Italian political world, on the other hand, accused him of excessive understanding toward terrorists. So he was, after all, in the best position to see things from both sides. The South Tyrolean events helped him develop the sensitivity of a water diviner with regard to the attacks: he saw only too well that they were playing the game of those who would have to repress them. There had been many episodes, over the past twelve years, that couldn't be understood except by supposing that somebody, some corrupt element of the government, was trying to score his own goal in order to justify the extent of the reaction. Magnago would never be able to prove it, obviously. And the delicate negotiations he'd been conducting with Italian governments for years had never allowed him to share these suspicions with his interlocutors, far from it! Yet he was certain that he was right. Only once, at the end of a customarily friendly interview with Aldo Moro, had he dropped a hint to see the effect it would have, ready to retract it if it had fallen into the void.

"And what if there were someone who didn't want Italy to become a real democracy?" Magnago had said. Moro, whose voice was normally so soft and clucking it was hard to make out his words as it was, had said nothing. However, he had looked at him with a deep, weary, understanding expression, and then half closed his eyes in an imperceptible but unequivocal expression of assent. From that moment on, Magnago had the certainty that he was right: there was a plan to destabilize democracy, and there were those who knew about it. But Silvius Magnago continued to be unable to share this conviction with anyone, just like the physical pain with which he'd lived since 1943— a lowering of the eyelids being his only proof.

And there is no point in wasting time on something that can be neither discussed nor tackled. There were already so many urgent issues to solve, complex regulations to be elaborated. For Magnago, especially now that relations with the Italian government were being normalized, there was another threat hanging over his *Heimat*, one that risked, in the long run, eating into its identity. It was the most destabilizing, most invasive, most dangerous phenomenon of all: inter-ethnic mixed marriages.

Yes, of course, he himself was the product of a *Mischehe*, but his parents had married when the entire undivided Tyrol was still part of Austria. Times when there was no need to defend the *Heimat* traditions against assimilation.

Now those times were over, and it was essential that a census be taken of the ethnic communities of Alto Adige, that they be quantified and clearly divided from one another: especially schools and cultural and language institutes, because it was only by separating South Tyrolean culture and language from the Italian ones that you could protect them effectively. The clarity of ethnic boundaries: after so many turmoils, it was the only way to maintain social peace.

It was the same as in collecting stamps. The place of *Sachsendreier*[46] or a *Schwarzer Einser*[47] was in the historical stamps album, and not in the one for World Fauna, in the bird subcategory. Order, cataloguing: South Tyrol needed the best skills of a stamp collector. Mixing and confusion between the communities would lead, once more, to conflagration and chaos.

The perforation gauge of the stamp was in good condition, as was its coating. Silvius Magnago replaced it in its album with a contented sigh. It wasn't yet the right time to issue public declarations on the subject, but this would be the next political battle the father of South Tyrol's autonomy would be fighting with his entire authority. The moment would soon come to say it out loud: *Mischehen* between Italians and Germans would spell the end of South Tyrol.

The lieutenant-colonel who read out to Vito the extract from the regulations was a couple of years older than him but seemed younger. His pale innocent eyes made it hard to imagine him with weapons in his hands, in action in a mountain pass or in a raid. As a matter of fact, none of this had ever happened to him: he'd arrived in Alto Adige only recently, when the worst was over.

He'd summoned him into his office and addressed him with the formal courtesy of Turin residents or shy people in positions of authority: and he was both those things. He'd taken the trouble to make a copy and wanted Vito to read it in person. Not because he thought he wasn't aware of its contents, but because everybody had great esteem for this non-commissioned officer, so he wanted to treat him with respect.

[46] Saxony, a Red worth three pfennig. It was the first stamp issued by the Kingdom of Saxony in 1850.
[47] A Black. The first stamp to be issued by the Kingdom of Bavaria in 1849.

Moreover, it was a delicate, intimate matter, so it might help to have the support of a piece of paper.

"Umberto of Savoy, Prince of Piedmont, Senior Lieutenant of the Kingdom. By virtue of the authority bestowed upon us; in view of the legislated royal decree, etc, etc . . . In view of the deliberation of the Council of Ministers; with regard to the proposal of the Minister of War, in agreement with the Minister of the Interior and the Exchequer; we have sanctioned and will promulgate as follows . . . "

Vito was sitting opposite him. The officer was leaning over the desk, pointing with his finger at the lines of the text he was reading. He smelled of cleanliness. Hanging on the wall behind him was the portrait of President Giovanni Leone, the face of a rodent in a thick black frame.

"Article 1. In the royal Carabinieri force, third-degree marshals and sergeants may be authorized to marry without any limitation of degree provided they have completed nine years of service and reached the age of twenty-eight . . . And you meet all these requirements," the lieutenant-colonel added.

Vito nodded.

"Article 2, which deals with corporals and selected Carabinieri, doesn't concern you, and neither does article 6. Articles 3, 4 and 5 define the quota of married Carabinieri allowed in the barracks. Article 7 is good news: married soldiers from the royal force of Carabinieri are entitled to free medical assistance from the doctor in charge at the stations."

"Excuse me, Colonel, but why 'royal'?"

"It's an attribute that has never been changed, it's still valid for us when we swear loyalty . . . " he indicated the portrait of the bespectacled rat behind him, " . . . to the Italian Republic. It's Article 8 the one that . . . " He paused.

When they have to give bad news, shy people need to be doubly courageous: to face their interlocutor, and themselves.

" . . . concerns you."

Vito had gotten distracted. He was remembering what his mother had told him when he'd been home on leave, two weeks earlier. She hadn't beaten about the bush. "It's either them, or us."

Them: Gerda and Eva. Us: her, all the relatives, and every single resident of the city and, actually, of the whole of Calabria.

"Article 8. The misconduct involving public scandal among members of the families of the married staff of the Royal Force of Carabinieri will lead to the dismissal of the soldier with termination of current duties upon proposal of his Legion commanders and the decision of the general command of the force."

The lieutenant-colonel read everything in one breath, like a schoolboy, never raising his blue eyes.

"Written in Rome on 29 March 1946. Umberto of Savoy. De Gasperi, Brosio, Romita, Corbino. Chancellor: Togliatti."

There was nothing else to read. But the officer still continued to stare at the sheet of paper.

It's either them, or us. That's what Mariangela Anania, née Mollica, had told her son. And all the Calabrians, even though they'd been divided by feuds, rivalries, arguments and obscure interests for centuries, had now united to condemn the marriage between Vito and an unmarried mother. A complete unanimity that hadn't been seen since the times of Magna Graecia or the Phoenicians. And in the face of the formidable compactness of the verdict pronounced by his living fellow countrymen, but also—his mother had made it clear—the dead ones, as well as future generations, for Vito the regulations of the Force were very small in comparison. What obstacle could it possibly find to oppose his love for Gerda, that wasn't already there, unmovable, insurmountable, like a boulder fallen on a mule track?

The lieutenant-colonel raised his gentle eyes. "The sister of a terrorist, an unmarried mother . . . Sergeant Anania, where did you find a woman like that?"

"Gerda has never done anything wrong."

The lieutenant-colonel sighed: powerless rather than annoyed. He was also sorry. "You can put it whichever way you like, Sergeant, but these are the regulations. Public scandal; misconduct. It's all in your situation. No superior will ever grant you permission to marry her. Obviously, you can do it as a free citizen but then you would be dismissed. The decree is very clear on this point."

Vito had spent his entire adult life respecting the regulations of the Force. With pride, self-denial, team spirit—things that no civilian could ever understand. Therefore, there was nothing he could say. When he left the lieutenant-colonel's office, he met Genovese. The Neapolitan had already opened his mouth to make a crack, but when he saw his expression, his lips tightened. There it was, the effect of the face of a man in love, the one you get when you're already running toward trouble: and Anania had clearly run straight into a wall. Genovese slowly moved his head down, then up, then down again, as though obtaining the confirmation he'd long been awaiting. He patted him on the shoulder twice with unexpected, rough tenderness, then turned on his heels and left.

Vito remained alone in the corridor.

To be married. Him and her. That's all they wanted. But how, when everything was against them? Above all they mustn't lose heart. They loved each other. That's all that mattered.

So they would dismiss him. Never mind. The Force wasn't the whole world. They'd still be able to manage: Gerda was a cook and he also had a profession, he was a qualified accountant. He would find a job and after a while she'd be able to stop sweating in the kitchen, and he'd make sure she never wanted for anything. Eva would go to school nearby and they could finally all live together. He would adopt her and give her his name: Eva Anania had a good ring to it.

They'd be happy, the three of them. They'd have other children too, and Eva would be pleased, all little girls like to cuddle younger siblings. They would love her so much that she'd never be jealous.

As for his mother, his mother just needed time, she'd change her mind sooner or later. As soon as the first grandchild was born she'd forgive everything, he already knew that.

Vito spoke intensely, softly under the sheets.

Gerda listened without saying a word. She clung to him and her hands sought him. She was hungry for him, for his mouth, she wanted to feel him move inside her, they would share a bed for the rest of their lives, but now she couldn't wait.

Vito was ready immediately, as he always was for her. He turned her and held her tight as she arched her back. Going inside her was so easy, my God, so essential.

Afterwards, Vito fell asleep.

Gerda held him like a child, his head tucked into her chest. She looked at the chair next to the bed where he had put his sergeant's uniform. He'd folded his trousers with precision, the red stripe right across the middle of the chair, the shoulders of the shirt hanging on the knobs. Her Vito was so tidy, so responsible, so reliable. A man of honor. She stroked his black hair. It was thinner than when she had first met him. So many times she had touched his forehead, the back of his neck, his eyebrows, that if she were suddenly to become blind she would recognize his hairline from a thousand others by touch. Gerda gave a deep sigh, and Vito's head rose with her breast.

She knew what had to be done.

When Vito woke up, Gerda was standing by the window, smoking. He looked at her and felt fear. Her voice was different, her face was different, her eyes were different. While he was sleeping, Gerda had already entered an after state that was very different from the one before.

She said, "I've made up my mind."

She didn't say: if you give up your Carabiniere uniform, you'll lose yourself and everything you believe in. And she didn't say: your mother has only you, this isn't your land, you'd always be unhappy here and die from homesickness. Nor did she say: tell me that what I'm about to say isn't true, convince me, insist that we should be together.

Instead, she said: I'm the one who doesn't want to marry you, I've thought about it for a long time, I can't live with you, we're different, it would never work, and I know that if we had other children you wouldn't love Eva anymore.

She raised her shoulders, and the movement almost made her collapse. She lit another cigarette even though she hadn't finished the first one.

Vito sat on the bed, silent.

Gerda puffed the smoke with vigor, blowing it far away, as though trying to hit the mountains beyond the window.

Vito still said nothing.

Gerda finished the cigarette.

Vito could never have imagined that it would be so difficult to look into her eyes.

And Gerda knew she had done the only thing that could have been done and should have been done when he didn't say: no, my love, light of my life, I love you, we'll overcome this and any other difficulty we come across in our long life together, don't leave me and I'll never leave you. Instead, he said, "But I want to be the one to tell Eva."

He said goodbye to everybody one by one. Sepp, Maria, Eloise, Ulli. He also went to the maso where Ruthi had gotten married, and took a little toy for her newborn baby. He said he'd asked for a transfer. He'd been away from home for too many years. His mother was elderly, he was all she had left, and it was time to go home. Nobody asked any questions. Nobody said, and what about Gerda? Maria hugged him and gave him *Schüttelbrot* and *Kaminwurz* to take to his mother, as well as the various grappas she had distilled: pine needle, raspberry, gentian. She didn't give him *Graukäse*: it wouldn't have reached Calabria in good condition. Sepp had carved a wooden box for him; he could keep all his souvenirs from Alto Adige in it, but the real souvenir was the fragrance that wafted out when you opened it, the fragrance of forests, of *Stube*, of haylofts. Ulli was crying and wouldn't let go of him. Eva wasn't there.

She was on the peak of Nanga Parbat. She was sitting on the wooden beams under the roof crossing, her legs swinging from the barrier. She was looking at the courtyard between the barn and the house, at the hens scratching on a heap of manure, at the dozing cat. She remained like this, motionless, during all the goodbyes. She was seen only when they got out to take photos with Vito—everybody wanted one with Vito, but there wasn't enough light in the *Stube*.

Gerda ordered her to come down.

His head leaning back and wrinkles on his forehead, Vito watched her without a word.

Eva climbed down from the barriers of the wooden balconies of the hayloft. On any other day, Vito would have gotten angry with her because it was dangerous to climb up and down three levels like that, she could hurt herself. Instead, he remained silent as he watched her come down the front of the old hayloft, her bare legs peering out of her dress, her scraped knees, her ankle socks. She landed with a little jump in front of the cowshed window and Vito went to her, held her tight in his arms, and said something to her. Eva wasn't listening, she was too busy thinking: he seemed different from the others, but actually he's the worst.

At the station of Villa San Giovanni, the rusty platform roof stands out against a wall covered in graffiti. ALCAMO AUTONOMOUS BRIGADES. NORTH PALERMO CURVE shits.

(Lower case). Beyond the platforms, there's a big shopping center with a very large green sign worthy of Salgari: THE PEARL OF THE STRAIT

It's connected to the station by a raised pedestrian passage. Lots of people go up and down its iron steps. There's a brand-new escalator right next to it, but it's still and, I suspect, never activated; but it's a cheerful, brilliant primary red, exactly the color of Marlene.

The Messina family gets off here. I imagine they're visiting Calabrian relatives and will spend Easter Monday with them before going back home. We say goodbye warmly, the lady gathers her many bags, the husband shakes my hand with the vigor of an ex-policeman, the daughter gives me a nice smile, and I'm left alone. In the compartment, in the carriage, perhaps even on the entire train.

Beyond the purple waters of the Strait, Sicily looks as if it's leaning against the setting sun, a dark mass over which long clouds hover. The train starts again toward its final stop and, at that very moment, the sun disappears behind the island beyond the sea, which has now turned a wan grey.

A blue glow emanates from the opening in the handbag on

the seat next to mine: there's an SMS. I pull out my cellphone and look at it. It's Carlo, he writes:

HOW ARE YOU? HAVE YOU ARRIVED? I LOVE YOU.

I look at it for a long time then, I don't even know why, I press the key under the screen which asks: DELETE?

I look out of the window. The outline of Sicily is growing darker and more blurred, now only defined by the lights of Messina. Then we cross the outskirts of Reggio Calabria. There are mass apartment buildings identical to those in the rest of Italy, illuminated by the yellow light of lamp posts. The night has fallen with almost tropical speed.

As the train pulls into Vito's city, I press: YES.

The station is almost deserted. I get out of the carriage with very few other passengers, unsteady on my legs as if after a long intercontinental journey. I've booked a hotel near the station, my suitcase trolley isn't heavy, so I should be able to get there on foot. I walk to the top of the platform, and that's when I see him.

He's exactly as I remember him. Not very tall, with a Phoenician nose, a soft, slightly crooked mouth. Vito, too, recognizes me at first glance and walks toward me. He's as young as he was then. He hasn't aged a bit.

It was the "license" that saved Gerda's life.

Or maybe she would have gotten through anyway, and the will to live would have forced her to regurgitate everything; or maybe somebody would have rushed into her room and stopped her. Or maybe, at the last minute, she would have remembered Eva and thrown the pills down the toilet. As it happened, Gerda didn't die thanks to the law on bilingualism, the cornerstone of the new provincial autonomy statute.

After years of South Tyroleans being forced to speak a foreign language in the public offices of their own land, the Package had corrected things. All the operators of public services had to produce a certificate of knowledge of both German and Italian: that was the so-called "license."

The law was compensating for a historical injustice, only it was a pity nobody had thought the practical issues through. What would happen to the Italian employees who didn't speak German well enough to pass the exam, in other words, almost all of them? Would they be fired en masse? And what about those who worked in public utility services, what would happen to them? Pharmacists, for instance.

Dr. Enrico Sanna had left his native Cagliari after university, and opened a pharmacy not far from Frau Mayer's hotel. Thirty years had passed since then, and all he had learned in German was to say hello and goodbye, "please, thank you, enjoy your meal" and a few other words. To understand the names of medicines, however, you don't need languages; hand gestures and facial expressions suffice to describe the symptoms of a headache or indigestion: he never considered not speaking German as an obstacle to his profession. His customers had never complained, either. On the contrary, in their dour way they'd always been warm toward him and his wife, who came from Barbagia and who had always felt at home among these people who were undemonstrative but true to their word. Until the day an official letter arrived for Dr. Sanna, requesting him to sit an exam to obtain the certificate of bilingualism.

Vito had been gone a couple of weeks. Gerda had returned to the kitchen. The food she prepared for Frau Mayer's guests was no less tasty, no less well cooked, garnished with no less care. When the waiters arrived with orders from the dining room, shouted "Neu!" and left notes on the counter, she was no less quick at supervising the cooking of a sauce, no less careful about basting the roast in the oven with the sauce, no less precise in slicing the roulé. However, during the lunch break, when the staff went down to eat and she, the faithful imitator of Herr Neumann, would remain alone in the kitchen in order not to leave the stove unattended, she sometimes happened to look at the bottles of detergent in Elmar's sink: it wouldn't be difficult to drink a whole one all in one go. Or at the meat knives: in her expert hands, these trusted blades would have no trouble finding her veins.

But the lunch break came to an end, the cooks returned to their counters, the hotel guests were hungry, and Gerda had survived another hour.

It was a day off, always the worst time. She was in her room, lying on her bed, but that was also unbearable, to stay like this right on the bed where she and Vito . . .

Suddenly determined, she got up, got dressed, and left the hotel. She went to the national health clinic, waited her turn amidst children with mumps and old people with diverticulitis and, when her turn came, she told the doctor about her problem: insomnia. The doctor saw her gray skin, the purple rings under her eyes, and prescribed her some benzodiazepine.

Are they sleeping pills?

Yes. With these she'd finally be able to sleep. Gerda went to the pharmacy. Was she waving the prescription like a samurai the sword with which he was about to perform harakiri? No. She'd put it into her handbag, with her face powder and her purse. But she was as determined to die as a Japanese warrior.

However, Dr. Sanna's pharmacy was shut. Gerda stood there, puzzled: it was four in the afternoon, it was a Monday, it wasn't Christmas. There was a sheet of paper full of official stamps attached to the lowered blind. It started with the title: PROVINZVERORDNUNG/PROVINCIAL DECREE.

Gerda looked around. There was a small crowd on the sidewalk outside the pharmacy. Old men, young mothers with their babies, drafted soldiers. They needed aspirin, mouthwash, anticoagulants, insulin. Condoms, thermometers, antibiotics, gauze, syringes, lice powder, sore throat sweets. Benzodiazepine to put an end to suffering. However, Dr. Sanna hadn't passed the bilingualism exam and so he couldn't sell anything to anyone anymore.

If Gerda had really wanted to, there were other pharmacies in nearby villages. But the determination that had led her thus far had lost its momentum.

So Gerda didn't die. But she started not wearing the woolen greatcoat. She would enter the refrigerated cell in her shirtsleeves, sweating, straight from the kitchen. The sweat would freeze on her instantly, burning her kidneys like an electric wire, but she would only remember to put something on when she was already out. Gerda belonged to her father Hermann's hearty brood, so she took a long time to get sick, but finally she developed a very high fever. When Frau Mayer went to see her in the attic room she got scared: her head cook was sweating and shaking as though she had cholera, and the pillow was covered in hair she was losing by the handful. She remained in bed for three weeks. When she was finally able to get up, Gerda still hadn't turned thirty but had large bald patches on her head. For months, she tied a handkerchief around it. Then her blonde hair grew back, but it was never as soft as it had been.

Gerda resumed her life of hard work. Everything was the same. Only, if anyone put the radio on in the kitchen, she would immediately turn it off. She gave Elmar the one in her room. Listening to music was more painful for her than anything else. If she met a man in a bar she wouldn't ask his name, and if he told her, she wouldn't listen anyway. There was only one name she wanted to hear. One morning, during a break, as she was preparing ingredients for the day's meals, she went out to the rear for a smoke; she was holding a ladle she'd forgotten to put down. Hannes Staggl was there, waiting for her. He'd put on weight, his red hair had splashes of gray, his eyelids were increasingly like those of a salamander. He was standing there, rooted in the middle of the courtyard of Frau Mayer's hotel, like the wrong frame in the middle of a film.

"*Figg lai mit mir,* Gerda," he said. Fuck only me. "That guy dumped you because he didn't love you, not like me. I was ready to pay for everything. Fuck only me from now on, and you and Eva will want for nothing."

Gerda took aim and hurled the ladle at her daughter's father. She hit him on the side of one eye. Hannes Staggl was lucky: ten minutes earlier, Gerda had been boning a side of beef with a cleaver.

For weeks, his eye remained half closed, blue and swollen, like that of an overage boxer. He told his wife that he'd opened the car door on himself. He'd finally sold his Mercedes and not yet gotten used to the door of his new Lancia.

When Gerda arrived at the little room where they lived during the low season, she found dozens of letters. She felt despair even just touching them. She threw them, unopened, into the wood stove. Many were addressed to Eva. She threw away those too, like she had thrown away the sausage with too much pepper in it.

Whenever Eva saw a tan (or even light grey, yellow or black) Fiat 600 climbing up the bends leading to the masi, her legs would feel paralyzed as though they'd sprouted roots, her breath would catch in her chest, and her mouth would dry up. If pumpkins could become carriages and some frogs be transformed into princes, then why shouldn't Vito appear in the square?

But it was useless. It didn't work. She was ten years old now, and no matter how hard she tried, she didn't believe in fairytales anymore.

The only solution was to stay put up in Nanga Parbat with Ulli, and to come down to the altitude of other human beings as seldom as possible. It's cold at fifteen thousand feet, you can't breathe easily, but at least you're high above desolation and homesickness.

Then, all of a sudden, almost from one day to the next, Ulli's voice started to change. At first, his childish soprano became a graceless croak, then, after a couple of years, it acquired the resonance of a tenor. Even so, he continued not to show any interest in girls, except Eva. In the morning, he'd wake up with a sticky pubis after dreams populated by strange animals.

At around fourteen, Eva began to feel men looking at her. Once, she was walking with Gerda down the main street of the town when a group of youths started to whistle. Gerda didn't turn around, certain as she had always been ever since she'd become a woman that the compliment was aimed at her. Eva met the excited, scared eyes of one of the boys and understood that, actually, they only had eyes for her, for the bare legs under the miniskirt, for the chest, already full, that was pushing against the blouse with the butterflies.

She looked at her mother. Gerda was walking with her back straight and her mouth tight, like a woman who doesn't respond to compliments. Eva parted her lips to explain the situation to her but then, excited, embarrassed, and with a vague feeling of betrayal, said nothing.

Kilometer 1397

It's not Vito but Gabriele, his son. He's come to pick me up at the station. He loads my trolley suitcase into the trunk of his Opel Vectra and, for an instant, I picture Carlo performing the same gesture. It feels like a year, but it was only two days ago.

It's too late to go and see Vito. The pain from the bone tumor keeps him awake at night and he manages to sleep only a little in the evening. Gabriele is now going to take me to the hotel, and I'll go to see him in the morning. As he drives, I can't help stealing glances at him. He also casts a furtive look at me. Caught red-handed, we burst out laughing.

Vito's son and I are laughing together in his car.

Imagine that.

He didn't say "Signora" or "Signorina," we've immediately used our first names as something right and natural. Gabriele talks as he drives. There's not much traffic and we're going fast but I can see nothing of Reggio Calabria. I have eyes only for the sharp profile and crooked mouth of the man who, ever since he was born, has been able to call Vito "Daddy."

He does know a few things about me. When he was a little over twenty, Vito told him: about the woman from up north he'd loved as a young man, and her little girl.

"And so I imagined this little girl with very blonde hair, almost white, like the children who arrive from Germany in the spring. And so you are."

"No, I'm not."

"You're not a blonde?"

"I'm not German from Germany. I'm South Tyrolean."

He looks at me. Serious, but with laughing eyes. "And that's something completely different . . . "

"Yes, completely different."

He looks so much like his father. He has the same slightly crooked way of laughing: half his mouth rises, stretches and widens, while the other half remains still as though waiting for the other to finish playing around—but without any impatience.

"And what else has he told you about me?"

"That he would have liked to know that you're happy."

I look away.

"Are you hungry?" he asks.

It's a little restaurant in a narrow alley, but where you can smell the sea. The ricotta rissoles and the mixed fried fish taste better than anything I've ever eaten, perhaps it's because I've not had a hot meal since Fortezza.

Gabriele is also a Carabiniere. He has two degrees, in Political Science and Law, and he speaks three languages, plus a smattering of all the languages from the places where he has been on a mission: Bosnia, Kosovo, Iraq.

When he was in Kosovo, the most important thing was greeting both Serbians and Albanians in the appropriate manner, without confusing them. Never order three coffees in an Albanian café by raising your thumb, index, and middle finger, because that's a Serbian greeting. You have to raise your index, middle, and little finger. If you make a mistake, they take it as an insult, and it's in nobody's interest to offend an Albanian. In Pec, he and his men raided a "girl farm." That's what the paramilitary called it. He doesn't want to say what he saw inside. He arrested the camp's boss himself and kept him under surveillance until handing him over to the emissaries of the international court. He was a middle-aged man, married, with a devoted wife and three daughters the same age as the women prisoners his soldiers were using like pieces of meat.

"It makes no sense."

"When I hear that kind of thing, I realize we were lucky in Alto Adige"

Gabriele nods. "Yes. Very lucky."

After coffee, I look up at him and smile. "You're not asking me."

"What?"

"If I feel more Italian or German."

"Why should I? It's as if you were to ask me if I feel more Calabrian or Italian. Or rather more Norman, Arab, Greek or Albanian."

I look at him and wonder what it would have been like to grow up with Gabriele as a younger brother.

* * *

When we reach the hotel, Gabriele turns off the engine. He remains silent for a minute before saying, "My mother also knew about you two."

"Your mother! How did she know?"

"It was my grandmother, she's dead now. When they got engaged she told her: my son's true love was another woman, he will never love you like that. But he will always respect you because he's a good man. Take it or leave it."

"And your mother took it."

Gabriele nods. "It wasn't an unhappy marriage. On the contrary."

He drags my trolley suitcase as far as the reception desk. Before leaving, he hands me a package. It's small, wrapped in brown paper, tied with a thin string. It's very old and smells of musty drawers.

"My father told me to give it to you when you arrive. You can use this," he says, handing me an old Walkman with headphones. We say goodbye with a slightly clumsy hug, like people who want to hold each other a little longer, but are too shy.

1978-1979

T hat phone call, the worst ever, didn't come in the middle of the night, or at the first light of dawn. It rang at a deceptively harmless time: right after lunch. Magnago had just finished coffee with his wife Sofia, and was about to go back to his office.

It was a familiar voice, with a Roman accent. It told him about the red Renault in the middle of Rome city center—right next to the headquarters of the two large political parties—and about the body under the blanket.

For some time now, Sofia had been having trouble remembering the names of things, or rather it was that they just refused to be found in her language. That thing with four legs that you sit on, she couldn't remember what it was called, yet she immediately gave it to her husband: she didn't know what they'd said to him on the phone, but she could see very clearly that Silvius was about to fall.

Magnago collapsed on the chair and put his hand to his forehead. He asked her to turn on the television.

There it was, the body curled up in the boot. The crowd of policemen. The priest giving the last rites. Over his bent neck, the famous face with its secret intelligence had a long beard after all the days of anxiety, terror, imprisonment. There it was in full, the destructive force of the hurricane. Aldo Moro had been killed.

Magnago hid his face in his hands. His wife was standing next to him. He leaned his forehead against her chest, and wept.

On that May 9, 1978, Gerda too was standing in front of the television. Frau Mayer, patrons, cooks, and assistant cooks were all watching the screen together, in silence.

Among them only Gerda, Elmar, and Frau Mayer had been present at the banquet which, so many years earlier, *Obmann* Magnago had hosted for Aldo Moro, in that very dining room. The rest of the staff had been hired later. Gerda recalled how they'd all stood in a row to say goodbye to the two powerful men. She couldn't remember the expression of the Italian, but then she recalled that he'd kept his eyes down while giving her his hand, and that it wasn't really a proper handshake: the grip of a defenseless man who certainly wasn't very strong. She wondered why they'd killed such a gentle man.

Besides, no man, powerful or ordinary, deserves to be shoved into the trunk of a car like that, like a thing.

That wasn't the worst day because every death is worse than any other for those who mourn it and, afterwards, there were many deaths in Italy, too many. However, in comparison, some of the attacks that used to take place in Alto Adige seemed like the firecrackers that explode several days after New Year's Eve is over. Nothing but insignificant bang bang from tiny little crackers, in comparison to what was happening in the rest of Italy.

In 1979, the *Tiroler Schutzbund*, an extremist faction few people had heard of, blew up the Wastl in Eva's home town for the umpteenth time. For the past forty years, the monument to the Alpini had been erected and destroyed, erected again and destroyed again, as though it had become the stake in a very long competition.

For a couple of years now, Eva had been a boarder in Bolzano, where she had been admitted to high school because of excellent grades at the end of middle school. After many arguments, she had persuaded her mother that she'd never become a cook. That morning, she walked past the intersection and saw young drafted soldiers in overalls and boots, armed with brooms and dust pans, collecting pieces of Wastl from the ground. They looked more like good little housewives than military forces deployed against a now-obsolete form of terrorism.

Nobody was interested in these things anymore, on either side, except for a few fanatics. A few months later, even the National Association of Alpini took the wise decision not to reconstruct the monument again, but to erect a granite bas-relief representing Alpini in peace service. Until it was built, the headless bust of Wastl would remain in its place on the pedestal. The bas-relief, however, was never sculpted, and the stub of statue is still there even now.

Eva was back home for her vacation when the small package arrived. It was wrapped in brown paper and tied with a thin string. Gerda went to open the door.

The names of the addressee and the sender were in neat handwriting. Gerda recognized it immediately. "I nimms net," she told Udo, the postman. I'm not taking it.

"But it's for Eva—"

"I'm her mother. I know she doesn't want it."

Udo nearly asked if she was sure. But she looked up at him with her transparent, almond-shaped eyes and stood there, motionless, staring at him. He said nothing. He took a pen out of his breast pocket and a form from the leather bag. He handed them to her, now avoiding her face. "Sign here."

Gerda signed. Then, suddenly gentle, she asked, "So what's going to happen to this parcel now?"

"I'll take it back to the sorting office and tell them you don't want it—"

"That Eva doesn't want it."

"—and they'll send it back."

Udo put the parcel back into his leather bag, folded the form, and slipped it with the other papers. He replaced the pen in his breast pocket after checking that it was closed securely. He was about to leave. The upper part of his body was already turning toward the road and his feet were about to follow when he had one last scruple. "Where's Eva, anyway?"

"Eva is asleep."

The brown parcel traveled backwards along the road it had taken to arrive at that spot: two thousand seven hundred and ninety-four kilometers in total, there and back.

D ear Sisiduzza,
       Today, you turn sixteen.
       It's an important day.
   All your birthdays are important days for me, and even
though I've not been able to see you again, I've never forgotten
any of them.

The hotel room has marble tiles and sponge effect walls,
with a fruit and flower frieze running along the top. The night
is quiet and, lying on a bed with an iron headboard, I have the
Walkman headphones over my ears.

Vito's voice. So young, so familiar. Every so often it breaks
with emotion and then it hurts to listen to it.

*Your mother and I couldn't get married for so many reasons,
I don't know if she's ever explained them to you, but that's not
important now. Things turned out the way they turned out and
nobody can go back. However, I want you to know that for me
you are not just . . . Gerda's daughter. You're also my Sisiduzza
and I love you very much, and just because I haven't seen you for
years doesn't mean that I've stopped.*

*I've written you so many letters but you never answered. I do
understand, you know, I'm not going to tell you off, you were so
little. What could you say to me? Perhaps you were angry with
me, and you had a perfect reason to be. But now you're grown-
up and it's different. If you want, I'd like us to write to each
other, perhaps even talk on the phone sometimes, you could tell*

me how things are going in high school, for example. I know
you've always been very bright, and I'd love to follow you in
your studies and along your path, I'm not very well-educated,
but your teachers will make sure they teach you, I just want you
to know that you can always count on me.

Now that you're growing into a woman, I think you will need
not to be alone, perhaps even more so than when you were tiny.
I mean, of course you have your mom, she loves you very much
and has done everything she could for you, even when things
were very . . . difficult for her.

There's a long pause. Vito clears his throat.

However, girls your age also need a dad and, if you want to,
I could be, well, let's say a kind of a dad, the one who gives you
advice, comforts you, perhaps even chides you when you make
mistakes.

Above all, someone who protects you.

I press the stop button. I stare at the Walkman. I press
rewind.

. . . one who gives you advice, comforts you, perhaps even tells
you off if you make mistakes.

Above all, someone who protects you.

Rewind.

. . . —one who protects you.

Rewind.

. . . who protects you.

Rewind.

. . . who protects you.

Rewind.

. . . who protects you.

Rewind . . .

There are bunches of grapes, lemons, and fruit I don't recognize. Poppies, roses, orange blossoms. Every so often, between a
fruit and flower, there's a Cupid. How long do I lie there, staring

at the frieze that runs high up along the walls? I have no idea. A gray light is beginning to filter through the window.

I can imagine him, a young non-commissioned officer in uniform, sitting at the table, talking into the microphone of the Geloso tape recorder. That fresh, affectionate, careful voice. It would have been there for me, but I lost it.

I lost Vito.

I lost him the way you lose at a fairground, when, instead of throwing the cloth ball straight and knocking down all the cans, so then they give you a prize, I threw but didn't win.

I didn't win a father. I didn't win him when I was born, or later with Vito. I didn't win a husband or children. I didn't win brothers or sisters who could share the difficulty of being my mother's daughter. I didn't win Ulli's love. They were right, the people at Ulli's funeral: they were saying, we lost him. I thought that wasn't true but, actually, yes, I did lose him. All my life I've been throwing cloth balls against cans but I've never been able to hit them, and now I think I've almost run out of balls.

I stretch, my arms knock down the parcel paper that the cassette tape was wrapped in. I pick it up. The address of the sender is on the back, like they used to do. It has been lying this side down in a drawer for so many years that it's still dark. The handwriting is neat, like that of a good soldier.

VITO ANANIA, VIA BOTTEGHELLE 17, REGGIO CALABRIA.

The side with the details of the addressee, however, is more discolored. It has obviously been in the light more. SIGNO-RINA EVA HUBER.

It was addressed to me. My name is, as a matter of fact, Eva Huber.

That name, it's me.

Above the address, in red, there's an oblique stamp: REFUSED.

Refused.

By whom?

Who?

I look up at the fruit on the freeze and recognize it now: it's a pomegranate.

It was she. She refused it.

She refused this package that was addressed to me, only to me, Eva Huber, and that's me, just me, not her, she has another name, she's another person, we are not the same thing, and yet she did this. I was sixteen years old and she told the postman to send back Vito's voice saying "I'll be the one who protects you."

I could have not lost Vito. I could have him here. Everything could have been different. But she had the postman write: "refused."

My solar plexus explodes with indignation.

It's all clear to me now.

It's her fault. It's all her fault. Everything, absolutely everything, is her fault.

I curse the day I was born, because that day Gerda Huber became my mother.

I go to the bathroom, throw cold water on my face, I am tired, tired but lucid as never before. Anger I've never known in my life presses on my chest like an iron hand. Tell her. I have to tell her.

Now the light streaming in through the window is pink and orange. It promises a beautiful day.

I go back to bed from the bathroom, sit down, pick up the phone, ask for an outside line, and dial a number. I have the implacable, precise movements of an assassin.

Gerda Huber has gotten up early all her life, and still does that now she's retired. After half a dozen rings, she answers.

I don't say hello. I immediately ask, why? Why did you get the postman to write "refused" on that package?

She says nothing

Maybe she was already awake, or maybe the phone has dragged her out of her light, pensioner's sleep.

I didn't even say: hi, it's me.

She takes a while to react while I throw other words at her, like blades, until she finally understands what I'm talking about.

"How do you know?"

"I'm in Reggio Calabria. I've come to see Vito, who's dying."

"How . . . ?"

Instead of answering her, I carry on. "Imagine if someone had prevented you from having a father. Your father. When you were a child. And even later, when you were older. Think. Think what it would have been like."

1992

When was the last time Gerda had seen her father? At Peter's funeral, a quarter of a century earlier.

These corridors were at such strange angles. You went straight ahead and ended up colliding with a window, and not a straight one but crooked. Even on the outside, the new retirement home had a façade full of oblique lines, triangular balconies, strange spires on the roof.

For a long time, the town had been waiting for the new *Altersheim* to be built. Perhaps because the population had increased, or perhaps because death had grown lazy, the old retirement home was always overcrowded. The waiting list was very long, families waited years to obtain a place. And, since there was only one way in which the occupant of a room could vacate it, it wasn't nice to wish for it. Now, finally, with a new building, there were far more beds and the waiting list diminished.

The town council had spared no expense in building it, partly because with the financial autonomy of the province there was more than enough money, to the point where one sometimes wondered how to spend it all. The architects who had planned it were pleased with their innovative work, the walls that met with daring perspectives, the large rooms that were never square or rectangular, but diamond, trapeze, scalene triangle-shaped. Unfortunately, moving amid those sharp corners could be very difficult for the guests; and anyone who brought furniture from their homes, so they could spend the end of their lives in their own beds, found that there was no way of putting them within those misshapen lines. But imagine an old people's home mentioned in architectural journals. What prestige!

Of Hermann Huber's children, Gerda was the only one the management of the *Altersheim* was able to track down: one was dead, the other abroad and no one remembered her married name. She was the only one left, at least the only one living in the town.

That's what the voice on the telephone had said in Frau Mayer's office, and she had personally gone to the kitchen to tell Gerda somebody urgently wanted to speak to her. The illness that had struck her father was in its final stages, the voice also said, he was no longer responding to therapy, and was on the danger list. If she wanted to say goodbye for the last time, she shouldn't waste any time. Unless she preferred to go there afterwards, in order to carry out the paperwork that would make the room available for the next person on the list.

Frau Mayer had left her alone in her office during the phone call. At eighty years of age, the Aztec green of her eyes was still magnetic, and just because the plait around her head was now white, it was no less perfect, on the contrary, it was even better sculpted, if such a thing were possible. And, since Gerda had become more essential and compact, she and Frau Mayer had started looking like each other, as happens with old couples. A little under fifty, Gerda was still a beautiful woman, but she no longer triggered in men the longing she once did, and this, no use denying it, had allowed Frau Mayer to be more kindly disposed toward her. When Gerda told her that she needed to be away for a day, she didn't object. She just commented that she didn't know her father was still alive.

"I didn't either," Gerda replied.

She walked down the corridor that led from the front door of the retirement home to the stairs.

The lower floors overlooking the garden were occupied by guests able to feed themselves, read Dolomiten, fall in love, throw angry scenes of jealousy at one another. On the upper floors were those who were not self-sufficient. The closer or more probable the departure of a guest, the closer their room was to the sky.

Gerda followed the instructions she was given at the reception desk and turned right, but found herself outside a bathroom door: she'd gotten lost. This happened to all visitors the first time they came in: it was easy to misunderstand the directions indicating right and left with all those unexpected turns in the corridors. Gerda retraced her steps, deciding to bypass the elevator and use the stairs instead. She was already halfway down the corridor when she came across a small crowd. A dozen people, care workers, guests, and visitors were gathered around a tall, gaunt figure, agile on his crutches in spite of his age, unmistakable. Gerda was startled: her *Obmann*!

"I guarantee you this, *gnädige Frau*,"[48] Silvius Magnago was saying to an elderly lady in a wheelchair, "osteoporosis in the hips doesn't affect your spirit. Believe me, I know what I'm talking about. If intelligence were in one's legs, then I'd be half an idiot."

And the Frau in the wheelchair burst out laughing like a girl who could have gotten up and danced.

Drawing close to eighty, Silvius Magnago was no longer either the president of his province, nor the *Obmann* of his party, of which he only kept an honorary presidency. A few months earlier, in June, Austria had given Italy a declaration which stated that the Italian government had fulfilled its obligations toward the German-speaking minority in Alto Adige. The official term for this certificate was: Discharge Receipt. A legal term, an accountant's term, like a shopping receipt, not

[48] Dear lady.

one fit for a hero—and perhaps therein lay Silvius Magnago's historical success. His own task fulfilled, he'd found himself another one: visiting the retirement homes of the province and surprising people his own age with the gallows humor no one had ever detected during his years of political activity.

Magnago indicated the cigarette in a young male nurse's hand. "The management has forbidden me from bringing cigarettes, they say they cause cancer. But in the Lana home they've allowed me to, and you know why? They have a very long waiting list there so they need a hand."

A brief silence, then a collective giggle, liberating, almost wild.

Gerda approached, a lump in her throat. Seeing him there before her, she suddenly felt like the little girl who'd seen him with the crowd at Castel Firmiano eating out of his hand.

"Herr Obmann . . . !" she whispered.

Magnago saw her, gallantly turned around, and shook the hand she herself was surprised she had the courage to proffer. "Beautiful lady, you're too young to be living here. Are you visiting a relative?"

"My father."

"Good for you. We old people need young people not to leave us on our own. How is your father?"

Gerda's mouth felt dry. Thankfully, at that very moment, after making a great effort to walk across the corridor with a stick, an octogenarian started telling the *Obmann* that he'd wanted to meet him in the flesh all his life.

With a long finger Magnago pointed at his own skinny chest. "In the bone, perhaps, but, sorry, there isn't much flesh left . . . " He said it like an experienced comic actor, deadpan, with a stern mouth. The public enjoyed it and burst out laughing again.

Confused, Gerda had already walked away.

The smell of disinfectant and bleach masked the discharge of a dissolving body. However, the air was still, like when death isn't far away. Hermann's shoulders were still broad and square; at the end of the long legs his daughter had inherited, his feet touched the tip of the bed. The arm stretched out on the sheet, with an inserted drip, was still muscular. He was asleep.

Standing at the door, Gerda hesitated. It was a large, bright room, although of an irregular shape. The space between her and the form on the bed seemed very wide to cross. For a long time, she stood looking at him from a distance. She needed an effort of will to approach, take a chair—of a daring tubular design—place it by the bed, and sit down.

Hermann gave no sign of noticing her presence. The windowsill was covered in figurines made with the soft part of the bread. They stood out against the light, like a little nation against the sky: beyond the glass pane, lenticular clouds with blurred edges drifted across the azure, propelled by the *Föhn*. Gerda didn't call the man who, for a time, had been her father, didn't try to attract his attention. She remained silent and motionless, as though her emotions too had been sterilized with bleach.

How long she remained like this, she didn't know. After a while, her father opened his eyes. He noticed her presence and turned to her. He stared at her with an opaque look at first then, once he'd focused, it became as brilliant as that of a child.

It was her.

Yes, yes, it was her.

The almond-shaped eyes. The high cheekbones. The soft mouth that only knows kind words.Hermann lowered his eyelids with a moan of relief, satisfaction, comfort."*Mamme . . .*," he whispered, with his eyes shut. He'd been waiting for her for so long. A lifetime.

KILOMETER 1397

G abriele has come to pick me up and taken me to his parents' apartment. His mother opens the door. She comes up to my shoulder, has short gray hair that must have once been curly, a heavy build. But she also has luminous green eyes, and music in her voice. "Here you are, finally! You've no idea how much my husband has been look-ing forward to seeing you!"

Embarrassment? Jealousy? Not even a hint. On the con-trary, she comes closer and drops her voice. "Please don't be offended, I'll pretend I don't know who you are. I don't want him to think I'm upset."

I don't know what to say but she doesn't need me to say anything. She continues, "I'll just finish making him comfort-able in the living room, please give me a moment, we're a little slow, I'm not a little girl anymore, either."

She goes beyond a frosted glass door, the only source of light in a corridor with a dark stone floor.

There's a smell of sauce.

"Would you like a coffee?" Gabriele says.

"Yes, please."

"I'll go and make it."

I put a hand on his shoulder. "Please, don't leave me alone."

He lowers his head in agreement; he's not surprised. He puts a hand on mine as I look at him gratefully.

There are various honors hanging on the corridor walls. Gabriele sees that I'm looking at them, and switches on the light.

They are all certificates conferred upon Vito Anania.
BRONZE MILITARY MEDAL FOR LONG SERVICE
SILVER MILITARY MEDAL FOR LONG SERVICE
GOLD MILITARY MEDAL FOR LONG SERVICE
GOLD CROSS FOR SENIORITY OF SERVICE
KNIGHT OF THE ITALIAN REPUBLIC
MAURITIAN MEDAL
There's also a mention in dispatches, with grounds. I start
to read it.

Alongside the Special Operations Group, he cooperated success-
fully with his superior in charge of carrying out complex and risky
inquiries into organized crime, concluding with the discovery and
reporting of 20 persons with records for criminal association, respon-
sible for 8 extortions, 17 explosive attacks, 7 aggravated damages
and other minor crimes, 2 of whom were arrested while dictating
over the line the details of delivery of significant sums of money.

"What does 'dictating over the line' mean?" I ask Gabriele.
"That they were on the phone." His eyes laugh a little but
not his mouth, which remains serious.
Vito's wife comes back through the glass door. She's wearing a jacket and putting a handbag across her body. She says to
her son, "I'm taking advantage that you two are here, so I can
go shopping." To me, as if I'm already part of the family, she
clarifies, "We can't leave him alone anymore." Then she smiles
in such a way that I can't help smiling myself.
"She's here."
Gabriele opens the glass door and lets me in, then I think
he goes to the kitchen, but I can't remember.
He is lying on the sofa on a dozen cushions, a shawl over his
legs that are resting on a pouf.
"Eva . . ."
He's so old. He's so ill. Only his eyes are the same, the rest
of him is ready to die.

"You came."

I can't even say his name. He motions to me to come closer. I cross the room; he looks at me, and looks at me, and looks at me.

"You're so beautiful."

Never before have I realized just how much I look like my mother.

What do you say in these cases? When you see a man who over thirty years ago . . . I don't know.

So I ask, "How are you?"

"Well . . . as you can see . . . "

"Do have a lot of pain?"

"A little, at night . . . "

He taps gently on the sofa, as though inviting me to dance.

"Come, sit down, tell me about yourself . . . Everything, I want to know everything."

Here we go, I think, now he's going to ask me if I'm married, if I have children. Instead, he asks, "So, what work do you do? I'm sure you have a good career. What did you study at university?"

He has the same voice as when he read me the exploits of the Malaysian Tigers, only fainter.

I shake my head. "I didn't finish university. I organize events."

"Events?"

I tell him I was studying law, that I wanted to qualify in employment law, but that in my second year they hired me at a public relations company. So I didn't take any more exams, started my own business, and now organize events, and I'm doing well financially: I've bought myself a nice apartment. My mother is happy that I don't do the job of a slave, as she puts it.

Vito doesn't comment. He doesn't tell me off for not studying, he doesn't say he's disappointed in me. And he doesn't say: if I'd been there, I would have helped you choose differently.

He nods slowly, as though thoughtfully contemplating the already fixed course of things. It's clear, however, that my answer has made him sad.

Neither does he ask if my mother is married. He just wants to know how she is. I tell him. "Does she know you're here?"

"I told her this morning before coming. But . . . I think I went about it the wrong way."

Again, he nods, in that slow way of his. Something else he doesn't say: give her my best.

He asks about the people he used to know. It becomes increasingly easy to talk. I tell him about everybody. The last one I tell him about is the hardest. Vito's eyes cloud over and, for a while, he can't find the words except his name: "Ulli . . . "

We remain a long time without speaking, and it's almost lovely to be close together in silence, the memory of the little boy with roebuck eyes between us.

He asks about Nanga Parbat. He remembers the name of our hiding place! The old hayloft was demolished, I say, Sepp and Maria's grandchildren have built a new one, and now the cowshed looks like a research lab.

I tell him about Sigi and his son Bruno, who's become a *Schütze* like his father, and about the parades where he wears a 19th-century three-cornered hat over dreadlocks and piercings. It's so easy to talk to Vito. He also tells me about himself, about his family. But I can see he's getting tired. I'm about to tell him but he pre-empts me.

"You look tired," he says to me.

I nod. "I haven't slept since . . . I can't even remember."

He puts a small cushion on the blanket that covers his legs, looks at me, and gives it two little taps, an affectionate invitation. As if to a cat or a little dog. Or to his little daughter.

I take off my shoes, put my head in his lap, stretch my legs, and make myself comfortable. He puts an arm around my shoulders, and plumps up the cushion under my neck.

"I listened to the tape," I say softly, looking up at the ceiling.

"Did Gabriele give it to you?"

I slowly move my head. "I would have liked to receive it when you sent it."

"You have it now."

The belly I'm leaning against resounds with his quiet voice, like a drum. I close my eyes with a deep sigh.

"But it's late now," I say.

"It's not late. It's just later."

Sleep creeps up on me like a thief: it was next to me but I didn't see it until I was in its clutches. I can still hear Gabriele coming into the room with the coffee, and Vito saying, "Eva will drink it afterwards. Now, she's asleep."

KILOMETER 0 - TODAY

And now I'm hugging my mom because nothing and nobody can make up for what we have lost, neither those guilty of these losses, nor those who, directly or indirectly, were their origin or cause. In the end, when all the calculations have been done and it's clear who has taken what away from whom and why, and credits and debits and the whole double entry of faults and resentments is in order and precise, the only thing that counts is this: that we can still hug each other without wasting a single instant of the extraordinary luck of still being alive.

I returned home on the plane, I flew over Italy in a couple of hours, my nose stuck to the window: I feel as though I have caressed the entire small peninsula I can now see from above.

I immediately went to see my mother. I told her about Vito. She looked at me, she didn't speak immediately. Then she said, "You must have missed him very much."

Words I've been waiting for for thirty years, yet I only realize it now that I hear her utter them. I tuck them inside myself, like a treasure.

"And what about you? Have you often thought about Vito?" I then ask.

My mother does something strange: she takes her bare feet out of her house shoes, and crosses her big toes. She looks at them for a long time. "I've thought of him every night before going to sleep."

*

I've slept over at her place. The roads are icy, there's a sudden frost. She's fallen asleep on the sofa, her head under the cushion Ruthi has embroidered, her mouth, still beautiful, half open. It almost hurts to look at her, but it's a good pain.

And I think: Gerda *schloft*. Gerda sleeps.

EPILOGUE

There is the time that flows around us, toward us and through us, time that conditions us and shapes us, the memory we cultivate or shake off—our History. Then, there is a sequence of places in which we live, between which we travel, where we are physically, places made of roads and buildings but also trees, horizons, temperatures, levels of atmospheric pressure, the major or minor speed with which the water of a river flows, altitude—our Geography.

These two trajectories, linked partly by fate and partly by free will, meet every instant and in every place at a spot, like in a Cartesian graphic cosmos, and the sequence of these spots forms a line, a curve and sometimes, if we're lucky, even a pattern which, if it's not harmonious, then at least it's one you can make out.

This is the shape of our lives.

One morning, in spring 1998, following the Schengen agreement, in the presence of Italian and Austrian authorities, the frontier barrier between the two countries at the Brenner Pass was removed. There was no longer a physical border separating Südtirol from Austria, its lost Mother Country.

It's a shame, though, that this event that had been dreamed of for almost eighty years, which had been claimed with blood and denied with military force, now had almost no more relevance in a world shaken by globalization. If History had meant to play a practical joke, the date was appropriate: the first of April.

*

Eva has made a decision. If there is another census of linguistic belonging, when she fills in the *Sprachgruppenzugehörigkeitserklärung*, in the box "ethnicity" she will write: CHINESE.

After all, her mother was born in Shanghai.

NOTE

Within the obvious limitations of an invented novel, I have tried to be as faithful as possible to historical events. In particular, the episode of the raid is based on episodes of the round-up that took place in Montassilone/Tesselberg (Val Pusteria) in September 1964, as reported by eyewitnesses. The Alpini officer who gave the order "shoot them all," and the fact that that order was part of a wider strategy, was reported in an interview given by retired General Giancarlo Giudici and published in the newspaper *La Repubblica* in July 1991: he had been the young lieutenant-colonel who directed the operation—and who disobeyed the orders.

The chapters dedicated to Silvius Magnago are largely based on the excellent book by Hans Karl Peterlini: *Das Vermächtnis. Bekenntnisse einer politischen Legende* (Raetia, 2007).

In order to meet the demands of fiction, I have allowed myself to pretend that the decree signed by Umberto of Savoy regarding "acceptable" mixed marriages for Carabinieri was still in force in 1973. In reality, it was repealed in 1971. Similarly, I have brought forward by one year, to 1963, Mina's return to TV two years after the birth of her son.

I would like to specify that the rules of South Tyrolean

dialect, especially in its written form, are much simpler compared with official German.

Finally, an observation on the terms "Alto Adige," "Alto Adige resident," "Südtirol" and "South Tyrolean": precisely because a non-secondary element of the issue was what the Province had the right, or the obligation, to be called, the names were not used, except rarely, in any neutral way. In general, I have followed the rule according to which you say Alto Adige when you're speaking from the Italian point of view, and Südtirol from the German point of view, and which defines Alto Adige residents and South Tyroleans as respectively Italian and German speakers. But the current usage of this rule has many exceptions; therefore, in writing, I have mixed things up a bit.

And if this sometimes causes confusion, then welcome to Alto Adige/Südtirol!

ACKNOWLEDGEMENTS

This book wouldn't exist without my mother. As an Italian holidaying in Alto Adige since the late 1960s, she has given me an interest in and respect for the residents of a land of which, even nowadays, many Italians love the geography, but know nothing of the history.

Moreover, I wish to thank the many Carabinieri, in service as well as retired, veterans of the fight against Alto Adige terrorism and of peace missions abroad, who have told me stories of life in the force: "usi obbedir tacendo," they have asked me not to mention their names; the chef Albert Pernter who opened the doors of his kingdom to me, the kitchen of the Hotel Post in Bruneck; Alois Niederwolfsgruber, for the stories of the coming out of gays in the mountains; Mirella Angelo and Giovanni Monaco for their hospitality and Sicilian-style sardines; Stefan Lechner for organizing the historical research; all the Italians, the Deutschsprachigen and the ladins who, in Alto Adige/Südtirol have always made me feel at home, most especially the Senoner family of the Putzè maso in Santa Cristina di Val Gardena, Annemi Feichter (die liebe Omi) and Dr. Manfred Walde; finally, the many friends who, with intelligent patience, embarked on the reading of the gradually evolving manuscript, providing advice, precious criticism and encouragement—too many to list them all, but they know who they are.

Many thanks—Donkschian.

About the Author

Francesca Melandri is a screenwriter and novelist. This is her English language debut. She lives in Rome, Italy.

EUROPA EDITIONS BACKLIST
(alphabetical by author)

Fiction

Carmine Abate
Between Two Seas • 978-1-933372-40-2 • Territories: World
The Homecoming Party • 978-1-933372-83-9 • Territories: World

Milena Agus
From the Land of the Moon • 978-1-60945-001-4 • Ebook • Territories:
World (excl. ANZ)

Salwa Al Neimi
The Proof of the Honey • 978-1-933372-68-6 • Ebook • Territories: World
(excl UK)

Simonetta Agnello Hornby
The Nun • 978-1-60945-062-5 • Territories: World

Daniel Arsand
Lovers • 978-1-60945-071-7 • Ebook • Territories: World

Jenn Ashworth
A Kind of Intimacy • 978-1-933372-86-0 • Territories: US & Can

Beryl Bainbridge
The Girl in the Polka Dot Dress • 978-1-60945-056-4 • Ebook •
Territories: US

Muriel Barbery
The Elegance of the Hedgehog • 978-1-933372-60-0 • Ebook • Territories:
World (excl. UK & EU)
Gourmet Rhapsody • 978-1-933372-95-2 • Ebook • Territories: World
(excl. UK & EU)

Stefano Benni
Margherita Dolce Vita • 978-1-933372-20-4 • Territories: World
Timeskipper • 978-1-933372-44-0 • Territories: World

Romano Bilenchi
The Chill • 978-1-933372-90-7 • Territories: World

Kazimierz Brandys
Rondo • 978-1-60945-004-5 • Territories: World

Alina Bronsky
Broken Glass Park • 978-1-933372-96-9 • Ebook • Territories: World
The Hottest Dishes of the Tartar Cuisine • 978-1-60945-006-9 • Ebook •
Territories: World

Jesse Browner
Everything Happens Today • 978-1-60945-051-9 • Ebook • Territories:
World (excl. UK & EU)

Francisco Coloane
Tierra del Fuego • 978-1-933372-63-1 • Ebook • Territories: World

Rebecca Connell
The Art of Losing • 978-1-933372-78-5 • Territories: US

Laurence Cossé
A Novel Bookstore • 978-1-933372-82-2 • Ebook • Territories: World
An Accident in August • 978-1-60945-049-6 • Territories: World (excl. UK)

Diego De Silva
I Hadn't Understood • 978-1-60945-065-6 • Territories: World

Shashi Deshpande
The Dark Holds No Terrors • 978-1-933372-67-9 • Territories: US

Steve Erickson
Zeroville • 978-1-933372-39-6 • Territories: US & Can
These Dreams of You • 978-1-60945-063-2 • Territories: US & Can

Elena Ferrante
The Days of Abandonment • 978-1-933372-00-6 • Ebook • Territories: World
Troubling Love • 978-1-933372-16-7 • Territories: World
The Lost Daughter • 978-1-933372-42-6 • Territories: World

Linda Ferri
Cecilia • 978-1-933372-87-7 • Territories: World

Damon Galgut
In a Strange Room • 978-1-60945-011-3 • Ebook • Territories: USA

Santiago Gamboa
Necropolis • 978-1-60945-073-1 • Ebook • Territories: World

Jane Gardam
Old Filth • 978-1-933372-13-6 • Ebook • Territories: US
The Queen of the Tambourine • 978-1-933372-36-5 • Ebook • Territories: US
The People on Privilege Hill • 978-1-933372-56-3 • Ebook • Territories: US
The Man in the Wooden Hat • 978-1-933372-89-1 • Ebook • Territories: US
God on the Rocks • 978-1-933372-76-1 • Ebook • Territories: US
Crusoe's Daughter • 978-1-60945-069-4 • Ebook • Territories: US

Anna Gavalda
French Leave • 978-1-60945-005-2 • Ebook • Territories: US & Can

Seth Greenland
The Angry Buddhist • 978-1-60945-068-7 • Ebook • Territories: World

Katharina Hacker
The Have-Nots • 978-1-933372-41-9 • Territories: World (excl. India)

Patrick Hamilton
Hangover Square • 978-1-933372-06-8 • Territories: US & Can

James Hamilton-Paterson
Cooking with Fernet Branca • 978-1-933372-01-3 • Territories: US
Amazing Disgrace • 978-1-933372-19-8 • Territories: US
Rancid Pansies • 978-1-933372-62-4 • Territories: USA

Alfred Hayes
The Girl on the Via Flaminia • 978-1-933372-24-2 • Ebook •
Territories: World

Jean-Claude Izzo
The Lost Sailors • 978-1-933372-35-8 • Territories: World
A Sun for the Dying • 978-1-933372-59-4 • Territories: World

Gail Jones
Sorry • 978-1-933372-55-6 • Territories: US & Can

Ioanna Karystiani
The Jasmine Isle • 978-1-933372-10-5 • Territories: World
Swell • 978-1-933372-98-3 • Territories: World

Peter Kocan
Fresh Fields • 978-1-933372-29-7 • Territories: US, EU & Can
The Treatment and the Cure • 978-1-933372-45-7 • Territories: US, EU & Can

Helmut Krausser
Eros • 978-1-933372-58-7 • Territories: World

Amara Lakhous
Clash of Civilizations Over an Elevator in Piazza Vittorio •
978-1-933372-61-7 • Ebook • Territories: World
Divorce Islamic Style • 978-1-60945-066-3 • Ebook • Territories: World

Lia Levi
The Jewish Husband • 978-1-933372-93-8 • Territories: World

Valerio Massimo Manfredi
The Ides of March • 978-1-933372-99-0 • Territories: US

Leïla Marouane
The Sexual Life of an Islamist in Paris • 978-1-933372-85-3 •
Territories: World

Lorenzo Mediano
The Frost on His Shoulders • 978-1-60945-072-4 • Ebook •
Territories: World

Sélim Nassib
I Loved You for Your Voice • 978-1-933372-07-5 • Territories: World
The Palestinian Lover • 978-1-933372-23-5 • Territories: World

Amélie Nothomb
Tokyo Fiancée • 978-1-933372-64-8 • Territories: US & Can
Hygiene and the Assassin • 978-1-933372-77-8 • Ebook • Territories: US & Can

Valeria Parrella
For Grace Received • 978-1-933372-94-5 • Territories: World

Alessandro Piperno
The Worst Intentions • 978-1-933372-33-4 • Territories: World
Persecution • 978-1-60945-074-8 • Ebook • Territories: World

Lorcan Roche
The Companion • 978-1-933372-84-6 • Territories: World

Boualem Sansal
The German Mujahid • 978-1-933372-92-1 • Ebook • Territories: US & Can

Eric-Emmanuel Schmitt
The Most Beautiful Book in the World • 978-1-933372-74-7 • Ebook •
Territories: World
The Woman with the Bouquet • 978-1-933372-81-5 • Ebook • Territories:
US & Can

Angelika Schrobsdorff
You Are Not Like Other Mothers • 978-1-60945-075-5 • Ebook •
Territories: World

Audrey Schulman
Three Weeks in December • 978-1-60945-064-9 • Ebook • Territories: US
& Can

James Scudamore
Heliopolis • 978-1-933372-73-0 • Ebook • Territories: US

Luis Sepúlveda
The Shadow of What We Were • 978-1-60945-002-1 • Ebook • Territories:
World

Paolo Sorrentino
Everybody's Right • 978-1-60945-052-6 • Ebook • Territories: US & Can

Domenico Starnone
First Execution • 978-1-933372-66-2 • Territories: World

Henry Sutton
Get Me out of Here • 978-1-60945-007-6 • Ebook • Territories: US & Can

Chad Taylor
Departure Lounge • 978-1-933372-09-9 • Territories: US, EU & Can

Roma Tearne
Mosquito • 978-1-933372-57-0 • Territories: US & Can
Bone China • 978-1-933372-75-4 • Territories: US

André Carl van der Merwe
Moffie • 978-1-60945-050-2 • Ebook • Territories: World
(excl. S. Africa)

Fay Weldon
Chalcot Crescent • 978-1-933372-79-2 • Territories: US

Anne Wiazemsky
My Berlin Child • 978-1-60945-003-8 • Territories: US & Can

Jonathan Yardley
Second Reading • 978-1-60945-008-3 • Ebook • Territories: US & Can

Edwin M. Yoder Jr.
Lions at Lamb House • 978-1-933372-34-1 • Territories: World

Michele Zackheim
Broken Colors • 978-1-933372-37-2 • Territories: World

Alice Zeniter
Take This Man • 978-1-60945-053-3 • Territories: World

Tonga Books

Ian Holding
Of Beasts and Beings • 978-1-60945-054-0 • Ebook • Territories: US & Can

Sara Levine
Treasure Island!!! • 978-0-14043-768-3 • Ebook • Territories: World

Alexander Maksik
You Deserve Nothing • 978-1-60945-048-9 • Ebook • Territories: US, Can & EU (excl. UK)

Thad Ziolkowski
Wichita • 978-1-60945-070-0 • Ebook • Territories: World

Crime/Noir

Massimo Carlotto
The Goodbye Kiss • 978-1-933372-05-1 • Ebook • Territories: World
Death's Dark Abyss • 978-1-933372-18-1 • Ebook • Territories: World
The Fugitive • 978-1-933372-25-9 • Ebook • Territories: World
Bandit Love • 978-1-933372-80-8 • Ebook • Territories: World
Poisonville • 978-1-933372-91-4 • Ebook • Territories: World

Giancarlo De Cataldo
The Father and the Foreigner • 978-1-933372-72-3 • Territories: World

Caryl Férey
Zulu • 978-1-933372-88-4 • Ebook • Territories: World (excl. UK & EU)
Utu • 978-1-60945-055-7 • Ebook • Territories: World (excl. UK & EU)

Alicia Giménez-Bartlett
Dog Day • 978-1-933372-14-3 • Territories: US & Can
Prime Time Suspect • 978-1-933372-31-0 • Territories: US & Can
Death Rites • 978-1-933372-54-9 • Territories: US & Can

Jean-Claude Izzo
Total Chaos • 978-1-933372-04-4 • Territories: US & Can
Chourmo • 978-1-933372-17-4 • Territories: US & Can
Solea • 978-1-933372-30-3 • Territories: US & Can

Matthew F. Jones
Boot Tracks • 978-1-933372-11-2 • Territories: US & Can

Gene Kerrigan
The Midnight Choir • 978-1-933372-26-6 • Territories: US & Can
Little Criminals • 978-1-933372-43-3 • Territories: US & Can

Carlo Lucarelli
Carte Blanche • 978-1-933372-15-0 • Territories: World
The Damned Season • 978-1-933372-27-3 • Territories: World
Via delle Oche • 978-1-933372-53-2 • Territories: World

Edna Mazya
Love Burns • 978-1-933372-08-2 • Territories: World (excl. ANZ)

Yishai Sarid
Limassol • 978-1-60945-000-7 • Ebook • Territories: World (excl. UK,
AUS & India)

Joel Stone
The Jerusalem File • 978-1-933372-65-5 • Ebook • Territories: World

Benjamin Tammuz
Minotaur • 978-1-933372-02-0 • Ebook • Territories: World

Non-fiction

Alberto Angela
A Day in the Life of Ancient Rome • 978-1-933372-71-6 • Territories:
World • History

Helmut Dubiel
Deep In the Brain: Living with Parkinson's Disease • 978-1-933372-70-9 •
Ebook • Territories: World • Medicine/Memoir

James Hamilton-Paterson
Seven-Tenths: The Sea and Its Thresholds • 978-1-933372-69-3 • Territories:
USA • Nature/Essays

Daniele Mastrogiacomo
Days of Fear • 978-1-933372-97-6 • Ebook • Territories: World • Current
affairs/Memoir/Afghanistan/Journalism

Valery Panyushkin
Twelve Who Don't Agree • 978-1-60945-010-6 • Ebook • Territories:
World • Current affairs/Memoir/Russia/Journalism

Christa Wolf
One Day a Year: 1960-2000 • 978-1-933372-22-8 • Territories: World •
Memoir/History/20th Century

Children's Illustrated Fiction

Altan
Here Comes Timpa • 978-1-933372-28-0 • Territories: World (excl. Italy)
Timpa Goes to the Sea • 978-1-933372-32-7 • Territories: World (excl. Italy)
Fairy Tale Timpa • 978-1-933372-38-9 • Territories: World (excl. Italy)

Wolf Erlbruch
The Big Question • 978-1-933372-03-7 • Territories: US & Can
The Miracle of the Bears • 978-1-933372-21-1 • Territories: US & Can
(with **Gioconda Belli**) *The Butterfly Workshop* • 978-1-933372-12-9 •
Territories: US & Can